Three's Company

Three's Company

ELENA GRAF

PURPLE HAND PRESS

Purple Hand Press
www.elenagraf.com
© 2025 by Elena Graf

This is a work of fiction. Names, characters, places, and incidents are the product of the author's imagination or used fictitiously, and any resemblance to actual persons, living or dead, businesses, institutions, companies, events, or locales is entirely coincidental.

Trade Paperback Edition
ISBN-13 978-1-953195-26-5
ePub Edition
ISBN-13 978-1-953195-25-8

Cover photo © Freepik.com, used by license.

07.25.2025

To Elaine, who encouraged me to explore this idea

Note

For a character guide to the inhabitants of Hobbs, Maine, please visit: https://elenagraf.com/hobbs-characters/

Chapter 1

Ignoring her ex-wife's frequent warnings about pine sap dropping on her car, Maggie Fitzgerald parked in the woods. Her Subaru hybrid had seen better days, and Maggie knew the sticky patches on the finish would eventually drive Liz crazy. She'd be out there, scrubbing them off with a solvent-soaked rag. Smiling at the thought, Maggie finally mustered the energy to get out of the car.

Today had been her busy day, when she taught three ninety-minute classes with hardly any break. She'd eagerly accepted the scheduling when the department head had suggested it because it gave her Fridays off. Long weekends might be the goal of every college student, but for the professor, it meant multiple classes on at least one day. Add a faculty meeting to the day's calendar, and exhaustion becomes inevitable. Maggie pulled the ridiculously heavy bags from behind the driver's seat. Electronic editions of all the texts were available, but she still used physical books. The idea of transferring the highlights and notes gathered over thirty-five years of teaching always seemed too overwhelming.

Lugging the bags to the stairs leading up to her apartment, she heard a sharp crack, followed by another. Puzzled for a moment, she finally identified the blows of a kindling axe. Through the side door of the garage, she saw a tall, white-haired woman splitting pine logs into neat baguettes. As usual, Liz was so involved in her task she was oblivious. Maggie took the opportunity to watch her unobserved. The gangly, flat-chested teenager she'd met in college over fifty years ago had grown up to be an attractive, exceptionally tall, but otherwise well-proportioned woman.

Sensing that someone was watching, Liz finally stood up and looked around. She made a little face when she saw Maggie peering at her through the door. A smile followed, then a wave inviting her to come out. Liz glanced at her gold watch. Even though she mocked it as a cliché, she always wore the retirement gift from Yale

New Haven because it was useful. "You're late today." It pleased Maggie that Liz kept track.

"We had a department meeting to decide next semester's curriculum."

"I thought you said you were going to take a break."

"I haven't decided yet. According to student surveys, my classes are still popular." Last year, at seventy, Maggie had come out of retirement for the second time. Teaching and directing theater again were invigorating. All those young faces focused on her, laptops and cellphones momentarily forgotten, was second only to holding a theater audience in thrall.

"Being appreciated is good, I suppose, but not a compelling reason to go on teaching." With a flick of her wrist, Liz planted the kindling axe in the weathered gray log, where a thousand blows had left a crazy crosshatch pattern. She rubbed her arm with a grimace.

"Hurt yourself?" Maggie asked sympathetically, reaching out to touch the spot.

"Ripped the biceps tendon throwing bags of salt pellets into my truck. I could feel it tear."

Maggie gritted her teeth sympathetically. "When did this happen?"

"While we weren't talking." After Maggie had heard Liz planned to marry Lucy, she'd stopped speaking to them. If not for Maggie's cancer recurrence forcing a conversation, there might still be silence. "Maybe you should see a doctor," Maggie suggested.

Liz warned her away from this subject with a sharp look. Like most doctors, she hated to be a patient and hated unsolicited medical advice even more. "Not much they can do. When it gets so bad I can't stand it, I'll see a surgeon."

"But Liz, *you are* a surgeon."

"Which is exactly *why* I don't want surgery. I know every step in the procedure, the side effects, the percentage of failures. Plus, I'm a coward. I even hate shots." Maggie studied Liz's face. The stoic woman she used to know would never admit any fears. Maybe Lucy was right. Liz had changed since the shooting.

Maggie couldn't even imagine the terror of being held hostage by a stoned, angry young man. Being forced to kill him in self-defense was even more unimaginable. When people called her a hero for taking down a shooter who'd killed so many kids, Liz hated it. Most people didn't understand, but Maggie did. She'd watched Liz mourn for days after shooting the chipmunk that had been eating her tomatoes. Liz was no killer.

"Kind of warm today," Liz said, batting away some mosquitos that had gathered because they'd been standing still. "How about a gin and tonic?" She grinned the slightly off-centered grin that had won Maggie's heart all those years ago, making the answer obvious.

"Sure. Sounds wonderful."

"Come inside, and I'll make you one."

Liz grimaced as she wiggled the axe to release it from its snug position in the log. "Hate to say it, but I might have to quit splitting wood. Sam's been after me to get a pellet stove."

Maggie didn't want to hear about Sam. In fact, she'd prefer to write off what they'd had together as a rebound relationship. Not long after Sam left, she'd landed in Hobbs between projects and invited Maggie to lunch. Knowing she was hurting one of the kindest people she'd ever known, Maggie had turned her down. Her feelings for Sam were too complicated, and she wasn't ready to face her.

Unaware of Maggie's thoughts, Liz continued talking about the painful subject. "Did you get the email about the barbecue at the pond?"

"Yes, I got it, but I'm not going."

Liz raised her head in exaggerated surprise. "I thought you and Sam parted on good terms."

"We did...mostly. She's moving on, and I'm trying."

Liz gently touched Maggie's arm. "Everything changes, Maggie. You can't stop it."

"I know, but I wish I could." Maggie shrugged off Liz's hand to throw her long, white hair over her shoulders. The heat was making it annoying today. A couple of times that summer, she'd been tempted to surprise everyone and cut her hair short again.

"Sam's leaving for Dallas at the end of the week," said Liz. She'd never known when to quit. "Probably won't be back till spring. I'm sure you'd like to say goodbye."

"I said goodbye when I moved out. How many times do I need to say it?"

The adamance of her response startled Liz. "Maggie, you left her. She didn't leave you." When Maggie didn't respond, Liz shrugged and headed into the garage. Maggie followed and watched Liz run a sharpening stone along the axe edge. She glanced at the carefully organized peg board with an outline of each tool so it could be returned to its place.

"Liz, I'm not a hypocrite. I know Sam is your friend, and you go back a long time, but I can't forgive her. She left the door open for a killer and kids died."

Liz carefully wiped the axe blade with oil before hanging it up. She peered at Maggie. "Sam didn't kill those kids."

"But even you said what she did was stupid."

"Because it was, but she didn't mean any harm. Let it go." Liz was suddenly distracted. Maggie followed her line of vision and saw she was eyeing her bags on the step. "Want me to carry those bags up for you?"

"I thought your shoulder hurts."

"It does, but only with percussive stress like chopping kindling, or when I try to raise my arm over my head." Looking pained, Liz demonstrated. "Weight doesn't bother it."

Maggie watched Liz carry the bags up the stairs and leave them outside the door of her apartment. After she descended, Maggie planted a quick kiss on her cheek. "Thanks, Liz."

As if Maggie's lips had left an impression, Liz gingerly touched the spot. "You're welcome, but you're going to hurt yourself hauling all that stuff around. Why don't you switch to digital books?"

"It takes time to transfer my notes, and I have too much to do." Liz looked skeptical. Even Maggie knew the excuse was lame. Since her granddaughters had gotten older, they didn't need her hovering nearby. After decades of lecturing college students, class preparation took little effort. Liz paid to have Maggie's apartment cleaned along with the rest of the house, so there was little housework to do. If not for teaching, Maggie would be playing bridge at the Hobbs Activity Center with the other bored seniors.

"I can help you," Liz offered.

Maggie tried not to look suspicious. "That's a kind offer, but don't you have enough to do?"

"I do, but I worry about an old bag like you becoming a cripple."

Maggie landed a playful punch on Liz's good arm. "Play nice," warned Liz, drawing back in exaggerated pain, "or I won't make a G&T for you."

"Who cares? I can make my own."

"Sure you can, but you know mine are better!"

Maggie raised her hand to punch her again, but Liz clamped her into a tight hug. Maggie struggled for effect, then leaned into the embrace. Liz was sweaty from splitting kindling, but her body next to hers felt good. Her familiar scent recalled how she smelled after sex. Maggie had never felt safer than when lying in Liz's arms after making love. As she inhaled the aromas of clean perspiration and laundry soap, Maggie felt a surge of nostalgia for those better days.

"If you promise not to hit me, I'll let you go."

Maggie agreed and Liz released her. "We don't have a group meal on the schedule tonight, but I bought an enormous sirloin, and the garden has been incredibly productive this year."

Maggie drew the obvious conclusion. "You have too much food, so you want me to come help you eat it?"

"Exactly. What do you say?"

Maggie had been too tired from the long day to stop at the store on the way home. "Lucy's been so busy since you got home from your travels. We haven't had much chance to talk, so...."

"So, that's a yes?" Liz leaned against the door to the house. "Well then, come on in!"

***

Lucy smiled when she saw Maggie's car parked in the woods and pulled in beside it. If Liz said anything, she could count on Maggie to defend her. She liked having an ally when Liz got too bossy.

Before heading in the direction of the voices down the hall, Lucy hooked her clerical collar on the banister post and hung up her black jacket. "Hi, ladies," she said, coming into the kitchen. "How was your day?"

"Okay." Liz bent to kiss her. "We're having G&Ts. Want one?"

"No, thanks, but if you're tending bar, I'll have a glass of wine." Lucy dumped her bags at the foot of the stool beside Maggie. Liz interrupted mixing the drinks to hold up Lucy's book bag.

"Okay, ladies. For the last time, carrying this much unbalanced weight can hurt your back, your hips, your knees, and..."

Lucy held a raised finger to her wife's lips. Liz sputtered for a few seconds before falling silent. "Liz, for the last time. Let me take responsibility for my own body." Lucy gave her a stern look before removing the finger. "Thank you."

"Wow, Lucy. You go, girl!" Maggie pumped her fist in affirmation.

"Okay, but don't complain to me about your aches and pains," Liz grumbled. She took a bottle of pinot grigio off the shelf on the refrigerator door and poured a glass for Lucy.

Maggie reached over and patted Lucy's arm. "I like my ink on paper too. They can throw all kinds of digital stuff at me, but I will still read real books."

"EBooks are *real* books," Liz protested. "It's the text, not the medium."

"Uh-oh, I hear a Professor Stolz lecture coming on," said Maggie, turning her back to Liz to show she had no intention of listening. "Lucy, how was your day?"

"Oh, my word, I don't even know where to begin. Reshma turned her ankle hiking with her girlfriend. She can't drive, so I took over her pastoral care visits. Susan went to a reunion of the nuns in her postulant class. Tom is visiting friends in Connecticut. Like I was when I first came to Hobbs, I was on my own. But I'm almost five years older and didn't realize how much work it is." Lucy picked up the glass of wine Liz had put in front of her and took a sip. "It's nice outside, if a little warm. Why don't we sit on the deck?"

"Great idea," Liz agreed. "You go out. Let me throw some snacks on a tray."

After Lucy and Maggie settled on the cushioned wicker furniture, Maggie said, "You look fried, Lucy."

Lucy exhaled a long sigh. "I am. What was I thinking to okay leave for both Susan and Tom at the same time? I've barely caught up after being away for the summer festivals. Obviously, Reshma spraining her ankle was not in the plan."

"I don't know how you do it, managing a church, a counseling practice, keeping up nearly a full-time singing schedule, never mind doing publicity for your book."

"Oh, the book. Now that the haters have moved on, it's finally finding an audience, not that I'm doing anything to help it. Another thing I can't get to."

"I've been there. When I was teaching, directing plays, and on the board of the Webhanet Playhouse, I was always running behind. And you're an opera star, flying all over the world. The travel alone must be exhausting."

"It is, but I know my time to sing is limited, so I'm willing to do it. And Liz manages everything while I'm on the road, transportation, tips, dinner reservations."

Maggie raised her glass. "Smart move, Lucy. That's a good role for her. Keeps her out of mischief."

Lucy smiled but didn't want to encourage criticism of Liz. "She's so good. She makes sure I'm fed and watered like a thoroughbred."

"Well, you are. That voice of yours is special. That's why you're back in demand after such a long absence." Maggie glanced away shyly, which meant she wanted to say something she wasn't sure would be received well. "Lucy, I know you're so busy, but once, you offered to give me voice lessons. I know we only had one or two, but my singing improved. You're a great teacher, Lucy. You turned Denise Chantal into a star."

"Denise is getting there, but she still has plenty of challenges. Her vocal cords are the same length they were when she identified as a male. No amount of training can change her range or the timbre of her voice. All I can do is help her develop a feminine nuance."

"Which you've done so well."

Maggie was being so complimentary today. Lucy wondered what was on her agenda, but she'd play along and see. "Denise is truly gifted, but transitioning from being a countertenor has overshadowed her talent. Her record company is still trying to exploit it."

"Hey, it's how it works nowadays. Anything to get traction in this competitive entertainment world." Maggie smiled coyly. "You wouldn't maybe...I mean, would you, if you can find the time..."

Lucy instantly understood that Maggie wanted to resume their lessons. "Sure. I know how hard it is for older singers, especially women. We're not only drier *down there*. Our voices dry out too and lose their brightness."

"I've noticed, but with my cancer history, Liz says hormone replacement is out of the question."

"For me too. My mother died of ovarian cancer. But my voice has darkened, which is natural as we age. That's why I'm being pushed toward the dramatic soprano repertoire. My mother would be horrified. She thought Wagnerians were so pretentious."

"I don't know as much about opera as you two, but I think I understand," said Maggie. "It's hard to be typecast."

"Even more, when you're as small as I am. I don't have the physical reserves of those massive Brünhildes, or the stage presence. It's one thing to play a consumptive courtesan, quite another to make a convincing warrior maiden." Lucy stuck out her elbows and curled in her fists in a body builder pose. "Plus, I'm sixty now."

Maggie waved dismissively. "Oh, you're just a baby. I have eleven years on you. Wait till you get to be my age."

"You look terrific, Maggie. I hope I look as good at seventy-one."

Maggie demurred at the compliment, but it was true. Maggie knew how to make the most of her assets. Her makeup was always artful. She dressed with an eye for the dramatic and wore colorful, large-rimmed reading glasses as a fashion accessory.

Liz emerged from the house with an abbreviated charcuterie tray. She'd also brought Lucy's wine and a vacuum bottle of gin and tonics.

Maggie watched her approach with obvious affection. "This is what I love about living here with you two. It's so civilized."

Liz set down the tray and slipped off her crocs. "Except when it's not."

Taking off her pumps, Lucy swung around on the wicker sofa and placed her feet in Liz's lap. "A foot rub would be greatly appreciated." She wiggled her toes, knowing the bright red polish would get Liz's attention.

"My lady, your wish is my command." Liz began to gently knead the ball of Lucy's foot.

"Lucy, how did you train her to do that?" Maggie asked enviously.

"I didn't. She started doing it while I was studying for my comps. She was seducing me with foot rubs while giving me the Cliff notes version of the books I was reading."

"While Lucy was studying for her comps, I read a lot of theology books." Liz rolled her eyes.

"Bullshit, Liz. You loved it. But seducing Lucy with foot rubs was inventive and much more subtle than I would have expected of you. Usually, you just charge ahead."

"Well, Lucy was a hard case, and I was desperate."

"Yes, I bet you were. You probably tell everyone how I deprived you when we were married. Evidently, you've met your match in Lucy."

Lucy felt her cheeks warm because it was true. "In Liz's defense, I was playing hard to get. I was still wrecked from Erika's death."

"I still can't believe she's gone," Maggie said sympathetically. "If I'd found my spouse unresponsive, I'd totally freak."

"Thank God I had the presence of mind to call Liz, and she came right away."

"Liz is good in emergencies," Maggie said, smiling in her direction. "When things are falling apart, Liz is as steady as a rock."

"Gee, thanks, Maggie. I think that's the nicest thing you ever said about me."

"You know it's not. You have many good qualities, including making the best G&Ts."

Liz whipped her phone out of her pocket.

"What are you doing?" asked Maggie.

"Recording this conversation."

Maggie threw back her head and implored the sky, "Oh my God! Liz, you'll never change!"

"I don't know, Maggie," said Lucy. "I've seen lots of changes in her. Haven't you?"

Maggie was silent for a long moment. "Actually, I have. Mostly positive. Must be your doing."

Lucy shook her head. "I don't deserve the credit. Liz has been working hard since the shooting and has made progress. I'm proud of her."

When Liz swallowed audibly, Lucy guessed she was reliving some of the unpleasant memories she'd had to face. After a long moment focusing on the colorful border below, she obviously changed the subject. "Luce, did I ever tell you I once let Maggie give me a pedicure?"

"Yes, you did, but I still find it hard to believe."

"Oh, it's true all right," Maggie confirmed. "You should have seen her squirm…like a toddler getting a haircut."

"She said my feet were frightening," said Liz.

"Well, they are," Lucy agreed. "Beastly things…with claws!"

"Luce, don't talk to me about claws. When you grow your fingernails for a performance, you are downright dangerous!!!"

Maggie's face had been following each of them like players in a tennis match. "You two are so funny. I kind of miss silly arguments like this."

Liz refreshed Maggie's glass from the carafe. "Well, join in. Not like you don't have anything to say."

Maggie sat back and gazed into the garden. "Actually, I don't have anything to say. I'm grateful to be here with you. It's a beautiful place, and I missed both of you while you were gallivanting around Europe." She watched Liz massaging Lucy's instep. "I've been on my feet most of the day. That looks so relaxing."

"Then switch places with me." Lucy swung around, leaving Liz's hands poised in the air.

Liz jumped up and headed to the door. "Let me wash my hands."

"I took a shower this morning," Lucy protested indignantly to Liz's back as she disappeared into the house. "I'm not dirty!"

Maggie's eyes followed Liz. "I wonder if she has any idea how insulting she is when she does things like that."

"Oh, I doubt it. Of course, the handwashing is a habit from her job. She washes them so much, they're chapped, even in the summer." Lucy realized she was telling Maggie something she already knew.

"Yup, and they're like sandpaper because she refuses to use hand cream."

Lucy didn't want to encourage criticism of Liz. She moved to one of the Adirondak chairs and patted the arm of the sofa. "Come on, Maggie. Your turn."

"You sure?" asked Maggie, eyeing her suspiciously.

"Of course. It's just a foot rub."

Liz returned and plopped on the sofa. She took Maggie's feet into her lap and began the massage. Within minutes, Maggie looked like she was in ecstasy.

"Feel good?" Liz asked.

"You have no idea."

***

Liz focused on the foot tendons in the arch. Maggie leaned back and sighed, mesmerized with pleasure. Now that Liz knew she had a receptive audience, she decided to push the invitation to Sam's picnic. "I'm really looking forward to seeing everyone at Sam's party."

Maggie opened one eye, but she could glare with one better than most people could with two. "When have you gotten so lovey-dovey with Sam? You were furious when we got together."

"I was not furious," Liz protested. "I thought it was a bad idea. As things turned out, I was right." Liz added a "so there" nod of her head, but Maggie had closed her eyes again, so she missed it. Liz could feel the slight movement of Maggie's muscles that indicated she was thinking of getting up, so she tightened her grip on her foot.

"Sam had a good thing going in Hobbs and she blew it. Not only did she make her life miserable, she ruined mine too."

Liz stared at Maggie because she was finally admitting the real reason she held a grudge against Sam. Liz glanced over to where Lucy sat and could tell she was thinking the same.

"Maggie, I know things didn't work out with Sam the way you hoped," said Lucy kindly, "but she'd appreciate you coming out to the pond to wish her well before she leaves."

"What is this? A conspiracy?"

"No," protested Lucy. "Just some friendly words of advice."

"I'm not a hypocrite," Maggie replied flatly. "You two go. I'm sure you'll have a great time."

"But Maggie, it won't be the same without you," said Liz.

The tag teaming did it. Maggie yanked her bare feet away from Liz and sat up. "Nothing, and I mean nothing, will ever be the same again. Don't you get it?" She jumped up, grabbed her shoes, and went into the house.

"Well, that went well." Liz sighed and began getting up.

"Let me go," Lucy offered.

"Actually, neither of us should go. If you do, she'll accuse you of ministering to her or trying to shrink her. If I go, she'll say I'm siding with Sam because we're old friends. No matter what, we're wrong."

"Liz, she's angry and hurt. She had so much invested in that relationship with Sam, and circumstances beyond her control ripped it away. Try to understand."

"I do understand. But that's life. I didn't want to shoot Peter Langdon either, but I had no choice. Maggie is a saver. She collects perceived hurts like some people collect coins or stamps. Occasionally, she takes them out and drools over them like Golem."

Lucy gave Liz her 'I'm being so patient' look. "Yes, we both know Maggie holds grudges. It's easier for some people to blame others silently than do the hard work of dealing with their own issues." Liz might have little use for therapy, but she admired how Lucy's training helped her understand complex emotional situations. Not only did her high EQ make her a good priest, it also made her an affecting singer. Lucy never sang just words and notes.

"I'll talk to her," Lucy said, slipping on her pumps. While she was gone, Liz used the time to call her service and return calls from her patients. In a short while, Lucy returned with Maggie.

"I'll go with you to Sam's," Maggie said petulantly.

Liz couldn't help exploiting the victory. "Look, Maggie. Sam didn't do anything to deliberately hurt you. She invited you to come along when she moved to Chicago. She's working as an architect again. Making new friends. She's moving on."

"I can't move on," Maggie admitted. "Her stupidity screwed up my life. We had a good thing going right here in Hobbs. She wrecked it."

"That's the truth, isn't it?" Liz said.

"Liz..." Lucy started to say with a warning look.

"I know, right?" Maggie said. "With Liz, it's always beat it in with a two by four."

"No, Maggie. That's not fair," Lucy replied. "Liz can be blunt, but she is telling the truth. Blaming Sam isn't going to change anything."

Maggie crumbled and put her face in her hands. Liz realized she was crying and moved over to sit beside her. She made soothing circles on her back until the tears stopped and Maggie sat up.

"You okay?" Liz asked solicitously.

"Yes, I'm fine. I just find it hard to talk about Sam. I might have gone with her, but in Hobbs I thought I found my forever home. I'm too old to start over. Sam's young. Her friends are much younger than I am. I have no place in the world she's creating for herself."

"Can't you be happy for her?" Lucy asked gently. "She thought her architectural career was over. Now, she has a second chance to do what she really loves, like me singing again."

After Lucy finished speaking, Maggie stared at Lucy for a long time. "I know you're right. I just feel so old and useless...thrown aside by my daughter and my much younger lover. No one needs me anymore."

Lucy sat beside Maggie and took her hand. "That's not true. We need you. Your students need you. Now that you're acting again, your audience needs you. You bring richness to the lives of others. Without your contributions, all those people would be poorer."

Maggie's tone was flat. "Nice speech, Lucy. I said I would go to Sam's. What else do you want?"

Lucy exchanged a look of barely constrained frustration with Liz. "Nothing," she said, getting up and moving to another seat. "Thank you for listening."

Liz rose. "I'll get dinner started."

Chapter 2

Fishing brought out Liz's most territorial instincts. Under her eyebrows, she watched Sam cast perilously close to where she'd sunk her lure. "Watch it, Sam."

"Don't worry, Liz. I see where you are."

"Girls, it's a big pond," said Brenda, reeling in her line. "Plenty of room for everyone. Don't fight."

"Not a fight yet," Liz assured her, giving Sam the eye. "I'm used to the way Sam fishes. As soon as I find a good spot, she tries to horn in on it."

"You're the only one catching anything," Sam complained. "And dammit, it's my pond."

Brenda laughed and pointed at the houses around the perimeter. "I think those people might disagree with you. As far as I know, you all own this pond."

"They're never around, so I sort of claimed Jimson for myself. They'll never know."

"Well, Sam, I wouldn't say that too loud. I am the police chief, and it's my job to enforce the law equally."

"Oh, Brenda. You know I'm just kidding." Sam shaded her eyes against the sun and gazed around the pond. "And now, I'm like them, one of the hated summer people."

"We watch all your homes equally," Brenda assured her.

Sam reeled in, but this time, she cast far from Liz's line. "It doesn't look like Maggie's too happy to be here. Hell, even being an actress, she can't pretend."

"I don't know," said Liz, turning around to look at Maggie sitting on the dock with the others. "I think she's doing a pretty good job of pretending, if that's what she's doing."

"Did you make her come, Liz?"

"Now, Sam, you know Maggie. Do you really think anyone can make her do anything?"

Sam's laugh was cynical. "Nope. Tried everything, including sweet talking her. Maggie does what she wants."

"Right," Liz agreed. "But since you asked, Lucy did talk to her. I don't know what she said, but Maggie came of her own volition. She wanted to say goodbye before you fly off to Dallas."

"Are you going to be living there, Sam?" asked Brenda, poking in the paper container of nightcrawlers from the general store. They wiggled away from her fingers as she tried to grab them. She was the only one fishing with live bait today, but it wasn't giving her any advantage. Liz had caught three big lake trout with her favorite lure.

"The company that hired me will put me up in an apartment while I'm working there," Sam explained, "but you can be damn sure I'm not moving to Texas permanently. Honestly, I hate the South. Weird vibe down there. Plus, the women look at me funny."

Liz reeled in a little. "They're more traditional in the South. The women want to be thought of as ladies...like any of us would qualify."

Brenda snickered. "We can, when we want to. Like you Liz, when you get dressed up in your power suit to intimidate people."

"Who are you to talk about intimidation? You wear a uniform and carry a gun."

"You carry a gun too. People just don't see it."

"I can see why Sam might be uncomfortable in the South," Liz said. "In my grown-up job, I often ended up there for medical conferences. It's not like Maine, where all the women dress like us. At least, Sam doesn't look so strange, now that she's let her hair grow out on the shaved side."

Sam sneered at Liz. "I'm there to do a job, not win a beauty pageant!"

"Well, you look more professional without the dyke haircut," Liz insisted. "Besides, those asymmetric haircuts are out of fashion now." She pointed to her own hair. "Lucy even convinced me to get rid of my grunge style."

"But I bet she was pissed when you decided to shave your hair on the sides," said Sam.

"Lucy didn't love it at first, but now, she says it looks good on me." Liz preened to show off her haircut.

"You two and your dyke haircuts," Brenda muttered. "I'll just keep mine long. No fuss, no muss. I brush it in the morning, tie it back, and I'm good to go."

"But you have to keep dyeing it," said Liz. "Isn't that annoying? I used to help Maggie color her hair. Years ago, when we were in college. After she was diagnosed, she quit. Guess the cancer scared her out of the illusion that she's a blonde."

"You didn't advise her to stop?" asked Brenda.

"Nope. She read an article online and decided that day. Took a while for her hair to grow out. She hated that part. Me too, especially her bitching about it."

"And you wonder why I don't stop dyeing mine," said Brenda. "Never mind that I have all those smart-ass new officers joining the force. I can't look old." Liz turned around and studied Brenda. She kept fit, which made her look younger than her nearly sixty years, but she wasn't fooling anyone with the dye job.

Liz recast in another direction. "You're both kids. Wait till you get to be my age."

Sam scrutinized Liz's hair. "The white looks good on you, Liz. Just weird how it changed so fast after the shooting."

"Trauma will do that. I never believed that it could turn hair white, but here I am, living proof."

"Let's not talk about the fucking shooting, if you don't mind," said Sam irritably.

"You brought it up," Brenda pointed out.

"Doesn't mean I want to talk about it." Sam disconnected her lure from the swivel. "Brenda, can you spare some bait?"

"For you, Sam, anything," said Brenda, handing Sam the container of crawlers. "If you want, Liz, you can try them too."

"No, thanks. The fish like me today. Why screw up a good thing?" Just as Liz said it, she got a strike. She reeled in and pulled up another good-size lake trout.

"Uh-oh. I see Olivia waving at us," said Brenda.

"They probably want us to come in and get the grill going," said Sam.

Brenda started reeling in her line. "Sam, don't you find it weird to have so many exes here? You dated Olivia, Amy, *and* Maggie. What have you got? You're a real chick magnet."

Liz smirked. Sam lightly punched her thigh. "You're just jealous. You bragged you weren't the marrying kind but look at you! You go from one wife to another with barely a break. Liz, I think your stud days are over."

Liz grinned slyly. "I don't know about that..."

"Don't even think it," said Brenda. "Lucy would kill you if you strayed, and I mean *dead*."

"Nah, she loves me too much. Besides, she's a priest. She believes in 'Thou shalt not kill.'"

"Yeah? I wouldn't test that theory if I were you," said Brenda. "And I still want to hear how Sam feels with three exes sitting on her dock."

Sam shrugged. "I try not to think about it. Besides, if I were that bad, they wouldn't be here. I never did anything to hurt them. Olivia just moved on when I left. Amy split up with me because she wasn't ready for another relationship. The only one who's still mad at me is Maggie. I don't know why. I asked her to come with me. I offered to sell her the house for pennies. She wasn't interested. And *she* left *me*, not the other way around!"

"Your love life is so complicated, Sam," said Brenda. "I couldn't keep track of all those women, and I wouldn't dare have them hanging around afterward. Cherie would kill me. Commandment or no."

"Sam's just a modern woman," said Liz, coming to Sam's defense. "The kids nowadays are into all sorts of relationships. They have fuck buddies and friends with benefits, and God knows what else. I bet Sam already has a new girlfriend." Liz nudged Sam with her elbow. "Right, Sam?"

"I'm not saying," Sam insisted, bringing her hook into the boat. The line dribbled water on her jeans. "Anyway, it's none of your damn business."

"That means she's got a hot babe in Chi-town," Liz whispered loudly behind her hand.

Brenda sniggered.

"Okay, guys," said Sam, hooking her spinner on one of the rod guides. "Time to call it a day. The ladies are counting on us to do the grilling, and we can't let them down."

"God forbid," muttered Liz.

***

Maggie was only half-listening to the conversation. On the other side of the circle, Olivia was holding court, pontificating on the Democrats' chances of winning the election. Of course, they were all in for the last-minute replacement candidate, hoping that she could prevail despite tight poll numbers. Olivia, from her long involvement in Republican politics, could always be counted on for an alternative perspective. "You can't just be against someone. You've got to have a positive message, and God knows she's trying. 'Forward' is more positive than 'We're not going back.'"

"Do you really think she has a chance?" Cherie asked hopefully, but her striking blue-green eyes betrayed her anxiety.

"I don't know," said Olivia. "Is this country ready for a female president? Last time they ran a woman, it didn't go well."

"But it was so close, and Clinton won the popular vote," said Amy, Olivia's partner. "Without those shenanigans, between the Russians and the Bernie bots, she would be our president, and what a different world it would be."

Olivia sighed so deeply it could be heard over the slap of the waves against the dock. "They'd been building a case against Hillary from the time Bill was governor of Arkansas. The drip, drip, drip of news stories about her emails. And they kept harping on her likeability. And this time, the candidate is both a woman and black." Olivia quickly glanced at the woman to her left. "I'm sorry, Cherie, no offense."

"I'm not offended," Cherie protested. "Those are two strikes against her, which I know better than any of you."

"And you don't even look black," Olivia said tactlessly. "With that blond hair and those blue eyes, who'd ever suspect?" Everyone was so accustomed to Olivia's blunt opinions, no one even raised a brow.

"You're right. When I tell people I'm black, half the time, they don't believe me. Up here, many people don't know what to do with a biracial woman. Is she black or white? It's not that way in the South, where they have the 'one-drop rule.' A single drop of black blood means you're not white. Of course, now you can spit in a tube and send it somewhere to have your DNA analyzed. I'm sure some of those angry white boys waving confederate flags would be shocked to find out the truth about themselves."

"Serves them right," pronounced Olivia without a scintilla of sympathy. "Idiots!"

Maggie subtly shook her head. Olivia still thought her opinion mattered more than anyone's. Somehow, she'd convinced the others too. But for all her officious ways, Olivia could always be counted on for intelligent conversation. She'd come from nothing, but had earned scholarships to Ivy League schools, and clawed her way up to the top of the financial industry. And she wasn't the only high achiever. Liz had been chief of surgery at Yale. Her bestseller on breast cancer was in its sixteenth edition. Lucy was back on the roster of the Metropolitan as a principal soprano. Maggie had been the darling of Broadway for a couple of seasons before becoming a tenured professor at NYU. Each woman at Sam's party had racked up multiple accomplishments before they'd come to Maine.

In her cynical moments, Olivia described their little group of former luminaries "a bunch of old has-beens." It wasn't fair. They might have stepped back from responsibility and fame, but each of them continued to make a difference in people's lives. Like many older women, they were powerhouses of knowledge and experience. And like almost all older women, they were nearly invisible.

"Maggie, what do you think?" Maggie awoke from her thoughts and saw Lucy smiling in her direction.

"Are we still talking about the election? I'm cautiously optimistic, but it's going to be close."

"I'm afraid you're right," Olivia agreed. "But we can't give up."

Maggie heard the splash of water and the squeal of oar hooks as the fishers returned to dock. Sam hopped out and skillfully tied up the rowboat. Liz climbed on to the dock with three large fish looped together. She proudly showed them around. Lucy applauded. Maggie said, "Don't tell me you're going to clean them now." Across the circle of chairs, she could hear Lucy sigh.

"No, I'll just gut them and throw them in Sam's refrigerator. I'll finish cleaning them when we get home." She went off whistling an opera tune. For all her knowledge and sophistication, Liz was basically as simple as a child. Little things could make her so happy.

"The water is too warm, and the fish are lazy today," Sam said, setting her rod and the others against an old sawhorse.

Brenda shaded her eyes against the sun. "I never have luck when the sun's this high. And I was using live bait, which almost always works." She opened the little paper container and flung the contents into the pond. The worms protested by wriggling wildly as they made their descent.

"Hey! Why did you do that?" Sam asked. "I could have used them tonight!"

Brenda patted Sam's shoulder affectionately. "Sorry, buddy. I didn't think."

They were commiserating about how bad the fishing was when Liz returned with a plastic bag full of fish heads and innards. "Sam, should I dump these in the pond or on the compost heap?"

"Pond. The compost heap draws enough critters. The raccoons love fish guts. Fishers too."

When she'd first moved into Sam's house on the pond, Maggie had made the mistake of adding meat or fish scraps to the compostable waste. Growling and spitting, the skunks and racoons fought over the tastiest scraps. While Sam was away supervising a construction site, Maggie had heard deep breathing and was certain there was a peeping Tom in the yard. She'd called Liz, hoping she'd come over and defend her, but she'd laughed and said, "Maggie, that's no human prowler. It's a bear. They're hungry when they come out of their dens in the spring. Rotting meat is a delicacy because it's easy to chew. You're not throwing meat scraps on that pile, are you?" When Liz used that tone, Maggie found it impossible to lie to her.

When Sam and Liz went off to get dinner ready, Lucy relocated to the chair next to Maggie's. "Are you having a good time?" she asked solicitously.

Indecisive, Maggie tilted her head from side to side. "Mostly. It's nice to be with my friends again, but strange to be here now that Sam and I are no longer together. Like a return to the scene of the crime."

Lucy laughed softly. "There was no crime committed. Sam was here for you when you needed her."

"But now she's gone."

"Yes, but it had nothing to do with you. Please try to remember, her leaving wasn't to hurt you."

"Yup. I was just collateral damage," muttered Maggie. She could feel Lucy's eyes on her, studying her the way she might in a therapy session.

"Can you try to be happy for Sam?" Lucy asked gently. "Her

career is rebounding after she thought it was over. I can say from experience what a gift that can be."

"I know, Lucy, but no one left you for another opportunity. I've been left by women twice for something better." She gazed at Liz, who was tending the grill with Sam. "Lucy, I know I should forgive her...and Liz. That's all I talk about in my therapy."

"That's because forgiveness is about *your* peace. A better relationship with Sam or Liz is a side benefit, but the most important thing is you feeling good about yourself."

"That's what Gloria keeps saying, but sometimes, I want to think out loud with a *real* friend." Maggie gazed intently into Lucy's green eyes, hoping she would get the message.

"You know where I am," said Lucy and patted her hand. "Now, come back and join the conversation. I know you have strong opinions on this subject."

"I most certainly do!" Maggie declared.

"Then come on. Pull up your chair and join us."

❋❋❋

Sated from eating delicious food and a little tipsy from wine, Lucy was content to curl up in the rear seat and drowse on the way home. They'd briefly scuffled over the seating arrangements. Liz worried about the precedent it would set, but Lucy didn't care. She didn't have to assert her position through where she sat. Being petite, she often volunteered to sit in tight places, even on the drivetrain hump, if necessary.

The best thing about being in the back seat was being spared from conversation. After socializing, Lucy felt talked out. She huddled into Liz's hoodie, the ratty one she kept in the truck for when the wind on the beach was brisk. Lucy needed it more often than Liz because she felt the cold so keenly.

She allowed her lids to droop and listened to the soft voices drifting from the front seat. The sound was comforting and reminded her of when she'd first met Liz and Maggie. Back then, she was the third wheel to the couple in the front. Now, their roles were reversed. Lucy was the wife, and Maggie merely a "friend of the family." As the newly confirmed rector of the Episcopal church, Lucy had known few people in Hobbs except the church staff and vestry members. The church ladies had plied her with casseroles and invitations to tea, but it was obvious they were currying favor with the new rector. Maggie, however, seemed to have no agenda other than wanting a playmate. A fellow "recovering Catholic," Maggie was one of Lucy's first converts to the Episcopal Church. When the elderly music director retired, she'd happily replaced him.

In the beginning, Liz saw Lucy primarily as Maggie's friend. Liz had no use for "girly things" and rolled her eyes when Maggie and Lucy came home with their thrift shop finds. She'd thought even less of Lucy's religious role, but as a life-long opera fan, she certainly liked her classical voice. She'd sobbed after Lucy sang the "*Liebestod*" for her in the harbor because the sublimation had failed. Lucy had sung her heart out. The beauty of her performance had come close to satisfying Liz, but it wasn't enough. The physical consummation they'd both craved had hung excruciatingly out of reach.

The realization abruptly woke Lucy. She strained to hear the conversation in the front seat. They were making plans for the trip to New York for the Met's opening night gala. Maggie would look after the house and gardens as she did while Liz and Lucy were in Berlin, Salzburg, and Aix for the summer festivals. At the last minute, Lucy had replaced the ailing soprano singing in Bayreuth's production of *Lohengrin*. Thirty years ago, Elsa von Brabant had been Lucy's debut role at the Met. The performance had also been a rescue mission. It was more than coincidence that Morales wanted her to audition along with Denise for *The Mahler Two*, setting the stage for her comeback. Despite all her mother's carefully laid plans, Lucy's career had always turned on serendipity.

"The Met Gala sounds like so much fun," Maggie was telling Liz in a dreamy tone. "And where do I get to wear my gowns anymore, except at the Playhouse? At least, they don't care that they're out of style."

"Oh, I love wearing my old gowns," said Lucy, sitting up. "People think they're so cool and retro."

Liz engaged her eyes in the rear-view mirror. "I thought you were asleep. We were trying to be so quiet."

"I was just dozing. Too much good food and wine." She leaned forward between the front seats. "Maggie, I might still be able to get you tickets to the gala."

"Oh, I'd love to, but the semester is just beginning. It throws the students off when the professor takes a break at the start of a course. Maybe another time, when we can plan it."

"You're sure?" Lucy asked. "It would only take a phone call."

"I'm sure." Maggie turned and smiled warmly. "I look forward to when you're away, and I have the place to myself. I enjoy sitting in the garden. The kids like going to the beach. They *love* spending the night sleeping under the moose quilts." In the rear-view mirror Lucy could see Liz's sharp look. Maggie saw it too. "What? Did I do something wrong?"

There were parts of the house that Liz considered private, her office being one, and their third-floor bedroom being another. No one was allowed in either room without an express invitation. Lucy could practically feel Liz's disgust at the idea that people were roaming the house without her permission.

But in Maggie's case, the boundaries were fuzzy. She'd once shared the master bedroom with Liz. The invaders in question were Maggie's grandchildren. Liz loved Katrina and Nicki like her own. Maggie began speaking rapidly. "You said I could use your kitchen whenever I wanted and to make myself at home. Ellie said she wouldn't bill for washing the extra linen, but I did offer to pay the difference."

Lucy watched Liz as she tried to formulate a response. "The dirty sheets and towels aren't the issue," Liz finally said. In her tone, Lucy could hear how annoyed she was. Obviously, Maggie could too.

"Liz, if I've overstepped, I'm sorry. I know you love the kids. I didn't think you'd mind."

"It's fine, Maggie," Liz said, but it clearly wasn't. There was silence for the next few miles. "In fairness," Liz finally said, "we never discussed entertaining on the property. Of course, I don't mind you using our kitchen or bringing Katrina and Nicki into the house. But what if you meet someone who interests you, and you want to bring them home?"

Lucy was grateful for the ambiguous pronoun, which avoided the contemptuous spin Liz would have put on the word "him." Liz still couldn't forgive Maggie for dating men while they were together in college. When Maggie admitted she'd slept with a young actor to punish Liz, it had ended their marriage. "On second thought," Liz added, "if you intend to get involved with a man, go to his place. Don't bring him to our house."

"Liz!" Lucy reached around the headrest and pinched Liz's shoulder. "First, you offer Maggie a place to live, then you put unreasonable restrictions on her."

"Then we need to set some ground rules," said Liz tersely. "I won't have strange men in my house."

"Our house," Lucy gently reminded her.

Maggie was clearly unnerved by Liz's statement, but she spoke calmly. "Yes, we probably should have discussed having guests. We were all getting along so well, I never thought of asking. I just assumed..."

Lucy could see Liz's shoulders rising. She interrupted before a bad situation became worse. "Sounds like we should talk about company and the use of the house while we're away. But we don't have to do it tonight. We had lots of fun at Sam's, but I think we're all tired."

Unfortunately, Liz wouldn't let it go. "How often have you had the kids stay over?"

"Oh, just twice. The first time, they stayed with me in the apartment. Katrina thinks the sleeping nook is just the coolest thing. Nicki likes to snuggle."

"Me too," said Lucy, and then thought, *Why am I giving her so much information?*

"Me three," Maggie said. "Liz hates for anyone to touch her when she sleeps. I tried to reform her, not with much success, I might add."

Liz's eyes focused on Lucy in the rear-view mirror, daring her to say another word. "Some people never change," Lucy said lightly. "But let's set a date to iron out how to deal with your guests, Maggie. How's Tuesday night?"

"Can't. I have an evening class. Wednesday?"

"To be clear, Maggie," Liz said. She was clearly trying to smooth things over, but her stern tone still sounded stern. "This doesn't apply to the kids. They're family, and they're always welcome."

"Thanks, Liz. They feel the same. They love coming to see Grandma Liz." Maggie was clearly playing on Liz's unfailing loyalty to family and friends. Lucy watched the expression in Liz's eyes soften.

"Why don't we take them out on the boat this weekend? The Wet Lady could use a run. I can give you something for your seasickness. Are you free on Sunday afternoon?"

Maggie quickly checked her phone. "Yes, as a matter of fact."

"How about you, Luce?"

Lucy blew an exasperated jet of air so hard that red strands of hair flew up. Sunday after services was her downtime. She resented her afternoon being booked with a planned event.

"Sure," Lucy replied in a flat tone.

Liz completely missed or ignored her lack of enthusiasm and

went on making plans. "We can put in at the Scarborough marina, so Alina and Steve won't even need to drive down."

Unlike Liz, Maggie wasn't tone deaf. "You sure about this, Lucy?" She looked through the divider between the front seats.

"Whatever you two think. I'm just the passenger." Lucy sat back to take herself out of the conversation while Liz and Maggie went on planning the outing.

Liz stopped the truck in front of her bay and opened the door with her remote. "Do you need help bringing in your stuff, Maggie?"

"Thanks, Liz. I've got it." Maggie collected her cooler and bag of plastic storage containers from the seat next to Lucy. She caught her gaze. Lucy smiled to dispel any worry on Maggie's part. In return, Maggie apparently felt generous. "Thanks for talking me into going to Sam's. You were right. It was fun."

Lucy's smile, being held so long, was making her face hurt. She opened the door on her side to get out of the truck.

"Will you be working at home on Wednesday?" Maggie asked before she headed into the garage with the cooler.

Lucy had to think for a moment. Once a month, she did her sermon prep in the office, but that was last week. "Yes, if something doesn't come up."

"Mind if I stop by for a cup of coffee?"

"That's fine," said Lucy casually. "Just text me first, so I'm decent." Maggie's eyes swept Lucy's body, undressing her almost like a man would. Unnerved, Lucy forced herself to speak in a level tone. "If this is about the rules for company, Liz should be here."

Maggie shook her head. "No, it's about something else."

"Want to give me a hint?"

"Nothing to worry about," said Maggie, blowing her a kiss. "I'll tell you on Wednesday. Have a good night."

Chapter 3

Lucy wasn't sure if the ringing she'd heard was real. She sat up and listened more carefully, then decided she'd imagined the sound and went back to work. Usually, there were a couple of lines in the Gospel that jumped out as inspiration. This week's reading from Mark was a hodge-podge, including the famous line, 'For what will it profit a man to gain the whole world and forfeit his life?' Lucy scrolled down to see all her false starts. She always kept them lined up on the page in case she found herself stumped. If she were desperate enough, she could usually develop one of her earlier efforts into something.

Her phone suddenly lit up with a banner indicating a text message. *Are you there? You said you'd be home today. Your car is in the garage.*

Lucy didn't even have to look at who'd sent the message. Only Liz or Maggie would know that Lucy's car was in the locked garage.

Yes, I'm home, upstairs, working on my sermon.

Can you be disturbed? I'm at the garage door.

Lucy glanced at her watch. It was almost lunchtime. She'd wasted most of the morning answering church emails and text messages. No wonder she couldn't write this sermon. She wasn't making any progress, so why not allow the interruption? *I can take a break*, she texted.

Good. I'll make you lunch.

Maggie wasn't leaving her any choice. Since Lucy had lost so much weight after Erika's death, people presumed she needed to be fed copious amounts of nourishing food.

When Lucy opened the door, Maggie looked her over from head to toe. Lucy was wearing a T-shirt and capris, her usual casual outfit in the summertime. She'd brushed her hair and tied it in a loose ponytail but hadn't bothered with makeup. As usual, Maggie was carefully dressed, coiffed, and wore a full complement of makeup.

"Lucy, I'm so jealous," Maggie began, and Lucy instinctively braced herself. Maggie's theater-trained elocution and cleverness with language made her highly effective at landing a verbal punch, usually when Lucy was least prepared. "How can someone look so good with absolutely no effort?" Her hazel eyes were full of warmth, which implied she wasn't criticizing Lucy for neglecting her appearance. Lucy opened the door wider, and Maggie stepped into the house. "You look flummoxed, Lucy. Having a tough time with your sermon?"

Maggie's observation took her by surprise. From practicing therapy, Lucy had become so adept at hiding her feelings that opera directors occasionally had to remind her to show them. Then she realized she hadn't been particularly expressive. Maggie simply excelled at reading facial expressions and body language.

"It hasn't been a productive morning. Church business and pastoral texts and emails sucked up my time. When I finally sat down to write, my brain was so jangled I couldn't focus."

"I've been there. Sometimes, it's best to step away for a while and do something else." Maggie glanced toward the kitchen. "I promised you lunch. Mind if I peek into the refrigerator?"

Lucy stepped aside and indicated the way with her hand. "I'm pretty sure Liz left me some leftovers to heat up. She usually does, but there's probably not enough for two."

"It's nice that she takes such good care of you." Again, Lucy's ears went on alert to pick up any hint of sarcasm. *This is ridiculous,* she told herself. *Give the poor woman the benefit of the doubt.* "People tell me surgeons aren't known for it," Maggie continued, "but Liz got a double dose of the responsibility gene. She doesn't want you to fade away like you did in that awful winter. It was scary how much weight you lost."

"Grief can do that to a person. I was lucky to have so many people who care about me."

Maggie's eyes sought the floor. "I'm ashamed to say I wasn't one of them. While everyone was pitching in to help keep you and Emily going, I abandoned my best friend when you needed me most. I'm sorry, Lucy. I was just so angry and suspicious."

Lucy's eyes widened. She hadn't expected to hear a confession today. She tapped Maggie's arm to get her attention. "We all made mistakes. I survived. Now, come on. Let's see what we can find for our lunch."

While Maggie poked around in the refrigerator, Lucy found herself admiring her trim, shapely rear. Maggie kept herself fit by doing yoga and walking. She was in better shape than women decades younger. Maggie turned around suddenly. Lucy quickly changed the focus of her gaze, but not fast enough. Maggie, who never missed a trick, raised an eyebrow and cocked her hip. Lucy's cheeks flamed.

In the exchange of gestures, they'd had an entire conversation without speaking a single word. Maggie smiled, apparently to let Lucy know she wasn't taking it seriously. "I found the roast salmon Liz left for your lunch." Maggie held up a plate covered with plastic wrap. "You were right. It's not enough for two, but it would make some tasty sandwiches. Work for you?"

"Great," Lucy agreed, relieved to be talking about lunch instead of her sneak peek at Maggie's butt cheeks.

"Good. I love salmon salad. I don't make it as often because I like to make my own mayonnaise, but it's too much work for one person."

"You're not going to do that now?" Lucy asked, concerned because she was suddenly ravenous. The only thing she'd eaten today was some Greek yogurt.

"Don't worry, Lucy. Since I've been living alone again, I've decided making your own condiments is a foodie's affectation. Old-fashioned Hellman's is fine for a quick lunch. Even Julia Child thought so."

Maggie hummed a Broadway tune while she worked in the kitchen as if it were her own. Usually, she grumbled about the way Liz had rearranged things since she'd moved out, but she didn't complain or ask where anything was. Not that Lucy could help. She still opened drawers and doors until she found what she needed.

By now, Lucy had recovered from being caught admiring Maggie's anatomy. *All women check out one another*, she told herself and stole a few quick looks at Maggie's rear to assure herself there was no harm in it. She relaxed into listening to Maggie's tuneful humming. Despite Maggie's request to resume their singing lessons, neither of them had found the time. Maggie had a good voice, but it was largely untrained. Lucy made a resolution to remind her of the offer.

In less than ten minutes, Maggie had produced sandwiches worthy of a photo in *Food and Wine*. At the first taste, Lucy moaned appreciatively. Liz was an amazing cook, but Maggie had been professionally trained, and it showed.

"Good?" Maggie asked, fishing for compliments despite Lucy's obvious enjoyment.

Lucy covered her mouth because she was chewing. "Oh, my word, delicious! Thank you so much."

While eating silenced Lucy, Maggie took the opportunity to explain why she'd come. "You're probably wondering why I'm bothering you on your sermon prep day," she began casually. "I have two things on my mind…" Maggie's pregnant pause was clearly for effect. "The first is Liz's birthday, which, if you remember, is coming up this weekend."

Of course, Lucy remembered. She'd already made reservations at the Eventide Oyster Company restaurant in Portland, a birthday tradition predating their marriage.

"My last birthday before seventy was a hard one for me," Maggie admitted, "and I'm sure it will be harder for Liz, who thinks she'll never get old. We should do something special to cheer her up. We could invite some of her friends to join us on the boat. I'm willing to make a gourmet picnic lunch for all of us. I promise it will be special."

Of that Lucy had no doubt. "Sounds like fun. What can I do?"

"Bring the wine and drinks?"

That was an easy assignment. Liz kept a well-stocked wine cellar and bought cases of soft drinks at the discount club. "Maybe you can choose some wine from the basement before you go?" Lucy suggested, knowing Maggie would be flattered to be asked.

"I can, and I can call Cherie, Olivia, and Tony. If you could let Tom know…. I think that's plenty."

"I agree. We don't want to sink the boat."

"You could also pray for good weather since you have an inside line with the Almighty." Maggie raised her eyes, then winked rakishly. She was being positively seductive today. Lucy wondered what was going on. Her roaming eyes hadn't been *that* suggestive.

"Okay, now that we've decided our plans for Liz's birthday, what else?" Lucy asked between bites.

Maggie put down her sandwich, indicating she was now giving their conversation her complete attention. Everything she did was always scripted down to the smallest detail. Her hazel eyes suddenly filled. Lucy studied her to make sure these weren't stage tears. "What's wrong?" she finally asked.

"Lucy, I've missed you so much! It's not easy for me to make friends with other women. I always saw them as competitors, even in school. As an actress, it was worse. Have you ever gone to a casting call?"

"No, but I did lots of vocal competitions before my *Fach* job in Stuttgart."

Maggie looked puzzled. "I have no idea what that is."

"The *Fach* system classifies singers by the range, color, and quality of their voices. When a singer is hired by a German opera company they are expected to learn and be able sing any of the operas in their *Fach*."

"Really? What's your *Fach*?" Maggie almost said it right.

"I was a *jugendlich-dramatischer Sopran*, a young dramatic soprano. My favorite roles were Desdemona in *Otello* and Cio-Cio San in *Butterfly*. Back then, Stuttgart wasn't big on Italian opera, so I sang the lighter Wagnerian roles too."

"Fascinating," Maggie said but didn't sound like she thought so. She'd finished her sandwich and wiped her fingers on the napkin. "Do you speak German with Liz like Erika used to do?"

"Sometimes, but not often. Liz only speaks German to me when she doesn't want others to know what we're talking about."

"Figures."

"Maggie, why are you so critical of Liz?"

"I guess I still haven't completely forgiven her for choosing you over me." At least, it was an honest answer.

"Do you feel like we're competing?" Lucy asked cautiously. "I know that's a stupid question, because we've been involved with the same woman, but I mean otherwise?"

"Oh, Lucy. Sometimes, I *hate* you, not because you're with Liz now, but because you're so beautiful and talented. You have a magnificent voice and such genuine warmth. It's irresistible. Everyone loves you!"

Lucy was startled by the direct assessment. "My looks came from my mom. She was a model. Yes, I have natural talent, but my mother worked damn hard to train my voice. I sang exercises until I was hoarse. She taught me how to smile, not like a movie star, but from the heart."

"Your smile is your trademark. But you can see why any woman would be jealous of your gifts."

"As you know, I have plenty of faults. I didn't discourage Liz from flirting, which was as bad as inviting her."

"I should have stopped it, but I understood what you were

doing. That's what all women are socialized to do, to deflect sexual attention in a way that doesn't offend. We're trained to coddle male egos and let them down gently when we're not interested."

Maggie was giving her an out, but Lucy didn't take it because it didn't fit the situation. If Liz had been available, she would have fallen for her from the moment they'd met. But Liz had come to the carols and lessons service with her pretty, elegantly dressed wife. Since Liz was taken, Lucy had recalibrated her sights and focused on Erika, who was available. No matter how candid they were being, Maggie didn't need to know any of this. Instead, Lucy said, "None of us were blameless in that situation. I think Liz has come to regret her flirting."

"Really? I wish she'd tell me."

"Oh, I think she will. Give her time."

"I've waited a long time, Lucy. It still hasn't happened."

"That doesn't mean it won't. Liz has worked hard since the shooting. She's had to face many regrets, not only killing Peter Langdon."

"She hates therapy. How did you convince her to do it?"

Lucy smiled slyly. "I have my ways."

"I bet you do." Maggie responded with an equally sly smile. Her brows puckered and she looked contrite. Like everything Maggie did, it was theatrical. "Lucy, I want us to make a fresh start. We can't erase the pain of the past, but we can try again. It was so much fun hanging out with you at the playhouse, prowling the shops. I miss all that."

"The fall is my busy season because of the deal I made with Tom, but in the winter, I'll be home more, and we can go shopping."

"I hope so. Lately, I've decided I absolutely *hate* everything in my closet."

Lucy took out her phone. "Let me look at my calendar. I don't know if it will be this week, and next, I'll be in New York for rehearsals."

Maggie touched her arm. "Lucy, I know you have your hands full. You've had a busy summer between the festivals and Brad Taylor's foundation."

Lucy saw an opportunity to make a point. "It would lighten my load if you got involved in the foundation. Tony Roselli is having a great time performing with us."

"I know, and I really miss performing. Let me think about it."

Best to leave the suggestion here and move on. Maggie would become resistant if pushed too hard. Lucy understood that overcoming a lifetime of social expectations wasn't easy, but Maggie compensated by going overboard.

Maggie started picking up the lunch dishes. "I just needed to talk to you. The truth is, I don't make friends easily. I've missed you, Lucy. I need you. Please give me another chance." Admitting this was a big share. Lucy knew she should take the opportunity to reinforce Maggie's honesty. She glanced at the clock over the kitchen sink. If she pushed herself, she could get her sermon written.

"Maggie, if you give me an hour or two after lunch, I'll finish my sermon, and we can go shopping this afternoon."

Maggie bent and looked into Lucy's eyes. "I don't want to put you under more pressure."

"You're not, and a time constraint will force me to get my sermon done. I miss you too. Give me two hours. Then we'll go to the shops."

Maggie hugged Lucy close. "Can't wait!"

✳✳✳

Momentarily trapped pulling the slinky dress over her head, Lucy would never know that Maggie was admiring her bra. Whenever they went out to try on clothes, she was fascinated by Lucy's unapologetically sexy underwear. She could get away with wearing intense colors like scarlet or deep purple because they wouldn't show through her black clerical blouse. The frothy lace of her silky, deep-plunging, front-open hot pink bra showed the tops of her shapely breasts. Maggie felt a sudden compulsion to touch them.

Her own breasts had always been smaller than she'd liked. During the double mastectomy to remove her cancerous breast and the other that could be fertile ground for a recurrence, Liz's brilliant protégée had followed her instructions to the letter, preserving most of the sensitivity. The plastic surgeon had used larger implants to give Maggie the figure she'd always wanted. But Maggie's breasts weren't real. Lucy's were, and they were absolutely perfect.

Lucy finally managed to free herself from the dress, removing the temptation from Maggie's view. She emerged from the strangling garment with her red hair going in every direction. She pulled out the tie and shook out her hair. Maggie watched her try to smooth it back, imagining styles that would suit that red mane.

"I think I'll pass on that dress," said Lucy. "It's not worth permanent confinement. Plus, it didn't look right on me. Too tight everywhere."

"But Liz would love it. She'd never take her eyes off you."

"Oh, I don't need to wear clingy dresses to get her attention. She just can't help herself." Lucy's statement was completely factual without even a hint of bragging because it was true. Whenever Lucy was around, Liz's eyes were riveted to her.

"Do you buy your underwear to keep her interested?" Maggie asked in a deliberately casual tone, despite her barely restrained urge to caress the perfect orb of flesh straining the confines of the silky bra.

Lucy continued to stand there in her revealing underwear, apparently unaware of how desperately Maggie wanted to touch her. "I've always bought my lingerie and underwear for myself, no one else."

"Most women do. Sexy underwear turns on the wearer as much or more than the beholder."

Lucy looked thoughtful. "It's more than that for me," she said.

"When I was traveling so much and laundering clothes in hotel bathrooms, I bought what they used to call 'drip-dry' underwear. After the rape, I felt used and ugly. I couldn't stand to look at myself in the mirror—hard for a performer, as you know. Then a friend suggested I buy myself some sexy underwear. At first, I could barely stand the feel of it, but eventually, I got used to wearing it. I've worn it ever since. Now, I'm probably Victoria's Secret's best customer."

"There are cheaper places," confided Maggie behind her hand.

"I'm sure I know every one of them," Lucy replied cheerfully. "Even though Liz knows the whole story, she accuses me of having an underwear fetish."

"Ignore her. What does she know? I had to beg her to replace her white cotton panties when they wore out. You have a perfect body for fancy underwear. Your boobs fill out those "C" cups perfectly. You could be a model like your mother."

One of Lucy's auburn brows tilted slightly. Maggie wondered if she'd sensed from the excessive compliments that she'd wanted to touch her. Hopefully, she'd think the flattery had a different motive.

Lucy merely said, "Thanks." Another woman might have added a self-deprecating remark, but not Lucy. She put on her sundress, removing the scenic view. "What do you say to an early dinner?"

"Liz won't mind?"

Lucy shrugged. "As you know, Liz looks out for herself very well."

They gathered up the things they'd taken in to try on to return to the lady at the door. On the way to the car, they discussed where to eat. Some of their favorites were on limited schedules due to lack of workers to serve tables and prepare food. "If he gets back in and makes good on his immigration threats," said Maggie, "who's going to stand in the hot sun and pick the crops? You can bet it won't be those Proud Boys."

"I pray every day we don't go back there, but it's so close. I really worry. It keeps Liz up at night."

Maggie started her car. "I know. I see the lights in the house going on and off in the wee hours of the morning. Since I'm awake anyway, I think about going over to see if she wants company. But I know she's probably in the media room listening to music at full volume and wouldn't hear me ring the bell."

"It's very weird to hear my voice that loud. I worry that the volume will affect her hearing, but she's a doctor and says she's not concerned."

Maggie shook her head. "Of course, she's not. She's always tempting fate. But I'm not surprised the election is keeping her awake. She and her mother had their morning political chat until the old woman became so deaf that phone calls were impossible. I'd listen to Liz and Erika out on the porch, babbling in German about the state of the world. Didn't have a clue what they were saying, but I'm sure it was interesting. I miss Erika." Maggie felt awkward, realizing she'd just told Lucy that she missed her deceased wife. "Sorry. Wasn't thinking."

Lucy looked sad but not offended. "I wonder what Erika would say about these times. Nothing good, I'm sure. After living in East Germany before the end of the Soviet Union, she despised authoritarianism."

"She and Liz bonded over the guilt from the past. As you know, Liz's father fought for the other side in the war. As long as I've known her, she's been struggling to understand how the Germans allowed Hitler to come to power. Now, we know."

Lucy reached out and touched Maggie's shoulder. "We should decide where we want to eat. Carrying the world's burdens requires fuel."

Maggie thought for a moment. "Down the Hatch? Their chowder lobster roll special is the best. Liz will hate us for not including her. It's one of her favorite eateries."

"So? Let's call her and see if she can join us. She might not like to shop, but she loves to eat!"

Lucy took out her phone and called Liz. She turned away to look out at the salt marsh while she waited for her to answer. Maggie understood the need for visual relief after sorting through too many racks of castoff clothing. "She's coming," Lucy announced after getting off with Liz. "She'll be here in a few minutes."

They headed to the restaurant. As they sat waiting for Liz to arrive, Maggie said, "Thanks for coming out with me today, Lucy. I'm probably keeping you from getting packed for your trip, which I'm sure is a big deal."

"Not really. I used to travel so much I've got it down to a science. Casual clothes for rehearsals. Enough dresses or suits for dinners and business meetings. A gown for the opening night gala and each performance of the Requiem. Because it's a religious work, I'll try to avoid brilliant colors or necklines that show too much cleavage."

Like they'd been given permission, Maggie's eyes instantly dropped to the space between Lucy's breasts. "Does it really matter?"

"No, but everyone knows I'm a priest, so they look at me differently. Even before I was ordained, I was careful about what I wore when I sang a religious work."

Liz's truck prowled past Maggie's Subaru on her way to find a place to park. She rolled down the window and called out. "Get a table. I'll meet you inside."

Down the Hatch was iconic shoreline dining. Long tables with benches for "family style" dining meant diners sat wherever they could. The napkins were a roll of paper towels suspended from the ceiling. The salt and pepper shakers were beer bottles with nail-pierced caps. The condiments, including the tartar sauce from a plastic squirt container, sat in a galvanized bucket on the table.

It was early for the dinner crowd, so they easily found space for the three of them. The neighboring diners at the table were just finishing their meal. They departed leaving piles of used napkins, empty steamer shells, and bright red lobster fragments. Maggie looked at the remnants with disgust. The tourists never knew how to clean out a lobster properly, leaving behind meat, and the green to-malley and orange roe, considered delicacies by lobster aficionados.

"Hey." Liz sat down and swung her long legs over the bench. "I was done for the day. Just catching up on paperwork. Thanks for the invite."

"We only invited you so you can pay," said Maggie.

Lucy stared at her in horror. "That's not true!"

"Of course, not, but Liz is a control freak, so she always offers to pay."

"In that case, Maggie, I'll give you the bill," Liz said lightly. "I just checked your portfolio. It's going gangbusters."

Lucy turned to Maggie in surprise. "You let Liz look at your portfolio?"

"She has trusted access to all my accounts."

Lucy's auburn brows dipped to the base of her nose. "How long has this been going on?"

Maggie shrugged. "Since we got married. I never changed it."

Lucy glanced at Liz, looking for an explanation.

"I just keep an eye on things to make sure Olivia isn't taking any big risks with Maggie's money. I look at yours too. What's the big deal? Erika used to let me do it for her too. That's why she could leave you that big pile of money." That finally seemed to satisfy Lucy. She busied herself with studying the chalkboard that listed the specials. "They have fried oysters today. I think I'll have those."

"I'm going to have a lobster roll *and* fried oysters!" Liz declared. "My mother loved them. Whenever she came to Maine, which wasn't often, she *had to* have them."

"I remember," Maggie said.

Lucy sighed. "I wish I'd had a chance to meet your mother."

"No, you don't," Liz corrected. "She hated Maggie because she was too much competition. I can't even imagine how nasty she'd be to you." Maggie stared at Liz, who obviously had no idea how insulting she'd been.

The waitress took their orders and came back with Liz's beer and two individual bottles of pinot grigio for Maggie and Lucy. The wine was the cheap mass-produced kind.

Watching Maggie's look of disgust, Liz said, "Not the place to order wine. But they always have good local beers on tap. How do I turn you two into beer drinkers?"

"I think it's too late for that. Don't you agree, Lucy?"

"Oh, I'll have a beer with Liz on a hot day," said Lucy. "I find it refreshing. But would I go out of my way to order it? No."

"In Maine, we live in the land of brewing opportunity!" She studied the bottle in front of her. "But I don't think I'll order this IPA again. Too bitter." She made a little face.

"Order something else," Maggie suggested.

"Nah, I always finish what I start, unless it's so awful I just can't."

Maggie wondered what that said about their marriage.

Chapter 4

Ginny, the practice manager, finally put down her tablet. "I think that's everything, Liz. You are officially off duty." Bobbie Lantry, the practice's nurse practitioner would be covering for Liz while she was away. So far, the new arrangement so Liz could travel with Lucy was working. As soon as Lucy's agent confirmed a booking, Ginny rearranged Liz's schedule. Bobbie saw Liz's patients and Amy provided backup. Before leaving Hobbs, Liz always met with the staff because anything so tightly wound had the potential to quickly unwind.

"Unlike last time, I'll be in New York, not out of the country, so there's no time difference and you can easily get in touch."

"Either way, we can handle it, Liz," Amy assured her with a friendly pat on the arm. "You need to trust us." The cardiologist's placid personality had a calming influence on the practice. As a former surgeon, Liz kept everyone on their toes. The staff seemed less anxious under Amy's leadership.

Since Liz had agreed to scale back her involvement in the practice, it had undergone important changes. Since the death of her longtime partner, Bobbie had come back full time. Active practice had invigorated her. She'd taken on mentoring their refugee nurse, Teresa Gai, who was training to be a nurse practitioner. Cherie had mostly taken over Hobbs Family Counseling from Lucy, advantageous because as a PA, she could write scripts. Liz still leaned heavily on Ginny, who'd come with the practice when Liz had bought it over ten years before. New hires were instructed to take care of her under all circumstances. "We can't ever afford to lose Ginny," Liz lectured all new staff. "She knows where all the bodies are buried."

Liz had been watching the clock. After the meeting was over, she'd drive home to pick up Lucy, who'd be anxious because they were having dinner with Roger Weinstein, her agent. Unfortunately, a cardiac emergency had kept Amy on the phone, so they'd started late.

Liz's phone vibrated on the desk. Of course, it was Lucy, wondering where she was. "Excuse me," said Liz, and tapped open the call. "I'm leaving in two minutes. I promise."

"Ok-a-a-y," said Lucy, signaling she was trying to be patient.

"You'd better go, Liz," Ginny urged. "You know Lucy means what she says." Liz glanced around the room. Everyone knew so much about the others, and their better halves, even their extended families. At Yale, Liz would have found the blurred lines between the personal and the professional horrifying, but in a small town like Hobbs, no one had much choice. Your doctor was your neighbor, your friend, the president of your club, and sometimes, even the person who showed up to do emergency plumbing. But Liz wouldn't have it any other way.

"All right, team. Ginny is right. My wife will have my hide if I don't get home," said Liz getting up. "You know where to reach me."

Amy got up too and affectionately patted Liz's shoulder. "Don't worry. We won't call you unless the place is on fire."

"God forbid!" Ginny said. "Remember that awful fire at Cliff Manor? Liz almost didn't get married because of it."

Bobbie gave Liz a nudge. "You'd better go. You know Lucy has a temper."

Liz, who was unlocking her gun safe, turned around. "Bobbie, how do you know?"

Bobbie looked sheepish. "I've heard Susan talk about it."

"You need to tell your lady friend that she shouldn't be talking about her boss like that." Liz grinned but she meant the warning.

"Susan would die if she knew I'd told you."

Liz laughed. "Okay. I won't tell on you...*this time.*"

Liz chased everyone out of her office and hurried out to her SUV. When she got home, she saw the garment bags with Lucy's gowns draped over the porch railing. She wasn't joking about wanting to get on the road.

"Glad you finally decided to show up." Lucy wasn't usually given to sarcasm, so she was clearly annoyed.

"Don't worry. We'll get there in time."

Lucy climbed into the passenger seat. "It's a Friday in September. The traffic will be horrendous. Let's go."

Liz hurried into the house and down to the basement to secure her gun in the safe and do a last check that all the doors were locked.

"Liz, please don't do that to me again," Lucy said when Liz got back in the car. "I know that doctors can be detained by emergencies, but please try to be on time when we're leaving for an engagement." She'd used her calm therapist's voice, but Liz had no doubt she was furious.

"Luce, I'm sorry I was late, but next time, please don't schedule a dinner date on the day we're travelling. It's five hours to New York when there's no traffic."

"I just wanted to get the meeting with Roger over and done. Now that I've gotten serious about singing, he's gotten worse, not better."

"I get it. You're a hot property now. He wants to make money on you while he can. He hears the clock ticking."

"I hear it too, but that doesn't mean either of us can do much about it. If he wears me out, it will just end my career sooner."

Liz didn't like to hear that kind of talk. "You know I won't allow that to happen."

Lucy reached out to pat her thigh. "Sweetie, I love you for being so protective, but you're not helping when you push after I say I don't think I can't do something. The Bayreuth thing was important, but like you always say, I need to pace myself."

"Okay, Madame Bartlett, then sit back and relax and let your trusty chauffeur drive you into the city. Mind if I put on some music?"

"Fine. Just no opera."

Liz streamed light classical music through her Bluetooth. As she'd predicted, the southbound traffic was light. While they were passing through Connecticut, Maggie called to say that the water timer in the garden had gone off on schedule.

Liz tapped the button on the wheel to end the call. "I'm glad Maggie is home, holding down the fort."

"Have you noticed how hard she tries to make herself useful?" Lucy said.

"Yes, now that you mention it, she often goes beyond the call of duty. Maybe she feels she needs to justify living rent free in the garage apartment. I don't know why. I let other people live there for nothing. I think she just wants to feel useful."

"Hmm. It's more than that," Lucy said. "I just haven't figured out what it is yet."

❋❋❋

Maggie elbowed aside some dishes that had been unloaded from the dishwasher but never shelved to put down the plate of cupcakes. Finding a place in the refrigerator to store the stew she'd brought for dinner had been a challenge. There were so many storage containers with leftover food. Maggie had been tempted to go toss anything that looked suspicious. At least, she could dump the expired condiments, but this was no longer her house, and certainly not her home. No wonder Alina had been pressuring her to move in with them. Things had gotten completely out of hand.

She decided to be a respectful guest and try to ignore the chaos and filth, but she worried about the example being set. At thirteen, Katrina was old enough to see the difference between her mother's housekeeping and when Maggie had lived with them.

A little dust or disorder never bothered Maggie, but she insisted on a clean kitchen. Her mother, despite a full-time job and four children, had kept their tiny Cape Cod scrupulously clean. Her brothers and sister had elbowed each other for space at the table and fought over the last scrap of meat, but her mother's kitchen was always spotless.

In college, Maggie rebelled against her mother's compulsive cleanliness and turned the dorm room into a disorderly mess. She was always behind on her laundry. When she finally did it, the clothes remained in piles until she wore them. She never put away her clothes and slept under an ever-growing stack of blouses, skirts, and jeans. Liz, who'd been raised to strict housekeeping standards by her German grandmother, finally reached her limit. In a fit of disgust, Liz did all of Maggie's laundry and put away her clothes. Having order imposed was a game changer. Maggie hadn't known where to begin. By tackling the disaster, Liz had solved the problem for her. In appreciation, Maggie had taken Liz straight to bed.

Smiling at the memory, Maggie wondered if organizing the mess in Alina's kitchen was the impetus she needed to reset her environment. While she waited for her daughter to return from picking up the girls, Maggie put away the relatively clean dishes. Anything questionable she put in the dishwasher. She pulled out the trash can from under the sink and began going through the refrigerator. She'd wash the shelves and bins another time, but one needed immediate attention. She was scrubbing it when Alina walked in.

While the girls tackled their grandmother, their mother took in the newly decluttered kitchen. Maggie distracted the girls with the fancy cupcakes decorated with buttercream violets that she'd brought. "Wash your hands, please," Maggie ordered, hypersensitive to hygiene after her repulsive task. When she turned around, she found her daughter glaring at her.

"What made you think I wanted you to clean up my kitchen?" she asked in a cold, accusatory tone.

"I think that's obvious," Maggie said, then wished she hadn't. Alina could melt down under the mildest criticism. Since her daughter's bad reaction to a medication switch, Maggie had been more careful. She was used to managing Alina's mood swings since she and her sister had arrived from Romania over thirty years ago. Life in an overcrowded orphanage had traumatized her and her sister. Sophia had recovered well enough to go to medical school and become a doctor, but Alina still needed bi-weekly therapy and medication. Sophia probably would have made a more emotionally stable parent, but it was Alina who'd gotten married and had two children. After Liz had explained epigenetics, Maggie worried that the horrible conditions in the orphanage could have altered her daughters' genes and those of their descendants for generations.

Alina could get past her triggered responses when she tried. While Maggie replaced the food on the clean shelf, she guessed Alina was calming herself with one of the cognitive therapy techniques she'd learned from Cherie Harrison, who'd taken over her therapy and medication.

"I'll take that out for you," Alina offered, watching Maggie tie up the bulging trash bag. Maybe Alina had figured out the task would help her recover her composure.

Maggie smiled, hoping her daughter would see that she wanted to make peace. "Thank you."

After Alina left, Maggie could finally turn her attention to her granddaughters. The girls were demolishing the plate of cupcakes. Nicki's tongue was purple from the buttercream pansies. Maggie sat on the stool beside Nicki and smoothed her long dark hair. Her granddaughters bore little resemblance to their hazel-eyed, fair grandmother. Nevertheless, she considered them "bone of her bone and blood of her blood." She craved their scent and the touch of their young skin just like any grandmother. The thought made her pull Nicki closer.

"I love you, Nicki," she whispered, kissing the top of the girl's head.

"I love you too, grandma," Nicki crooned. Katrina slipped off her stool and came over to get some hugs.

"Yes, they miss you," Alina said, returning. She replaced the garbage bag in the can. "They keep asking when you're going to move back in."

Maggie continued to pet the girls. She didn't care if some of the brightly colored icing transferred to her fancy sweater.

"Let's talk about it later," Maggie advised, not wanting to upset them.

"Girls, you've had enough sugary treats," Alina said in a relatively mild voice. The trip to the garage had calmed her. "Why don't you let me and grandma talk for a while?" Katrina grabbed another cupcake and took off. Nicki lingered, unwilling to leave her grandmother's arms. Alina shot her a stern look, and the girl reluctantly followed her sister.

Alina waited a few moments until she heard the bedroom doors close.

"I apologize if I overstepped," Maggie said.

"No, you did me a favor, and I should be grateful." Alina released a long sigh. "I let it get out of hand. It became so bad I didn't even know where to start."

So, what Maggie had suspected was true. "Maybe you should hire a cleaner. Between you and Steve, you have a good income."

Alina's dark eyes focused on her. "We do, but we also have a big mortgage." That was an obvious dig because Maggie was holding the note.

"I'm sorry, sweetie, but Sam insisted that I sell the house to you at the actual value."

"What does Sam know about real estate?" Maggie was surprised at Alina's bitterness toward Sam. They'd always seemed to get along so well.

"As an architect, she knows quite a bit. And Olivia, who's my financial advisor, agreed. You're buying the house for practically a zero-percent mortgage when rates are high. If you had to pay what the banks are charging now, you couldn't afford it."

"You're right, Mom." Maggie had a flicker of hope that today was one of Alina's reasonable days. Then her daughter added, "as always."

Maggie needed to draw on her acting skills to resist reacting. "How about I pay for the cleaner? Even once a week would help keep things under control."

"You already pay for the girls' babysitter after school and all their school fees. I'm not a charity case, Mom."

"No, but you could clearly use some help. You have a busy, responsible job. You work long hours."

Alina laughed. "Ironic that you'd pay for me to have household help, when Liz is paying for yours." It was an assumption on Alina's part, but one that happened to be true.

"Liz pays Ellie to clean the whole place. I throw in extra tips and money for cleaning supplies. The poor woman works so hard. She's trying to put her daughter through college."

"You ladies have quite the little commune down there." Alina had meant it sarcastically, but she sounded almost envious.

"Yes, I guess we do. It works for us."

"I could never live with my ex and another partner."

"It's different with women," Maggie said, realizing the truth of her words as she spoke them.

"You could live here. I promise I'll never throw you out again."

Maggie involuntarily shuddered at the memory of that awful night. After listening to the shouting and crashing objects above her for over an hour, she'd interrupted a fight between Alina and her fiancé. Terrified, the girls had cowered with her in the basement apartment. When Maggie had gone upstairs to try to reason with her daughter, she became even more infuriated. She'd gone down to the basement, scattering the girls like frightened chickens before throwing Maggie's belongings into her bags. Maggie still wondered how the tiny woman had found the strength to bring them out to the driveway.

"My medication is under control now," Alina assured her,

bringing her back to the present. "I promise, Mom. It will never happen again."

Maggie looked into her daughter's eyes, knowing her PTSD and dependence on medication made such promises impossible to keep. "It's not just you, Alina. That little apartment is dark and cramped. It makes my Village apartment in New York look like a palace. Besides, you're establishing a new relationship. The girls don't need me like they once did. It's time for me to move on."

"But you can do so much good here. When you were living downstairs, the place never got out of control like this."

"Alina, despite what the Republican vice-presidential candidate says, post-menopausal women do not exist to take care of their grandchildren. I am not a domestic servant. I have a PhD from Yale, and I teach college students. Besides, I'm not exactly the best housekeeper myself."

"But Mom, the girls miss you. I miss you!" Alina suddenly looked much younger than her thirty-four years. Maggie could see the little dark-haired waif who'd gotten off the plane from Romania, clutching her sister's hand. Then as now, she looked so frightened and vulnerable. Maggie swept her up in her arms. At first, Alina seemed startled by the sudden display of affection, but she hugged back fiercely.

"I miss you too, Alina, but Hobbs isn't far. This works for me. Trust me on this."

Alina finally let her go. "But, Mom, look what happened when you trusted Sam to provide a place for you to live."

Maggie had her issues with Sam, but Alina's criticism rankled. "She offered me the use of the house while she's away, but it's too isolated. I was frightened being there all alone. Look, Alina, things seldom turn out as we plan. The best we can do is adjust. It's the key to survival. Trying to keep things the same never works."

"But there you are, back with your ex."

Maggie tried to hide her frustration. Alina might be emotionally damaged, but like her sister, she was perceptive and whip smart. "Liz...and Lucy have always been there for me, even in my darkest hour. Why wouldn't I go to them?" Maggie listened to the words she'd just spoken, realizing their import for the first time.

"But, Mom, we're your *family*."

"Alina, they're my family too," Maggie replied gently. "It doesn't make you and the girls any less. You know I will help you and support you in any way I can. That was the pledge I made to you and Sophia when your father and I adopted you. But you are both adults now, and there is only so much I can do. Please say you'll accept my offer to pay for a house cleaner."

Alina's dark brows had dipped toward her nose while Maggie had been speaking. Finally, she nodded. "Thanks, Mom. I appreciate it."

"Now, do you mind if I continue to straighten up here a little? I can't eat in a filthy kitchen."

"I'll help you," Alina volunteered.

"Okay, sweetheart, but go change out of your work clothes first."

Chapter 5

Drying the last of the pans, Lucy enjoyed the comforting sounds in the house. There was a gentle clatter as Maggie put away the serving dishes. In the living room, Liz was stacking wood next to the stove. How easily they'd fallen into sharing the chores of keeping their household going. Maggie had taken over most of the meal preparation, freeing Liz to do more of the outside work. Lucy and Liz alternated kitchen cleanup, which they both hated. Splitting the responsibility made it less of a burden. Liz always said that life was easier for a couple than a single person. Lucy was learning that three worked even better than two.

Lucy was glad to finally hang up the dishtowel. "Maggie, do you plan to watch the vice president's interview tonight?"

"Of course! I wouldn't miss it."

"Would you like to watch it with us?"

"I've heard some people have been organizing watch parties. Do you think the three of us qualify?"

"Why not? I'll open another bottle of wine. Liz can share some of her salty snacks. That counts as a party, doesn't it?"

When Liz came into the kitchen, Lucy told her that she'd invited Maggie to watch the *Sixty Minutes* interview.

"Funny. While I was out in the living room, I was thinking about hanging a TV. I could put it on the wall where we have the painting of the old barn, and it won't be intrusive. I don't know why I resisted the idea so long."

"You wanted to reserve the room for socializing and reading, not TV," Maggie reminded her.

"We could watch the interview in the media room."

"It's too big. And it's where I practice," Lucy protested. "When I watch the news, I want a cozy place to curl up."

"I designed the media room for watching movies and streaming live performances. What do you think of a TV in the living room?"

Liz raised her hand. "All in favor, say…" Maggie and Lucy raised their hands and said 'aye' in unison.

"Good. I'll work on fishing the wires tomorrow. Meanwhile, we could invite Maggie to watch in our upstairs TV room. Okay, Lucy?"

Lucy understood that Liz was asking permission to bring Maggie into one of their intimate spaces. "Sure, I'll go up and get it ready. Meanwhile, you can round up some treats. Maybe Maggie can go down to the wine cellar and choose a bottle."

"White?" Maggie asked, looking at Lucy, then Liz.

"I don't care which you pick," said Liz. "I'm going to drink beer."

Lucy rolled her eyes. "As long as you don't get into a drinking game with your whiskey."

"Hmm," said Liz, stroking her chin. "Depends on what the drinking game is. Let me think about that."

"Skip the whiskey. I don't want to have to carry you up the stairs."

The absurdity of the thought made Liz laugh. "That's why we have an elevator…for moments of infirmity…and when we grow old together."

"Never mind, Liz. Stick with the beer. Maggie and I will share a bottle of wine."

"Pinot, of course?" Maggie glanced at Lucy.

Lucy nodded, thinking how nice it was to have an ally, especially one who understood her preferences so well. Then she realized the person they were conspiring against was her wife, which felt disloyal and wrong. Maggie went down to the basement to pick out the wine. Lucy turned to Liz. "Do you feel like Maggie and I gang up on you?"

Liz shrugged. "I'm used to it."

"Liz, that's not what I asked."

"Sometimes, I feel outnumbered, but I know you're only teasing." The adult, analytical Liz had answered Lucy's question, not the sensitive tomboy who could be easily wounded by a sharp word from a woman.

"I'm on your side," Lucy reminded her and stood on her toes to give her a kiss. "If you ever feel like the teasing hurts, you'll let me know, right?"

"Of course, but I never feel you're *not* on my side. I know you love me."

Lucy mentally gave Liz a gold star for the right answer.

Maggie finally returned with the wine. "You have so many bottles of Chardonnay and Sauvignon Blanc that go to waste down there. I brought up a pinot because it's Lucy's favorite, but we really should work on reducing the stock of the others. White wines don't keep long."

"Good point, Maggie," said Liz. "Now if you can just convince my wife."

"I don't need convincing. Next time, Maggie, bring up whatever you'd like to drink." After Lucy said it, she felt Liz studying her curiously.

They settled into the guestroom they'd converted to a TV room. Lucy realized that apart from when the children visited, no one had been invited to join them in this private space. Usually, Liz would stretch out on the sofa and lay her head in Lucy's lap, but with a guest present, she'd be more formal. She tore into the bag of salty chips, rattling loudly until Lucy gave her the side-eye. Liz instantly dumped the bag into the bowl and offered it around. Soon, they were all crunching anxiously.

"Well, she's certainly sticking to the script," Liz said. "I don't understand why she can't articulate how her administration would be different from Biden's. Basically, she's saying it will be the same in substance, only with her stamp on it. I'm worried."

"You're not the only one," Maggie agreed.

As the interview continued, the three of them stress ate all the salty snacks.

***

Liz cursed the double sole plate that resisted penetration with her most powerful drill. She had every tool known to man, yet sometimes a project simply defied her. She rested her arms for a moment. Holding the drill overhead had made them ache. She poked in the hole she was trying to drill and saw that she was almost there.

She'd always believed if she was going to start a project it should be done right, which was why she was installing a new outlet for the living room TV. She'd already cut out the drywall for the new wiring, installed the outlet housing, and hung the TV mount on the studs. Now, if she could only get this damned hole drilled, she'd be home free. The drill showered shavings on her arms as she leaned on it. Finally, the bit broke through. She attached the new cable to the fish wire, but it hit a snag. "Fucking pain-in-the-ass project!" she growled.

Maggie came into the living room. "Liz, I can hear you swearing all the way in the kitchen."

"Why the fuck did I ever think this was a good idea?"

"It is a good idea. Having another TV makes perfect sense."

Liz eyed Maggie cautiously. "Glad you approve. We didn't always agree about decorating this house."

"I admit I found your 'Maine cabin in the woods' look a little over the top. I wanted more modern seating in here, not this big old leather furniture. But I know you like it, so it's okay with me."

Liz raised a brow. "And when did you come to this conclusion?"

"When I lived at my daughter's and then at Sam's and realized how good I had it here. Even though you didn't let me touch this room, you let me decorate other spaces to my taste."

"And you filled it up with your tchotchkes, which drove me crazy."

Maggie gently stroked Liz's shoulder. "Which you were kind enough to tolerate." She gazed around the room fondly. "If I lived here again, I would be more restrained. Part of adding my things to the space was to establish I belonged. Most of my stuff from the

New York apartment ended up in the barn because you didn't like it."

Liz sensed an argument brewing. "You know that's not what happened. You moved into a fully furnished house. We just didn't need some of your things, and you chose what would go into storage. I even put some of my stuff away."

"Yes, you did." Maggie reached up to kiss Liz on the cheek. "And I appreciated it then and now."

Liz turned a suspicious eye on Maggie. "You're not planning to move anything in here, I hope."

Maggie laughed. "I wouldn't dare to even think about, but I did like the painting we had hanging over there." She pointed to a space that now held a watercolor of a scene from Acadia. "I still have it, if you're interested."

"Maybe," said Liz, still frowning.

"I see you finally got the wires through."

"Sam double-plated the bottom," Liz explained, "so I had to drill through two thicknesses." She brandished her carbide-tipped bell hanger bit. "Even this monster found it tough going."

"But you did it!" Maggie gave Liz's shoulder a congratulatory pat. "Is there anything I can do to help? The braise is in the oven, so there's nothing to do in the kitchen for a while."

"You? You're going to help? Is this the same woman who refused to learn how to reset the water conditioner just so I could come over to do it?"

Maggie winked. "Works every time. But I don't mind helping you if you need an extra pair of hands. You used to let me help you. Don't you remember?"

Liz did remember. "So why do you play dumb when it comes to technical or mechanical things?"

"It's a strategy I learned from my mother...stoking the male ego was the way you got things done. But it doesn't always work on you. You're not a guy, even though sometimes you like to act like one. You're a competent beautiful woman."

Liz glanced in the direction of the kitchen. "Maggie, have you been drinking while you're cooking?"

"No, and the recipe doesn't call for wine. Now, what can I do?"

"You could hold on to this cable while I wire up this outlet." Liz deftly stripped the cable and handed it to Maggie. "At least you're taller than Lucy. Half the time she can't reach things, and I need to bring in a ladder."

"Lucy can't help that she's short. God made her that way. She has plenty of valuable traits."

Liz gazed at Maggie from under her brows. "When did you become such a big Lucy fan?"

"Oh, I've always been a Lucy fan. Remember I was her friend before you were. You used to think she was silly. I always suspected you thought I was silly too."

"No comment," said Liz, screwing down a wire.

"See? You did, didn't you?"

"I know you're not silly, Maggie. And even though you didn't always believe in your intelligence, I did." Liz pushed back the wires and screwed the outlet into the box. "Okay, now for the hard part."

"What's that?" Maggie asked on cue.

"I need to install the new breaker in the panel. I've done it before, but every time I wonder if this will be the one time I electrocute myself."

Maggie's eyes widened with fear. "Maybe you should call an electrician?"

"No, I know what to do, but just to be safe, I'll cut the power to the panel. You could hold the flashlight for me, if you have nothing else to do."

"I said I'd help you, Liz. Show me where I need to be."

Liz waved her on. They went downstairs. Liz handed Maggie her flashlight and showed her where to focus it. She threw the main breaker, and all the basement lights went off. As she slipped the breaker into place, she could feel Maggie's anxiety. Pushing against all the current that wanted to flood back into the house, Liz had to lean against the main breaker to turn on the power. When it switched into position, the basement lights lit.

Maggie looked incredibly relieved. "If you turned off the power, does that mean the stove went off too?"

"Yup. You should probably go upstairs and turn it back on."

Maggie left. Liz double checked all the connections before she went back upstairs. She had the TV mounted by the time Maggie returned to the living room. "Need any more help?"

"No, just connecting the TV to the internet." She switched on the news station that Lucy preferred to watch. The news coverage of the upcoming election was showing on every channel nonstop, so Liz turned it off. "Well, we know it works." She pushed the TV back into its final position and stood, hands on hips, to admire her handiwork.

Maggie looped her arm through Liz's. "You already have a cozy space upstairs. You didn't need another place to watch TV. You did this for me, didn't you?"

"It was no big deal."

"Liz, I'm trying to say thank you."

Liz turned and saw that Maggie's eyes were misty. "You're welcome," Liz said and put her arm around her.

Chapter 6

From her perch at the kitchen island, Liz half listened to Lucy and Reshma debate whether to wear their collars and rainbow stoles to a rally in Kittery. Officially, the Episcopal Church advocated the separation of church and state. Taking sides for a political party could jeopardize St. Margaret's status as a non-profit, never mind alienating the substantial number of Republicans in the congregation. Most had stayed, despite the progressive theology of its rector, but Lucy was always walking a fine line to avoid offending them.

Liz finally interrupted. "Want to know my opinion?" They all turned around to look at her. "This isn't like the rallies for gun reform or Black Lives Matter. It's clearly political. Go as private citizens and leave the collars and stoles home."

"Thank you for your pronouncement, Dr. Stolz," Maggie said sarcastically. She was wearing large dramatic glasses this morning, making her look owlish. "How is it that you have advice for us but can't bother to come along?"

"You know I'm not the demonstration type. I haven't carried a sign for or against anything since the Indian Point protests back in the sixties."

"She means the 1960s," Maggie unnecessarily explained to the others. "Back then, protesting nuclear power plants was a thing."

"Someone snapped my picture, and it landed in the newspaper. My teacher said, 'Liz, if you want to get into medical school, lay off the politics.' And he was right. He was the same guy who told the class, 'Yes, government by the people. Too bad the people are so damn stupid.'"

"He would get into a lot of trouble for saying that now," Reshma observed.

"Then too, but none of us would have reported our teachers. We were as subversive as they were."

Maggie arched a perfectly tweezed brow. "Hard to imagine you being subversive, Ms. Young Republican. You sometimes forget I remember you when."

Liz shrugged. "I have subversive creds. Back in high school, I was reading all those radical theologians the Church later defrocked or silenced…Hans Küng, Edward Schillebeeckx, Karl Rahner, and Teilhard, of course."

Reshma's dark eyes grew big. "You were reading theology in high school?"

"Liz started reading theology in the *seventh grade*," Maggie bragged.

Liz gave her a stern look. "You didn't know me then, Maggie, and that information is no one's business."

"Liz only pretends she's not interested in religion," said Lucy. "But I know differently. Erika told me all about it."

"Maggie needs to learn when to keep her mouth shut," Liz said, eyeing her. "Lucy doesn't need any ammunition."

Reshma interjected, "Liz, I studied those twentieth-century theologians in seminary. I'd love to discuss them with you."

"Sure, Reshma. You're welcome to come over to drink whiskey with me any time."

"Dr. Liz, I'm not a big fan of whiskey, but I am open to acquiring new tastes."

"Better watch out, Lucy, or Professor Atheist there will corrupt your curate," Maggie warned.

"I'm not worried. Reshma is wicked smart and knows her own mind. And I wouldn't mind being part of that conversation myself. I learn a lot from listening to Liz."

"I'll leave the theological discussions to the collars," said Maggie. "I had enough of it back in college. Not my thing."

Liz glanced at her watch. "Ladies, you should probably decide what you're doing and get going soon."

"We can't convince you to join us?" Lucy asked.

"Nope. Not carrying a sign. Plus, it doesn't look good for the practice if I run into people I know."

"Always looking out for your business," Maggie said in a disparaging tone.

"Damn right, I am. I know this election is important, but afterward I still need to keep Hobbs Family Practice going."

"So what are you going to do with your afternoon, Dr. Stolz?" asked Maggie.

Liz grinned. "I'm not telling. Otherwise, what's the point of getting rid of my wives?"

Reshma looked surprised.

Lucy gave Liz a long, penetrating look.

Maggie merely smiled.

✳✳✳

Sitting in the back seat of Lucy's SUV, Maggie listened to the women she collectively called "the collars" talk softly in the front. Before Liz had insinuated herself into the conversation, Reshma had argued against wearing their collars to the rally. Although Lucy was both Reshma's boss and mentor, she listened to the young woman with more than token respect. Like Liz, Reshma had the ability to build her case step by step and exhibited a natural authority that made others want to follow her leadership. Someday, she would make a great rector.

Maggie thought of her own students. Not many of them measured up to Reshma's abilities, but Maggie had long ago resolved not to get into complaining about the sorry state of the youth. For one thing, as she aged, they grew younger and younger. Now, she could literally be their grandmother. Most were respectful, but others showed their boredom during her lectures by scrolling their phones. Cell phones didn't exist when she first began teaching at NYU. Now, all the focus was on preparing students for careers. She felt lucky that the local schools still wanted a teacher with a PhD in theater arts from Yale, but, as Liz pointed out, they'd be plain stupid to turn away someone with Maggie's credentials.

"Lucy, if Liz came the rally, would it really damage the reputation of Hobbs Family Practice?" Reshma suddenly asked.

"It might," Lucy said. "It could impact St. Margaret's too, if people in the congregation find out we are at this rally. Liz was right about leaving home our collars."

"But many might approve of what we're doing," countered Reshma.

"But you can see how hard it is to know where to draw the line. Many of Liz's ideas about keeping the personal separate from the professional come from a different era. When she was in medical school, women were trained to internalize and adapt to the hierarchical male power structure. They wore tailored suits like men. They asserted their authority like men. Unfortunately, some of them didn't respect or support other women." Lucy's tidy summary impressed Maggie, especially because Lucy had been too young to feel the impact of the time she was describing.

"That is so interesting," said Reshma. "I used to love to listen to my professor, one of the first women to be ordained in the Episcopal Church around the time Dr. Liz would have been a surgical resident. Professor Cotton couldn't find a church to hire her, so she went on for her theology degree and taught. Many women of my generation don't realize how different it was for women or how hard our elders fought for our rights. We've always enjoyed them, so we take them for granted."

Maggie leaned forward so she could speak through the break in the bucket seats. "That's what I love about you, Reshma. You see the big picture."

"Thank you for noticing. Being a refugee gives me a different perspective. I had to study to become a citizen. I'm not sure schools still teach all the things I needed to learn."

"They used to," Maggie said. "I have no idea what they teach now."

"But as a professor, you are with young people."

"Maybe it's discussed in political science or history classes, but not in mine."

"That is a shame," said Reshma. "Look at all the politics in Shakespeare."

Maggie realized that Reshma had a point. Some of Shakespeare's plays couldn't be understood without some historical and political context. "Reshma, I always learn something when I'm with you."

"Thank you, Maggie. I feel the same."

"We are very lucky to have Reshma," Lucy said. "For all her gifts, she's also humble, a necessary quality in a priest. She knows she doesn't have all the answers. I certainly don't."

"But you have a PhD in theology," Reshma said, "and you've had transformative life experiences."

Maggie laughed softly. "Hard to get to be Lucy's age and not have life rough you up."

"Yes, but many people don't learn from life's difficulties," Reshma said wisely. "Mother Lucy has. I think that's why her compassion has such depth."

Maggie sat back so she could see Lucy's reflection in the rearview mirror. Her face was flaming. Maggie tapped her shoulder. "You know Reshma's right. You turned the horror of being sexually assaulted into something positive. You became a priest and earned a brown belt in Jiu Jitsu. Take the compliment. You earned it."

Lucy turned to her passenger. "Thank you, Reshma. But I can't take all the credit. I had a lot of help from my friends."

Maggie's guilt about how she treated Lucy after Erika's death returned. She'd complained when Liz left to start Lucy's generator during an ice storm. She'd sniped at Liz when she'd brought Lucy home after she'd collapsed over Erika's grave. *That's not how friends treat one another.*

Lucy sensed that Maggie had left the conversation to entertain her own thoughts. Her green eyes engaged Maggie's in the mirror. "You okay back there, Maggie?"

"Yes, fine. Just thinking."

"Help us look for a parking space. This place is packed."

The park where they were holding the rally was swarming with people carrying signs. If this crowd was any indication of how the election would go, they would win. But they'd been burned before when an accomplished, competent woman ran for the nation's highest office, only to discover the hidden misogyny in the electorate.

They finally found a parking space, but it was snug. Lucy was a good driver, used to driving in big cities like New York and Boston. She managed to nudge in between two trucks. "Sorry, Reshma, but you'll have a tight squeeze. You're slim and flexible, so do your duty for the old ladies."

"Neither of you are old," Reshma scoffed. "Your bodies may have years behind them, but you have young minds and hearts."

"Such a schmoozer." Lucy had picked up that expression from Liz, who used it often.

"But I am sincere," Reshma protested, gingerly opening the door. "It was you, Mother Lucy, who taught me to always smile when I tell the truth and to say it in the kindest way possible."

Lucy caught Maggie's eye in the mirror. "See what I have to put up with? Being reminded of everything I say?"

"Lucy, I get it from my students. What they don't get is it's all a work in progress. What's true one minute may not be true the next."

"Don't get Reshma started on the relativity of truth. She loves to discuss deep subjects."

"And why not? I have the benefit of having a real theologian as my rector. I should be asking you such questions."

"You'd be better off talking to Liz, who actually studied philosophy."

"After what I heard in your house this morning, I may take her up on the invitation. I had no idea a doctor would even think about such things."

Maggie said, "Liz is not your typical doctor. And if she invited you to drink whiskey with her and discuss theology, she meant it."

"Then I look forward to it." Like a snake collapsing its skeleton, lithe Reshma squeezed out of the car. Lucy unloaded the campaign signs they'd yanked up from the mouth of the driveway on their way out. Reshma reached out to carry them. "I used to say, 'a deacon's role is to serve.' Now, I should probably say, 'it's a curate's role.'"

"A curate's role is to learn," Lucy corrected gently, "and you do that without prompting."

Reshma offered a little bow. "Thank you."

They hiked a distance to where the rally was assembling. All the access roads were lined with cars. *This is a good sign,* Maggie told herself. Lucy elbowed her way through the crowd so they could hear the speakers. When Maggie looked around, she saw that the other attendees were mostly gray-haired. Where were the young people? Of course, there were some, but the majority were old social justice warriors like herself. As the speaker led a chant of "we're not going back!" Maggie felt genuinely afraid for the first time.

❋❋❋

Liz stripped off her plastic gloves and tossed them into the bucket. She'd come down to the boat to enjoy the beautiful autumn afternoon. Oiling the hatch could wait for a day when she felt like working. She stretched out in her sling chair and put her feet up on the side wall of the lower deck. She wondered how the rally was going, but she was glad she hadn't gone. As much as she loved Lucy, she sometimes needed time to herself. Other people were fine in small doses, but, if necessary, she could live without them. *Well, not really. I couldn't live without Lucy.* She hadn't loved anyone so passionately since she first fell in love with Maggie back in college.

The thought clouded Liz's pleasure in the lazy afternoon. Why had she let Maggie get away? Twice. Sam often said if she'd tried harder, she could have saved the marriage. As much as she adored

Lucy and wanted to have sex with her at every possible moment, she still loved Maggie. It was so confusing.

Maggie's response when Liz had installed the TV had come as a surprise. She'd recognized that Liz had done it to accommodate her, and she was grateful. Lately, she'd been skipping opportunities to put Liz down. Maybe Maggie had finally forgiven her, although it seemed unlikely. She seemed to hold grudges forever.

Liz sighed and unwrapped the lobster roll she'd picked up on the way down to the harbor. She took a bite and closed her eyes in pleasure. The taste reminded her of the Friday evening ritual of a lobster roll picnic on the jetty to watch the sunset. That was before Maggie had shown up in her office with a broken ankle and once more became the center of her life.

Liz had given up so many things she used to love. Before Liz got involved with Maggie again, Liz had a standing dinner date with Tony Roselli, the manager of the Webhanet Playhouse. She'd given up membership in her hiking club and the mineral society because outdoor activities didn't interest Maggie.

Thinking about all the things she missed was impinging on her enjoyment of her lobster roll. She opened a beer from the cooler to wash it down. Just as she finished the last delicious bite, she noticed a familiar SUV enter the harbor parking lot. A tall woman got out of the vehicle and headed down the stairs to the dock. Liz instantly recognized the Hobbs police chief from her long, confident strides, but there was something different about her. She walked down to the floating dock, and Liz finally figured it out.

"You cut your hair," said Liz with exaggerated shock when Brenda climbed into the boat.

"Cherie did it. What do you think?"

Liz walked around her friend to get the full picture. Brenda's hair had been blunt cut to her jaw.

"Looks good. I like it."

"Cherie was practicing on the kids, and I volunteered to be her next victim."

"Brave woman, but I wouldn't call it being a victim. She did a nice job. Brenda, you swore you'd never change your hair. What prompted this?"

"I'm tired of dyeing it, and with the kids, I don't have the time. All my friends have gone gray, so why not me?"

Liz gave her a congratulatory shoulder pat. "Welcome to the club! But you always said you don't want your officers to think you're an old lady."

"Fuck them. I shouldn't let a bunch of kids dictate how I wear my hair."

Liz pulled her head back and made a shocked face. "Well, good for you! Yes, fuck them. It's your hair." Liz pulled over her chair and pointed at it. "Take a seat." She opened the storage bin, took out another sling chair and opened it for herself. "Beer?"

"Sure. What are you drinking?"

Liz pulled a bottle out of the cooler and showed Brenda the label. "It's kind of like that red ale you like. Want to try it?" Benda nodded and Liz reached for the opener tied to the cooler handle. "Too bad I didn't know you were coming. I would have bought a lobster roll for you. I just ate mine."

"I'll take a rain check." Brenda said and looked around. "What did you do with your wife?"

"She went to a rally in Kittery with Maggie and Reshma."

"Must be nice to be able to show your political stripes. As police chief, I could never do it. No one should ever know my party affiliation except my family and closest friends."

"I'm surprised Lucy agreed to go. She's got plenty of Republicans in her congregation."

"Hobbs used to be majority Republican. Now..." Brenda see-sawed her hand. "Slight favor to the blue team."

"All those transplants who came up during the pandemic...people who always wanted to live in Maine retiring early...workers who thought that work at home gig would last forever. I'm sure buyer's remorse is running high right now. But the great exodus drove real estate prices through the roof. Good for us, I guess."

"Just glad I got my mortgage before the rates shot up."

Liz put her feet up. "How can people even afford to buy a house now? That's why Maggie is holding the mortgage for her daughter. Only problem is, it's not helping Alina's credit rating, which really needs rehabilitation after her ex-husband crashed it."

"That's too bad, but we do what we need to do," said Brenda.

Liz watched Brenda taste the beer. "Like it?"

"It's good, but I should tell you that I *never* complain about free beer." Brenda grinned. "When my officers buy me beer at the Irish Pub, I always thank them. Means they'll buy me one next time too."

"Smart policy. Keep the troops happy. Works every time."

"How's it going with Amy taking over your practice?"

Liz shrugged. "No complaints. She's doing a good job. She's steady and calm, not one of those top-down, command, control, coerce leaders like I was back in the day."

"Even you learned to tone down that chief of surgery attitude."

"It didn't fit with my retirement plans. When I came up here I was in full-scale rebellion against corporate medicine."

"At least, you dress normally now. The hiking shorts and the Keens in the office might have been a bit much."

Liz pouted. "I love my Keens. I still wear them in the summer. Just not every day."

"Proving a point has its limits. Glad you knew to quit while you're ahead. Otherwise, it gets preachy." Brenda took a long slug of beer and nodded her approval. "Still working, having Maggie over there?"

"Good so far. She looks after the place while we travel. I don't mind coming home to her meals."

"I know. I look forward to Cherie's cooking. And she's a great mom. I'm so relieved that adopting the kids solved our problem. After you told me all the risks, I didn't want her to get pregnant.

Especially not after my long-Covid heart problems almost put me out of a job."

"Well, you're doing great now. Plus, you've got Amy looking after you now. She knows more about hearts than I do."

"Yeah, you're more an expert on heartbreaking than fixing."

"Hah. Very funny." Liz studied her old friend. "Brenda, I'm warming up to your new hair style. I really like it."

"Thanks, Liz. I'm glad you think it works. Even if it didn't, I couldn't tell Cherie I hate her haircut. Poor woman was so anxious her hands were shaking. I was afraid she'd cut my ear off!"

"Cherie is the best PA I ever had. If she cut off your ear, she'd sew you up right."

"That's not reassuring, Liz."

"Just saying she's good at wound care." Liz gazed out into the harbor. "Brenda, I miss our fishing trips. My birthday cruise was fun, but with the ladies and the kids on the boat, we couldn't do any serious fishing. The whole summer got away from us with Lucy singing in all those festivals. I mean, it's fun to be in Europe, but summer in Maine is why we live here."

"I know. I miss fishing too, but with the kids and the house, it's hard to get away."

"Everything's changed. I miss you. I miss Sam. Since Maggie moved back, I'm being smothered with girly stuff!"

"Don't lie, Liz. You love the attention. Two pretty women totally focused on you. You are in heaven. Admit it."

Liz frowned. "It's not exactly like that. They gang up on me sometimes, and I don't know how to defend myself."

Brenda laughed as if it were the most hilarious thing she'd ever heard. "Don't bullshit me, Liz. You know exactly how to deal with them."

"No, I don't. Separately, they frighten me. Together, they scare the shit out of me."

"You're serious," Brenda observed, her blond brows dipping. "Is that why you're hiding down here?"

"Maybe," said Liz, taking a long pull on her beer. She drained the bottle and opened another one.

"Liz, we can plan a fishing trip, but I can't bring Sam back. Sounds like she's gone for good."

"Not sure about that, but she's not here now, so we need to figure it out on our own. Let's go fishing on Monday. It's my day off. Yours too, right?"

"Yep, I could use a break. Things are so tense with this election coming up. Whenever I go into the breakroom, I can feel it. People always take sides, but this feels different."

"I know what you mean, and I agree, but there's nothing we can do about it except cast our ballots."

Brenda nodded and stared into the harbor. "I'll check the weather report for Monday. I think it's supposed to be nice."

"Good. The Wet Lady can use a run. I'm putting her into dry dock next week."

"That's early for you."

Liz narrowed her eyes. "Maggie gets seasick and doesn't enjoy the boat."

"Why does that matter?"

Liz realized it was a good question. "It doesn't. Lucy loves going out on the boat. She enjoys fishing, although she complains it's smelly, which it is. But I'll leave her home on Monday. It will be just us."

"Sounds good," said Brenda. "It will be good to get out on the water before it gets too cold." She engaged Liz's gaze. "With all the shit going on in the outside world, we need to do the things that make us happy."

Liz saw the frank worry in Brenda's eyes. Although it wasn't cold, she felt a chill.

Chapter 7

Sophia Krusick looked through the back window overlooking Liz's vegetable garden. "This place is bigger and much nicer than I'd imagined."

"I told you, darling. If only you'd come up earlier, you'd have saved you so much worry."

Seemingly ignoring what her mother had said, Maggie's dark-haired older daughter continued to take in the view of the garden. "Liz's chrysanthemums are beautiful this year."

"She planted some flowers in her vegetable garden to improve the view."

Sophia finally turned around. "That's why I wasn't really worried, Mom. I know Liz looks after you."

"You do? How?"

"I know you're not going to tell me what's really going on with your health. When your tumor markers are due, I call Liz for the results...if she hasn't already called me."

This was the first Maggie had heard they'd been communicating. Put off balance by the subterfuge, Maggie sat down on the sofa. "So that's why you stopped harassing me for the test results. Maybe I shouldn't have given you two access to my health information. I never expected you to go behind my back."

"Mom, I'm your daughter. I have a right to know, and it's not like she's telling someone who won't understand. I'm an oncologist, and Liz is one the country's leading breast cancer specialists. Two medical professionals discussing a patient of mutual interest. Perfectly normal."

Used to doctors keeping things from her, Maggie was doubtful. "I don't know about that."

Sophia sat down opposite her mother. "We have your best interests at heart, but I don't recommend you tell Alina. She has enough to handle."

"That goes without saying, but I think this relationship is good for your sister. With Steve around, she's much calmer."

"Except when she drinks with her meds and flips out. Thank God, Liz and her PA got her straightened out. Sounds like the last time was a real doozy."

You have no idea, thought Maggie. She'd never told Sophia all the details of that awful night. She wondered if Alina had been honest with her sister. Maggie would find it hard to admit something so humiliating. And yet, when she'd invited herself to Liz's place, she'd confessed the whole sordid story to Lucy, who'd listened without a word of judgment.

"The kids were really frightened, so was I."

"Alina is tiny, but in an adrenalin rage, I bet she could really hurt someone. What was the fight about?"

"I have no idea. You know it doesn't take much to provoke her. I never understood why she's so volatile, and you're so calm and level-headed, even as a child."

"She depended on me. I couldn't afford to fall apart. That orphanage was so crowded. No one paid attention. If I didn't look after Alina, no one would."

"That's interesting," Maggie said, reaching for her wine glass. "Did you figure that out on your own?"

Sophia looked impatient. "Of course. Who has time for therapy?"

"You sound like Liz. She hates 'shrinks' as she calls them."

"Since medicine figured out how to deal with mental illness chemically, there's less respect for talking therapy. Some people do benefit, like my cancer patients who are alone and have no one to listen to their terror over their illness. In that case, a therapist is like a paid friend."

"I have friends, but I went back to therapy. It's helping me understand why I keep making the same mistakes."

"Glad it works for you, Mom." Sophia replied dismissively. Her eyes had been studying the connector to the main house. "Can you just go through that bridge into the house?"

"Yes, but it's locked on both sides. Liz gives me my privacy and never comes in without asking first."

"So, she's a respectful landlord. I love Liz, but you must admit it's an unconventional arrangement."

Maggie raised her shoulders. "As you can see, it's a lovely place, quiet, picturesque setting, probably better than anything I can rent in town. God knows the price is right. Liz says it's not a legal apartment, so she can't charge the people who live here."

"That's a kind excuse for her generosity." Sophia reached for her wine and took a sip. "None of my business, Mom, but wasn't it humiliating to crawl back to your ex?"

That was out of line, but Sophia had always been outspoken, probably why she was able to get what she needed for herself and her sister in that Romanian orphanage.

"Honestly, Phi, it was more humiliating to be thrown out of my own house by your sister." There, she'd said it. Sophia didn't look particularly surprised. So, Alina *had* told her.

"But you were happy living with the girls," said Sophia. "They loved having Grandma there to make them treats."

"And I enjoyed it too...for a time, but they're growing up and don't need me as much. Plus, I have better things to do than be a domestic servant for my daughter and her fiancé."

"Ouch," said Sophia. "And you're right. I'm glad you've gone back to teaching and directing. It's good for you. You're too young to sit in a rocking chair."

"And..." Maggie paused dramatically. "I was going to announce this at dinner, but I'll tell you now. They are reviving *Suddenly Last Summer* at the State Theater this winter, and I've been cast in a leading role."

"Oh, Mom, that's great. You love Tennessee Williams. Which character are you playing?"

"Mrs. Veneble, of course. I'm long past being cast as an ingénue."

"I'll come up for the opening night if I can. Send me the dates, so I can arrange for time off."

"That would be wonderful." Maggie glanced at the clock in the kitchen. "Drink your wine, dear. We're due at Liz's in a few minutes."

In the kitchen of the main house, Liz was fussing over her lobster scampi. Maggie nudged her way between her ex-wife and her younger daughter, who was putting the finishing touches on a vegetable casserole she'd brought. "How can I help?" Maggie asked.

"If you wouldn't mind draining the pasta…"

It was no surprise that Liz already had the colander positioned in the sink. Liz ran her kitchen like an operating room. Everything was prepared in advance and laid out in the order it would be used. Maggie would have made rice with the scampi, but Lucy preferred pasta and Liz always catered to her. Maggie dumped the Cavatappi into the enormous bowl Liz had waiting on the island. Liz topped the pasta with the scampi and dusted it with chopped parsley.

She turned to Sophia and scooped her into a hug. "And now, I can finally say hello to my favorite oncologist."

"Oh, your favorite is your old friend, Bev Birnbaum."

"Well, yes, but why can't I have two?" Liz affectionately clapped Sophia on the shoulder. "Welcome back. It's been too long. Pour yourself some wine."

Maggie's granddaughters bolted into the kitchen. Nicki wrapped her arms around her grandmother's waist and squeezed tight. Katrina was at an age when she was becoming more formal and waited for an invitation. The happy chaos in the overheated, slightly steamy kitchen was delightful, but Maggie knew Liz wouldn't tolerate it long. She herded her family into the dining room.

Although she knew Liz wouldn't like it, Maggie asked Lucy to say grace. They passed their plates to Liz to serve. The silence while they ate proved how tasty the scampi was.

"Liz, did you pick the lobster yourself?" Maggie asked.

"Of course. Buying picked meat is cheating. Plus, who knows how long it's been hanging around in the fish store."

Maggie was about to accuse Liz of being a purist, but it wasn't true. Liz sometimes took shortcuts, but never with lobster. If she could, Liz would eat it at every meal.

"Emily really wanted to be here," said Lucy, "but her class schedule wouldn't allow it."

"That's so cool that they made her a professor when most people are just graduating from college," Sophia said.

"Now, everyone in this family is a doctor," said Alina ruefully. "I'm beginning to feel like a dummy."

Lucy gazed at her sympathetically. "I used to feel that way too, but unless you're an M.D. like your sister, those letters after your name don't mean much."

Alina frowned at Sophia, sitting across from her. "I invited my sister to stay at my house, but she likes it here better."

"I came up to visit Mom. I'll stay with you next time," Sophia replied diplomatically.

"If you're cramped over there in that little sleeping nook, you're welcome to sleep in one of the guest rooms," Liz said, entering the fray. Maggie knew she was being generous, not competitive.

"That's kind, Liz," Sophia said, "but I'm really looking forward to spending time with mom. Another time." Maggie was touched by her daughter's loyalty and the acknowledgement of the sovereignty of her household. She might live next to her ex-wife, but she wasn't living *with* her.

"Maggie, do you mind if I borrow Sophia for a while after dinner? We need to catch up on a few things." Maggie guessed the subject was professional. Liz had used her influence to help Sophia land positions in some of the country's best cancer hospitals.

"No, it's fine. You cooked. I'll help Lucy with the dishes."

❊❊❊

Liz turned on the propane stove on the enclosed porch. There, she and Sophia would have privacy for their talk. Her stepdaughter had asked Liz to support her application for a position at Dana Farber, where she'd done a fellowship before taking a job in New York. Although they had a warm relationship now, when they'd first met, they'd clashed over Liz's conservative approach to Maggie's breast cancer. Sophia had wanted every treatment possible, including chemo and radiation. Liz had advocated a more measured approach.

Once the room had warmed up to Liz's satisfaction, she returned to the kitchen to find Sophia. Maggie caught her putting her whiskey bottle and her favorite crystal glasses on a tray and gave her a stern look. "Don't overdo it," Maggie warned. "I'm making breakfast tomorrow, and I expect you both to be there."

Sophia rolled her eyes. "Yes, Mom."

"Don't worry," Liz assured Maggie. "I'll make sure she gets home safe. It's not far."

Maggie pursed her lips at the understatement. Liz handed Sophia the tray to carry out to the porch. Liz opened the door to the porch. The blast of hot air that greeted them felt good on such a chilly night. "Used to drive me nuts when I was an adult, and my mom tried to mother me," Liz said.

Sophia settled into one of the wicker settees. "I complain, but I'm so glad they rescued us from that awful orphanage. Mom and Dad probably saved our lives."

Liz dropped an ice cube into each glass and poured the whiskey. "How is your Dad?"

"Better. They're managing the prostate cancer with Eligard. I told him a prostatectomy was the way to go, but having erections is important to him."

Liz shook her head. "Old men and their erections. Some of my female patients curse the day Viagra was invented."

Sophia grinned. "I bet. Most older women just want to be left in peace."

"Not all of them," said Liz, thinking of Lucy. "I'm sad to hear your father's not doing well," Liz said, "I've known him for over fifty years. I wasn't happy when your mother married him, but I'm sorry he's suffering."

"He's in much worse shape than Mom."

Liz frowned in sympathy. "I'm sorry, Phi. I know you and your father are close."

"He was the one who encouraged me to go to med school. Mom didn't discourage me, but I think she would have liked me to get married and have a bunch of grandchildren like Alina."

"No disrespect to your sister, but you would have made a better parent."

"Honestly, I just wasn't interested in having kids. Maybe because my early childhood was so awful. And you know how it is when you're a woman trying to build a medical career. Even now, you're expected to put everything you have into it. That slogan, 'You can have it all,' is pure bullshit."

"People look down on Lucy for putting her child up for adoption, but what choice did she have? Unfortunately, it didn't save her singing career."

"It's a tough choice between being a mother and excelling at something, whether it's opera or medicine. Men don't need to choose. It's better now, but not much. I can't even imagine how bad it was for you before time limits on duty and the match system. How did you do it?"

"By being smarter, tougher, and better than the men. Lucy's trying to cure me of some of my less desirable behaviors." Liz raised her glass. "Good luck with that!"

"Unfortunately, there's still misogyny. It might even be worse now."

"It's backlash against women's success." Liz studied her stepdaughter. "I never knew you were such a feminist."

"I'm not really. I don't have time for politics. I just see the obvious inequities that still exist, despite the sacrifices your generation made for us."

"You're welcome and thank you for recognizing what the old ladies did for you. Many women your age don't. Overturning the right to an abortion was a wakeup call. Hopefully, they stay awake and make the right choice in this election."

"I wouldn't hold your breath," said Sophia.

"I know. I'm worried too." The political situation was so depressing. Liz decided to turn the conversation to something more positive. "How are the negotiations with Dana-Farber going?"

"Oh, they offered me the job, but I haven't accepted yet."

Liz was surprised. Only a few weeks ago, Sophia had been raving about this opportunity. "Why not?"

"It's a great hospital, but I've been there, and I'm not sure I want to go back to Boston. I've done the big push for my career. I'm almost forty, and I want more out of life."

Liz tucked her chin into her chest. "So, maybe marriage and kids to make your mother happy?"

Sophia mocked horror. "No, not that. But more time for myself. You know, work-life balance."

"Okay. That's fair." Liz put down her whiskey glass and considered how to word her proposal. "The Mass General satellite in New Hampshire is looking for a chief of oncology. It's a good regional cancer center connected to a nationally known hospital network. It would give you portable management experience."

"Why didn't you tell me before?"

Liz shrugged. "I thought the Dana-Farber job was a done deed."

"Do you really think I have a shot at being made chief?"

"Sure you do. You have a great education and experience at some of the best cancer hospitals in the country. I know the board chair, if you want more information."

Sophia's negotiation face gave way to her natural enthusiasm. "Would you? I'd really appreciate it."

"Good. I'll call Dr. Andersen tomorrow. Another reason to stay sober tonight." Liz added another ice cube to her glass. "Dover is only twenty minutes away...at least the way I drive. Sure that's not too close for comfort?"

"No, I'd love to be closer to Mom and Alina. I've missed them. I enjoyed being in Boston and New York, but I need the trees."

Liz got up to turn down the thermostat. The porch was getting too warm. "I don't know if I could live in a big city again. I guess I could if I had to."

"I was surprised Mom adapted so well to living in Maine. She lived in New York for decades." Liz looked up and saw Sophia studying her with a frown. "How's she doing?"

"Healthwise or in general?" asked Liz.

"Both."

Liz thought for a moment. "You see her numbers. They're excellent. She's still protective of the implants, but she's fully healed now, and everything looks good."

"She seems to have settled in here."

"She was frightened to live alone at Sam's place. She admitted it the first time Sam went to California to interview for the museum competition. Maybe she could have managed Sam's travel, but not her moving away. The shooting changed a lot of things."

Sophia scrutinized her with the eyes of a physician. "And how are you doing, Liz? You've had your share of challenges."

"Oh, please, Phi, don't sound like my wife."

Sophia laughed. "Sorry. I'm just curious...and concerned. It's not every day a civilian has to shoot a mass killer. Mom said you took it hard in the beginning."

"I did, but I'm okay now...I think. Working on gun safety initiatives helps me channel my regret and anxiety into something positive. There are residual effects. I've never slept well, but my sleep is worse since the shooting. Of course, some of the sleep disturbance could be menopause related. See what you can look forward to?"

"Can't wait. Periods are a pain in the ass."

Liz smiled. "You say that now, but your hormones start to dry up, so does everything else...your skin, your throat. It even affects your voice."

Sophia looked surprised. "Hadn't thought of that. How does Lucy deal with it in her singing?"

"With her family history of ovarian cancer, hormone therapy isn't a solution. She's careful to hydrate and warm up before she sings."

"It's all so complicated, isn't it?" Sophia drained her glass.

"That's why doctors have jobs. Although Emily keeps telling me we'll all be replaced by AI." Liz refilled their glasses. "Last one for both of us, but we can pace ourselves and sit out here for a while."

"I think when Mom's ready to go, I should spend some time with her."

"Yes, I'm sure she'd like that. She's missed you."

"I've missed her too, but you know how it is when you're building a career. Finding time for friends and family is so hard." Sophia raised her glass to Liz. "Thanks for telling me about the job in New Hampshire. But most of all, thanks for taking care of Mom."

"She takes care of herself, so it's no bother."

"Even though she's your ex?"

Liz shrugged. "We may not be married any more, but I still care about her."

"She's lucky," Sophia said.

"Me too," Liz murmured into her glass.

✸✸✸

"Oof!" exclaimed Lucy when Nicki suddenly landed on her lap, knocking the wind out of her.

"Nicki!" called Maggie from across the room. "You're not a baby. You shouldn't be jumping on Lucy like that. You'll hurt her."

Lucy's arms instinctively encircled Nicki, and her hand rose to cover the girl's silky dark hair, protecting her from the blows of her grandmother's sharp words. She hugged Nicki tight. Since the day two decades ago when Lucy had handed over her infant daughter to the well-meaning social worker, she'd craved to hold young children against her body.

"Nicki! Get off Lucy right now!" Maggie insisted with a fierce look.

The girl clutched her tighter, burying her face in the space between Lucy's breasts. "It's all right, Maggie. She didn't hurt me." But it wasn't true. When Nicki squirmed, her sharp bones dug into Lucy's thighs. Tomorrow, they'd probably be black and blue.

"L-u-u-cy," the girl crooned softly.

"Yes, sweetie?" asked Lucy, bending her head to hear.

"Can I stay here tonight? Please? I want to sleep in the moose room."

Lucy glanced across the room to where her wife sat. "Sure. Why not?" Liz said with a shrug, "The more, the merrier."

"You need to ask mommy if you can stay," Lucy said in Nicki's ear. The girl came out of hiding to cautiously regard her mother.

"Mommy, can I stay at Grandma Liz's house tonight?"

"*May* I stay," Maggie corrected in a gentler tone than she'd been using. "Kids can't get enough of you, Lucy. I don't know what you have."

Lucy laughed but thought, *They're drawn to me because I'm soft and have large breasts, so I make a cozy nest.* If Alina's fiancé weren't present, Lucy might have shared those thoughts. A male presence changed everything. Who knew what men thought when women talked about breasts? And Steve wasn't Lucy's only concern. Maggie no longer had real breasts. During the double mastectomy after her last cancer scare, they'd been replaced by implants. Lucy had caught her admiring her breasts when she thought she wasn't looking and wondered if she was jealous.

Lucy kissed Nicki's silky, dark hair. "We can bring them home after church on Sunday. That will give you most of the weekend to yourselves."

Alina glanced at her fiancé. The gleam in his eye meant he was probably already imagining the sex they would have without the children in the house. "How can we turn down an offer like that? Babysitting and transportation," he said. "Thank you."

Liz got up to refill Lucy's wine glass. "The police chief and her wife became mothers in their fifties, and they're still getting used to the whole thing. We babysit their kids, so their moms can have a date night."

Alina peered at Steve. "Hear that? Date night. Hint, hint."

Steve ran his hand through his graying hair. "Okay. I'll take you to dinner in Portland tomorrow night, a nice place. You can get dressed up, if you want."

"Check out the events at the State Theater," Maggie suggested. "I can get you tickets."

Nicki's bony rear was becoming painful, so Lucy tried to gently nudge her off her lap. She sat up so quickly she nearly clocked Lucy on the chin. "I'll tell Trina we're staying here." When she left, Lucy missed her warm presence.

"I should have asked if you're okay with it, Maggie," Lucy said. "I know you were looking forward to spending time with Sophia."

"If you're keeping them, I'll have plenty of time with Phi. Believe me. The moose room has more appeal than Grandma's place."

"And I don't have to drive up to Scarborough tomorrow to see my nieces. Win-win." Sophia ignored her sister's penetrating look.

Steve got up. "We should be going. It's an early morning at the news studio." He reached for his fiancée's hand. "Come on, honey. Let's get out of their hair and let them get the kids to bed. You know what a project that can be."

Liz got up too. She patted Steve's shoulder. "I don't envy you being the only male with all these women."

Steve laughed. "What man wouldn't want to be with a bunch of beautiful women, who also happen to be great cooks?"

Liz kissed him on the cheek, and he blushed a little. "You're such a charmer. No wonder Alina loves you."

Lucy turned down Maggie's offer to help get the girls ready for bed. "You go spend time with Sophia. She came all the way from New York to be with you. And it's fun for me to play mom. This is the part I missed."

"You're sure?"

"Yes, she's sure," Liz said, returning. "Now, get out of here. Sophia turned down more of my favorite whiskey to be with you, so go!"

Maggie looked reluctant to leave. "I don't want to miss anything."

"Of course, we'll talk about you as soon as you're out the door." Liz grinned.

"Oh!" Maggie rolled her eyes. "Come on, Phi. They're throwing us out. Let's go!"

The girls loved the spa bathtub in the master bathroom, so there was no argument over bathtime. Lucy convinced them to abandon the movie they'd been watching in the TV room with the promise to sing to them. Since the shooting, she'd expanded her repertoire of classical and popular lullabies to soothe Liz on the nights she couldn't sleep. Of course, the girls weren't any more content with one song than they'd be with one story.

When Lucy finally headed to bed, she found Liz reading. "Thanks for letting the girls stay over and getting them to bed," said Liz.

"I love them and love spending time with them." As Lucy undressed she felt Liz's admiring eyes and quickly slipped her nightgown over her head. "Don't get any ideas. I'm way too tired."

Liz put her tablet aside. "It's okay. I'm tired too."

Lucy got into bed and gratefully insinuated herself into Liz's open arms. "Lucy, you're a wonderful mom," Liz whispered into her ear. "I know you're trying to make up for missing Emily's childhood, but you don't have anything to prove."

"Oh, yes, I do." Lucy snuggled against Liz's breast because at times like this, she needed mothering too.

Chapter 8

Liz scanned the dining room of the Front Porch, searching for Tony Roselli. He jumped up from his seat and waved vigorously. He was grayer than when Liz had last seen him six months ago. He'd also put on a few pounds, probably from stress eating during the tense election like every other LGBT person in Southern Maine. He enfolded Liz in a warm embrace. "I thought you'd forgotten me."

"Never," Liz assured him.

She'd met Tony during her first vacation in Maine. She'd always been a Broadway musical fan. When she saw an ad in the tourist newspaper for a revival of *South Pacific* at the Webhanet Playhouse, she had to buy tickets. She'd arrived at the summer stock theater with a New Yorker's chauvinism and low expectations, but the production had amazed her. The next day, she'd sent a laudatory note and enclosed a significant check. The music director himself called to thank her. They were on the phone for over an hour, trading stories of great performances they'd seen. It was the start of a friendship that would change Liz's life. Tony's complaints about his doctor retiring had alerted Liz to the family practice for sale in Hobbs. She'd left her partner and beautiful home on Long Island Sound and moved to Maine.

Tony dramatically kissed Maggie on each cheek. In his world she was a diva, based on her two seasons on Broadway playing the lead role in *Les Mis*. Until the divorce, Maggie had served on the board of the Playhouse. Tony kept talking about wooing her back to perform and rejoin the board, which was why Liz had invited her to lunch.

"Two of my favorite ladies," Tony said, pulling the chair out for Maggie like a perfect gentleman. Like Maggie, he always moved in a deliberate and theatrical way. While Tony fussed effusively over Maggie, Liz quietly seated herself and studied the specials menu.

"Why bother with the menu, Liz?" Maggie said. "You always order the same thing."

Liz smiled but didn't look up. "Not always. I can be flexible."

Maggie laughed, covering her mouth after making the most unladylike snort. "Flexible is not a word I'd ever apply to you."

"Oh Maggie, you have to admit she has her moments," Tony said loyally. "Not many, but she does have them."

"You let him talk like that to you, Liz?"

"It's alright, Maggie. Tony's known me for a long time too, not as long as you have, but a long time. I make allowances for old friends."

"For him, but not for me?"

While they bickered, Tony massaged the pencil moustache over his upper lip. "Seems like nothing has changed. Seeing you together, I need to remind myself that you're no longer married."

Maggie turned to him. "Unfortunately, we exhibit all the worst characteristics of an old married couple."

"Actually, it's endearing." He affectionately patted Maggie's hand. "Glad you're back in Hobbs, dear. You look divine! And your health is good, I hope."

"It is. My ex takes good care of me." Maggie affectionately stroked Liz's arm.

"Well, you couldn't have a better doctor than Liz. Too bad she's cut back her hours because of Lucy's travel."

"Ginny knows to make exceptions for old friends like you, Tony. You don't really have trouble getting an appointment, do you?"

"No, just complaining because you think you have to fix everything." When Tony grinned, his moustache went along for the ride. "Where is Lucy today?"

"In Portland for her quarterly meeting with the bishop."

Tony rolled his eyes. He'd had to listen to Liz's complaints about Lucy's bishop. "Did you remind her about the fundraiser?"

"She says she's on board, but you need to work out the schedule with her agent."

"That's great news," said Tony, signaling the waiter. "Let's get some drinks and we'll make a plan." Under his breath, he said, "Of course, if the former guy gets in, I'm sure they'll cut the grants to arts organizations. We finally got out of the red after being shut down for Covid. Now this."

Liz raised her crossed fingers. "It's not over yet."

Tony smiled flirtatiously at the waiter who appeared at his side. He seemed to know every gay man in Webhanet, but the permanent residents were a tight-knit community. They kept the gay bar going during the lean winter months. Liz recognized the exceptionally handsome waiter as one of the stars of the drag show. Out of costume, he didn't look particularly feminine or even gay.

When the waiter left to get their bottle of wine, Tony got down to business. "I thought we could recreate the program of our last fundraiser. People still talk about that night." At the cast party after the last big fundraiser, Erika had publicly asked Lucy to marry her. There hadn't been a dry eye in the house.

"I'm afraid we can't recreate the situation that made it so memorable," said Liz with a sigh.

"No, sadly we can't. But we can show our Pride. That's why I'd like to move the fundraiser from the end of the season to June."

Liz pulled out her phone to check Lucy's singing schedule. "Madame Bartlett is free the first two weeks of June. After that, it's off to the races."

"I'd like to reprise that number from *The Witches of Eastwick* that we did for the Cathedral concert," Tony said. "People loved it. We just need an alto."

In unison, Maggie and Tony turned to Liz. "Don't look at me like that. I only sing in the shower." Liz sat back with her arms folded on her chest. "Can you imagine my patients seeing their doctor, flying around on stage, pretending to be a witch?

"Why not?" asked Maggie. "Lucy's a priest."

"Lucy's a professional singer, and so are you. That's different.

Tell Lucy to call in a favor from Denise Chantal. She owes her big time. She wouldn't have a career without Lucy's coaching."

"But Liz, you have such a good voice. You'd be spectacular." Maggie turned to Tony. "I'll work on her," she prompted.

Their drinks appeared. "You know, Maggie," Tony began, "I'm supposed to talk you into joining the Gun Victims Fund tour. Apparently, your ex thinks I can convince you even though she can't."

"Oh, Liz knows I'm as stubborn as she is. The more she pushes, the more I resist. Lucy's been working on me too. I want to help, but I can't do anything this semester. Maybe next year."

Tony nodded in Liz's direction. "So there's the answer. Is 'maybe' good enough?"

"I'll take it," said Liz. "As long as I don't have to sing."

Tony stroked his moustache and smiled. The little twinkle in his dark eyes meant he'd merely paused his efforts. "Maggie, I hope you won't take offense, but I'd like to do 'An Evening with Lucille Bartlett' event. There are lots of opera lovers in Webhanet."

"With all the gay men here, I'm sure there are. No, I get it. Now that Lucy's singing at the Met again, she's a superstar. But if you consider reviving Lloyd-Webber's *Sunset Boulevard* for me, I won't hold it against you. Playing old has-beens is my specialty."

"That's actually a good idea, but I don't like that kind of self-talk," said Tony. "You'll always be Maggie Fitzgerald. I'm sure your *Suddenly Last Summer* will make every gay man's heart break. You are the ultimate Williams heroine."

On cue, Maggie delivered the famous line from *Streetcar Named Desire*. "Whoever you are—I have always depended on the kindness of strangers."

"Maggie excels at playing deranged old ladies," Liz said dryly.

"Just the right amount of faded beauty," Tony agreed, playing along. "You can just see her in an adaptation of *Great Expectations*."

"So kind of you two to remind me of my advanced age."

"We love you, Maggie," Tony assured her. "Liz and I aren't far behind."

The waiter reappeared, eagerly poised to take their order.

"So, Liz, will it be lobster again?" Tony asked.

"No, I think I'll have the mussels Meuniere today."

"Funny," said Maggie. "Me too."

"Me three," said Tony and smiled indulgently at the young waiter.

✻✻✻

As they drove home from their lunch date with Tony, Liz didn't speak. Maggie knew that Liz found small talk difficult. She spoke when she had something to say, but during their marriage, Liz's long reflective silences had driven Maggie crazy. She was chatty by nature, and she often wished Liz would say something, anything, to fill the quiet.

Maggie occupied herself with enjoying the sights as they drove north to Hobbs. Since she'd left the board of the Playhouse, she seldom came down to Webhanet. The town had broken away from Hobbs in the 1980s to become a destination resort, a kind of Provincetown North. The result seemed so contrived—deliberately trendy, happy, and *gay*. Rainbow flags flew in front of every iconically New England storefront. The wares they sold were absurdly expensive and touristy, including the tiny pots of blueberry jam or bottles of maple syrup that no one ever opened. At least, Hobbs was a real town with a grocery store and a school, not just pretty, little shops and upscale restaurants.

The dry spell at the end of the summer had caused the leaves to fall early this year, but here and there, a hardy maple stubbornly hung on to shreds of its brilliant foliage. Fortunately, most of the "leaf peepers" had gone home, and there was little traffic today. Even so, Liz didn't defy the posted speed limit on Route 1 like she usually did. The change was so obvious, Maggie felt she had to say something.

"Liz, I'm impressed. You're driving at a reasonable speed."

Liz shrugged. "We're in no hurry today. We both have the day off."

"But usually, you have to prove you can outrun the police, and if you can't, talk them out of a ticket."

Liz looked thoughtful. "Lucy doesn't complain about my driving like you did. There's no fun when you don't get called out for being naughty."

Maggie studied Liz and saw that it was a completely unguarded statement. "Then Lucy is smarter than I am. I thought I could re-form you. Instead she accomplished it by doing nothing."

"It's elementary behavior modification. If you don't reinforce a problem behavior it might disappear on its own. That is, if the person is made aware of it."

"Tell me that you weren't aware that speeding is a silly disregard of the law."

"I've always felt compelled to defy the odds. That's probably why I chose surgery as my specialty. Each difficult procedure was like a dare I couldn't turn down. But I didn't speed to see if I can evade the cops. I just hate pokey drivers, and sometimes, I'm just in a hurry to get somewhere. As I get older, I wonder why? Time passes. Why should I try to make it go faster? I'll arrive at the end of the road soon enough."

Only Liz could turn a topic like speeding on local roads into a reflection on life and death. Back in college, Liz's depth had attracted Maggie. She wasn't vapid and superficial like Maggie's theater crowd. Liz was a thinker, who'd taken a full load of philosophy and theology classes along with the required pre-medical courses.

Maggie envisioned the tall, skinny girl, who'd always worn her long hair pulled back and never wore makeup. She had good bones and so much potential, if only she would do something for herself. Maggie was surprised when she'd first met Liz's mother and saw her turned out in the latest fashions and tastefully made up. Liz freely admitted that her disregard for her appearance was an act of rebellion.

By the time they'd reconnected after forty years, Liz had mostly gotten over her need to be contrary. She'd never be "feminine" in the conventional sense, but at least she no longer looked like a walking ad for L.L. Bean's outdoors division. Today, she wore slacks and a cashmere sweater that clung just enough to show her attractive figure. Mascara and a dash of blush accentuated her natural good looks. Liz rubbed her cheek. "Maggie, I can feel your eyes burning a hole in the side of my face. What's going on?"

"I was thinking how beautiful you are, and how much you've changed since college."

Liz smiled. "Well, thank you. Funny how five decades will do that. You look pretty damn good yourself. I'm always proud to be with you." Liz was sparing in her compliments, so Maggie could always trust that they were meant.

"Thank you, Liz. I feel the same."

"But not always. You used to be embarrassed by the way I dressed in college. Maybe that's why you hid me."

"I didn't *hide* you!" Maggie protested indignantly. "We were all in the closet in those days.

"Yeah, like vampires, only coming out at night." Liz was given to hyperbole for the sake of humor, but her assessments were accurate. She glanced at Maggie. "How did it make you feel when Tony said he still sees us as a couple?"

After a moment of reflection, Maggie said, "Sad mostly, but I understand. People don't like disruptions in their social networks. They prefer things to be settled. Every time there's a breakup or a divorce, they feel like they need to choose sides. They lose friendships, even their place in the community."

"Is that what you lost when we broke up?"

"Of course, that's why I moved up to Scarborough. It was humiliating to go from being the wife of the town doctor to being a spurned woman."

"Maggie, you drive me nuts with this insistence that I broke up the marriage. You left me."

Maggie faced front. "I did, didn't I?"

"I get it. We all tend to edit our stories to make us feel better about ourselves."

"We do. And you're right."

"Thank you," said Liz, looking surprised to have won so easily.

"But to get back to your question about Tony," Maggie continued. "I guess when people say they see us as still being married, it means they saw us being right together."

"That's because we were," Liz said. "I didn't want a divorce."

Maggie shook her head. "I heard you say it, but I didn't *know* it. If I did, I didn't want to believe it. I was so blinded by my jealousy of Lucy I couldn't see or hear anything, not her apology, not when she gave me absolution for my infidelity, not my therapist, who advised me to try to work it out with you."

"Why were you so jealous? It was just an impulsive kiss. I was always flirting with Lucy."

"Liz, that was more than flirting. You wanted her in the worst possible way. Whenever we were together, your eyes were on springs. I could feel you lusting for her."

"Oh come on, Maggie. That's an exaggeration."

"Really? Okay, maybe a little. You always drool over pretty women, but this was different. You know how you go insane when I sleep with men? Your attraction to Lucy was like that for me. I knew I couldn't compete with her. She was your ideal woman, beautiful, feminine, always kind, everyone loves her, and on top of that she was an opera singer."

"Yes, she was all those things, but I loved you, and I still love you."

Maggie reached out and patted Liz's thigh. "I know, Liz. I still love you too."

"If you hadn't pushed me by sleeping with that kid, I think we could have worked things out."

"Sam kept saying the same thing."

Liz shook her head. "I wish you never got together with Sam."

"You were jealous."

"Yes, a little." It was irrational, given all that had happened, but it pleased Maggie to think Liz was possessive of her. "I was more worried that it wouldn't last. Sam's relationships never do. I don't know why. It's not a conquest thing for her. She just can't seem to find the right woman."

"Obviously, I wasn't the one," said Maggie. "Sam is kind and loyal. I think she thought she loved me, but more than anything she felt sorry for me when the cancer came back. She was so dear and attentive. I felt I had to pay her back for her kindness."

"Well, Maggie, I have to say that's a dumb reason to get involved with someone."

"Why? There are worse reasons. You asked me to marry you because you wanted to prove the cancer hadn't scared you away."

Liz spoke quietly. "You know that's not true. I loved you."

"I know you did, but Sam was in love with the picture of us together, me being her little wifey cooking her meals and being attentive when she came home at the end of the day. You know, like how our moms were trained to be." Maggie glanced out the window. "I don't know if Sam ever really knew me."

Liz turned into the access road that led to the house. "Does anyone *really* know you, Maggie?"

"Maybe not," Maggie finally admitted.

"Well, you don't make it easy. You're always on. You're always trying to act the way you think people expect you to be. Most of the time, I can see through the act, but sometimes, I'm not sure what's real."

God help me, thought Maggie. *She sees through me.* Then she realized that had been exactly why she'd been attracted to Liz. It hadn't been her looks or her brilliant mind or the fact that other people thought she was a genius. She was drawn to Liz because she really wanted to know her, the real Maggie.

"Okay," said Liz, parking in front of the garage. "Now, where have you gone?"

"Nowhere. I'm right here with you."

"That's good. I was worried you were having a stroke or something." Liz grinned.

"That's not funny, Liz."

"I know, especially not after what happened to Erika." Liz clicked the remote to open the garage door, so they could go in through the garage. "Want to come in for a cup of coffee? The wine at lunch made me sleepy."

"Sure. I should be getting dinner started anyway."

***

Bishop Greene's greeting was theatrical and effusive. "Lucy, it's so good to see you!" He flung out his arms and enfolded her in a warm embrace. They didn't always agree on policy, but Lucy never doubted the man's affection for her. She'd mostly forgiven him for pushing her ex-lover on her as a curate and for insisting that he perform her marriage ceremony. By a stroke of luck, Covid had solved the wedding problem. Hopefully, he would never realize how much she resented his well-intentioned interference.

The bishop showed Lucy to a seat while his assistant brought in a tray with coffee and cookies. "I know you have a weakness for these almond cookies, Lucy, so we got them especially for you."

"That's so kind, Jim. Thank you."

"Anything for our Lucy. You're making us quite famous as our 'singing priest.'"

"As long as I'm not the Singing Nun. The church defrauded her of all her earnings, leaving her with nothing when she left the convent. She later came out as a lesbian and died after making a suicide pact with her lover."

The bishop's handsome face darkened. "I hadn't heard that."

"It's old news...from the bad old days, when we were all in hiding and consumed with guilt."

"Unfortunately, the Christian nationalists would be glad if we all went back into the closet. It's terrifying." He mocked a shudder. "I'm sure it's tense in Hobbs with the upcoming election and the polls being so close."

"That's an understatement. I'm trying to model calm, but honestly, I'm scared too."

"I understand. I'm in the same position." The bishop steepled his fingers. "But let's talk about happier things. I hear from Tom Simmons that things are working out with your shared rectorship. He likes not being burdened with full leadership, and St. Margaret's gets the benefit of his long experience. Win-win." Liz often used that expression, but when the bishop said it, it sounded like no one was winning. "No matter how many times Tom claimed he just wanted to retire, I think he missed being in leadership, but in only six years he reaches the mandatory retirement age."

Lucy heard the bishop implying that she should be planning for Tom's departure. "By that time, I'll probably have to stop singing, and if not, it may be time for a younger person to step in to lead St. Margaret's."

"Yes, look at our new presiding bishop, the youngest ever!"

Lucy scrutinized Bishop Greene. He was only in his early fifties. She wondered if he had higher ambitions. Maybe he should be worried about his present position. After numerous schisms over ordaining women and LGBT, membership in the Episcopal Church had steeply declined. Some dioceses were merging to pool resources and eliminate redundancy.

But the bishop was already on to another topic. "I follow your performances, Lucy. I stream them when I can. I always proudly think, 'that's our Lucy.'"

"Thanks, Jim. I never knew you were such an opera fan."

"I've always enjoyed it, but my husband follows you religiously." There was some irony in that statement. The bishop's husband was also a priest. "We were hoping to make it down to the Met for one of your performances, but we discovered you're not singing this spring." Through his exaggerated disappointment, the bishop peered at her as if he suspected something.

"That's because they're not staging any operas in my *Fach*. The manager tried to talk me into singing *Fidelio*, but the role requires a bigger voice than mine."

The bishop looked puzzled, but Lucy was not about to explain the technical reasons for turning down Fidelio or how insulted she was when Liz had told her that she was too femme to play such a heroic role. Although he always seemed interested, Lucy suspected he was just making conversation.

"Well, we hope to see you perform soon."

"I'm singing in *Die Tote Stadt* at the Boston Lyric Opera in February."

"Oh, even better! Closer to home." He mimed tiny clapping. "And I see your book is now getting positive reviews."

"The conservatives trashed it, hoping to drive it into obscurity, but thankfully, they seem to have lost interest. Academic theologians are finally giving it some attention. Erika encouraged me to get a doctorate to give it more credibility, but she always hoped the book would be a popular success."

"I never read any of Professor Bultmann's philosophy. Over my head, but I understand she was brilliant. Did she influence your thinking?"

"Erika was brilliant, but it was Liz who taught me to think critically. Without her editing, my book wouldn't have been as good or as clear."

"I envy you having the stimulation of such brilliant minds."

"And now, we have another professor living in our in-law apartment. Liz's ex is teaching at UNE again." As soon as she'd said, Lucy wondered why she'd brought up Maggie. Unfortunately, the mention stirred up an old concern.

"I remember we had to time your wedding to accommodate

the one year waiting period after Liz's divorce." Lucy decided not to remind him about the more difficult conversation about whether she'd been the cause of the breakup. "Isn't it strange to be living with your wife's ex right next door?"

"Everyone asks me that question, but Maggie and I were close friends before the marriage dissolved. It took time for the dust to settle, but now we're on good terms again."

"I don't pretend I understand lesbian culture. You always seem to remain friends after a breakup. What's that about?"

Lucy shrugged. "Maybe because there are so few of us, we can't afford to lose anyone we care about. Honestly, I don't understand how gay men can trade partners so easily. The sexes are just very different."

"I remember that you wrote about the competing interests of men and women in your book. Very illuminating."

"For women, bonding is about much more than sex. That's not to say sex isn't important. I believe in a healthy sex life, but physical intimacy for women is much more than genital stimulation."

"For men as well," he reminded her with a significant look. He glanced at the little clock on his desk. "Fascinating conversation, Lucy, and we haven't even touched on some of the topics I wanted to discuss. We should get down to business. Unfortunately, I don't think we have enough time to discuss it all. How about we meet on Zoom next week? I'll have Cindy set it up." Lucy wasn't looking forward to another interview with the bishop, but she had no choice.

She wasn't trying to hide anything, but she resented the bishop's meddling disguised as pastoral concern. The arrangement she'd worked out with Tom was delicate enough. She'd promised him he could spend the winter months in Florida with his husband, which limited the time that Lucy could be away. Her agent was furious that Lucy was refusing high-profile engagements during the busiest season, but that was the price she paid for trying to keep her feet in both worlds.

She had an inkling of one of the topics the bishop wanted to discuss. Someone in the diocesan office had hinted that he was thinking of appointing her a canon for outreach through the performing arts. It was an entirely honorary role, but it would give Lucy an official church job if the arrangement with Tom fell apart. So far, the bishop had nothing to complain about. During their meeting, the review of the financials and attendance data proved that St. Margaret's was running smoothly.

When Lucy arrived home, she parked in the garage, noting that all the vehicles were there. She wondered what Liz and Maggie were doing. Given the time of day, she guessed it probably had something to do with cooking.

Maggie caught her in a hug when she came into the kitchen. "Just in time," she said, landing a kiss on Lucy's cheek. "We're just about to sample my new carrot cake recipe."

Liz was sprawled on the bench, still wearing her "good" clothes, so they hadn't been back from Webhanet long.

Lucy carefully took off her collar and hooked it over the finial of one of the chairs. She had only worn it a few hours. She could wear it again, so she didn't want it crushed. Liz had carefully pressed the fine linen. Although she was meticulous, she wasn't as skilled with an iron as Erika. "How was your date with Tony?" Lucy asked.

"Fun..." Liz replied, "...and productive. Tony managed to convince Maggie to run for the board of the playhouse. She's a maybe on the foundation tour."

Maggie instantly looked apologetic. "I'm sorry, Lucy, but I signed up for a full schedule of classes this fall. I'm thinking of cutting back or even taking a break in the spring."

Liz whipped out her phone to look at the calendar. "Brad's been talking about an event to coincide with the performances in *Die Tote Stadt*. It's just Boston. I'm sure Reshma and Susan can hold down the fort for a few days."

"We can talk to them," Lucy said, seeing the logic of Liz's

planning. "Susan says she wants to come on board full time. Let's see if she really means it. The church doesn't pay as well as teaching or offer the same level of benefits."

"Now that she has Bobbie as her sugar mommy, Susan doesn't have to worry about money as much," said Liz, looking up from her phone. "If they marry, the practice will cover Susan's health insurance."

Maggie gave Liz a sharp look. "If Susan has any brains in her head, she won't end up dependent on someone else."

Lucy wasn't surprised by Maggie's strong reaction. In her desperate search for security, Maggie had turned over the helm of her life to others, first her husband, then Liz. When those relationships had imploded, she'd been required to give up her home and fend for herself. Fortunately, Maggie had been smart and resilient enough to further her education, enabling her to support herself as professor and live, as she'd always dreamed, among the New York theater crowd. Lucy saw for the first time what an enormous risk Maggie had taken when she'd sold her New York coop to move in with Liz. Against all instincts, she'd given up her hard-won independence out of love. No wonder the loss of the relationship was so devastating.

Lucy's hunger distracted her. Her meeting with the bishop had overlapped with lunch, but he'd only offered the almond cookies that were now only a memory. The tantalizing smell of the carrot cake baking hung in the air. Lucy helped herself to a cup of coffee to slake her appetite while they waited for it to cool enough to eat. "Your cake smells delicious, Maggie. I can't wait."

"No icing on these samples. It will still be too warm. The cream cheese would melt."

"Doesn't matter," Lucy said. "I'm sure it will be delicious."

Liz sat up and put her legs under the table so Lucy could sit down. "How did your meeting with the little prick go?" Lucy shot her a disapproving look. She'd given up scolding Liz for calling the bishop names because it only made her come up with more creative and insulting ones.

"He didn't get to everything he wanted to discuss, so we'll meet on Zoom next week." Lucy briefly explained the canon scheme. "It's only a rumor at this point, but the person who told me about it is in a position to know."

"Your concerts at the cathedral bring in lots of money," observed Maggie. "Sounds like he just wants to ensure you perform there on a regular basis."

"But being canon has prestige and looks good on a curriculum vitae."

"Like you care," Liz said, staring into her coffee cup, which meant she wanted more. "St. Margaret's was supposed to be your last posting."

"But I still have ten years before mandatory retirement. Who knows?"

"Lucy, what aren't you telling me?" Liz said. Lucy could feel her staring into her ear.

"I'm saying it would be an honor to be a canon. And I don't need to be bribed into performing at the cathedral. I enjoy doing it. And it doesn't always have to be me performing. With Maggie's and Tony's contacts, we could draw from a wider talent pool. The Cathedral has great acoustics. People might be glad for a program of events. If, God forbid, he gets in again, you can be sure his administration will cut funding to the arts."

"Tony said the same thing, and he's right. Used to be Republicans generously supported the arts. Now they see creative ventures as 'woke'."

"Reminds me of Hitler's campaign against degenerate' art," Liz said glumly, "which was basically, destroy everything you don't understand."

"Some people at the college say we've been over-compensating for past racism by awarding most of the scholarships and grants to people of color, but righting a great wrong sometimes requires going overboard." Maggie tested the cake with her fingertips. "Needs a few more minutes."

"I could eat it warm," Lucy said, her eyes coveting the fragrant cake.

"Warm, maybe, but not steaming hot," Maggie said, putting her arm around Lucy's shoulder. "Be patient. Did you have lunch? I can make you a sandwich."

"Thanks. I can wait."

Liz got up to make herself another cup of coffee. "We've been talking about having a watch party the night of the election. I have a full schedule that day, so we thought we'd break into the stash of frozen goodies we put up from the harvest. We still have a few trays from last year that should be used up. We figure if we use pre-made food, we can manage a big crowd without a lot of work."

"Why can't we just bring in pizza?" suggested Lucy.

Liz stared at her as if she'd spoken heresy. "Lucy, people come for the food."

"They come because they love you…and they're afraid to refuse."

Maggie's hazel eyes grew wide. "Now, there's an interesting thought."

"That's terrible," said Liz. "It makes me sound like some kind of mob boss who intimidates people to keep them in line."

"No, sweetie. That's not what I meant. I'm only saying that you have a lot of power because people look up to you."

"Maybe Liz should run for office." Maggie cut a small section out of the cake pan and divided it into three. "It will cool faster," she explained, "Sorry it's so crumbly."

Leaning against the cabinet while her coffee brewed, Liz looked pensive. "Olivia has been after me to run for office since Covid, but I'd make a terrible politician. I don't know when to keep my mouth shut."

Maggie put the cake on plates. "That's true, but someone needs to speak truth to power. No one shuts you up when you have something to say."

Liz glared at Maggie.

Lucy felt obligated to defend her wife. "Liz is direct, which can be an advantage. She knows how to make a good case. When she testified to the legislature on gun control, the press was talking about it for days. Sweetie, maybe you should consider running for something."

"Thanks, but I have enough on my plate. Let someone else do it."

"That's what everyone says," Lucy said mildly.

"Lucy, whose side are you on?"

"Your side, always." Lucy gave her wife a radiant smile, and her scowl instantly faded.

Oh, Liz, you're so easy, thought Lucy.

Chapter 9

"Still stomping in sawdust from your shop, I see," Maggie said when Liz came in to refill her water bottle. Sitting in the breakfast nook with a cup of tea, student papers piled on the table, Maggie looked as relaxed as if she lived there. "Good thing Ellie is a saint and never complains."

"I pay her to clean my house. That's her job." Liz held her bottle to the refrigerator spigot. "Why do you even care? You don't have to clean it up."

"Just because Ellie cleans for you doesn't mean you should go out of the way to make a mess."

"I took off my shoes at the door, and I vacuumed myself off as best I could. What else should I do? Woodworking makes sawdust. Why do you always complain about what I do?"

Maggie looked reflective. "Because you expect it," Maggie finally said.

"Well, you could stop."

Maggie looked like she'd never considered that possibility, but she did now. "But that's how you know I pay attention to you and what you do. And you really should sew that sweatshirt cuff before it falls off."

Liz inspected the frayed, partially detached cuff of her old sweatshirt. "Geeze, Maggie. Leave me alone. I'm not bothering you. Go back to grading your papers or whatever you're doing."

"Give me the shirt. If you won't sew that cuff, I'll do it."

"I know how to sew," Liz protested.

"You sew everything like a surgeon."

"I am a surgeon, and it works, doesn't it?" Liz's water bottle finally filled. She turned around to find Maggie standing right behind her.

"I'm sorry, Liz. You're right. I should stop picking on you. I know it probably doesn't sound like it, but it's how I show I still care." Maggie's hazel eyes were misty with affection.

"Maggie, I'd hug you right now, but I'd get sawdust on your pretty sweater."

"It doesn't matter." Liz tried to hold her body away and hugged only Maggie's neck. "If you give me that shirt and a needle and thread," Maggie said, "I'll sew it while I'm waiting for Lucy."

"Don't you have to go soon?"

"No, we have time. The rally doesn't start until eleven."

Liz rummaged in the junk drawer and came up with the small sewing kit she kept there for emergencies. She slipped off her sweatshirt. The T-shirt she wore beneath was equally ratty and had holes around the sleeves. She hoped Maggie wouldn't get the idea to sew that too. She didn't know how she'd feel standing there in only her sports bra.

Maggie shook the sweatshirt over the kitchen waste pail to get rid of most of the saw dust.

"You'll still get it on you," Liz said.

"Doesn't matter."

Leaning against the countertop, Liz watched Maggie sew tiny, precise stitches. "Where's Lucy?"

"She had to take a phone call. She said she'd be right back, but that was ten minutes ago."

"See what it's like being married to a priest? She's always on. They keep having meetings about 'clergy burnout,' but they never figure out what to do about it."

"What can they do? Life happens, and with this election coming up, everyone is stressed."

"Yes, they are. I've been writing so many scripts for anxiety meds it's not funny. And I can't even send the people for counseling because there's such a shortage of mental health workers. That's why Lucy works non-stop, and I'm losing my best PA ever to her practice."

"Really? Cherie's quitting Hobbs Family Practice?"

"Not exactly. She's still working there two days a week. Amy has decided we should hire another doctor. She likes that young D.O. who was living with Bobbie while she was going to school."

"I thought you said you weren't going to hire more osteopaths."

"Maine doesn't have any medical schools except the osteopathic college. And I've changed my mind about D.O.s. Cathy and Bill give our patients excellent care. Their philosophy might be weird to my way of thinking, and their training is a little different, but they're good doctors."

Maggie looked up from her sewing. "Congratulations, Liz. Once you've decided something, you can be so stubborn. You don't often change your mind."

"I'd never change my mind when it comes to giving my patients the best care, but I realized that my prejudice against D.O.s made no sense." Liz realized that Maggie had stopped sewing and was staring at her. "What? Do I have sawdust on my face?"

"No, I'm just realizing how much you've changed. Maybe being married to a priest, who's also a therapist, is good for you."

Liz inspected her fingernails as she considered what Maggie had said. "I think that's part of it. What really changed me was Peter aiming that gun at me. Like most people, I don't think about dying all the time. We couldn't go on with daily life if we did. But I almost died that day, which is a damn sobering thought."

Maggie continued to scrutinize her before returning to her sewing. "I understand what you're saying. The BRCA mutations could make my cancer recur at any time, so my mortality is always right in my face. Often, I need to deliberately think of something else, or I'd be paralyzed."

"You're okay, Maggie. Stop worrying."

"Easy to say. Harder to do."

"I get it, but you're such a good actress you've got everyone fooled."

"Can't fool myself though." Maggie neatly knotted the thread and rooted in the sewing kit for something to cut it. Liz opened a drawer and took out a pair of scissors. "Thanks." Maggie replaced everything neatly in the little sewing box. She got up and held the sweatshirt so Liz could put her arms into the sleeves.

After she put on the shirt, Liz turned and enclosed Maggie in a bear hug. "Sorry. I forgot about the sawdust."

"I don't care. The hug feels good. I miss affection more than sex."

"In that case, I'll have to give you more hugs."

Maggie squeezed her tight. "I'd like that."

After Liz let Maggie go, she brushed off the dust she'd left behind. "There. Not too bad."

Lucy hurried into the room. "Sorry about that. Maggie, are you ready to go?"

"Yes," said Maggie, "but I made profitable use of the time."

Liz held up the newly repaired sweatshirt sleeve. "She sewed my shirt."

"About time someone fixed that shirt. You know, Liz, you could go with us. We need a good turnout at this rally."

"Sorry, Luce. Not my thing." She grabbed her water bottle. "See you later."

❋❋❋

Maggie could relax when Lucy drove. Unlike Liz, she generally observed the speed limit and drove with two hands on the wheel. Smoothly merging into southbound traffic, Lucy suddenly said, "It was so nice of you to sew Liz's shirt."

"I can never figure out why she doesn't do it herself. She can sew perfectly well, probably better than I can. But she'd always ask me to sew on her buttons or mend a tear, like it was some service 'her woman' was supposed to perform."

Lucy's eyes remained focused on the road, but Maggie sensed

she was listening as attentively as always. "Maybe she sees it as an act of love," she finally said.

"Who knows with Liz? But you're probably right."

"I'm sure she's happy you fixed that old shirt. It's her favorite."

"It's been washed so many times it has no nap left to attract sawdust. I bought it for her in the L.L. Bean outlet on our way back from Acadia after one of our anniversary camping trips. We were approaching the Freeport exit, and I asked her to get off."

"And she was okay with that?" Lucy glanced in Maggie's direction. "She hates to shop."

"It was early in our marriage, and she still indulged me. She left me to browse and went off to look at fishing equipment. She doesn't mind shopping for things that interest her or when she's looking for something she needs."

"Yes, I've noticed. You've known her for fifty years. Maybe you can help me understand some of her quirks." The idea that Lucy would ask for her advice was oddly touching, especially because Lucy was a therapist and had probably figured out all the vagaries of Liz's behavior.

As Maggie studied Lucy's perfect profile, she noted that the jealousy she'd once felt had since given way to admiration. No wonder people stared at Lucy. By any standard, she was simply beautiful. "Lucy, I miss our thrift-store treasure hunts. I know I'll be a bundle of nerves on election day. Why don't we go shopping to get our minds off the drama?"

"Sounds like fun. I need to check my calendar." Lucy took her phone out of her pocket and handed it to Maggie. "Here, take a look."

Maggie studied the phone. "What's your passcode?"

"Liz's birth date."

Maggie said it aloud as she input the numbers. "Nine, fourteen, fifty-five. Not enough digits.

"Zero nine."

"Oh, of course!"

Maggie scrolled to the November calendar. "Looks like you have that afternoon free."

"Okay. Block it off, so I don't forget and book something."

Before Maggie returned the phone, she found herself in the camera roll. "Sorry. I shouldn't be looking at your pictures. Nice shots of Emily."

"It's okay," said Lucy, turning with a grin. "I have nothing to hide. I don't take nudies in the bedroom."

Maggie chuckled. "I doubt you would. Doesn't sound like you."

"Oh, I've been tempted, but my phone is always somewhere people can find it, like on my desk at work. Not that people can get in without the password, but if they did and saw anything lewd it would be bad."

"Lucy, you're full of surprises. And I thought I knew you!"

Lucy's laughter was musical, as if she'd learned it for an opera. "We all have secrets, Maggie. For years, no one knew about Emily's existence. The court documents were supposed to be sealed. Her father was a control freak, and I never wanted him to interfere in her life. I was afraid to even think about her, as if he'd discover her existence telepathically. It was like I was keeping the secret from myself! Liz knew I'd been pregnant because she's a doctor, but she kept it from everyone, even Erika when we were dating."

"Liz never even told me," Maggie confirmed. "I was so surprised when you came over to tell us about Emily. Well, just me, because Liz already knew."

"I didn't expect her to cover for me, but she did. Liz takes professional confidence seriously. I wonder if they still teach ethics in medical school. She says things are all different now."

"I've listened to her complain about how medicine has changed for years. She says young doctors lack curiosity because if they don't know something, they can look it up online. Medicine won't be the same when her generation retires. We're lucky to have her. She watches my tumor markers like a hawk. If I lose an ounce, she's all over me."

"She cares about you like she cares about all her patients," said Lucy, glancing at Maggie after changing lanes. She might be careful, but she had no patience with slow drivers in the passing lane. "Liz might play tough, but things do get to her."

"When we first got back together, a boy who'd been her patient since he was young got killed in a car crash. She was really broken up about it. But her act is good. I use her as a model when I direct actors playing doctor characters."

"*Most* of the time her act is good."

"But you see through it," said Maggie. "So do I. That's probably why she keeps us around. Someone needs to call her on her bullshit."

Lucy laughed. "Yes, exactly, and she won't put up with it from just anyone."

"Hell no. Most people are too afraid of her. Even Sam." Maggie sighed deeply. "I wonder how she's doing."

"Don't you hear from her?"

"Not really. She never was a big talker, and she hates talking on the phone, so I'm not surprised. Plus, she's in her glory out there, teaching architecture, building the great monuments of the twenty-first century."

"Liz hasn't heard much from her either."

"I'm sure she just wants to put Hobbs in the rear-view mirror."

"I'm not sure about that," said Lucy, looking thoughtful. She wasn't alone in that opinion. Lately, several people had made similar remarks to Maggie. She supposed they were trying to give her hope, but the fact was, she was finally ready to move on.

"You really think she'll come back?" Maggie asked.

"Maybe. But probably not soon. She's enjoying the revival of her career and needs to take advantage of it while she can. I didn't expect to have this second act, either."

"I think it's your third act, Lucy. Being a priest was your second act."

"True. I was never good at Math." Lucy turned and gave Maggie one of her incandescent smiles. "I missed singing. I'm sure Sam loves being able to design things other than beach houses. Amy's brother, who's an architect, says that Sam will have a significant place in the history of architecture. Maybe it's not the worst thing that the shooting drove her out of Hobbs. Like they say, God works in strange ways."

Maggie stared at Lucy. "You're not saying God wanted a bunch of kids to die so Sam could be an architect again?"

"No, of course not. But Sam had a role to play that day."

"Liz doesn't believe things happen for a reason," said Maggie.

"I don't either. As a person of faith, I don't believe everything that happens is God's will, but if we pay attention, we can see connections. We all make choices, like when Liz left Yale and bought the practice here in Maine. Look at how that impacted all of us. You left New York to explore the chance you missed to be together the first time. Liz encouraged Erika to buy the beach house. Sam moved up here on Liz's recommendation."

Maggie added to the litany of events that had changed their lives. "Part of the reason Liz chose to come to Maine was because Erika was already teaching at Colby. She and Tony were the anchors that kept her here in the early days when her practice was struggling. The ancients thought it was fate."

"Did you know that Liz was living in Hobbs when you accepted that gig at the Webhanet Playhouse?" Lucy asked.

Maggie shook her head.

"Morales was scheduled to conduct the performance when Denise's friend got her the audition, but I never knew he was such a fan of mine. Suddenly, I'm singing again. Oh, Maggie, you have no idea how hard I tried to keep my career going after Alex had me blacklisted. The harder I tried, the worse it got. Thank God Susan was there to scrape me off the ground. And look. Now she's here too!"

Maggie had heard the whole story before, but it felt like she was listening with new ears. "I know how it feels. I kept trying to get back into Broadway, and it never happened. Then I spent all those years trying to get pregnant. The fertility treatments really screwed up my body, which probably contributed to my getting cancer. And this is the weirdest part. While I was getting them at Yale New Haven, Liz was there *the whole time*. Of course, she'd changed so much from when we were in college, I probably wouldn't have recognized her."

"Because you weren't supposed to connect...yet."

"Guess not," Maggie agreed.

Lucy turned at the York exit and took the cutoff to make the left turn on the divided overpass. "Interesting conversation," she said. "At least, it took our minds off this election anxiety."

"At this point, I'll talk about anything to avoid politics."

"Do you think everyone is as nervous as we are?"

"From what I hear my students saying and the other faculty, you bet."

"God help us if he gets in again."

"Lucy, is that a prayer?"

"You bet. One of many!"

＊＊＊

Lucy peeked through the vestry door to see the size of the congregation. With only two days before the election, the church was packed. Both sides had come to pray for their candidates. Lucy imagined them sorting themselves like wedding guests, the bride's family on one side of the aisle, the groom's on the other. Some congregants always sat in the same place as if they paid rent for it, like in some of the oldest New England's churches, where the ancient family names were preserved on small, brass plaques. At the summer chapel, few people dared to sit in the places marked with the Bush family's names, as if they expected a member to show up and claim it.

Wealthy Republicans had asserted their position in WASP society through membership in the Episcopal Church, but those were different times. In the 1950s, Margaret Chase Smith had called out anti-communist witch hunter, Joe McCarthy, in her famous "Conscience Speech." Lucy drew on her example to summon courage to speak on the upcoming election. No matter what she said, she'd be walking a fine line.

Fortunately, the Gospel assigned for this Sunday, also the feast of All Saints, provided a perfect theme. Mark's description of Jesus answering the scribe's question about the great commandment made a perfect starting point: "You shall love your neighbor as yourself." It sounded easy, but it wasn't always.

"You can feel the tension out there," said a young voice behind her. Lucy turned and saw Reshma, her concelebrant this morning. The young curate's smile beamed like sunshine on a bright fall morning. "but I am sure you will know exactly what to say. You always do."

"I'm still riding the high from yesterday's rally." Despite the crowd, Reshma and her girlfriend, Tiffany, had managed to find Lucy and Maggie. Afterwards, Maggie had invited them for wood-fired pizzas at When Pigs Fly. When Tiffany joined them, Lucy always let Maggie choose the restaurant, trusting a foodie would know the places that met the standards of a culinary school graduate.

"I'm wondering how you'll navigate this sticky subject," Reshma said. "Several times this week, I've managed to choke on my foot. Our candidate is the first woman of color to run for the highest office. Sometimes, I find it hard to restrain my enthusiasm. And please don't say it's because I'm young."

"Reshma! I wasn't going to say that. I'm just as wound up as you are. We all are. There's so much at stake."

"I can understand poor people voting against the president's party because of inflation or rents becoming astronomical. But our people are mostly affluent, if not wealthy. What's their excuse?"

Lucy shrugged. "Some have always belonged to the party. Others will never vote for a woman, especially not a black woman. Many don't believe he will do the outrageous things he says."

"Oh, I think he will," Reshma said flatly. "They have it all planned, and they learned from last time. I'm really worried for people like Denise."

Lucy scrutinized Reshma, trying to determine if her concern for her trans former girlfriend was personal or political. "Fortunately, Denise is living in Milan now, although Italy has its own right-wing, anti-LGBT government."

"What made everyone lose their minds like this?" Reshma asked as if she really expected Lucy to have an answer.

Lucy exhaled a long breath. "I don't know, but it's everywhere. Maybe it was Covid. People felt they'd lost control over their lives. They resented the shutdowns and the masks."

"And the vaccine mandates," said Reshma. "I saw as a child in Africa how preventable diseases got out of control without vaccines. Why can't people listen to reason?"

Lucy saw that Reshma was becoming increasingly agitated. She patted her arm. "We can't go into this service all worked up. Pray with me for peace." She reached for Reshma's slender hand and closed her eyes. "Gracious God, who calms the raging waters and stills the threatening winds, please quiet the souls of your servants, Reshma and Lucy, so that they may go forth to do the work of your holy Church. Amen."

"Amen," Reshma repeated.

"Hopefully, nothing I say will make someone walk out this morning."

"You never know."

"No, you don't. Every word is an excuse to take offense. But we can only do the best we can. Now, come on, let's join the procession."

Still holding Reshma's hand, Lucy led her out of the sacristy.

Chapter 10

Maggie returned the sweater to the rack. Her reconstructed breasts were too firm and didn't have the natural sag to make it hang correctly. Lucy, with her perfect breasts, could wear such a thing, but the retro-redux mock turtleneck wasn't really her style.

In her seventy-plus years of life, Maggie had seen so many styles come and go. Sometimes she couldn't place a particular fashion in its era, which was why she embraced them all. Her formula was simple. If the colors and shapes looked good together, she wore them. Her eclecticism was really a form of disregard for the opinions of others. She tried not to give away her secret when people complimented her for being so chic.

After two hours of treasure hunting, she and Lucy had hit most of the worthwhile thrift shops on the Post Road. Maggie's feet ached. She just wanted to sit down somewhere and have a drink. The idea of a crisp Sauvignon Blanc and a pile of perfectly fried calamari was tantalizing, but they wouldn't have much time to enjoy them. Tonight was the election watch party. As usual, Liz had everything well organized, but they couldn't leave it all for her.

Lucy came out of the dressing room with the colorful jacket Maggie had insisted she try on to brighten her wardrobe. She had no criticism of Lucy's off-duty outfits. Her concert gowns were stunning. Some went back to her first career, but the garments were classic and gorgeous. Many had been designed by prominent couturiers of the day. When Lucy dressed to go out in one of her chic, clingy dresses and spiked heels, she was downright sexy, but her work wardrobe could certainly use some pizazz. A dark suit over a black clerical blouse might look professional, but it was so dreary.

"As a female rector, I always feel I need to assert my authority," Lucy had explained.

"Lucy, I can understand why you might have felt that way when you were new, but you're established now and can take more risks."

"I know, but even those pastel collared shirts that Erika bought me to wear in the summer don't feel right." Since Erika's memory had been invoked, Maggie didn't have the heart to say that the seersucker blouses looked dated, whereas Lucy's usual summer choice, a sleeveless, form-fitting black blouse, was almost sexy. "Honestly, I'm just lazy," Lucy said. "The dark suits are like a uniform I can put on without thinking. Between singing practice and a walk for exercise, my mornings are busy."

Maggie watched Lucy return the jacket to the rack. "You didn't like it?"

"It's nice. I guess I'm not in a shopping mood today."

"But we came here as a distraction from the election," Maggie reminded her.

Lucy looked near despair. "It's not working."

"Did the jacket fit?"

"Yes, perfectly. And you were right. It would look wonderful with my clerical blouses." Lucy had worn a black turtleneck to get the effect.

"Buy it," Maggie advised.

"I don't know..."

"You can always return it later."

Lucy hesitated before taking the jacket to the cash register. While they waited for the volunteer to come to the desk, Maggie inspected the garment. The label from a high-end European brand meant that it had been expensive. The workmanship, including bound buttonholes, was impeccable. The fabric was a tapestry of exotic fruits in rich colors, reds and oranges dominant, but there was enough black to blend with her clerical blouse. The combination, which would complement Lucy's hair, would be stunning.

Lucy paid the cashier the price on the ticket—ten dollars, a steal for a jacket from that trendy brand, but that's why they shopped in thrift stores.

"Do you need a bag?" asked the white-haired woman at the register.

"No, but if you can spare the hanger, I'd be grateful."

"Of course," said the woman in a kind tone. "We end up with so many hangers, we bag them up and give them away." She lowered her voice. "We get a lot of clothes from estate sales. They come in with the hangers." That was the creepy part of thrift store shopping. You never knew if the items came out of some dead woman's closet. But did it really matter whether it was a castoff from someone who'd grown tired of her wardrobe or someone who'd left this world? Either way, its original owner no longer needed it, and it was now some other woman's treasure to find.

Lucy's speculative look implied a question was imminent. "Are you ready to take a break?"

"I thought you'd never ask. How about a drink and some snacks at the new brew pub?"

"Perfect!" Lucy agreed.

Although the restaurant was within walking distance, they decided to take Maggie's Subaru so they wouldn't have to come back for it. At that time of day, there was no hope of making a U-turn, which meant a brief drive in the wrong direction. Along the way, they passed a knot of people waving political signs. Maggie beeped her horn and opened the passenger window so Lucy could give them a thumbs up. The driver behind them aggressively shouted loud profanities that caused the sign carriers to shrink back from the curb.

"I still can't decide how I think this election will turn out," said Lucy, raising her window. "The local support seems to be for our side. The attendance at her rallies is enormous. Why are the polls so close?"

"I wonder why can't they see he's insane, maybe even demented? Instead, they think there's something wrong with us. Calling us childless women cat ladies is so juvenile. The contempt for women is what you'd expect from an adolescent boy. Is it a case of arrested development?"

"Maybe sometimes," Lucy said, taking the question seriously. "More likely, low expectations creating generations of fragile male egos."

Maggie watched a woman with a red hat bark at the sign-holders. "What about the women? That's the part I can't figure out. Why do they keep voting for him?"

"Liz says it's because they derive their status from men."

The pub was coming up on the right, but they could see from the road that the parking lot was already full. "We could skip the snack and have a drink at home," Maggie suggested. "Liz could probably use some help getting ready for the party."

"That's a good idea.'

Maggie signaled to change lanes but had to wait because the traffic was so heavy. "I hope Liz has some wine chilling. I'm so anxious, I could drink a whole bottle!"

"Except you'd wake up feeling even worse," Lucy reminded her.

"What are you doing to keep from crawling the walls?"

"I pray."

"Seriously, Lucy."

"I mean it. I'm cautiously optimistic, and I try to remain hopeful." Lucy was speaking slowly to sound calm, but the raised pitch of her voice betrayed her anxiety. "I tell myself I've done everything I could. I've donated to candidates until I'm broke. I've gone to rallies. I've called voters in red states, written dozens of postcards. At this point, there's nothing else to do but pray."

"There are a lot of Evangelical Christians on his side. I bet they're praying too."

Lucy sighed audibly. "I'm sure they are."

"So which prayers will God listen to?"

"Good question. I hope it's not theirs. They believe the Beatitudes show weakness."

"If he wins, will that prove you wrong?"

"No, only that there is still so much work to do."

✻✻✻

Lucy was glad to be heading home. She'd only agreed to have a drink in town because Maggie looked like she needed a break. Given the choice, Lucy preferred not to dine in local restaurants because she inevitably ran into a church member. The constant possibility of an ambush made her feel like she had no privacy.

When they got home they discovered Liz wasn't there. They were expecting quite a crowd tonight, so it was good that they'd skipped the brew pub and came straight home. Lucy checked her phone for a message from Liz but found none. "I guess we're on our own."

"I'm not worried," Maggie assured her confidently. "We know the plan."

Lucy wasn't worried either. Her wife was the most organized person she'd ever met. Drawing on their store of frozen food processed during the season's last harvest would save time. Worried about the food supply if the former president could threaten the food supply, Liz had bought a second industrial-sized freezer on sale and filled it to capacity. She'd built more shelves to hold canned goods.

Lucy could see the influence of Liz's Depression-era grandmother in the feverish preparation for a possible shortage. But the annual ritual of food processing was more than a practicality. Like a church liturgy, it was a re-enactment. When Liz cooked vats of fruits and vegetables and filled the shelves with jars of preserved foods, she was keeping her grandmother's memory alive.

"Do you remember Liz's grandmother?" Lucy asked, thinking how convenient it was to have someone who'd known her wife for over fifty years.

Maggie stopped setting out serving spoons. "I do. I spent a lot of time with Liz's family when we were in college."

"What was she like?"

Maggie brought her wine to the table. "Grandma Stolz was tiny, under five feet, probably. She was a typical *Hausfrau*, who wore house dresses and wrap-around floral aprons. There were always baked treats in her kitchen. Her hands were never still. She was always knitting or crocheting something. She had pale blue eyes like Erika's. When she gave you 'the look,' you knew she meant business. People often thought she was fierce and unwelcoming, but she doted on Liz."

"She often says her grandmother was her real mother."

"I'm sure you've heard her say she'd be a serial killer if not for her grandmother."

Lucy chuckled. "Sometimes she says it so convincingly I believe her."

"I used to think she had it easy because her family was affluent when she was growing up, but her mother was a piece of work. Her Dad never got past the trauma of being on the Russian front during the war."

"We all had our challenges growing up." Lucy thought of her father's early death from a heart attack.

"Do you think Liz will ever get past the brutal training to become a surgeon?"

"She's trying."

Maggie helped herself to a piece of cheese. She made sure that the refrigerator was always stocked with good cheese, not the industrially produced stuff from the dairy counter, which Lucy appreciated. "She's different with you. Are you deliberately trying to change her?"

"Nope. Instead, I try to meet her where she is and encourage her to be her best self. She modifies her own behavior. Make sense?"

Maggie thought for a minute. "Yes, kind of. It explains why all my efforts to change her only made her dig in and do things to deliberately annoy me."

"Funny how that works. I mean, I call her on things she does that aren't kind or appropriate, or don't portray her in the best light. When I explain it, she listens to me."

Maggie sipped her wine thoughtfully. "She trusts you not to hurt her," she finally said. "Everyone she's loved has hurt her, but not you."

"I'm sure I have, but not deliberately."

Maggie drew a long breath. "There are lots of things I wish I could do over, but it's too late now."

"You can't undo the past, but you can forgive yourself and let go of the regrets."

"You're still young, Lucy. When you get to be my age, you have so many regrets. You've done damage that can't be undone, hurt people who can't forgive you because they're no longer with us. Some things just can't be forgiven. Liz can say she forgives me for abandoning her in college, but if I look twice at a man, her head explodes. Maybe one lifetime isn't long enough to make everything right."

Lucy took a moment to reflect. "Maybe not, but the person who most needs forgiveness is always you. That's why confession is such a common religious practice."

"That didn't work for me."

"I know. I gave you absolution after you slept with that young actor, but you still carry around the guilt."

Maggie squirmed in her chair. "Sometimes, it's hard to be around you, Lucy."

"Why?" Lucy asked anxiously.

"You see everything. Most people try to keep some things private, but you see it all."

"Just my training and some common sense. Nothing special."

"I think it's more than that." Maggie glanced at the clock over the sink. "We need to get moving. And *where* is Liz?"

❋❋❋

Liz carried in the beverage cases two at a time. She'd bought the beer and soft drinks in cans to save weight in the deposit bags. This was an occasion for swilling down alcohol, not savoring the fine points of artisan microbrews. Besides, her guests never complained about the free food and drink they were offered.

Arriving in the kitchen, she launched into the drinking song from *La Traviata*. Lucy found the accompaniment on her phone and joined in on cue.

When they finished, Maggie applauded enthusiastically. "How did you cure her of being shy about singing?"

"I didn't. She cured herself. Liz is basically a ham. Didn't you know?"

Maggie parked her oversized reading glasses on her head and studied Liz. "She is, isn't she? That shy act is false modesty."

"Not completely," Lucy countered. "Liz is a perfectionist. If she can't do it exactly right, she can't have an audience."

"But why haven't you explained to her that she's not a tenor?"

"Oh, she knows," Lucy said, smiling at her wife. "I've suggested developing her head voice, but basically she's not interested. She has a hefty chest voice. She can reach all the tenor notes except those way down into the baritone range. She loves singing tenor parts, so why spoil her fun? She says singing soprano is femme."

Maggie burst out laughing. "Seriously? Aren't you insulted?"

Lucy shrugged. "Why? It's true, and being a femme isn't bad."

Liz had been listening to this whole conversation with her arms crossed on her chest. "Are you done talking about me in the third person, so I can apologize for being late?"

"Sure," said Lucy, getting up to give Liz a kiss. "We were a little worried you'd abandoned us. I wish you had called or texted." Lucy's arm encircled Liz's waist and remained there. The gesture felt proprietary. To demonstrate she belonged to Lucy, Liz moved closer until their hips touched. "Okay, Liz. You obviously need to explain why you're late. Go ahead."

"Cathy's kid got into a car accident, and she had to leave, so I was seeing her patients. And I stopped to pick up more beer and soda." Liz checked the stove temperature and looked under the foil covering the trays Maggie had arranged on the counter. "Thanks for organizing things, Maggie. I knew I could count on you to get things started."

Maggie turned up her cheek for a kiss. "Do you think we'll have enough food?"

"Oh, I think so. Cherie cooked a real Louisiana gumbo. Olivia's making cold apps. Brenda is picking up some pizza, and Tiffany is bringing the pastries." Liz rubbed her hands together. "So, let's rock and roll. How about more singing?"

"Wow," said Maggie. "You're so cheerful. You must think she's going to win."

"I'm trying to stay hopeful. The truth is, I'm scared shitless."

"No," said Lucy, covering Liz's mouth with her hand. "Don't say that. Don't even think it! We need to stay positive!"

Liz started saying gibberish behind Lucy's hand to vex her. "What I was going to say is," Liz said after Lucy removed her hand, "the polls are so damn close, it could go either way."

"Ladies, ladies," Maggie interrupted, "In an hour, we're going to have over a dozen people here and we need to be ready." The oven beeped to announce it had come up to temperature. Maggie slid in the trays. "I've got this, Liz. You do what you need to do, I've got this covered."

Liz headed to the garage to take the big cooler down from the rafters and brought it into the media room. She was filling it with beer and soda, when Reshma and Tiffany arrived.

"Lucy had us put the pastries on the porch to stay cool," said Tiffany. "Okay with you?"

"Perfect."

"What can we do?" asked Reshma. She pushed back the sleeves of her colorful sweater, showing she was ready to work.

"We're going to have an overflow crowd. Help me bring in the folding chairs I brought up from the basement."

Reshma followed Liz, but Tiffany stayed behind, taking in the media room with its rows of home theater seats and enormous screen. "Wow, this is amazing!"

"None of my business, Reshma," said Liz in a low voice, "but I wouldn't let her get away with slacking off. That kind of role play sets a bad precedent. Take it from one who knows."

"I can manage, Dr. Liz," Reshma assured her.

"Come on, Tiffany," Liz called over her shoulder. "We need all the strong arms we can get."

Tiffany struck a bodybuilder's pose. "Coming, Dr. Stolz."

"Good woman," Liz said, patting Tiffany's shoulder, "but everyone either calls me Liz or Dr. Liz. Okay?" The young blonde gave her a big smile and nodded.

Liz showed them where the chairs were and left them to their task. When Liz came into the kitchen, Olivia was giving orders. Hands on her hips, Maggie was clearly furious about the interference. Liz's ex and the town manager had trained in different culinary schools and sometimes clashed over food management. Liz interposed herself between the two. "Sorry, Liv, but this is *Maggie's* kitchen." Stunned faces turned to look at her, and Liz realized the implications. She hurried to amend her statement. "I mean, Maggie is head chef today, and everyone needs to follow *her* orders."

Liz ignored the continuing stares. She waved to Amy, who followed her former boss's orders without question.

"Well, I proved again I can put my foot in my mouth," Liz said, pulling an eight-foot folding table out of the room behind the massive screen.

"Olivia needs boundaries," said Amy. "You did the right thing."

Liz was relieved that Amy was exercising her impeccable tact. She helped open the table without any need for instruction, while Liz explained the plan for arranging the alcohol and other beverages. "We'll leave space on the tabletop for Olivia's cold apps and snacks out here so people can graze. I'm sure there will be lots of stress eating while we watch this thing unfold."

"I'm sure," Amy agreed. "Need more help? Otherwise, I'll go back to the kitchen and make sure Olivia's behaving herself."

"I'm sorry if I got her wound up."

Amy shook her head. "She gets full of herself and needs to be reminded of her place."

Liz arched a brow. "Is that how you keep her in line?"

"You know as well as I do, there's no keeping Olivia in line, but if I don't push back, she'd run all over me."

"As long as it's working for you... Understand, I'm not asking about your personal life." Despite Liz's stated policy to keep out of her staff's business, she was always curious about what went on at home. She found her newest partner a challenge because she was so maddeningly discrete.

Amy's dark eyes glittered with amusement. "Of course, you are, Liz, and it's fine as long as you don't ask me about what we do in bed."

Liz bit her lip to avoid smiling. Amy had now confirmed that she and Olivia were sleeping together, not that anyone doubted it. "None of my business," Liz declared with too much adamance to be believed. She stood straight and shook her head. "I seem to be saying that a lot today."

Amy laughed aloud. "Then you must be giving too much advice. It's okay, Liz. People know you."

"That's what I'm afraid of. Do I sound like a crabby, old woman?"

Amy chuckled and patted Liz's shoulder affectionately. "Don't worry. It's a lot of pressure to have all these people coming to your house. And we're all on edge waiting to find out what will happen. You have every right to be crabby."

Liz glanced at her watch. "I need to check on my casseroles."

The atmosphere in the kitchen, when they arrived, was peaceful, probably because Cherie, who was also a therapist, had arrived. Her honeyed Louisiana accent was naturally calming. Liz leaned down to speak in Cherie's ear. "I see you've soothed the savage beasts."

"No, music calmed them. Maggie has been leading us in old protest songs like 'Blowing in the Wind,' and 'Where have all the Flowers Gone?"

"Like a trip down memory lane," said Olivia, but it didn't sound like a compliment.

"Not for you, Liv, but I can still hear the bell of the campus chapel ringing when the war in Vietnam ended. Remember, Maggie?"

"Watch it, Liz. You're telling everyone how old we are."

"What difference does it make? They already know."

Brenda came in with the pizzas. Behind her were the fire chief, Paul Duvaney, and his wife. A few minutes later, Tom Simmons arrived with Jeff. Tony and Fred brought pies from a famous bakery in Webhanet. There was a scramble to find counter space to put them down. Susan and Bobbie brought potato and macaroni salad, so Liz shifted things around again.

When Maggie told her that the casseroles were ready, Liz clapped her hands. "Everybody! Listen up! Please help yourself to food. Then come to the media room for drinks. Let the party begin!"

"Or as they say at home," Cherie said, "laissez les bons temps rouler!"

Liz remained to make sure people were filling their plates to her satisfaction before grabbing one for herself.

"You always throw the best parties," said Tom, bending to speak near Liz's ear, as she helped herself to a bowl of gumbo. She was sorry she'd filled her plate. Her food got cold while she directed traffic in the kitchen, but she took pleasure in watching her guests enjoy themselves.

After dinner, Reshma brought in the artful pastries Tiffany had created. Tony sat down at Liz's baby grand piano and began playing Broadway tunes. Maggie and Cherie stepped up to the small stage to belt out some Roger and Hammerstein favorites. They encouraged Lucy to join them, and they sang duets and trios. Lucy sang

"Climb Every Mountain" from *The Sound of Music*, which brought everyone to their feet.

Maggie grabbed Liz's guitar from the stand behind the piano. "Play," she ordered. Liz tuned the guitar and launched into Cohen's "Hallelujah" followed by Judy Collins favorites.

The party atmosphere had made the gathering feel more like a celebration instead of the anxious wait for the election results. Despite the singing and laughter, Brenda fell asleep in the last row of home theater seats. Liz sat down beside her. "She was up half the night with Keith," Cherie whispered across her sleeping spouse. "Poor baby has been having panic attacks. When he's scared like that, he only wants Brenda because she has a gun. He thinks that's the only thing that can protect him." Cherie mocked a shudder.

Liz sighed. "Unfortunately, Keith might be right about that."

"Oh, Liz, don't tell me that after my sister was shot by that trooper, my kids' mother was shot by their father, and Keith's classmates were shot right in their own school. Honey, I've seen enough gun violence to last an entire lifetime. I'm just glad my kids have Aunt Simone with them tonight. She knows how to comfort my babies. She sings to them. Always works."

"Works on grownups too. You calmed down a lot of jittery people with your old folk songs."

"People love those protest songs. We should bring them back."

"Hopefully, we win, so there's no need."

"Liz!" called Tony, closing the keyboard cover and getting up from the piano. "Shouldn't we turn on the election coverage? It's almost seven o'clock. Polls are closing in some states."

Liz took a vote to decide which channel to watch. They agreed on CNN. After she navigated to the channel, Liz settled into the empty seat between Lucy and Maggie and reached for their hands. Maggie glanced at Lucy before taking it. "Well, here we go," Liz said, watching the election scoreboard appear on the screen.

Chapter 11

When Lucy awoke it was pitch black, as dark as when she'd gone to bed sometime after midnight. She was tempted to roll over and doze for a few minutes. Then she remembered what had happened, and her eyes flew open. "Alexa, who won the election?"

The charming female voice declared, "The AP called the election for Donald J. Trump at 5:34 AM."

Lucy felt a cold, gray feeling and an ache in the pit of her stomach, like the morning after Erika died. Sleep had brought a respite, even some pleasant dreams. Consciousness made reality impossible to deny. Although there had been no call, the results had been obvious before they'd gone to bed. One state after another in the "blue wall" fell. Once it was obvious Pennsylvania had gone red, they'd finally awakened Brenda to tell her the bad news. She sat bolt upright, a seasoned first responder ready for any emergency. "No fucking way!" she'd declared, speaking for them all.

The party, which had begun with so much cheer, began to break up. "It's a gut punch," Chief Duvaney said, collecting his wife and the dishes they'd brought. In a somber mood, people collected the trays and plates they'd brought. They were silent as they left their house except for murmurs of thanks to their hosts.

Remembering the sad scene, Lucy's mind instinctively began reciting the prayer in times of tragedy:

O Lord our God, source of all goodness and love, accept the fervent prayers of your people; in the multitude of your mercies look with compassion upon all who turn to you for help; for you are gracious, O lover of souls, and to you we give glory, Father, Son, and Holy Spirit, now and forever.

Her hand reached across the king-sized bed to find Liz, but her space was empty. The sheets were cold, indicating she'd been gone for some time. No doubt she was downstairs, cleaning up from the party. Lucy put on her fuzzy slippers and polar fleece robe and headed downstairs. She found Liz in the media room collecting stray trash into an orange transfer station bag.

"Don't tell me you came in here to sing," Liz said in a flat voice.

"No singing this morning." Lucy plopped into one of the home theater seats near the front. "Not too much mess," she observed, watching Liz fill the green bottle-deposit bag with beer and soda cans.

Liz sat down beside her. "I don't want to leave it all for Ellie. I'll ask her to come by this week to give the place a good cleaning. People seemed to be having a good time...while it lasted, but now, the party's over."

Lucy knew Liz wouldn't sit long. When she was anxious she had to move. She got up to tie the bags she'd filled.

"We still have a few months of sanity," said Lucy, drawing a hopeful tone from her head, not her heart. "Take a break from your cleanup to have a cup of coffee with me."

Lucy salivated at the thought of the coffee dribbling into her cup. She desperately needed the caffeine this morning. She hadn't over-imbibed, but her head was pounding. At least, if she'd enjoyed some wine, it might be worth the headache.

She'd just taken her first sip of coffee, when arms engulfed her from behind.

"How long have you been awake?" Lucy asked, turning to accept Liz's kiss. "Maybe I should ask if you ever went to bed."

"Oh, I went to bed shortly after you went upstairs. You even woke up long enough to ask me to spoon you because you were scared."

Lucy remembered now. She'd felt so cold after the election shock. Liz's body wrapped around her was the only thing that could warm her. "Did you get any sleep?"

"I dozed for a couple of hours, but I was wide awake a little after five. I came downstairs and turned on the TV. When I saw the electoral map was a sea of red, I turned it off again. They hadn't called it yet, except for Fox News, but the result was obvious."

Lucy put down her coffee and snuggled against Liz's shoulder. "It wouldn't be so painful if we hadn't had so much hope!" Out of nowhere came a deep, visceral sob, no tears, just her body shuddering, like dry heaves after a drunken college orgy. Stroking her back and kissing her hair, Liz kept murmuring, "It's okay."

"It's not okay," protested Lucy, shaking Liz's arms. "It's a disaster!"

"Yes, it is, but it's what they wanted and now they have it."

"*I* didn't want it. *A lot* of other people didn't want it! What about *us*?"

"We get to suffer along with them." Liz heaved out a long sigh. "That's what I resent the most. I'd hoped I could retire eventually and travel with you. I never thought I'd be spending my golden years fighting fascism. Never mind waking up every morning wondering what new chaos I have to face."

Lucy gave Liz's waist a final squeeze before letting her go. "Go make yourself some coffee, and let's decide what to do today."

"That's right. It's Wednesday, sermon day."

"I don't have to write one. The others are taking worship this week." Lucy took her coffee to the breakfast nook and slid across the bench to leave room for Liz. From that position, they could both see the bird feeder outside the window. Lucy watched a pair of cardinals scatter the smaller birds.

Liz scrolled through her phone. "I have no appointments until one." One day a week, the practice was open in the evening for working people who couldn't see the doctor during the day. The doctors rotated coverage. This was Liz's week.

Lucy checked her calendar too. "I think I rescheduled all my meetings. I was prepared for the worst, so I planned a sick day. Tom's taking pastoral care."

In a stern voice to wake up the AI speaker, Liz demanded a weather forecast. "Wow, that's warm for this time of year. Maybe we can go for a walk on the beach." Liz cut some slices of the blueberry bread Maggie had left for their breakfast and brought it to the table.

Taking a piece, Lucy said, "We should invite Maggie. She'll be upset too."

"After I finish my coffee, I'll go over and ask."

"I could call her." Lucy picked up her phone, but Liz put her hand on her arm.

"The ring will wake her. Send her a text instead. If we haven't heard from her by the time I finish my coffee, I'll go over and knock on her door."

After Lucy sent the text, she scrolled through her phone and saw the usual endless list of emails and texts from parishioners asking advice and pastoral care. As if there wasn't already enough pain in the world, the incoming president had promised revenge and cruelty to immigrants. His campaign had made clear that the only people who would matter now were white, Christian males. Lucy put down the phone and covered her face with her hands. "Fuck!" she said. "Fuck, fuck, fuck!" Liz's mouth was gaping when Lucy uncovered her eyes. Although anger could inspire some salty language, Lucy tried to set a good example by not dropping the F-bomb.

"If it makes you feel any better, I second that," Liz said, sitting down beside her.

"Liz, how can you be so calm?"

Liz transferred a piece of blueberry bread to her plate. "When he won in 2016, I screamed at the top of my lungs. Maggie thought I'd lost my mind. I feel different this time. We all knew it was going to be close, and we lost. The American people voted for this guy, knowing full well what they're getting... a guy who publicly talked about the size of Arnold Palmer's dick, who condoned the murder of his own vice president. My attitude is, you wanted this, you got it. When he destroys the country, it's on you."

"Except the rest of us will suffer."

"Unfortunately, that's true," Liz admitted. "But we know what's coming. They don't. It will be the shock of their lives but fuck them. They deserve everything they get."

"Liz..."

"No, I mean it. I don't give a shit anymore. I gave to the campaigns until it hurt. Unlike you, I didn't carry a sign at those silly rallies, but otherwise, I did everything I could. She still lost. They're never going to elect a woman president. I'm just done."

"Liz, we can't just give up."

"Yeah? Watch me. When Hillary lost, I wrote emails, called my representatives. Donated to the ACLU, Planned Parenthood, etc, etc. This time, I just don't fucking care."

"Liz, I know you. I know how much you care."

"I can't afford to care. I don't have the spit to do it again. Can you understand?"

Lucy nodded sadly.

❄❄❄

Liz hauled the trash out to the garage and carefully deposited each bag in the correct bin. She was committed to preserving the environment, but sometimes, sorting the trash could be a burden. She replaced the lids of the bins and listened carefully for any sounds from above. Overhead, a floorboard squealed, followed by the scuff of soft footfalls. Maggie was awake.

Liz climbed the stairs more slowly than usual because her bad knee was creaky this morning. She knocked softly on the apartment door, then strained her ears listening for sounds of activity. Finally, the doorknob turned, and Maggie peeked out from the partially opened door. She'd obviously just awakened and wasn't expecting visitors because she wore no makeup and her long white braid was loose and messy. She looked relieved to see it was Liz.

"Good morning," Liz said.

"I don't know if I'd call it that, but here we are, dammit."

"Mind if I come in?"

Maggie opened the door wider. With a little whimper, she flung herself into Liz's arms, almost knocking her off balance. Liz was glad for the sturdy railing Sam had built around the landing. "Oh, Liz, how could this happen?"

"People are too damn stupid to know better," Liz said gathering her close. Maggie clung tightly. She smelled like sleep and her favorite cologne, Madame Rochas, an old-fashioned scent that Maggie's mother had worn. There was also a faint whiff of stale wine. Liz wondered if she'd had more to drink after leaving the party. Liz had poured herself a neat whiskey and knocked it down, but she'd cut herself off after one.

Maggie finally released her. "Things are kind of a mess, but come in."

Liz peeked into the apartment, relieved to see the place didn't look that bad. Pots remained in the drainer near the kitchen sink. Maggie had just gotten up, so the queen-sized bed was unmade. The little desk was littered with books and papers. Otherwise, the apartment was relatively neat.

Maggie gave Liz's arm a little tug, encouraging her to step inside. "Want a cup of coffee?"

"Sure, if you have some to spare." Liz shut the door behind her.

In the kitchen, Maggie held the coffee pot up to eye level. "Looks like there's a cup left for you." Maggie was a coffee snob. When they'd lived together, she regularly told Liz how much she despised single-serve coffee makers. Now that she was living alone, she'd gone back to her trusty French press. "Have a seat, Liz. You don't have to wait for an invitation. It's your house."

"Yes, but this is your space." Liz pulled out a chair from the two-person dining table.

"I've never known you to stand on ceremony."

Liz shrugged. "Lucy says that it's important to observe the

amenities with those who are close to us. We shouldn't be nice to strangers and then take the people we love for granted."

"Does that mean you love me?" Maggie splashed half and half into Liz's coffee.

"You know I do."

Maggie looked up into Liz's face. "I love you too. But there are times when I could just shake you!"

"Goes both ways."

Maggie poured the last of the coffee into her own cup. "Should I make more?" She held up the French press.

"Only for yourself. I had a cup with Lucy this morning."

Maggie quickly relocated a stack of books to the floor and placed a coaster for Liz's cup. "You built this table, so I try to protect it."

"Thank you, but the top has about ten coats of polyurethane, so don't worry."

Maggie ran her hand over the polished maple. "It's beautiful, and I want you to know I value the furniture you build."

"Glad someone does. In my will, I left it to my niece, but maybe she doesn't want it. She already has a fully furnished house of her own." Liz inhaled a long breath. "When I'm dead, it won't matter, so I don't know why I even bother."

"Because you always try to do the right thing." Maggie turned to fill the electric teapot with fresh water to make more coffee. "But, Liz, I have to tell you. I still resent that you made me sign a premarital agreement."

Liz took a sip of coffee while she considered what to say. "It was what Harriet advised because we both have heirs. If I had to do it over again, I would have done it differently."

Maggie turned in surprise. "Really?"

"Yes, really, but I can't take it back now, and it did make our divorce easier."

Maggie dumped the spent coffee grounds out of the pot and replaced them with fresh ones. "It was easy because you just gave me everything I wanted."

Liz shrugged. "Your personal mementos weren't a hill I wanted to die on. Plus, I could see how much you were hurting."

Maggie's hazel eyes cooly studied her. "You actually noticed."

"Of course, I noticed!" Liz protested indignantly. She was glad the rumble of the electric teapot provided a distraction. The contents began to roil. The red light went out, and the pot switched off loudly. Maggie got up to pour water into the coffee press. On her return, she bent to kiss the top of Liz's head. "I know you care, Liz. That's why you're here this morning. You knew I'd be upset, so you came to check on me."

"I did, but I'm also on a mission. Lucy thinks we should practice self-care today."

Maggie looked in the direction of the main house. "Being a good pastor, I guess. But I like her thinking. What did she have in mind?"

"It's going to be unseasonably warm. We could take a walk on the beach, but first, I'll treat you to breakfast at the diner. You interested?"

"Why not? I don't have any classes until this afternoon. I'll need some time to shower and get ready."

"Yes, Maggie, but we're only going to the diner, not opening night at the Met. Can you step it up a little?"

"I can be ready in half an hour. Finish your coffee, so I can get started." Liz gulped down the rest of her coffee. As she was leaving, Maggie called after her, "Thanks for checking on me. Means a lot to me."

✳✳✳

Coming down the stairs, Maggie found Liz gazing up at her with a frank look of admiration. It had been years since Liz had looked at her that way, with a mixture of pride, delight, and, to Maggie's surprise, attraction.

"How do you always manage to look so good?" Liz asked, reaching out her hand as Maggie approached the landing.

"As you know, it's quite a process."

Liz continued to admire her, checking out her hair, which Maggie had put in a simple updo. Liz nodded her approval. "You said you'd be ready in half an hour, and you are. Must be a record."

Maggie gave her a playful smack. "Liz, don't spoil it. I was enjoying the compliment."

"As you should. You look beautiful." Liz gallantly raised Maggie's hand to her lips. She hadn't used this sweet, old-fashioned gesture since they'd started fighting over the kiss on the boat. "That's a great sweater," Liz added.

Knit from natural multi-color yarn, the oversized cardigan had been a real find. "It's from the thrift shop," Maggie said dismissively.

"I know, but no one else does."

"Lucy does." Maggie squinted to see through the windshield of the SUV idling in the driveway. "Where is she?"

"Letting Tom know she'll be out of pocket this morning."

"Poor woman," said Maggie sympathetically. "She's always on."

"You don't know the half of it, but things are so much better since Tom became co-rector. And once the school year ends in June, Susan will be coming on full time."

"You seem calmer too."

"I don't have as much to worry about. I've cut back on my office hours. Amy is ably managing the practice..." Liz's blue eyes narrowed as she watched Maggie's face. "You know I can hear what you're thinking. Why couldn't I do it while we were still married?"

"I didn't say that, Liz, and I wasn't even thinking it. You weren't ready then, and, in retrospect, I retired too early." Liz barely hid her surprise. "Don't look at me like that. I've had time to think too. I'm glad to be back to teaching. Tony was lobbying me last night about coming back on the board of the playhouse, and I'm seriously considering it."

Liz's face lit up. "That is great news. I'm so happy."

"And...I think I will go on the road with Brad Taylor's foundation. I'm only teaching one class next semester, and it can be partially online. I've spoken to the dean already, and she's on board."

"Excellent!" Liz raised her hand for a high five, but Maggie ignored it. She tried not to encourage Liz's boyish behaviors.

"You'll be coming on the foundation tour, won't you?" she asked Liz.

"Of course, I promised Lucy I'd travel with her to her singing gigs. She tells me I'm useful for carrying luggage and tipping people."

"You're good at looking after the details, but you know that's not why she takes you along. She wants to be with you, and she doesn't want to feel guilty about leaving you home alone."

"Hmm. Lucy doesn't do guilt much, but maybe you're right."

Lucy came down the porch steps, and Liz beamed at her wife. Oddly, Maggie didn't feel jealous. Inspecting her feelings, she realized the sight of Lucy made her smile too. As Lucy climbed into the passenger seat, Maggie got a glimpse of her backside shaped like an inverted heart. Lucy was so perfectly made that no other woman could possibly compete, and yet Lucy wasn't competitive or even impressed with her own beauty. She always seemed completely at home in her own skin. That's what Maggie really envied—Lucy's effortless acceptance of herself. She lived in her body like she loved it.

"Maggie..." said Liz, interrupting her thoughts. "You ready to go?" Liz's left brow was slightly cocked, which meant she'd probably noticed Maggie admiring Lucy's backside. Maggie cringed, waiting for Liz to say something, but she merely opened the driver's door and got into the truck.

"I'm looking forward to this," Maggie said, searching for her seatbelt in the back. "I haven't eaten at the diner in a long time."

"We haven't either," Lucy said. "In the summer, it's so packed with tourists, you can't get in. In the winter, it's closed half the time."

Liz turned the key, and the huge engine roared to life. "They can't get enough kitchen help or wait staff," said Liz. "That's why it's closed so much. When the former guy gets in again, and ICE scoops up all the immigrants, they'll be even more shorthanded."

"Yep, people thought food inflation was a problem," Maggie agreed. "Just wait until there are no immigrants to harvest the crops and he puts those tariffs on goods coming in from Canada and Mexico. Goodbye to French cheese and wine."

Backing up the truck, Liz smiled at Maggie in the rear-view mirror. "I should probably stock up on Irish whiskey. BTW, I think our dryer is on its last leg. Maybe we should replace it before he slaps tariffs on China and Taiwan."

"Is that really necessary?" Lucy asked.

"No, but if it craps out and it costs double or triple when we need to replace it, we'll kick ourselves if we don't. How's that stackable working in your apartment, Maggie? Okay?"

"Seems fine," Maggie replied. "None of my business, Liz, but you don't really need to worry about money."

"No, but I was raised not to waste it. And if he tanks the economy, all the wealth we think we have on paper could vanish like a puff of smoke."

"Why don't people realize this?" Maggie wondered aloud.

"Because we live in news silos," Liz said, assuming her usual role as explainer. "People listen to what they want to hear. And we listen to what we want to hear. It's like we live on two different planets. But it doesn't matter now. He won, and we'll have to live with it." Liz engaged Maggie's eyes in the rear-view mirror. "Maggie, tell Lucy what you told me about joining Brad Taylor's fundraising tour."

"Oh, she knows. I told her yesterday."

Liz gave her a dirty look to Maggie's reflection. "You told my wife before you told me?"

"I wasn't keeping it from you, Liz. We were out shopping yesterday, and we had lots of time to catch up, so I told her." Liz's scowl told Maggie she wasn't having this excuse. "Lucy and I meet weekly to go over music for church. She sits in on choir practice. We're together at home. Honey, you can't expect us not to talk." Maggie realized she'd just addressed her ex as 'honey.' She waited for another sharp look in the mirror, but instead Liz stifled a smile.

"It's been a long time since you've called me that, Maggie. Must be the post-election stress."

"Must be," Maggie agreed. She glanced at Lucy to see her response, but if she'd heard, she was pretending she hadn't.

When they arrived at the diner, there were only a few cars in the diner parking lot. It was close to nine-thirty, too late for the regular breakfast crowd and too early for the few tourists, who dribbled in after ten. Some of the seasonal people might still be packing up their summer homes, but most had left by now.

The counter waitress brightened when she saw them. Paula had been a fixture at the Hobbs Diner for a generation, but her trademark unnaturally red hair was only a memory. Paula had finally grown out her hair to gray. She was past retirement age, but like so many low earners, she couldn't afford to stop working.

Paula always had a cheerful smile for the diner's best customers. "Hey, doc!" Paula sang out when they came through the double doors. Flyers for local events, some already in the past, covered the glass.

Liz reached across the counter to take her hand. "Good morning, Paula. Is my table ready? I'd sit here, but, as you can see, I have fancy company this morning."

"Yes, I can see. You have *both* your ladies with you this morning." Paula beamed a smile at Lucy. Her warmth toward Maggie was more muted. After Maggie left town, people took sides. Paula lowered her voice and addressed Liz. "Bad news this morning. Thankfully, Maine went blue, except for those damn yahoos up north. Just wait till those potato farmers find out what he's going to do to *them*."

"They'll find out soon," Liz said confidently. "Meanwhile, we're going to enjoy the peace while we have it."

"I'll put in your orders if you give them to me." Paula handed menus to Maggie and Lucy. "I know what you want, Doc, but how about the ladies?"

Maggie ordered a ham and cheese omelet. The home fries at the Hobbs Diner were delicious, skins still on, crisped to perfection, but Maggie virtuously skipped them.

Lucy looked pensive while she studied the menu. Finally, she said, "I'm going to be bad and order Eggs Benedict Florentine."

Paula nodded her approval. "Good for you, Mother Lucy. Even a reverend has to be naughty sometimes."

Liz handed back Lucy's menu. "You know what, Paula, make mine a Lobster Benedict." Apparently, Liz intended to drown her sorrows in hollandaise sauce.

"I'll have one of the girls bring you coffee. Doc, take your ladies back to your table." The diner staff considered the corner table in the back to be Liz's because she often met with town leaders there. With its back to the industrial-sized coffee maker, the oversized booth offered a view of the entire place, enabling Liz to lower her voice when something needed to be kept confidential. Lucy slid into the circular bench beside her.

Maggie pulled out the chair opposite them. "Liz, this was a great idea."

"We need comfort food this morning. We should eat while we still have an appetite. God help us when he gets in."

An older woman brought a coffee carafe and poured three steaming cups of coffee. She unloaded two handfuls of packaged creamers from the pocket of her apron. The mountain of creamers was for Liz, who liked her coffee light.

"Good morning, Lois." Liz knew all the "girls" who worked in the diner. Lois must be close to eighty, another one who couldn't afford to stop working. "Paula took our orders at the counter."

"I know, Dr. Liz. I'm sorry for the wait, but they make the hollandaise for the Benedicts from scratch."

"Why I only order them here." Liz beamed her a smile. "And how are you this morning?"

Lois's face instantly changed from cheerful to stormy. "Ugh!

How can I be? What a disaster! Those men in their stupid red hats coming in this morning, gloating about 'owning the libs' and teaching the cat ladies a lesson. I swear it's all I can do to keep from spilling hot coffee onto their tiny balls. Love to do the same to *him*... with his weird mushroom thingy."

Liz chuckled. Lucy closed her eyes and shuddered. "Except after I heard that I couldn't unsee the image."

"Good for Stormy that she let us know how ugly and small it is," said Lois, making a face.

Liz roared hilariously. "Gotta love Maine women. They don't hold back."

Liz's hearty laughter seemed to brighten Lois' mood. "You have the right idea, Dr. Liz. The only thing we can do is laugh at them."

"Probably the best defense." Then humor left Liz's face. "Until someone gets hurt."

Lois' jaw stiffened. "I'll see if your meals are ready."

"I know we need to vent," Lucy said, "but we've been talking about politics nonstop for months. Why don't we give it a break and enjoy our breakfast?"

"Good idea," Maggie agreed.

Liz opened another cream pod and dumped the contents into her coffee. "Maybe we should go away for the weekend. I can try to find a cabin on Moosehead. The Aurora is supposed to be active all this week. Since they reported an increase in solar activity, I've been checking out some places up there. Saw some nice two bedrooms, right on the lake."

Maggie grew quiet, waiting to see if she'd be invited. Liz turned to her. "Mag, you free this weekend?"

"Let me check." Maggie already knew that she was free because her daughter and her fiancé were taking the kids to Massachusetts to visit his parents. She didn't want to seem too eager, so she took out her phone to look at her calendar. "Alina and the girls will be away, so yes, I'm free," she announced.

"Good," said Liz. "After we get back from the beach, I'll reserve a place, and Maggie, this one's on me."

Maggie appreciated the invitation, but she didn't expect Liz to foot the bill. "Thanks, but I can pay my own way."

"I know, Mag. But let me take care of us. It was my idea."

"All right, but then I insist on paying for breakfast!"

Liz responded with an expansive wave of her hand. "Be my guest."

Maggie quickly realized that Liz had tricked her into paying the smaller bill. Even off-season accommodations on Moosehead would be expensive. Why hadn't she remembered that Liz was always five steps ahead? Maggie drew breath to protest, but Liz cut her off.

"Forget it, Maggie. I'm not taking no for an answer."

"Well, well. The gang's all here," said a familiar voice. Maggie looked up into Brenda Harrison's blue eyes. Brenda took off her campaign hat. "Mind if I sit with you guys for a minute?"

Liz and Lucy moved deeper into the circular booth, so Brenda could sit beside them.

"Can I buy you breakfast?" Liz asked. "Oops. Can't. Maggie's buying this morning."

"Thank you, Maggie," said Brenda with a charming nod, "but my sweet Cherie cooked me a huge breakfast this morning." She patted her belly. "Almost didn't have the room after all that great food last night. Great party, ladies. Too bad it didn't end the way we'd hoped."

Lucy affectionately rubbed Brenda's shoulder. "We're all disappointed. That's why we're practicing self-care this morning. After breakfast, we're going to the beach."

"What a great idea! Wish I could join you, but after they bring my coffee, it's back to work."

"You should go to Tiffany's shop for coffee," Lucy suggested. "It would be good for her business for people to see the police chief there."

"I know, but she won't take any money. The kid works so hard. I don't want to take advantage of her. Plus, I like seeing Paula and Lois and my old friends. Look, I met you here." Brenda turned to Liz. "You know how it is when you have a prominent position in town. You need to spread yourself around, so people know they mean something to you."

"Everyone wants to give you free coffee, Brenda," Liz said. "My heart pumps piss for you."

Brenda looked to Lucy and Maggie for sympathy. "Is she always this friendly?"

Maggie shrugged. "Brenda, you know how she is. She's crabby about the election, like we all are."

Usually, Liz smiled after one of her dry insults to let people know she was only teasing, but the little pucker between her brows persisted. "Brenda, how's the vibe out there?"

While Brenda thought, she gazed out the window into the parking lot. "Quiet. Scary it's so calm. The streets are almost deserted. The last time he won, the good 'ol boys were out there, flying their flags and whooping it up about owning the libs. Not this time. Feels completely different. Weird, actually."

"Maybe they know something we don't?" Liz conjectured.

"Hmm. Good question. Maybe they're thinking 'oh, shit. Now, what did I do?"

"I doubt they're self-aware enough to have buyer's remorse," Lucy said.

Lois brought Brenda's extra-large coffee in a capped paper cup. Brenda got up and replaced her hat. Before she could get away, Liz stopped her. "Hey, we're going away this weekend. Keep an eye out, please."

Brenda focused on Maggie, apparently realizing that if Liz wanted the place looked after, she'd be going along. But the police chief was almost as good at hiding her reactions as Liz was. "Sure thing, Liz. Any place special?"

"Up to Moosehead to chase the Northern Lights."

"Sounds like fun. Have a good time."

Lois came with their breakfasts. Maggie's omelet looked so puny compared to what Liz and Lucy had ordered. Liz noticed and offered her some hollandaise sauce. "Bet it would be tasty on that omelet. They always drown the Benedicts." Liz didn't wait for an answer. She reached for Maggie's plate and spooned on some of the rich sauce.

"If you're going to be bothered making hollandaise from scratch, might as well make a lot," Maggie said.

"If you're going to consume all that cholesterol, might as well eat a lot," said Liz, cheerfully digging into her meal.

As usual, Liz finished first and started talking about their possibilities of sighting the Northern Lights over the weekend. She tracked the Aurora Borealis with web crawlers and apps.

While she was talking, Lucy's cell phone pinged in her pocket. She sighed. "I knew it couldn't last." Maggie could read on Lucy's face that the message was important.

Liz had been watching too. "Everything okay?"

Lucy locked her phone and tucked it into her pocket. "Not really. Tom ordered the sanctuary be kept open for people to pray after the election, and people are coming in crying and asking for me."

Maggie sighed. "Of course, they are. They call you *Mother* Lucy for a reason. Having *Father* Tom is not the same. Especially for all us women who were hoping this country was finally ready to elect a woman."

Liz looked anxiously at Lucy. "Do you need to go?"

"Not this instant. Tom and Reshma are dealing with it for now. But he's suggesting we hold a prayer service tonight, and I agree. Let's finish our breakfast. We can take a short walk on the beach. Then I need to go."

Liz's eyes gazed into Maggie's in a mutual exchange of sympathy. Of course, Liz wanted to protect her spouse from the non-stop demands on her time. As Lucy's friend, Maggie wanted to protect her too.

"Can I help with the service?" Maggie asked, although the music director didn't usually get involved in impromptu prayer services. "Maybe I could sing some comforting favorites like 'Amazing Grace.' Or even some of the old protest songs like we were singing last night. We might be able to get Liz to bring her guitar."

Liz made big eyes to discourage the idea.

"I think that's a great idea," said Lucy, picking up her fork. "Yes, we're all grieving the loss, but people need to vent their anger too. Songs of defiance would help. Congratulations, you're both assigned to the planning team."

"That you just formed...." Maggie replied with a wry smile.

"At this table, even as we speak. Now, let's enjoy our breakfast and go on our walk. We need to take care of ourselves first. Remember that."

"Lucy, you're really giving yourself that advice," Maggie said.

Lucy looked up from her plate. "You betcha."

Chapter 12

Despite the dusky dawns and the colorless landscape, Liz had always loved November. The naked trees and the stubble in the empty fields signaled it was time for the earth to rest. It needed a break as much as three friends escaping from the frantic election and painful defeat.

Liz glanced over at Maggie admiring the bare scenery. She occupied the passenger seat because Lucy had said she needed a nap. It was no surprise that she was exhausted after long days of consoling church members distressed by the election results. Lucy's congregation had reached the breaking point. First came the pandemic, then the shootings, and now this political calamity. Lucy kept being there for them, listening and absorbing their despair and anger in endless pastoral counseling and therapy sessions. Although Lucy had amazing endurance, Liz could see that she had no more left to give.

"Lucy's out cold," said Maggie, watching her between the bucket seats. "She looks as innocent as a child when she sleeps."

Liz adjusted the rear-view mirror to see into the back seat. Lucy's frothy hair spread over her shoulder like a red fan. Her small, freckled fists were snuggly tucked under her chin.. "She's so lucky," Liz mused with a smile. "As soon as she puts her head down, she goes right to sleep."

"But not you. When I got up last night, I saw the lights going on and off in the house."

"I was packing for the trip. When I can't sleep I try to make good use of my time."

"You always enjoyed the preparation as much as camping. I can remember you, days ahead, assembling the canned goods, filling the zip-lock bags with dry ingredients for muffins and cornbread. But, Liz, you can't keep going like this."

"I'm used to it. When I was a resident, my sleep was constantly being interrupted, so I trained myself to sleep lightly, but I admit that I don't bounce back like I used to."

"You can take a nap when we get there."

"First, we'll unpack the car. Then, I'll get a fire started, and then…"

"And then you'll take a nap," Maggie said firmly. "You need rest, Liz. In your mind, you're a superhero, but in fact, you're only human. And you're getting older like the rest of us."

"Gee, thanks for the reminder." Liz reached over to pat Maggie's thigh. "I'm glad you came. It will be fun. Maybe we'll establish a new tradition. When Lucy and Erika planned their wedding so they could honeymoon in Acadia during our annual camping trip, they didn't know it would end up being doubly sad. Besides, Maine is a big state with lots to see, and maybe we'll get lucky and see the Aurora this weekend."

"Remember the night you kidnapped me after I broke my leg, and we talked about seeing the Northern Lights?"

Liz smiled at the memory. "But I didn't kidnap you. I was only providing accommodations. There weren't any rooms available, and you couldn't make it to your third-floor walkup with that walking boot."

"Yeah, right," said Maggie dismissively. "You held me hostage until I fell in love with you again."

"All right, I admit it, but I'm surprised you've stayed in Maine. After we divorced, I expected you to hightail it back to New York. You always said you wanted to get back to Broadway."

Maggie turned in her seat to face her. "Let's be real, Liz. I was never going back to the New York stage except maybe a few Off-Broadway short runs. Here, I'm a big fish in a small pond. I can perform at the Playhouse. Through the board I can influence what we produce. I can direct and act in plays at the State Theater. Since

Alina moved up here to be near us, and now it looks like Sophia will too, Maine is my home."

"At least, Maine is a blue state.."

"True. We could be living in a place where they hate lesbians."

"Even the part of upstate New York, where you come from, is red now."

Maggie shook her head. "My parents would be rolling over in their graves. They came from union families and were die-hard Kennedy Democrats. But they loved this country. Voted in every election. Took us to patriotic parades. What America has become would break their hearts."

"My father was so proud of his American citizenship that when my mother asked if he wanted to be buried in Germany where he was born, he said no. But there were right-wing threats when we were young. Remember the TV ads against the John Birch society?"

"I wasn't focused on politics when I was a kid. I liked the singing in the old cartoons better. Plus, I had to fight with my brothers and sister over which TV station to watch. The older kids always won."

"I was the oldest, so I called the shots, except when my Dad wanted to watch a show. He was on the other side during the war, but he loved to watch *Combat*. Until I saw *South Pacific* at the drive-in, I thought wars only took place at night. Later, I learned they made the production sets dark so the explosions of the fake bombs could be seen on the low-res TVs." Of course, the technical aspects interested Liz more than the metaphor, but Maggie drew the connection.

"Those old shows were black and white, but it is always dark during wars. Look at Ukraine and Gaza."

"Let's talk about something else," said Liz. "I'm depressed enough by the election. I just want to enjoy the little peace we have left before he gets into office."

"Me too," Maggie agreed.

"And we should have a big Thanksgiving this year, go all out before he puts in tariffs and there are shortages of our favorite things. We can invite all our family and friends."

"Even the ones who voted for him?"

"Yes, them too."

"I think Alina is going to Steve's family for Thanksgiving. But now that Sophia's moving to New Hampshire, she'll come." Out of the corner of her eye, Liz saw the broad smile on Maggie's face. "Thanks for talking her into taking the job in Dover."

"I knew you'd like that. And it's a good move for her. Gets her good management experience and Mass General will look good as a ticket punch."

Liz could feel Maggie's eyes studying her. "Even when we were at odds, you always treated my daughters like your own."

"Because they are," said Liz. "Your kids may be adopted, but who is kin is more than a blood relationship. I'll always consider your daughters and grandkids my family. You too."

Maggie rested her hand on Liz's thigh. Her voice was thick when she said, "Thank you, Liz. I feel the same."

A sleepy voice came from the backseat. "Are we there yet?"

Liz imagined a young, freckle-faced girl asking the same question. She patiently explained to Lucy's image in the mirror. "Not yet, sweetie, but soon."

"Wake me up when we get there." Lucy pulled Liz's down jacket closer and went back to sleep.

"Do you think I'll wake her if I sing softly?"

"Nah, when Lucy sleeps, she's dead to the world."

Apparently inspired by the mention of *South Pacific*, Maggie began to sing "Bali Ha'i." The monotonous highway driving and Maggie's quiet singing were lulling Liz to sleep. So she opened the vent to let in more air. Fortunately, their exit wasn't far.

Their final destination was quite a distance from the highway. After navigating miles of rural roads, Liz finally spotted the landmarks mentioned on the website. She pulled into the muddy parking area outside the office and jumped out to get the keys. Their cabin was along the lake. They drove more than a mile down an unpaved road before they found the number that matched their key. Liz had chosen the location because it faced north across the lake, making it ideal for watching the Northern Lights.

Maggie leaned forward to look at the place through the windshield. "Cabin" was something of a misnomer. The large, recently built house had ship-lapped boards as siding, which gave it a rustic look, but other than that, everything about it was modern and looked almost brand new. "Pretty fancy. It's much bigger than I expected," Maggie said.

"It was the only one with a king-sized bed."

"Still can't stand being touched when you're sleeping?"

"You know I never liked being crowded in bed." Liz set the handbrake and looked through the bucket seats. "Lu-u-ucy," she crooned softly. "We're here. You can get up now and sleep in a real bed." Lucy sat up and blinked a few times.

"I'm fine now, but that nap felt good." She opened the door and got out. "Nice place," she concluded after a quick survey of the exterior. The meticulously mown yard and a stand of trees gave them privacy from their nearest neighbors. In the border in front of the wrap around porch, a few white chrysanthemums with overblown maroon centers had escaped the frost. One section of the porch was enclosed to make it usable in black-fly and mosquito season.

"How much is this place costing you?"

Maggie's question was impertinent, and Liz had no intention of answering it. "Not saying. I don't want to hear about it from my wife."

Lucy shrugged. "It's your money, Liz. I don't care what you do with it." With Maggie there, Liz wasn't about to remind Lucy that since they'd combined their assets, it was their money.

Liz handed some of the supply bags to Maggie and asked her to bring them into the cabin.

"What can I do?" asked Lucy.

"Bring in my computer bag, yours, and the other electronics. Can you manage that?"

"Though she be but little, she is fierce!" said Lucy, quoting Shakespeare. With her hands on her hips and a determined look in her eyes, Lucy looked fierce indeed. "I'll bring in the bags with snacks too."

"Just leave the heavy stuff to me," Liz warned. "I don't want to play doctor on this trip."

"You will anyway. You can't help it." Lucy yawned and arched her back like a cat. "Next time, can we take one of the cars instead of the truck? Kinda snug back there, even for me."

Liz brought the cooler into the kitchen, happy to see that all the appliances were full sized. There was even a dishwasher. This place was much more civilized than the tiny cabin in their favorite Acadia campground. The natural materials added to the cabin feel. The common room was paneled in knotty pine. A fieldstone hearth went up to the cathedral ceiling. The leather furniture looked comfortable, and the owners had thoughtfully provided a variety of throws. It wasn't exactly a traditional North Woods camp, but Liz decided it was close enough.

Maggie came out of the kitchen and saw Liz looking over the place. "Are you pleased with the accommodations?"

"I am, if you are. I put your bags in the room with the queensized bed. Didn't think you'd want the kids' room with the twin beds."

"You think?" Maggie said but instantly regretted the sarcasm. "Sorry. Trying to kick that habit."

Liz planted a soft kiss on Maggie's forehead. "Thank you. I can't always be the bad guy."

"You're always trying out for the role, so why not?"

"Maggie, would you mind unpacking the cooler," Liz asked to get her off this subject. She bent to inspect the wood stove and saw that the owners had left them kindling and fire starters. Liz hadn't known what to expect so she'd brought up firewood, which had been the justification for bringing the truck. She didn't want insects hitching a ride on the logs and infesting her car upholstery.

While Liz was busy with the fire, Lucy came out of the bathroom. "Whew! That's the last time I drink so much coffee before a long trip." She looked around the place. "Pretty fancy. Nothing like our place in Acadia, but I'll take it. After what we've all been through, we deserve a nice place, right, Maggie?"

"Yes, we do!" Maggie agreed enthusiastically, coming out of the kitchen. She glanced at the clock on the mantle behind the wood stove. "It's a little past one. How about some lunch?"

***

After lunch, Lucy called Tom. The anxious visits to the church and calls for pastoral care had tapered off. People were still stressed about the election results, but Tom assured Lucy that the remaining clergy could handle it. "Turn off your phone, Lucy. I've got this," he urged gently. Now, if Lucy and her companions could honor their pact not to discuss the election, the peaceful respite would be just what they needed.

Exhausted by the long solo drive, Liz went up to the loft bedroom to take a nap. She could have shared the driving if they'd taken one of the cars instead of her truck. In a pinch, Lucy could drive it, holding the wheel with rigid arms and white knuckles. Maggie wouldn't even touch it.

Refreshed by the nap, Liz encouraged her companions to take a walk around the compound. The trail along the lake was littered with leaves. While the oaks at home still held some maroon leaves, here the trees were completely bare. If the Aurora appeared later, they would have an unencumbered view across the lake. At that time of year, most of the other cabins were empty, so they dared to walk up on the porches and peek inside. They decided their cabin had been a good choice, and if they came to Moosehead again, they would rent the same unit.

Maggie took Lucy's arm. "Liz was saying we should make a new tradition since our annual camping trip to Acadia holds so many sad memories."

"I'm sure Erika's here with us in spirit," Lucy said.

Liz put her hands in her pockets because the wind off the lake was chilly. "Maine is a big state with lots of places I've always wanted to explore. Let's see how we like it here before we make any plans."

While Liz was busy in the kitchen making dinner, Maggie and Lucy sat side by side on the sofa, watching a vampire movie called *The Hunger*. Maggie had suggested it because she thought watching a scary movie would distract them from the real horror of the election.

"The 70s and 80s were an edgy period in movie making," Maggie said, in her authoritative, professorial tone. "Some films from that time are so gritty and over-the-top, like Ken Russell's movies. But some were just gorgeous like this one. I find the role of music in it so interesting. The score is not only for background or mood setting. It's a plot element." Lucy hadn't seen the movie since she was nineteen, but within the first few minutes, she could see what Maggie meant.

Liz had cranked up the fire in the wood stove so high it became too warm in the room. Lucy took off her socks and put her bare feet on the hassock.

Knowing nail polish drove Liz crazy, Lucy had painted her fingernails and toenails a deep, retro red that screamed for attention. Lucy believed in the value of sex for relaxation, and she intended to have lots of it this weekend. Poor Liz had no idea what she was in for.

Slipping off her mules, Maggie aligned her bare feet with Lucy's and wiggled her toes. Her nails were painted almost an identical shade. "Look, we match."

"Great minds think alike." Lucy turned to Maggie and saw that her pupils were wide and dark with sexual interest. Lucy wondered if hers were dilated too. She felt a tingling between her legs, followed by involuntary pulses that indicated she was aroused. *This can't be happening*, Lucy thought. *Maggie is my friend.*

Lucy faced forward, pretending to be engrossed in the movie, which was no pretense. Catherine Deneuve and Susan Sarandon in their prime were riveting. The Catherine Deneuve character began to play the piano accompaniment of the duet from *Lakmé*. "This music is so beautiful," Maggie said. "Such a shame it was so overused, even in an airline commercial! Lucy, can you sing it?"

"I can sing it, but I've never performed it. It's not really in my *Fach*." Fortunately, Maggie didn't ask Lucy to explain the *Fach* system again.

"Maybe you can teach me how to sing the other part, and we can sing it together."

Lucy found it curious that the voice lessons had resurfaced in this context. There were only a few great operatic duets for female voices but singing them always felt so intimate. This one was like a round, with the upper and lower voice interweaving, almost like women making love.

When the Susan Sarandon character asked, "Is it a love song?" Maggie turned to Lucy. "Good question. Is it?"

"I guess in a way it is."

Maggie moved closer until their thighs touched. Her warmth was exciting. Lucy felt telltale moisture gathering between her legs, but she kept her gaze locked on the huge TV screen.

In the movie, a drop of sherry fell on Sarah's T-shirt. Beside her, Lucy could feel Maggie holding her breath. They both knew the actress would soon pull off the shirt, revealing her perfect breasts. Miriam approached and began to kiss Sarah while the *Lakmé* duet played in the background.

Maggie reached for Lucy's hand. "It's so sexy, isn't it?" Maggie asked in a whisper. Her pupils were so large and black, Lucy felt she might fall into them. "Can I tell you a secret?" Maggie whispered near Lucy's ear.

Lucy gave her a cautious side-eye. "Sure," she whispered back.

"I bought a VHS copy of this movie. Back then, it was incredibly expensive, but I had to own it. When I was alone at home, playing housewife, I'd watch it and make myself come."

Fascinated, Lucy asked, "Did you imagine yourself as Miriam or Sarah?"

"Both, but mostly, I imagined making love to Liz." Maggie's whisper was barely audible. "She thinks I cut her off during those years because I thought she was stalking me. The truth is, I was afraid of what I might do if I saw her again."

Lucy gazed deeply into Maggie's hazel eyes. "That must have been so difficult for you."

"Oh, it was. Barry knew I was still in love with Liz. Coming on the inside was impossible, so he'd grudgingly rub me. Even then, it didn't always happen. Having an orgasm was such an event he'd ask if I was thinking of Liz when I came."

Now, Lucy couldn't help reacting. She blinked several times.

"Too much information?" said Maggie, interpreting the subtle movement as withdrawal.

"No, I was thinking that men couldn't satisfy me either. Even the musicians. You'd think they'd have a better sense of rhythm, but they don't."

"Most men are clumsy and selfish. They only care about their own pleasure." Maggie slouched a little, so their eyes were at the same level. "Did you have many relationships with men before you met Susan?"

Lucy, looking into Maggie's eyes, weighed whether to trust her. She knew that Maggie saved up information to use at the worst time. But they were in this deep, so why not? "Not really. Boys were always asking me out. When everyone else is flat chested, and you have big boobs, you're popular. But I was so busy practicing and going to singing competitions, I didn't have time for dating. When I finally had intercourse, it was mostly a non-event." Lucy thought back to her first sexual experience. The young tenor had a large penis, and the sex had been painful. She'd felt compelled to lose her virginity. Now, she wondered why.

"I know what you mean," said Maggie, moving even closer. "I've only been with two women besides Liz." Lucy knew about Sam but wondered who the other might be. "I had an affair with a director while I was doing summer stock," Maggie explained without the need for Lucy to ask. "I knew my husband was cheating and wanted to get back at him, but she was my only female lover between being with Liz in college and when we reconnected. I don't know why I kept going back to men. Just stupid, I guess."

"Not stupid," Lucy protested, defending Maggie from herself. "That's how we were brought up. We were taught to dream of marriage and a big, fairy-tale wedding, babies, and living happily ever after."

Maggie exhaled a long sigh. "If only we knew what we know now. I even got what I thought I wanted—the center-hall colonial in the right development, a successful professional with a promising career for a husband. The only thing missing was kids, so we adopted them. To an outsider, my life looked perfect, that is, until Barry left me for a younger woman."

"But you turned your life around. You went back to school for an advanced degree. You returned to the stage."

"I went back to grad school before Barry left. Being around theater people encouraged me to live the bohemian life that I'd always imagined. Liz and I would lie in one of our twin beds in our dorm and tell our dreams to the dark. She'd go to medical school while I supported her as an actress." Maggie grunted. "Shows how completely naïve we were." She looked at her hands as if they could tell her something important. "Only she had the strength and guts to live the life she wanted. To me, it looked too unconventional and insecure, so I ran."

"When Susan first kissed me, I ran too. I'd never even considered loving a woman. But I came back. I had to teach her how to make love, not that I knew what I was doing, either. But Erika was a very skilled lover, and...." Lucy's voice suddenly caught.

"And you really loved her," Maggie supplied.

Lucy took some deep breaths and finally recovered her composure. "Yes, I did, but differently from how I love Liz. We have a connection that has nothing to do with being married, or even sex."

"I know," said Maggie. "I can feel it. I could feel it when it first began. And you're right. I can't explain it either."

"But you had that kind of connection with her too." Lucy searched Maggie's eyes.

"I don't know if it was the same. We were each other's first. That's special and powerful."

Maggie studied Lucy's face like she'd never seen it before. "What if I told you that I'm attracted to you? That there were so many times when I wanted to touch you?" Maggie's eyes firmly held her gaze. She was skilled at reading faces and would instantly sense any evasion. "I know you're interested too. I've seen you check me out."

"All women do that."

"Except we're lesbians, or at least bi." Maggie's trembling fingers tentatively reached out and lightly caressed Lucy's nipple. Lucy felt it harden and tingle under her touch. Maggie's face was so close that Lucy could feel her warm breath on her lips. She closed her eyes because its proximity was making her dizzy. Then she felt the soft press of lips against hers. Maggie's mouth was open. Her tongue flicked against Lucy's lips, but after the brief contact, the warm lips moved away. Lucy opened her eyes to see Maggie's tender smile.

Before Lucy could respond, Liz called from the kitchen door, "Okay, kids. Dinner's ready. Come on now. You're not missing anything. The end of that movie is fucking awful!"

***

Liz loved sitting wedged between two ladies with red toenails. Like affectionate pets, Maggie and Lucy had draped themselves over her. Each of them smelled delicious after bathing in the huge spa tub in the master suite. Like flowers, they had distinctive scents. Just by turning her head, she could enjoy the aroma of either Madame Rochas or Chanel No. 5. Each inhale brought back delicious memories of sex with each of them.

Liz's companions were indulging her by watching the second installment of the new *Dune* series. They each knew that space opera franchises were one of Liz's passions. One of the ways she asked them to prove their devotion was to sit through them. Liz held a large bowl of popcorn in her lap while they munched happily. *Could life be any more perfect?*

Unfortunately, the question was a reminder of why they'd come to the lake. If the former guy hadn't won the election, they wouldn't need to escape from Hobbs or real life. They could have slept peacefully for another four years. Once he returned to office, they'd wake up every morning, wondering what new horror they'd have to face. The human nervous system wasn't built to take so many shocks.

Liz reached for her whiskey glass, but Lucy whispered a warning. "Take it easy, sweetie. I have plans for you tonight."

Liz smiled into Lucy's eyes. She glanced at Maggie to see if she'd heard, but her eyes remained on the big screen.

"I think I like the 1984 version of this movie better," Maggie opined.

Liz set the popcorn bowl on the table. "Yes, I guess I do too. For the time, the special effects were incredible."

"I was thinking about the acting. There were distinguished theatrical actors in the original." Maggie listed some of the luminaries: "Siân Phillips, José Ferrer, Patrick Stewart, Francesca Annis, Linda Hunt..."

Liz glanced at Lucy, wondering if she was as bored by their film discussions, as Maggie looked when they talked about opera.

Liz's phone on the coffee table began to chirp.

"What the hell is that?" asked Maggie. "I've never heard that sound before."

Liz reached for her phone. "That's my Aurora alert." She studied the screen to interpret the colorful map. "Orange means a high likelihood that the lights will be visible," she explained. "Ten minutes until maximum. Positions, people!"

Lucy pouted. "I'm cozy here. I don't want to move."

Liz gave Lucy's thigh an affectionate smack. "Come on, you lazy thing. Get up."

"Lucy, don't let her put you down like that!" Maggie's sharp tone made Liz and Lucy turn in unison.

Frowning, Liz recognized that Maggie was defending herself, not Lucy. She spoke quietly. "Lucy works harder than anyone I know. In fact, I have nothing but respect for her…" Liz kissed the top of Lucy's head. "but her ass is getting big from sitting on it all day."

Lucy playfully swatted her. "Liz means that part, and she's right," Lucy explained, pulling on her wooly socks. Groaning, she got to her feet. "Okay. We came to see the lights. Let's go."

After they shut off all the lights inside the cabin, they donned their parkas because the thermometer in the enclosed porch showed it was below freezing. Shivering, they sat tightly packed on the wicker settee while they waited in silence.

"Liz, how long will it take?" Lucy asked.

"We're on a fifteen-minute alert." With a flashlight, Liz checked her camera. She'd set it to long exposure to capture light too faint to be detected by the naked eye.

Suddenly, a streak of green danced in the sky, looping in on itself. A red curtain shimmered on the horizon, growing brighter as they watched. For twenty minutes, they watched the light show, huddling together for warmth and breathing clouds of vapor. Finally, the cold defeated them, and they went inside. Liz put more wood on the fire. They kept the lights off and watched from the front window for a few more minutes, but the beautiful colors had faded away.

"Wow," said Maggie. "That was truly amazing. I can scratch that off my bucket list. I guess now I can die happy."

"The Aurora is supposed to be active all weekend, so you get a reprieve, if you make it to tomorrow."

Lucy's arched brow indicated what she thought of Liz's lame attempt at humor. Given Maggie's cancer scares, it was also tactless. But Maggie played along. "Nice to know I'll be spared for another day." She looked at each of them in turn. "I don't know about you, but all this relaxing has made me tired. Liz, you don't mind if we watch the rest of the movie tomorrow?" Lucy's hand found Liz's and squeezed it, which meant she approved of the idea.

The others headed to bed while Liz banked the fire. After Lucy's warning, Liz expected a torrid night of wild sex, but when she slid into the soft king-sized bed, she discovered a different agenda. Lucy molded her body to Liz's and asked to be kissed everywhere.

"Everywhere?" Liz asked, teasing.

"Wherever suits your fancy," Lucy whispered. Liz's imagination ran wild, but Lucy's mellow attitude meant she probably wasn't in the mood for anything too unusual. She began at Lucy's sensual mouth and made an extra-long stop at her breasts before delicately kissing her way down to her crotch. Lucy indicated her appreciation with a loud moan. Fortunately, the loft was enclosed, so the sound wasn't projecting into the open chamber outside. Maggie didn't need to hear them making love in stereo. By the time Lucy came, Liz was so excited she only needed a light touch to bring her to a powerful climax. "Wow, that was big," Lucy said congratulating herself as well as Liz.

"Get up and pee," Liz ordered.

"No, I don't want to get up," Lucy protested. "I'm nice and warm."

"No UTIs on vacation. Wasn't that one after your wedding to Erika enough?"

"Oh, my word! That was enough to last a lifetime," said Lucy sitting up.

Liz retrieved her shirt from the floor and put on her lounge pants because the loft was chilly. She tossed Lucy her flannel nightgown.

"When you said you had plans for me, I was expecting you to trot out all your toys. Didn't you bring them?"

"Oh, I did," said Lucy, stretching lazily. "They're in that bag." She pointed to a small duffle, on the floor near the bed.

Curious, Liz opened it. "My God, Lucy, you've got everything in here! What did you do? Open your dildo drawer and dump the contents?"

Lucy giggled. "That's exactly what I did. I was so busy before we left, I didn't have time to be choosey."

Liz picked through the colorful silicone toys and bottles of lubricants and cleaners. When she looked up, she saw Lucy looking pensive. "Something wrong?"

"Liz, sit down."

The serious look on Lucy's face made Liz instantly comply. She sat on the edge of bed. "This sounds ominous. What's the matter?"

"I have a confession to make."

"Uh, no, Lucy. You're the priest, not me."

"Liz, I mean it. This is important."

Liz assumed an attentive posture. "I'm listening."

"We've agreed to have full transparency in our relationship, and I want to keep it that way." As Lucy scanned her face, Liz became increasingly anxious, but she maintained what Lucy called her 'doctor face'. Finally, Lucy said, "Maggie kissed me."

Liz had been controlling her face in case what Lucy revealed was serious. "When did this happen?" she asked cautiously.

"On the sofa this afternoon while we were watching *The Hunger*."

Liz chuckled, which seemed to put Lucy off balance. "Those scenes between Sarandon and Deneuve got you all horny? Especially with the flower duet from *Lakmé* playing in the background? I get it. I bought myself a copy of the movie and watched that scene again and again."

"Funny. That's what Maggie said."

"So what's the big deal? Lucy, *everyone* wants to kiss you."

Lucy stared at her. "I don't understand. When Maggie slept with that young actor, you lost your mind. You went to the firing range and shot everything in sight. You tried to force me to kiss you until I had to use martial arts to stop you."

"That was different. Maggie did it to get back at me. She knew it would trigger bad memories from college, so she did it to hurt me."

"She told me she did it to end the marriage."

"Which it did. Sleeping with a man was the one thing I could never forgive."

"So you're not angry she kissed me?"

"You mean jealous? No, I'm only disappointed I wasn't there to watch."

"Liz, be serious."

"I am being serious. As they say, 'payback's a bitch.' I kissed you when you were married to someone else, and now, Maggie has too. That makes us even. Hope she's happy."

"Liz, this wasn't about settling a score. I could feel how aroused she was."

"And you weren't? Did you want her to kiss you?"

Lucy dropped her gaze to the bedding and wouldn't look up.

"Luce...?"

"Liz, I love you with all my heart," Lucy declared with great ardor.

"I know you do. Lucy, I don't know what to say. You wanted Maggie to kiss you, and she did. No harm done. It was just a kiss."

"More than just a kiss..."

Liz studied Lucy, whose green eyes were large with worry. "You want her, don't you?"

Lucy lowered her gaze again.

"What if I said, I want her too?"

At that, Lucy looked up sharply. "You do?"

"Of course, I do. Lucy, I've never stopped wanting her. Maybe we should invite her up to finish what she started."

"Liz! We're married."

"So? I was married to Maggie too. I took a vow to be with her for the rest of my life. You think ceremonies and papers change your feelings about a person? Marriage is nothing but a legal transaction to ensure property rights and kinship."

"More than that" Lucy insisted.

"To you, maybe. You're a priest. That's what you're supposed to say."

"Liz, you were the one who insisted we get married."

"Because I knew how important it was to you. Poor Erika. You tried to make her wait until she married you."

"But I didn't make her wait."

"I know. Obviously, you can bend the rules when you want to." Lucy gave her another sharp look.

"She was needy after her mother died," Lucy said slowly. "We both knew where the relationship was heading, but yes, I broke my own rules."

Liz reached for Lucy's hands. "Honey, I'm not angry," Liz said evenly. "I'm not jealous. I think you wanted Maggie to kiss you, and she did. Hell, I want to kiss her too and fuck her right now, right here with you."

"I'm not interested in just a fuck. I don't believe in sex without love."

"Whoa! This is serious," said Liz. "Maybe Maggie should be part of this conversation."

"I'm afraid," Lucy murmured. "We already have so much chaos swirling around us. Why invite more?"

Liz shrugged. "Fine. We don't have to do it. And if we do, it doesn't have to be tonight." She knew that pretending lack of interest would force Lucy to reveal her true feelings.

"We don't have to do anything, but this feels like something we should explore. We should at least talk to Maggie and tell her you know about the kiss."

Liz held Lucy's cheeks and looked directly into her eyes. She could see the little brown and gold specks in the irises, and the enlarged pupils. Lucy might be protesting the idea of a threesome, but she was very aroused. "I'll go down and get her. You're sure?"

"Yes," Lucy said softly but with conviction. "I'm sure."

"She might decline."

"That's okay too."

❋❋❋

Before settling down to read, Maggie had made herself come to relieve the pent-up arousal. Snuggling beside Lucy and Liz during the movie and while they'd waited for the Northern Lights had only made it build. She was surprised to come so quickly and to find such an abundance of natural moisture.

Relieved of the tension, she was deeply involved in a thriller when a sharp rap on the door made her jump. Of course, it would be Liz. Lucy would never do something so invasive. Feeling sexy, Maggie had put on her sheerest nightgown. She pulled the comforter up to her chin before cautiously calling out, "Come in." Usually, she could read Liz, but the look on her face was a strange combination of threat and mischief.

Liz folded her arms on her chest and asked sternly, "Maggie, did you kiss my wife?"

For a moment, Maggie couldn't think of what to say.

"Did you or did you not kiss my wife?" Liz demanded.

"Yes," Maggie said almost like a dare, hoping Liz wouldn't perceive how anxious she was.

"May I enter?" The formality didn't jive with Liz's fierce look or her aggressive stance.

"Yes, of course. Come in."

Liz approached the bed and extended her hand. "Let's go."

"Where?"

"Upstairs. Come with me." Liz extended her hand more forcefully this time. The gesture was more threatening than inviting. Maggie held the comforter closer to her chin.

"Why am I going upstairs?"

"To finish what you started." Liz gathered air with her hand. "Come on. Let's go."

"Liz, have you been drinking?"

"The alcohol wore off a long time ago. I'm not kidding, Maggie. You're wanted upstairs. Lucy's orders."

Liz grinned, and Maggie finally lowered the covers. "You're serious."

"Here. I'll prove it." Liz pushed Maggie back against her pillow and assertively parted Maggie's lips. The passion of the kiss took Maggie's breath away. Liz hadn't kissed her like that since the early days of their marriage, when she couldn't get enough of her. Maggie reached up to touch Liz's breast, which made her break off the kiss. "Maggie, I want to fuck you in the worst possible way, but not here. Come upstairs." She stood straight and reached out her hand again. This time, Maggie took it. She tried to snatch the robe that lay at the bottom of the bed as she passed, but Liz steadily pulled her forward. "Leave it. You won't need it. Come on. I can't wait."

Maggie followed her to the stairs, hurrying to keep up with Liz, whose legs were much longer.

"Liz, wait! Are you sure Lucy is okay with this?"

"She says she is." Liz eyed her sternly. "If you don't want to do this, you can go back to bed, but I hope you'll come with me." Liz put her arms around her waist and pulled her close. The feel of her unbound breasts was exciting.

"I'll come with you," Maggie said.

"Good. Lucy's waiting for us." Liz stood aside and gestured with a deep bow. "Ladies, first." Maggie hurried because she knew Liz liked to pinch her from behind.

Lucy smiled and opened her arms wide. They were instantly a tangle of bodies, mouths, tongues and fingers. Maggie found Lucy's perfect nipple in her mouth and circled it with her tongue before sucking on it enthusiastically. Liz gently nudged her aside to enjoy the other creamy breast.

After more mutual exploration, Liz and Lucy were completely into making love to each other. Being made a spectator, Maggie decided to embrace the role and moved to the chair for a better view. Of course, she'd been curious about their sex life and now, she had a front row seat. The glimpse of Lucy's bright red pubic hair and the sight of her perfect heart-shaped backside bobbing up and down had aroused her in ways she hadn't imagined. She guessed if she touched herself, she'd find something she'd thought she'd never have again—an abundance of natural moisture.

Her eyes couldn't believe what they saw. Tiny Lucy deftly flipped Liz over on her back with one of her martial arts moves. She laughed merrily at Liz's surprise, but it was clearly some kind of dominance game they played. Lucy kissed her way down to Liz's crotch. Her tongue had barely touched Liz when she emitted a deep moan and arched her back.

"Well," said Lucy, sitting up, "now that we've gotten that out of the way, we can move on." She reached beside the bed.

"Uh, I don't think that's a good idea," Liz said. "Maggie doesn't approve of *devices*." Lucy turned around with a questioning look.

"Liz, don't you dare speak for me," Maggie protested indignantly, irritated by Liz's presumption. She was even more annoyed that Liz had interrupted the sex lesson. "I want to see what you two do in bed. Pretend I'm not here."

Liz raised her head from the pillow. "That's kind of hard, Maggie, with you sitting right there."

Maggie batted away her objection. "Ignore me. Get back to work."

Liz laughed and put her head down. Lucy reached over Liz again and brought up a small duffle bag. She removed a turquoise device, with a bulbous end on one side and a significant phallus on the other. Despite Maggie's deliberate ignorance of dildos, it was clearly identifiable as one meant for two. Fortunately, the business end bore no resemblance to the real thing apart from its shape. The jewellike color made it seem inviting, almost playful.

Lucy dribbled some lubricant on the active side and positioned it between Liz's legs. "Open up, lover. This is your favorite part." Liz flinched a little as Lucy began to insert it, but then a look of profound pleasure spread over her face. From sex with men, Maggie remembered that first moment of penetration. For her, that was the high point. The rest of the experience was usually disappointing, often boring. She often stared at the ceiling while her male partners labored over her.

Lucy lay on her back and opened her legs wider. They clung together, rocking in rhythm to one another's moans and movements. Liz withdrew and advanced, timing her thrusts to Lucy's responses. Lucy wrapped her legs around Liz's hips. "Deeper," she begged, and Liz drove into her. Finally, they both shuddered, first Lucy, then Liz just moments later. The act had left Maggie so excited she could have come with a single touch.

After Liz caught her breath, Liz rolled Lucy over on her back and allowed her to remove the thing slowly and gently. Still panting, Lucy beckoned. "Come join us."

Unsure, Maggie hesitated.

"Come on," Lucy insisted. "Don't think we're going to let you get away." Finally, Maggie approached the bed. Lucy rolled her on her back. The tiny, feminine woman was the aggressor, as she had been with Liz. Maggie perceived that Lucy called the shots in that marriage.

Her observations were interrupted when Lucy gently nudged her legs apart and sat cross-legged between them. She carefully spread Maggie's lips with her thumbs. "I like to see what other women look like. They're so beautiful…like flowers."

"Georgia O'Keefe thought so too," said Maggie. Being inspected unnerved her and she closed her eyes.

"I'm always curious because I've only been with three women," Lucy admitted. "Liz gets to look at lady parts all the time."

"I do not!" Liz protested indignantly.

Completely ignoring her, Lucy continued to explore Maggie's genitals. "You look like Liz. Pale and compact. Like a tight, little pink rosebud. Absolutely beautiful!" Maggie jumped when the exploring fingers finally touched her clitoris. "But a little dry, even though you have a good start. Liz, can you help us out here?"

Liz found a small jar in the duffle bag, ripped off the inner plastic liner, and handed it to Lucy.

"Brand new, and just for you," said Lucy, showing Maggie the contents.

"What is it?" asked Maggie, regarding the jar skeptically.

"It's a lubricant that Liz bought me for vaginal dryness, but I don't have that problem anymore. Like she says, use it or lose it."

"What's in it? I can't take hormones."

"It's just beeswax with propolis and honey, which gives it mild antiseptic qualities," Liz explained. "It moisturizes and lubricates the vulval tissues."

Lucy plucked out a glistening wad with her fingertip and applied the cream to both sides of Maggie's inner lips. Maggie was electrified by her touch. "Feel good?" Lucy asked, gently rubbing in the cream. "This will ease the dryness. It must be so uncomfortable," she added soothingly. But Maggie wasn't thinking of anything except the delicious sensations Lucy's caresses were producing. Her gentle fingers and hypnotic pace brought Maggie right to the edge of a climax, but then she stopped, holding her lightly between her thumb and forefinger. "Not yet, sweetie. Don't waste it. Liz has been waiting to give you the first orgasm."

Leaning against the headboard, Liz said, "Lucy, don't be cruel. Let her come."

"No, I know how much you want to take her." Lucy slowly penetrated Maggie, first with one finger, then two. "Oh, Maggie, you're so tight!"

"Let's see," said Liz, nudging Lucy gently out of the way. She slowly entered with one finger, then two. Maggie didn't like the look of her frown. "You are tight." Liz's fingers continued to explore her.

"Liz…" Lucy warned gently, "this is no time for a gynecological exam. We're making love."

As stubborn as Liz could be, she didn't argue. "Sorry, Maggie," said Liz and withdrew.

"Liz, make love to me like you did with Lucy."

They exchanged a look. Lucy rooted around in the duffle bag. "We have that small dildo we started with when you were so tight."

While Lucy searched for whatever she was looking for, Liz explained, "It had been decades since I'd slept with a man. It took a while to get used to being penetrated again. We'll try, Maggie. If it's painful, I'll stop right away."

After a moment of indecision, Maggie nodded. "Just be careful." She lay still, waiting to see what would happen next. Liz's tongue teased her right to the very edge. Maggie closed her eyes to focus on the pleasure. When she opened them, Liz's face was above hers. Her blue eyes were misty with desire like after they first got back together. Her desire radiated from her body like fire. She gently nudged her legs apart and gathered them around her. "May I?" she asked with a tender look Maggie hadn't seen for years.

"Yes, I want you inside me."

The thing pressing against her was a little cold, not like a real penis. "Just relax," Liz urged. "I'll go slow. Stop me if it hurts."

But it didn't hurt. Liz moved into her slowly, and it felt so good to be filled. The gentle rhythm was soothing. Maggie clutched Liz's shoulders, enjoying their strength. It had been so long since she'd held her naked in her arms. Liz slowly pushed into her until the dildo plumbed her depth. Gingerly, Liz lowered her weight. Pressed tightly together, they rocked with the same rhythm, Maggie rising to meet her lover. The dildo had finally warmed. It was smaller than a male organ and slicker because of the lubricant, and the thrusts weren't invasive like when a man was busy colonizing and taking possession of *his* woman. Maggie wrapped her legs around Liz's back so she could go even deeper. "I love you," she whispered into her ear.

"I love you too," Liz whispered back, "but I hope you can come soon because I'm so close."

The pressure momentarily made Maggie freeze. Realizing, Liz withdrew a little and started again. Feeling her deep inside, expanding her with each thrust, Maggie felt the orgasm begin and pulled Liz's hips closer. When the excitement reached its peak, she saw flashing lights and exploding stars and opened herself completely. A moment later, Liz's muscles tensed. She'd always been muted in her orgasms. She clenched her teeth and groaned before resting lightly on Maggie's body.

After Liz withdrew, she collapsed on the bed beside her. Lucy clapped. "Beautiful!" She kissed Maggie. "Did you enjoy it?"

"It was wonderful," Maggie said between ragged breaths. She waited until she stopped panting before she asked, "How did you make me come with that thing?"

"It's called a dildo, Maggie," said Liz, turning toward her. "Not that *thing*. But to answer your question, one of the virtues of Lucy's toys is they can improve on the real thing. There's a little nub in a strategic place that stimulates the clitoris during penetration." Liz picked up the dildo and showed her the spot.

"She makes it sound so romantic, doesn't she?" Lucy said.

"She's answering my question, so it's okay," Maggie said, looking thoughtful. "But feeling you inside me felt so good."

Liz sat up and crawled like an inchworm to the end of the bed. She rummaged in a backpack and produced a pad and a mechanical pencil. "Lesbians who reject dildos because they remind them of penises completely miss the point. Our genitals are built to enjoy penetration," said Liz and began drawing something like a cross between a stylized angel and a wishbone with wings. "This is what the clitoris really looks like. It's not just the little pearl under the hood. It goes through the labia majora and has these vesicles." She expanded the diagram, explaining how the different parts worked and fit together.

Maggie leaned her chin on Liz's shoulder. "I forgot how well you draw."

"She does, doesn't she?" Lucy agreed in an admiring tone.

Liz continued sketching. "In medical school, we were trained to draw what we saw during a dissection to reinforce the appearance and location of the structures in our minds. Same with what we saw under the microscope. Most of our books were text with illustrations. We had to learn the vocabulary, not just where things were and what they did. When you're up to your elbows in retractors and guts, you can't whip out your phone and point to a picture." Liz finished the drawing and held it up so Lucy could see it too. "When something penetrates your vagina, it stimulates this part of the vulva and more. If you're stimulated enough, you come. That's why foreplay is so important."

Maggie turned to Lucy. "Did you know all this?"

Lucy shrugged. "Liz used to give me little sex education lectures when I was working on my book. I learned so much."

"I know she's good for more than orgasms," Maggie said, gently pinching Liz's arm, "but I have to admit that one was a wow!"

Liz wiggled her brows suggestively. "Ready for another one?"

"Easy tiger. Give the old lady a break." Maggie leaned back against the headboard and sighed. "Liz, I'm surprised you're not running downstairs for something to eat. You're usually hungry after sex."

"Who says I'm not?"

✳✳✳

Liz volunteered to go on a snack run. She knew her wives—for lack of something else to call them—preferred white wine, so she decided to go with the majority and opened a bottle of pinot grigio. The juice tumblers she found in one of the cabinets were sturdy enough to endure the jaunt upstairs and lacked a stem to make the glasses as tipsy as those who drank from them. She didn't want to be changing wine-soaked sheets at that hour. She took one of the empty canvas bags in which they'd transported their supplies and added a box of crackers, a bag of chips, and some pre-sliced cheese that Maggie would surely complain about. They were supposed to be camping, so maybe she wouldn't.

Liz took her bag up to the loft, but when she opened the door, she discovered a worrying scene. Lucy was holding Maggie, while tracing sympathetic circles on her back and crooning soothing words.

"What's going on?" Liz asked, mystified. "When I left five minutes ago, everyone was smiling."

"Liz!" Lucy shot her an irritated look. "Can't you see Maggie's upset?"

"But why?" Liz stowed the canvas bag and sat down beside her. "Maggie, what's wrong?"

"She wants to tell you something," said Lucy, nudging Maggie to urge her to sit up straight.

Liz went into the bathroom and found a box of tissues. She

snatched a fistful and handed them to Maggie. "I didn't hurt you, did I?"

Maggie reached out and stroked her arm. "No, sweetheart. You were so gentle and tender. You didn't hurt me one bit."

Liz looked to Lucy for an explanation, but she shook her head and glanced at Maggie. "She needs to tell you."

"What the hell's going on?" asked Liz, mystified.

Lucy put her arm around Maggie. "Just tell her."

Maggie took a deep breath. "When I tried to have sex with Brad, I was so tight he couldn't get in. He kept trying. My God, did it hurt! I bled like a virgin. Finally, I had to ask him to stop."

Liz had always imagined Maggie's act of vengeance to be a defiant moment of heterosexual pleasure. Now she had to revise everything she'd thought about the breakup.

"Then what?" asked Liz bluntly.

"I gave him a hand job. He tried to do the same, but I was in so much pain I wouldn't let him touch me. After he came, I left him in his hotel room with the bloody sheets. I later found out he'd only slept with me because I was on the board of the theater. Afterwards, he bragged about it."

"So a kiss and tell on top of it," Liz said angrily. "I wish I had known, Maggie. I would have made sure that little snot never told a single soul."

"What would you do? Threaten him with your gun? That would only have gotten you in trouble."

"But it would have shut him up. Maggie, why didn't you come to me? Maybe I could have helped."

"You! When we agreed to get married, you refused to be my doctor."

"Then why didn't you tell Cathy? She's a gynecologist."

"I did, but she said it was normal aging."

"Most women have some vaginal atrophy after menopause, but

that doesn't mean you have to suffer or give up sex. I'm surprised at Cathy. I'll talk to her."

Maggie grabbed Liz's wrist. "Please don't. She didn't mean anything by it."

"Maybe not, but she shouldn't be dismissing the concerns of older women just because she's not there yet. I'm sorry, Maggie, but I need to betray your confidence on this one."

"All right, Liz, that's enough," Lucy said in a firm but even tone. "We just made love. Maggie told you one of her deepest, most intimate secrets, and now you're threatening her."

Liz realized Lucy was right. "I'm sorry, Maggie," said Liz. "That was insensitive of me."

Maggie looked at Lucy. "Wow, you sure do have her well trained."

Lucy didn't smile. "Take the apology, Maggie. She means it."

"I'm sorry too, Liz, but now you know what my big revenge was a bust. I was trying to get back at you for kissing Lucy, and all I did was make a fool of myself!"

"Oh, Maggie, that must have been so humiliating," Lucy said, enfolding her in her arms.

Liz found it ironic that the woman who'd perfected the art of saving face had it fail when she'd needed it most. She shook her head. "Sometimes, Maggie, you just need to get out of your own way."

When Maggie began to sob, Lucy shot Liz an irritated look. "This is no time for lectures. Have some compassion!"

"Compassion? That lie wrecked our marriage!" Liz protested.

"You wrecked our marriage by ogling Lucy!" Maggie shot back. "You couldn't take your eyes off her. You obviously stared at her boobs in front of our friends. It was so disrespectful to me, your wife, and to Lucy."

Liz took a deep breath before she spoke. "I'm sorry. You're right."

For an ever-lengthening moment, Maggie stared at her. "What?"

"I'm sorry I flirted with Lucy and embarrassed you."

"About time you apologized. Now, tell Lucy you're sorry too."

It irked Liz, but she apologized to Lucy.

"None of us was blameless in that situation," said Lucy with a sigh. "Now, let's forgive each other and move on." She got up and opened the bag Liz had brought up from downstairs. She distributed the glasses and poured three glasses of wine. Reluctantly, Maggie accepted a cracker topped with cheese that Lucy had prepared.

"Well, Lucy, you were right. She apologized. I guess you do know her better than I do."

"Liz isn't perfect, but she always tries to do the right thing," Lucy said in a humorless voice.

For a time, the only sound in the room was the crunch of crackers. They finished the cheese, and most of the bottle of wine. Liz held it up, but there were no takers. She put the bottle on the windowsill to stay cool and carefully folded the liner of the cracker box.

Maggie started to get up. "I guess I'll go back to my room."

"No," said Lucy, gripping her arm. "Stay with us tonight."

Great, thought Liz, another person to crowd the bed.

Maggie looked at Liz. "You okay with this?"

Liz shrugged. "As long as you stay on her side of the bed." She went into the bathroom to brush her teeth. A moment later, Lucy came in.

"Maggie went downstairs to brush her teeth."

"But she's coming back?" mumbled Liz with a mouthful of toothpaste suds.

"Yes, with my encouragement, and, Liz, please try to be more sensitive. That was a big share. You say you want to know the real Maggie. She's showing herself to you, but what you're seeing makes you uncomfortable."

Liz spat emphatically. "Don't shrink me, Lucy. It's been a weird night."

"Tell me about it."

They settled into bed, Maggie and Lucy on one side, Liz on the other. *Good,* Liz thought. *They can cuddle each other and leave me alone.* The fatigue from the long day and its emotional ending was making her increasingly grumpy. Lucy finally turned off the light. Liz had just closed her eyes when she heard them whispering in the dark.

"I'm not deaf, you know. I can hear you," she said tartly.

Lucy giggled. "Such a grouch. All right. We'll be quiet."

But a minute later, the whispering started again. Liz pulled the comforter over her head. It muffled the sound a little, but she was so tired it didn't matter. When she closed her eyes, she instantly fell asleep.

Chapter 13

Bright sunlight blazed into Liz's face through the skylight. Beside her she found only a pile of frigid sheets and blankets. Apparently, her sleeping companions were long gone. Usually, nervous energy would have awakened Liz by now. Wondering what time it was, she located her phone amid the clutter on the night table and discovered it was already past eight.

From the walkway outside the loft bedroom, Liz could see Lucy and Maggie sitting near the wood stove. The heat rising from below told her they'd found the kindling and started a fire. Busy trying to manage everything, Liz often forgot how competent her wives were. Individually, they were more than able. Together, they were formidable.

Liz strained to listen to what they were saying. Their conversation was animated, but they were speaking softly to avoid awakening her. They sat close and chattered as if they hadn't seen one another in years. Lucy rarely complained but she'd often talked about how much she'd missed Maggie. In her role as rector of a church, Lucy's relationships were complicated. Maggie felt competitive toward other women and tended to keep them at arm's length. She had many acquaintances, but few friends. For so many reasons, both women needed one another.

The détente since Maggie had come to live with them had been a pause in the conflict rather than a healing of the rift between them. Their deep friendship had never returned to normal. Maggie's resentment at being supplanted had always lurked below the surface. Liz could sense from watching the two women that something important had changed.

Lucy looked up and noticed Liz standing at the railing. "Good morning, sleepy head!" she called. "Feeling better?"

Liz stifled a yawn. "Much better. Thanks for letting me sleep. How long have you two been awake?"

"Not long," said Maggie. "Not even half an hour. You were snoring to beat the band."

"Sorry about that," Liz said, descending the stairs. "I was exhausted. Two wild women in my bed wore me out."

"Not us. Blame the emotionality of the week and the long drive," Lucy observed dryly. "I, for one, found our lovemaking invigorating."

"You're quite a bit younger than we are," Liz reminded her.

"Did you forget that you'd promised to make us blueberry pancakes this morning?" Maggie asked. "I can make breakfast if you're not feeling up to it."

"Nope. I'll do it. Let me get some coffee first." Lucy turned her face up for a kiss. Although Maggie seemed shy at first, she accepted one as well. Liz went into the kitchen and filled a pod with the special dark roast Maggie had brought. Idly, she watched the dusky liquid dribble into the cup. When she turned around she found two bright faces looking back expectantly. "Geeze. You two are worse than the kids. Can't you wait?"

"We're not looking for pancakes," Lucy quickly explained. "We had some of Maggie's apple bread while we were waiting for you to get up. We want to talk about plans for the day."

Liz almost jumped when she felt a hand seductively rubbing her buttocks, and realized it was Maggie. "Sit down and relax, Liz. I can make breakfast. I found your bag of premixed ingredients, in a logical place, as always." Her hand stealthily moved into the erogenous regions, forcing Liz to choose whether to focus on the welcome taste of her coffee or the sensations below. She chose the coffee. Probably a sign of age. "Catch you later, girl," said Liz moving away from Maggie's stimulating hand. Maggie's positively seductive smile woke Liz with a bang.

She took one of the empty seats at the table. "Okay. What are we going to do today? That is, if you don't have it all figured out already."

"In fact, we do," Maggie said, "but we'll discuss it with you because you like to think you're in charge."

Lucy giggled behind her hand.

"Okay. Ground rule number one." Liz raised a finger for emphasis. "No ganging up on me."

"She's right. Two against one isn't fair," Lucy agreed.

Maggie turned to Liz. "We know you hate conspiracies, even though you don't see them half the time."

Liz grunted. "I see them, but I don't want to give you the satisfaction of knowing you got to me. So, what's on today's agenda?"

"More sex, of course," Maggie said enthusiastically. Liz stared at her. When had Maggie ever been excited about sex? Even in the early days of their relationship she'd always waited for Liz initiate it.

"Besides sex." Liz broke off a piece from the slice of apple bread that lay on the cutting board.

Lucy nibbled on the remains. "It's supposed to be a nice day. Partly sunny and warm. We checked and the steamboat is still running. I booked us on The Katahdin for the one o'clock cruise. That is, if you want to go."

"I guess so." Liz's irritated tone drew a harsh look from Lucy, so she revised her response. "Sure. Sounds like fun," Liz said, but her smile was more like a grimace. She glanced at the clock over the sink. "If we're going on this boat ride, I should make breakfast."

"Have another piece of bread," Maggie suggested. "You can make the pancakes tomorrow. We're supposed to be resting, remember?" Maggie tapped her finger into the crumbs left on the cutting board. "We were going to sneak off to my room for a little fun while you were sleeping, but we didn't want to leave you out."

Liz shrugged. "I don't care if you two go off for a little aside."

"But I do!" Lucy declared. "I'm still your wife!"

Maggie shrank back into her chair. Liz swallowed her mouthful of coffee in a gulp. The outburst had taken her completely by surprise. "Yes, you are, Lucy. Maggie knows it too." Maggie was eyeing Lucy cautiously. "Bet you've never seen Lucy's temper," Liz continued. "Now you know it's not a myth."

"I'm sorry, Maggie," Lucy said in a conciliatory tone, reaching for her hand. "I don't know where that came from."

"I understand," Maggie said. "So much has changed. What made sense yesterday doesn't make the same sense today."

"Nothing's really changed," Liz said. "Since Maggie moved in next door, we've been living as a family. All we did was add sex to the mix. People act like sex changes everything."

"It does," Lucy said. "A woman's status changes when she loses her virginity, or a marriage is consummated, or she becomes pregnant."

"But a man's status doesn't," Maggie quickly pointed out.

Liz finally cut herself a real slice of Maggie's bread. "I'm not saying we don't have a lot to figure out. Only six years ago, your Church didn't allow same sex marriage. In the Church of England, we're not really married. Who gets to say what a marriage really is? If you ask me, it's about property, who the kids belong to, and inheritance."

"How romantic," Maggie said.

"Sorry, Mag. Unlike you, I never bought into those fantasies of fairy tale weddings. I decided early that I would never marry a man."

Lucy turned to Maggie. "I'm sorry I jumped down your throat. We came up here to relax. Let's just enjoy being together and have fun. We can have the heavy conversations when we get home."

"Works for me," Liz said.

"Me three," Maggie chimed in.

After breakfast, Liz took a long leisurely shower. The water was steaming hot and the proprietors had provided a variety of fragrant shampoos. Liz picked the least floral scent and lathered her hair. She was startled to feel small hands on her waist.

"Geeze, Lucy, don't sneak up on me like that!"

"You do it to me all the time. Turnabout is fair play." Lucy ran her hands over Liz's soapy breasts. "It's good for you to be challenged, Liz. Maybe I do let you get away with too much. I don't want you to get too comfortable in our little role play."

"How can I? You'll just flip me with one of your jiu jitsu moves."

"I don't mean only in bed," Lucy said, touching lightly between Liz's legs, an affectionate caress, not a real invitation. Given the recent changes, it could also be a territorial claim. "Liz, can you please move aside so I can have some hot water?"

"I'm done. You can have the bathroom to yourself."

Liz was relieved when she heard Lucy singing in the shower because it meant she was happy. Things might seem calm on the surface, but with Lucy, it was hard to tell. Lucy was skilled at keeping her inner turmoil to herself, but what they'd done must have shaken up her world.

While Lucy was writing her now infamous book on sex, Liz had watched her wife twist herself into knots trying to reconcile her progressive views with traditional Church doctrine. After struggling to justify pre-marital sex and same-sex marriage, Lucy persisted in confining valid sexual relationships to two committed people. The alternative had first come up when Erika shocked Lucy by suggesting she sleep with Liz. It returned to the conversation when Susan Gedney began seeing a woman whose partner had dementia. Whenever polyamory was mentioned, Lucy had firmly promised to keep an open mind. Until now, it had remained a mere hypothetical. Now, it was real.

Wrapped in an oversized, plush towel, Lucy emerged from the bathroom. "If you're all dressed, why don't you go down and keep Maggie company?"

"I'm thinking," Liz said.

"Uh oh. Are you having second thoughts about what we did last night?"

"No, but I worry that you will."

Lucy bent to put on her lacy panties, giving Liz a superb view of her breasts. If this subject weren't so serious, Liz would have demonstrated how much she appreciated them.

"I'm not completely sure what I think," Lucy admitted, "but it felt okay while we were doing it." Lucy closed her bra and pulled on her jeans. "How do you feel about it?"

"I'm okay with it if you and Maggie are. This could be a one-time event that we all enjoyed, or something else. Most of the time when three people fall into bed together, it's not planned, and people go back to their regular lives as if nothing happened."

"Is that what you want?" Lucy asked, obviously playing therapist.

"Not necessarily. I like having Maggie back in our life, but it doesn't mean she has to be in our bed."

"I don't know what I want," Lucy admitted, "but I'm sure I *don't* want anyone to get hurt."

"Neither do I."

Lucy struggled with her tight T-shirt until her head popped out from the collar. "Let's see how it goes. Okay?"

While they waited for Maggie to dress, Liz made sandwiches to take on the steamboat tour. She wasn't looking forward to it. Unless she was the pilot, being on the water made her twitchy. She forced a smile as they drove to the pier.

✻✻✻

Without inviting anyone to join her, Liz announced that she was going to explore the trail along the lake. Maggie sensed that they'd exhausted her tolerance for company. She could be social up to a point, but she regularly needed time alone and made sure she got it. Maggie, who usually thought of herself last, had always envied Liz's ability to take what she needed.

Maggie didn't mind having Lucy all to herself because she had so many questions. She opened a bottle of Lucy's favorite wine and prepared a cheese board. "How are you doing?" she asked, setting her offerings on the table near the sofa.

Lucy yawned and stretched. "I feel sleepy after being on the water all afternoon. I could take a nap."

"Maybe you should," Maggie said, instinctively accommodating her wishes.

Lucy's green eyes shrewdly studied her face. "No, let's talk. I want to hear what you think about all this. Sit down." Lucy sat back, demonstrating that she was ready to listen.

Maggie recognized the pose. "Oh, please, Lucy, I'm not one of your clients."

Lucy's eyes clouded with hurt. "Of course, not. I just want to compare notes with my friend...partner...lover. Sorry. I'm still figuring out what to call our new relationship."

Maggie was oddly comforted by the fact that Lucy, who always knew what to say, was unsure, too. "I'll settle for 'friend' because that's who I really need right now, someone who will listen because she cares about me, not because it's a job."

"I'm sorry, Maggie, but our jobs become second nature. Look at Liz, she's always playing doctor."

"Yup, still chasing us out of a cozy bed to pee after sex."

"She means well," Lucy said, "and so do I, but I'm not sure how much I can help. I'm on unfamiliar ground too." Lucy shifted uncomfortably and took a moment to think. "Maybe we should have talked about having sex before we invited you to bed, but as Liz said, a ménage à trois isn't something you plan."

"Not unless you're a predatory couple looking for a new thrill."

Lucy smiled. "I promise you my life already has more than enough thrills, and I didn't expect this any more than you did."

"But it does seem like a natural progression. You took me into your home without question. You welcomed me into your life together. Like Liz said, we have been living as a kind of family. But all this is so confusing! I mean, how do I fit in? Am I still just the ex, living in the in-law apartment?"

"That's up to you, Maggie," said Lucy. "What do you want?"

Maggie was momentarily annoyed at what appeared to be a therapist's trick until she realized it was an honest question. "Some of it's up to me. The rest is up to you and Liz. What does she want? Or you? What will you allow? This morning, you were quick to remind us that you are Liz's wife."

"I was surprised I suddenly felt so possessive. In fact, I am her wife, and I hope we stay married for many reasons."

"But who are we to one another? Am I like your "sister wife"?

Lucy laughed. "Liz is too much of a feminist to keep a harem. And sister wives only have sex with their husband, not with each other. Now that I've had sex with you, I'm not giving it up."

"Good because I enjoy making love to you. I don't want to give it up either." Maggie glanced at Lucy shyly. "I really like your toys."

"They're so much fun, aren't they? But Liz told me you weren't interested while you were married."

"Liz needs to keep some things to herself. But it's true. Dildos didn't appeal to me. I'd been fucked by a real penis for years. Why would I want a fake one? But that wasn't the real reason. Liz told me Jenny liked them, and I resisted them even more." Maggie realized how silly it sounded to turn down a bedroom suggestion based on a previous lover's opinion. When she tried to justify herself, she only dug herself in deeper. "I hated Jenny after she tried to talk Liz out of being with me. She told her I was a bad risk because of my cancer." When Lucy's eyes widened, Maggie realized how shocked she was. "You didn't know?"

Lucy shook her head. "No. That was an incredibly cruel thing to say."

"It was, and it was insensitive of Liz to tell me."

"It certainly was." In Lucy's sigh, Maggie heard an inkling of how much Liz could frustrate her.

"Liz will try anything once. I think she was disappointed I was so conventional."

"Did you ask her if she was disappointed?" asked Lucy.

Maggie shook her head. "The beginning of our relationship was all about my cancer. Her role as my lover and a doctor got all mixed up. And there was all the unfinished business from our past. Then she proposed to prove she'd stand by me despite the cancer. I probably should have turned her down." Maggie saw how actively Lucy was listening. "You are doing therapy, Lucy. Admit it."

Lucy shook her head. "No, I'm listening to my friend...my *best* friend. Maybe if you and Liz had listened more, you'd still be married."

Maggie sat up and thought about Lucy's words. As usual, she'd hit the mark. "We can't change that now."

"No, but you have a second chance."

"A third, really...if we continue this arrangement. I just can't get my head around how it will work."

"I can't either. There are so many things to figure out. I don't care what Liz says. Adding sex changes things. It's always been clear to me that you and Liz still love each other. Maybe this is how it needs to be expressed."

"Our feelings for each other were always complicated," Maggie said. "I was Liz's first lover. Nothing can compare to the intensity of that first time we fall in love. We keep trying to recreate it, looking for that one person who makes our heart sing. For you, Liz is the one. I saw the look on your face when you took her hand at the lessons and carols service. You didn't even know her name."

"I know," said Lucy. "Even I can't explain it, and I've tried."

"You were meant to be together," said Maggie.

"So were you. Forty years apart couldn't separate you."

"But what about us? We have Liz in common, but how are we connected? Are you really attracted to me?" Maggie couldn't believe she was making herself so vulnerable. What if Lucy said, 'no'? How could she ever recover from such a humiliation?

Lucy looked sad. "You mean you don't know?"

"Oh, I do, but I need to hear it."

Lucy moved closer and planted a soft kiss on Maggie's mouth. Surprised, Maggie didn't respond at first. Undaunted, Lucy teased her lips until they parted and eased Maggie down on the couch. The sensual kiss deepened. Lucy's breathing changed as she explored Maggie's mouth. She could feel and hear how aroused she was. She moaned when Maggie caressed her breast.

When Lucy finally allowed Maggie to take a breath, her green eyes were full of mischief. "There. Believe me now?"

Maggie smiled, and Lucy smiled back. "I need a lot of reassurance."

"I know," Lucy said. "It's okay. We're all insecure. Look at me insisting I be recognized as Liz's legal wife."

"Which I once was too. When we were still married, I once told Liz I found you attractive. She rolled her eyes."

"Of course, she did," Lucy said dismissively. "She thought I was silly and hated the idea that I was a priest."

"I think that was part of the attraction. She didn't understand it, and she couldn't control you. The other part was her butch-femme thing. We're feminine, so we're not supposed to be attracted to each other."

"Who cares what she thinks? We don't have to follow her rules. But I was mortified when you caught me admiring your rear."

Maggie laughed. "Why? I was flattered. I know how to get a man's attention, but attracting a woman is something else, especially a drop-dead gorgeous woman like you."

Maggie could see that Lucy wasn't taken in by the flattery. "It's not about looks. I just happened to hit the genetic lottery. Beauty doesn't last, and we're all fading. I'm much more attracted by what makes people who they are. I love what makes you, you, your effortless theatrical presence, your sense of style, your quick wit, the way you sing those old folk songs. No one sings 'Amazing Grace' like Maggie Fitzgerald."

"Thank you, from an opera star, that's a high compliment."

"And it's meant. Oh, Maggie, there is so much I love about you, including your persistent love for Liz. You fought for your mate, not always in ways that were effective, but you fiercely defended your marriage."

"You're being kind. I drove her away. First, I withheld sex, then... I'm embarrassed now that I told you about Brad."

Lucy took her head. "Don't be. That was a horrible secret to bear. Maybe now that Liz knows, she can help you."

Maggie was relieved that Liz knew about her sexual problems. She knew Liz would doggedly pursue a solution, but then her thoughts turned dark. "I bet she's gloating that it was humiliating."

"Maggie…" Lucy began in her kindest voice. "Liz is a doctor. She wouldn't wish pain on anyone, but especially not you. She loves you very deeply and would never wish you harm."

In Lucy's gentle gaze, Maggie saw a deep feeling, not desire like she'd seen in bed, more like the radiant look when she offered the communion bread. "Lucy, how can you always be so loving?"

"Sometimes it's hard because people make themselves so unlovable. With you, it's not hard because I love you."

"You really do, don't you?"

When Lucy nodded, Maggie's eyes began to sting. "I'm afraid."

"Me too."

A tear broke away and rolled down Maggie's cheek. Lucy got up and sat down beside her. "Come here and let me hold you." Maggie boldly snuggled against Lucy's breasts. "Now, I know why kids love it here. It feels so safe."

"I hope so, because it is. Oh, Maggie, you're safe with me. You try so hard to be what others want. Just be who you are." Maggie finally sat up so she could blow her nose.

"I'm afraid other people won't like the real me."

"I think you'd be surprised."

The door opened, and they both turned around. Liz took in the situation in a glance. "This looks serious. Should I go back out again?"

"No, you can come in," Lucy said. "You should be part of this conversation too."

"My ears were burning."

Maggie turned to Lucy. "See how full of herself she is? She thinks we're talking about her." Maggie launched into the chorus of "You're so vain."

Liz waited for her to finish singing before she said, "I know how you like to complain about me. How could you stand to be married to me for so long?"

"Maybe because I love you?" Maggie challenged.

"I think I will go back outside. It's too dangerous in here," Liz said, but instead, she headed to the kitchen.

"Coward," Maggie called after her.

"No, just getting a beer." She came back a moment later. "Oh, and I figured out where the thermostat is on the porch. We don't have to freeze tonight while we wait for the Aurora."

"Thanks, Liz," Lucy called to her as she retreated again. She turned to Maggie. "Why do you always pick on her?"

Maggie shrugged. "Bad habit, I guess."

"Maybe you should work on that," Lucy said with a little frown.

The criticism stung, but Maggie knew Lucy was right. "Maybe I should."

Lucy took Maggie's hands in hers. "Let's pause this conversation, but don't worry. We'll get back to it soon." She planted a quick kiss on Maggie's lips. "I promise."

❋❋❋

The conversation with Maggie had been exhausting. At least, Liz tried to figure things out before talking about them. Maggie needed to talk about her feelings to understand them.

Lucy was grateful when they went into the kitchen to prepare dinner and gave her a break.

She'd needed this respite as much as they did, but she was doing too much work on this trip. She was tired of mediating their disputes. She resented being the one to remind them that politics were off limits. This change in their relationship required processing, but they didn't need to do it all at once. She closed her eyes and tried to center herself.

After dinner, they settled in the common room to finish watching *Dune*. Although the thought of reprising last night's sexual adventures was enticing, no one seemed in hurry to rush off to bed. They resumed their positions in front of the big screen TV. Enrapt in the movie, Liz snarfed down popcorn by the fistful. Lucy had long since lost interest in the plot, and Maggie, sitting beside her, looked equally bored.

"Lucy, you look tense," Maggie whispered. "Would you like a shoulder rub?" The offer sounded too good to refuse. Maggie pointed to a spot on the carpet in front of her. Lucy sat cross legged while Maggie's skilled hands kneaded the tense muscles in her shoulders and neck. She moved aside Lucy's red ponytail and sensually kissed the back of her neck. Her hand stealthily slipped into Lucy's shirt. A fingertip traced the perimeter of her nipple, then gently pinched it. "You like that, don't you?" Maggie breathed into her ear. Lucy leaned her head against Maggie's crotch. Another pinch, harder this time, made her moan.

That finally got Liz's attention. "Okay, girls. Time to get a room."

Maggie smiled suggestively. "What? You're not interested?"

"The movie's almost over. Can't you wait?"

"Go on. Finish your movie," Maggie said, roaming in Lucy's shirt. "I'll keep your wife occupied."

"That's what I'm afraid of."

"No, you're not," said Maggie in a low, sultry voice. "You just don't want to miss anything."

"I don't, but we should go upstairs. I doubt the owners will appreciate their guests coming all over their furniture."

"Only you would think of that." Maggie got up and lightly caressed Liz's crotch.

"Maggie, I've never seen you so aggressive, but I admit I like it."

"I bet you do," Maggie said, kissing Liz. She reached down for Lucy's hand. "Come on, Lucy. Let's take your wife upstairs and show her how it's done."

Upstairs, Maggie wasted no time. She undressed Lucy to her purple lace underwear, then dropped her jeans and got into bed with her. Maggie tickled the top of Lucy's breasts with the tail of her long white braid. "If I'd known how luscious you are, I would have kissed you much earlier."

"We weren't ready."

Maggie's hand slid into the lace panties. "But now we are." As Maggie stroked her, Lucy could hear how wet she was. "I know what Liz likes, but what do you like, Lucy?"

"Everything you're doing feels wonderful. Surprise me."

The pace was more relaxed than the night before, but the climaxes were no less powerful. Lucy and Maggie asked questions about each other's likes and dislikes. Liz, who knew the preferences of both women, lay back and listened with a smile. A few of the things they said surprised her. Must be a femme thing, she concluded.

Finally spent, they lay in a heap until Liz's phone began to beep. "That's the Aurora monitor. Fifteen minutes to go. I'll turn on the heat." She jumped out of bed and pulled on her jeans without bothering with panties. "Well, come on! Let's go." She grabbed the pile of wool blankets from the closet. Maggie went into the kitchen to make hot cocoa from scratch with curls of dark chocolate melted into milk.

The porch was warmer than the previous night, but being uninsulated, it was still chilly. Bundled under the blankets, they watched a light show even better than the night before. Snuggled into Liz's warmth with Maggie flanking her, Lucy watched the sky shimmer with green and red curtains and banners. She felt peaceful and content.

When the lights finally faded from the sky, the three drifted off to do their bedtime chores. When they met again in the king-sized bed, Liz agreed to be the biggest spoon. With Maggie's arms wrapped around her, Liz's warm hands on her hips, Lucy fell into a deep, peaceful sleep.

***

"Are we going to church this morning?" Maggie asked casually as she prepared her coffee.

"We're on vacation," said Liz without looking up from her tablet.

"But I'd still like to go to church, wouldn't you, Lucy?" Maggie said, looking for support. Instead, she found a reflective frown.

"If you want…" said Lucy with a conspicuous lack of enthusiasm.

Maggie found the whole thing puzzling. "Lucy, it's Sunday."

"Yes, I know. But even I get a day off."

Liz rapidly tapped around her tablet. "Let me see if I can find one nearby." The nearest church was in Millinocket, a good half hour's drive away. The service was at nine, so they'd missed it. Liz found another church. She calculated the distance and how long it would take to get there, but there wasn't enough time. "Sorry, gang. I tried." She didn't look especially disappointed. Neither did Lucy.

Maggie wasn't about to give up so easily. "There's three of us. Lucy, couldn't you hold a service just for us? When we camped in Acadia, you were putting up signs for Sunday worship, inviting anyone who wanted to come."

Lucy wouldn't meet her gaze. "That was different."

"Why?"

"I was in a different place. I was a brand-new rector, full of enthusiasm. I'd just gotten married. Everything was going great, until it wasn't. Covid hit. Erika died. We had a school shooting. Liz had to kill a boy we'd both tried to save."

Maggie listened to Lucy enumerate the hardships she'd had to endure. "Okay I get all that, but what does that have to do with leading us in worship?"

Liz, who'd been studying her wife, over her tablet, piped in. "Working on her doctorate dented Lucy's shiny new faith."

"Is this true, Lucy?" Maggie asked, sitting down across from her. Lucy nodded. "Afraid so."

"Does that mean you can't celebrate Eucharist with us?"

Lucy let out a long sigh. "I can, but right now, my life doesn't reflect my ordination vows."

Maggie frowned. As music director and a volunteer on church committees, she'd worked with Lucy for years but had never seen this side of her. "Have you lost your faith?"

"Not exactly," Lucy said vaguely. "But it's not the same. I have a lot of doubts. Some of my beliefs are in conflict with the Church. And now that we've slept together, I really wonder if I..." Lucy's voice trailed off.

"Aren't there priests who are atheists?" asked Maggie. "The Church of England still hasn't okayed same-sex marriage. Some churches still won't accept women. There are conflicts everywhere. You always say God loves us, no matter what."

Lucy looked momentarily impatient, then sad. "Maggie, you want me to function as a priest this morning, but you don't want to hear what my priesthood compels me to say."

"Remember Susan's sermon at Reshma's ordination? She was right. God doesn't call perfect people to be priests. No matter how you think you've failed, you're still an ordained priest."

Liz did a slow clap. "Well said, Maggie. I'm impressed." She turned to Lucy. "Luce, she's giving you a run for your money, and you know she's right."

Lucy raised her eyes and sighed. "I can get my *Book of Common Prayer*. You don't need me to hold a morning prayer service. You're a lay minister, Maggie. You can lead it. If you poke Liz hard enough, she might help you."

Liz showed no sign of getting up from the couch. "Not a chance."

"Please, Lucy," Maggie begged.

Liz sat up and put her tablet aside. "Lucy, she's not going to let up. What do you need?"

"You know what I need. A plate and a cup. Bread, wine, some water."

Liz rummaged in their supplies and came up with some whole wheat pitas. They'd opened a ninety-dollar bottle of wine last night for dinner but hadn't finished it. Maggie found a crystal wine glass in a cabinet and a China plate. She set up a makeshift altar on the dining table and dared Lucy with her eyes to come to it.

Lucy reluctantly got up. "I don't have a stole but let me get my Book of Common Prayer."

Maggie and Liz took turns reading the scripture passages. At the kiss of peace, they embraced and kissed like lovers.

"Do you mind if I don't give a sermon?"

"Oh, I think you should," said Liz. "You always have something to say, and I'm sure you have some thoughts about what's happened this weekend."

Lucy glared at her. "All right, but I'll keep it short."

"That's fine."

Lucy bowed her head as she gathered her thoughts. Liz idly inspected her fingernails while they waited. Maggie began to wonder if it had been a good idea to force Lucy to do this.

"When I was in seminary," Lucy began, "lesbians and gay men were supposed to be celibate. Many people struggled with their sexuality. Some got depressed. Some left the church. It might seem better now. So much has changed, and yet it hasn't. We are pushing the envelope even further. I don't know where it will lead us, and there's much risk ahead. The Church's doctrines on sexual conduct are supposed to keep people from hurting one another. Unfortunately, they often do the opposite. I know that God loves us beyond our wildest imagination. I take comfort in the many passages in the New Testament about the primacy of love. Jesus tells us, it is the first and last commandment. Paul says, 'the greatest of these is love.' When I give you my body, I give it with love. When you give me your bodies, I accept them with love. That's all I can do. Somehow, I think God will understand."

Maggie reached over and took Lucy's hand. "And She will."

"Eucharist is meant to be a meal. This morning, Maggie set the table. Liz gave us the bread and the last cup of her ninety-dollar bottle of wine. Maggie, thank you for encouraging me to do this.

Usually, the two of you are feeding me. This morning I can feed you."

Lucy conducted an abbreviated version of the communion service. She never wore intensely colored nail polish for services. When she offered up the bread, her fingernails were a striking affirmation of her femininity and a clear break from the past. She broke the bread into three pieces, handing one to each of them. They consumed all the expensive wine because it had been consecrated.

After the service, they were silent, sitting in the living room, looking at the lake through the large picture window. They'd all been transformed by the events of the last forty-eight hours, but they had no road map. They were truly in uncharted territory.

Finally, Liz spoke. "So, is this going to be 'what happens at the lake, stays at the lake' or something permanent?"

Maggie and Lucy turned to stare at Liz.

"What's the matter?" asked Liz, trying to look innocent. She liked to say provocative things, but the only outrageous part of her statement had been its simple truth. "I've been in ménages before, but never a permanent one. Are we going to continue when we get home?"

Lucy's eyes were fixed on Liz's. "Why didn't you tell me you'd been in a threesome before? I've asked you."

Liz shrugged. "Do I have to tell you everything?"

"Yes, you do. That's what intimacy is. No masks. No secrets."

Liz gave her a tart look. "Impossible."

"But that's the purpose of erotic love, to seek to know someone as absolutely and completely as you can."

Liz raised her hand and made a sweeping gesture. "The Rev. Dr. Bartlett, noted theologian and sex expert, speaks."

Maggie could see that Lucy had no intention of allowing Liz's mockery to divert her. "And when did you have this ménage? Did it involve Erika?"

"Yes," Liz admitted after a long moment of consideration.

"Anyone else I know?" Lucy asked.

Liz refused to meet Lucy's penetrating gaze.

"Liz…" prompted Lucy in a firm voice.

"All right, dammit! I slept with Erika and Tom Simmons."

"Liz, you said you slept with Erika once."

Liz shrugged sheepishly. "I didn't tell the whole truth. All right?"

Sitting beside Lucy, Maggie could feel the tension in her body. "Gracious God, give me patience! What else?"

"Nothing else. That's it. Tom wasn't sure how he felt about women. Erika and I weren't sure how we felt about men. It was a different time. Everyone was sleeping with their friends."

"And you let me hire Tom without telling me this?" Lucy asked.

"Lucy, we didn't have that kind of relationship then. I didn't feel it was my duty to tell you I'd fucked Tom any more than it was to tell Maggie you'd been pregnant."

Maggie remembered tracing the silvery stretch marks on Lucy's soft belly. The delicate feathers were almost ethereally beautiful. How ironic that Lucy had been forced into motherhood, whereas Maggie had craved it, but couldn't conceive.

"You mentioned other ménages, Liz," Lucy said, peering directly into Liz's eyes. "Anyone else I know?"

"Jenny, but that was just fun and games, nothing serious."

"The arrangement with Erika and Tom was serious?"

"Only in the sense that we truly cared for one another. We were honestly seeking answers to questions about ourselves. Erika and I went back to women, other women. Tom discovered he wasn't heterosexual, but he lived in the closet for the sake of his career. After he got religion, we lost touch with him. Again, it was a different time, and we shouldn't judge the past by the standards of the present."

"How often did this happen?" Lucy demanded.

"For Christ's sake, Lucy. I don't remember! It was over forty years ago."

"May I say something?" Maggie asked meekly.

Lucy turned in her direction, but her eyes were pure steel. "Go ahead, Maggie," she said in a deliberately even tone.

"Liz is right. It was a different time. She was incredibly brave to live as a lesbian. I thought I was "liberated" as we called it back then, but I scared the hell out of myself when I fell in love with a woman. If I'd chosen to be with Liz, it would have upended all the plans I'd made for my life. It was a different time, Lucy. It was over forty years ago."

Lucy had listened, attentive as always, but she wasn't done with cross-examining Liz. "Did you sleep with Tom separately?"

"Yes."

"How do you feel about Tom now?"

"I love him like a brother. Lucy, men never interested me. But I believe in taking a scientific approach to things I don't understand. I'll do anything once."

"Sounds like it was much more than once."

"Oh, Lucy, give it up!" said Liz in frustration. She got down on her knees and rested her clasped hands on Lucy's leg. "Bless me, Mother, for I have sinned. I didn't tell you everything I did before I met you."

The parody of the Catholic confession ritual only made Lucy's frown deeper. "Oh! You're impossible!" She glanced toward the kitchen where wine bottles stood on the counter. "I know it's early, but I need a drink."

Liz leaned on her knee to get up. "We drank most of the good stuff, but I'll see what I can find."

"Maybe I should make some omelets," said Maggie, "before we get too inebriated."

"Sounds like a good idea," Liz called over her shoulder as she headed into the kitchen to get Lucy some wine.

✱✱✱

Lucy was happy to sit in the rear seat on the way home. She

didn't feel like talking to anyone and sitting in the back gave her an excuse to avoid conversation. Maggie was driving, spurred on by Liz's threat: "What if I dropped dead and there was no one to drive you home?" Surprisingly, Maggie had volunteered to take the wheel. They had to drive on local roads for quite a stretch, which gave her time to get used to handling a vehicle twice the size of her Subaru.

Maggie was a careful, steady driver, and Lucy felt comfortable enough to close her eyes. They'd probably think she was asleep, but she was praying because she needed the familiar structure. That morning, when she'd performed the Eucharist rite, she'd felt like a fraud, and it wasn't the imposter syndrome she'd felt after first being ordained. Then, she'd felt justified defying the Church rules against LGB priests because she thought they were unfair. When she was writing her doctoral dissertation, making the case for loving another woman had been difficult enough, and now she was in love with two?

When she and Liz had talked about polyamory in the past, it had been a scholarly debate. It came as no surprise that Liz didn't see anything wrong with it. She and Erika had always been up front about their disdain for marriage and monogamy. Erika had dismissed them as "tools the patriarchy uses to control women." *But where do you draw the line? Bestiality? Pedophilia? Snuff porn?*

If Liz could hear Lucy's thoughts, she'd call her out for sliding down the proverbial slippery slope. She'd regularly lectured Lucy on this logical fallacy while she was writing her dissertation. Lucy was sure she could have a perfectly reasonable conversation with Liz, but right now, reasonable was the last thing she felt. She had tasted Maggie, felt her fingers inside her, and come in her arms, and the experience couldn't be any more real.

Lucy didn't know whether to cry or scream. *Breathe,* she told herself. *Just breathe.* Meditation might work better than prayer, but she couldn't calm her mind. The thoughts were zipping by too quickly, tearing up a path along the way. She attempted to focus on her emotions instead. The fear was too threatening, so she chose anger. She felt betrayed by the people she loved most. No matter what Liz said, hiding things from others wasn't always about keeping professional confidences. The revelation about Tom and Erika had been too shocking for words. Yes, the love triangle was over forty years in the past, but that didn't excuse the lie of omission. At least Erika could have told her. Lucy was beginning to wonder if she could trust anyone.

Stop it! The little voice in her head said. *You love each of these people. They're flawed. Give them some grace.*

Glad to finally get a response to her prayers, Lucy talked back: *But how am I supposed to go home, put on my collar, and pretend I've honored my ordination vows?*

How have you broken them? By asking questions? Looking at something from a new perspective? You encourage others to question their beliefs. Why not you?

It's too much all at once.

Then rest. Come back to it tomorrow. Enjoy the view.

Lucy opened her eyes and gazed at the bleak landscape passing. Liz said that she loved the purity of the bare trees against the sky. Lucy preferred the lushness of the overblown summer leaves. She grieved when they fell. Only the bright red rose hips made the loss of the beach roses bearable. But the turn of the seasons was something she could count on, like the regular flow of the liturgical calendar. It was predictable and imposed order on the passing of time. That's what she feared most—the chaos their actions could cause.

Lucy reminded herself that she was good at rolling with the punches. When the social agency called to tell her that her daughter was seeking her birth mother, she couldn't leave a sixteen-year-old, neurodiverse girl in a homeless shelter. Although Erika had a hard time adapting to what she called "instant parenthood," she'd ultimately turned out to be a loving and supportive stepmother. Dear Erika, always so reasonable, so dutiful, so *German.*

If I could adapt, so can you. The female voice in Lucy's head was so clearly Erika's.

Lucy suddenly sat up, which got Liz's attention. "You okay back there?"

"Yes, fine," said Lucy, settling back again.

"Want to drive next?" Maggie asked, engaging Lucy's eyes in the rear-view mirror.

"No thanks. Liz already knows I can drive this thing."

Maggie glanced at Liz. "You do?"

"Yup, Lucy has driven it before. She's fearless."

Unexpectedly, a tear rolled down Lucy's cheek. "That's not true." She gulped before she whispered, "I'm afraid of the feelings we stirred up this weekend."

Maggie's worried eyes sought hers in the mirror. "Lucy, please don't be afraid. We love you!"

"I can't help it. I don't know where we're going. It feels so strange."

Liz's blue eyes were soft and sympathetic. "Don't worry, Luce. We've got you."

"I hope so," Lucy said, but the tears kept coming.

❋❋❋

Maggie carried the lighter bags into her apartment. She could have managed the others, but Liz was into her butch role. After insisting she bring in Maggie's bags, Liz surprised her by rolling them to the elevator and bringing them over through the bridge. On the other side, she banged on the door to the apartment. Maggie couldn't get there quickly enough, so Liz opened it with her key.

"Asserting your landlord's privilege?"

"Of course." Liz wrestled a large suitcase into the apartment. "Maggie, you need to learn how to travel light."

"Never going to happen, so don't hold your breath," Maggie said, pushing the largest bag out of the way. "Glad you were smart enough to use the elevator instead of proving how strong you are."

"Are you kidding? You two wore me out!"

Maggie gently pinched her arm. "Such a stud, trying to satisfy two women. Glad to hear we were too much for you. Proves we can still bring it." She leaned over and kissed Liz on the cheek.

"Thanks for arranging the trip. We didn't plan some of the activities, but I think we all had a great time."

Liz glanced toward the main house. "Not sure Lucy agrees."

"Liz..." Maggie began, hesitant to interfere. How many times had Liz nailed her for offering unsolicited advice?

"What is it, Maggie?" Liz asked in a surly tone.

"...if you don't mind my saying so, I think you need to spend some time with Lucy...alone. She feels threatened."

Liz gave her a sharp look. Then she frowned, considering what Maggie had said. "It's not you."

"I know it's not me. She's not worried about losing you...at least not to me. She won that battle long ago. She's worried about her role as a priest and how this threatens it."

Liz looked reflective. "I'm worried about that too. Studying at a progressive place like Union Theological forced her out of her comfort zone. She became a true believer after the rape because she needed a lifeline. Now, things aren't so certain anymore. I'm surprised she hasn't used her singing career as an excuse to bail out of St. Margaret's instead of setting up that convoluted arrangement with Tom."

"Telling her about your ménage with Tom and Erika shocked her."

"I never wanted her to know, but when she focuses those green eyes on you, it's impossible to lie to her."

"You were right to tell her the truth. You're such a straight arrow, and I love you for it." Maggie traced the curve of Liz's breast with her fingertips. "God! It feels so good to be able to touch you again."

Liz leaned down and gave her a sexy kiss. "Come over later?"

"We'll see. We've blown up Lucy's world, and she needs you right now. And if you don't mind even more advice, stop trying to reason her out of her feelings. That never works. Capisce?" Maggie said the word with a Bronx Arthur Avenue accent, not quite authentic, except to another New Yorker.

"Of course, I understand, Maggie," said Liz impatiently. "It's just that Lucy's always the one smoothing things over."

"And you don't like the role reversal. Honey, you better get used to it because we're all trying on different roles here."

Liz grinned and puffed up. "No kidding. I was damn proud to see you driving my truck."

"Honestly, I was often tempted, just to prove I could do it, but you're so protective of that thing, like it's solid gold or something." Maggie put her hand at the back of Liz's neck and pulled her down into a kiss. She was enjoying it so much she didn't want to let her go, but she forced herself to stop. "Liz, I love you dearly but go take care of your wife."

"You'll come over later if Lucy's okay?"

"Text me. Otherwise, I'm just as happy to sleep alone tonight. I sleep better. I have class tomorrow, and I need the rest. You're not the only one worn out by all that sex. It's more than I've had in years." Liz looked curious, no doubt wondering what Maggie and Sam had been doing all that time, but that was none of her business. Maggie nudged her. "Go, Liz. Lucy needs you. I'll be fine."

After stealing another quick kiss, Liz left. Maggie decided to unpack and start a load of laundry, otherwise she wouldn't have enough panties. On the trip, she'd kept changing them because they were soaked from the constant stimulation. *When was the last time that happened?*

She nibbled on some cheese and multigrain crackers, while she sorted her laundry. After all the eating on this trip, she could do without another meal. She was glad Lucy had nixed the idea of going out to dinner on the way home.

Unpacking her bags suddenly reminded her of returning after her abortive attempt to reconcile with Barry. His much younger girlfriend had dumped him, and he'd begged and pleaded with Maggie to try to work things out. Maggie was lonely because the girls were off at college. She'd never wanted to sell the Connecticut house, but now Alina had been launched, the divorce decree required it. Once she arrived in California, Barry once again proved that he was a selfish prick. He'd expected her to be attentive to his every need, cook him delicious meals, and lie prone in bed while he satisfied himself. After five miserable days, she'd come home angry and defeated.

When she'd told Sophia about the trip, her daughter had said, "Mom, how could you humiliate yourself like that? Dad left you for another woman. Don't you have any pride?"

Maggie had been stunned, especially because Sophia was so fond of her adoptive father, but she was pleased to have raised a daughter with enough self-respect to recognize when a woman was being used by a man. She wondered what her daughter would say if she knew she had returned to another ex. If the new arrangement was confusing to Lucy, who counseled people all the time, how would it look to Alina and Sophia or their friends?

Maggie didn't have any answers. She began to regret starting a load of laundry. To stay awake until it was done, she made a cup of tea. Sipping it, she wondered what her role would be in this new iteration of her relationship with Liz. She certainly couldn't stand beside her as the proud wife. Was she now the 'other woman,' like the secret mistresses that married men used to hide from polite society? Liz certainly wasn't hiding her. She'd been living right next door for months. Maybe nobody would question the arrangement, and they could just continue to pretend she was a tenant, living next door to her ex for convenience.

The washing machine pinged. Maggie got up to put her clothes in the dryer. The stackable washer and dryer in the apartment was so convenient. At least, one thing about this complicated arrangement was easy.

✳✳✳

The house was frigid because the heat had been shut off all weekend. Shivering, Lucy changed into a yoga suit and put two shirts over it including one of Liz's old Yale hoodies. She found Liz in the kitchen putting away the food they'd brought back from their trip. Lucy clamped herself to her warm body and announced, "I'm cold!"

"I have a fire going. Go sit in the living room." Impatient to get things back in order, Liz tried to escape from Lucy's embrace, but Lucy hung on.

"Come with me."

"Okay. I'll be right there," Liz promised. "Let me put the perishables in the fridge."

The fire was indeed roaring, but the cast iron wasn't hot enough to radiate heat, so Lucy wrapped herself in a colorful Afghan Liz's grandmother had crocheted. Liz smiled when she saw her. "You just gave me an idea. How's some grandma comfort food? I can make grilled cheese and tomato soup."

"Sounds wonderful. It's too late for a big meal, and I'm not that hungry."

Liz frowned with concern. "But you need to eat something, and so do I."

While Liz went to the basement to get the soup out of the freezer, Lucy pulled up the hood of Liz's sweatshirt and burrowed deeper into the colorful Afghan. She knew she was being a baby about the cold, but even in this familiar room in her own house, she felt oddly out of place. She often had that unsettling sense of dislocation when she returned from an extended singing trip, but they'd only been away for a long weekend. This weird feeling came from another cause.

She heard the microwave door close. Liz was defrosting the soup. Still bundled up, Lucy headed to the kitchen.

Liz laughed when she saw her. "You look like ET when the kids tried to hide him in the closet."

"Right now, I kind of feel like an alien, so I'm not surprised I look like one."

Liz's smile faded. Her warm hands took Lucy's. "It's going to be okay. I promise."

"How can you promise? Everything's changed. It used to be just you and me. Now…"

"Only one thing changed, Lucy. And it was never just you and me. Besides our family and friends, we have your church, your audience, my practice… We live in a community with lots of people."

"That's what I'm worried about. How do we fit in now? I was your wife, and our roles were clear."

"You're still my wife, and nothing will ever change that."

"Are you sure?" asked Lucy. Even to her own ears, her voice rising to the question mark, sounded shrill and young.

"I'm sure." Liz came closer and put her arm around her. Her hand found an opening in the Afghan and reached under Lucy's multiple shirts. Her warm fingertips pinched her nipple gently. "Mm. No bra. Love it." She weighed Lucy's breast in her palm. When Lucy turned her face up, Liz kissed her, just a touch of their lips at first, then more insistently. The fingers gently kneading her breast were producing the most insistent urges below.

Lucy pulled back from the kiss. "Let's go upstairs."

The microwave beeped. Liz reset it. "That can wait until we come back."

With the heat on, the bedroom was warm enough for Lucy to undress, but she shivered between the icy sheets. Liz stripped within minutes and enfolded her in her warm body.

"Just love me," Lucy whispered into her ear when Liz nudged her legs apart with her knees. She gently let down her weight on her, balancing carefully so that it wasn't oppressive. Lucy opened her legs wider to get more of the rocking pressure. She usually couldn't come this way, but the stimulation from so much sex had left her sensitive. The orgasm came on quickly and spread through her body like a bead of oil in warm liquid. She pulled Liz's hips closer to prolong the sensation.

"Wow, that was fast," Liz said when Lucy finally lessened her grip on her buttocks.

Lucy teased Liz's ear with her tongue. "You're not the only one who can come fast when you're excited." She reached down and gently stroked Liz. "Oh, you're so wet."

Liz closed her eyes when Lucy's touch became more insistent. Usually, she'd pace her strokes to keep Liz from coming too fast, but she felt her urgency. After the many positions and sex aids they'd used over the last days, the simple sex felt so real, honest, and intimate.

After Liz's breathing returned to normal, she opened her eyes and smiled. "Hello, wife," she said as Lucy gently stroked her cheek. "Did I tell you how much I enjoyed watching your hands this weekend? Thank you for the sexy nail polish."

"I know how much it turns you on," Lucy said, gazing intently into her eyes. "I love you."

"I love you too."

"We're going to be okay," Lucy said, half-statement, half-question.

"Yes, we are," Liz declared confidently. "We're going to be just fine." She tried to get up. "I need to see about dinner."

Lucy clung to her. "Not yet. Stay with me for a little longer, and let's talk." In her arms, Liz tensed. "Don't worry, sweetie. Nothing bad. I just want to visit with you alone for a while. I want to know how you feel about what happened. And before you say, 'don't shrink me, Lucy,' that's not why I'm asking."

That seemed to calm Liz somewhat. "I feel okay about what

happened. Like I said, it seemed a natural conclusion. I know it's confusing because we don't have any precedents. Well, I do...sort of, but it's not the same."

The long-ago triangular relationship with Erika and Tom was still fraught with emotion, so Lucy decided not to address it. "I want to feel comfortable with what we've done, but I'm not there yet."

"I know, and it's okay. We shouldn't pretend it's fine. No one should feel forced."

Lucy was relieved that Liz wasn't pushing her, but a nagging doubt remained. "Why wasn't I enough for you?"

"Oh, baby, you are more than enough. You are my goddess, my queen, my lady love. I am your knight, and I adore you!"

Lucy's heart swelled at hearing all the ardent declarations, but she said, "I only want to be loved, not adored."

"I love you with all my heart."

"See? That doesn't make sense to me. How can you love me with all your heart and Maggie too?"

"I know. I don't understand it, either."

"Can you understand that sometimes, I need to be alone with you. Just you and me. Is that okay?"

"Yes, we need time alone together. I can talk to you about things I can't discuss with Maggie."

"And I'm sure there are things you can talk about with her, you can't talk about with me."

Liz thought for a moment. "Yes, I guess there are, especially things about our past and how we fucked up our marriage. And I wasn't deliberately keeping any secrets from you about Tom and Erika. It all happened so long ago, and it never came up in conversation. Can you understand?"

"Sort of," Lucy admitted. "I was just shocked to hear it."

"People don't like to share things with someone who might judge them. You ride the monogamy pony hard."

"That's what the church teaches."

"I get it, but as you often say, 'one size doesn't fit all.'"

"It doesn't, but we don't have to try on every size to see if it fits." Liz looked puzzled, so Lucy kissed her. This had been an important conversation, but Liz would be hungry after sex as always, and the last time they'd eaten was the omelets at lunch. "Let's go downstairs. We can talk while we eat." Liz put on her pajamas and sweatshirt. Lucy slipped into her flannel nightgown and wooly robe. "Thanks for the sexy lovemaking and the talk," she said as they walked downstairs.

"You don't have to thank me. I love talking to you." Lucy smiled because that was the right answer.

The tomato soup needed another round in the microwave. While it heated, Liz prepared their sandwiches for the panini press. "Denise and I bonded over this meal," she explained, buttering the bread. "Her grandmother used to make it for her too. Both of us used to head to grandma's house when things got wild at home. It was always safe at grandma's."

"You were lucky you had a place to go. I know how special she was to you. That's why I wear her diamond ring, even though it's so big."

Liz smiled. "She was embarrassed by it too. I appreciate that you wear it." Knife poised in air, Liz suddenly turned around. "I wonder if Maggie still has the ring I gave her. I bought it in Connecticut on impulse. It's a good stone. Not as showy as yours."

"Liz! Please tell me you're not going to ask for it back!"

"I'd never do such a thing! It's hers to keep or sell or do whatever she wants to do with it."

"Knowing Maggie, she would never sell it. I bet she still has it in her jewelry box and takes it out and looks at it." Lucy thought how sad it was that she could proudly wear her diamond, while Maggie kept hers hidden away. It was a small thing, but emblematic of their strange situation. "I'm surprised Maggie didn't want to join us."

"She thought we needed time alone,"

Lucy's voice went up half an octave. "You asked her advice about us?"

"No, and I could see how uncomfortable she was offering it."

Liz raised the lid of the panini press to check the sandwiches. "I guess I should have sensed you needed some time alone, but I couldn't imagine a woman who can blast the roof off the Metropolitan Opera House being insecure."

"Liz, it's more than insecurity. We don't live on an island, although that's what it felt like up at the lake. Now, we're home, back to our ordinary lives, but everything's different."

Liz placed a plate with perfectly golden triangles filled with gooey cheese in front of Lucy. She salivated at the aroma of the buttery toasted bread.

Liz sat down with her plate. "This whole thing will take some getting used to. I think Maggie probably needs time to absorb it too."

Liz's sensitivity made Lucy feel suddenly generous. "If you want to invite her tonight, that's okay."

Liz dipped the corner of her sandwich into her soup. "No, let's leave it this way." She grinned. "My equipment needs a break."

✳✳✳

Lying in bed with her hands clasped behind her neck, Liz stared at the ceiling. Lucy was recovering from another orgasm with a little snooze. Liz had known from the moment she lay down that Lucy would ignore her pleas to give her "equipment" a break. When she felt insecure, Lucy needed a lot of affectionate, conventional sex.

The toys had been banished to their drawer. While Liz never minded indulging Lucy's device fetish, she was often grateful Lucy wasn't into something edgier like bondage or S&M. Liz was a self-confessed control freak, so the idea of being tied up never appealed to her. She was a coward when it came to pain, so that was out too. Lucy accused her of having a breast fetish, which she couldn't deny. The thought reminded Liz to give Maggie's reconstructed breasts more attention, especially knowing how sensitive she was about them.

Liz inspected the observation with curiosity and concern. She kept telling Lucy and Maggie that everything would be all right, yet she didn't believe her own propaganda. The dilemma was familiar from her medical practice. A prognosis was an educated guess, but she sometimes needed to sound more optimistic than she felt because causing her patients or their families unnecessary anxiety wasn't useful or kind.

During their marriage and while Maggie was going through cancer treatments, she'd often referred to Liz as her "rock." She probably had no idea how much it cost her to maintain this fiction. Maybe her wives thought she roamed the house at night because she didn't need sleep. That's what she told them after all. She was tough and had learned how to do without it, but it was her worry about them, their finances, and security that kept her awake. She wondered what they would think if they knew she was as riddled with doubts as they were.

As she thought about this newly reconfigured relationship, she realized there could be benefits. Maggie could reassure Lucy when she was needy. Lucy could call out Maggie when she became a drama queen. Maggie and Lucy could cuddle each other instead of crowding Liz in bed. Best of all, Maggie wouldn't feel any pressure to provide sex. Lucy was happy to provide enough sex for all of them.

Reviewing the practical aspects calmed Liz. Then she thought about the potential pitfalls, and her anxiety level ticked up again. What if one of her wives felt she wasn't getting her due? She was shocked when Lucy pulled rank as the *official* wife. For the sake of Lucy's role as the rector of a significant congregation, they needed to remain married. Hopefully, Maggie would agree. Her sensitive perception that Lucy needed private time indicated a stunning change from Maggie's irrational raving while their marriage was coming apart.

Liz tried to imagine how she would feel if Lucy and Maggie made love without her. And their damned whispering! It reminded Liz of kindergarten when the girls had teased her because she liked to play with boys. Now, she was living with two women who'd been the popular girls Liz had always loathed.

"Liz, you're thinking very LOUD!" Lucy said, touching Liz between her legs.

"I thought you were asleep," Liz said and kissed her.

"I just dozed off, but then I reached out, and my cuddle buddy wasn't there!"

Liz knew she meant Maggie. "It's a little late to invite her now. It's almost eleven. She texted a while ago to ask if we'd like her to make breakfast tomorrow."

"What did you say?"

"No thanks. You haven't practiced in more than a week. I thought you'd like to get back into your routine."

"Thanks for deciding for me," Lucy said cooly.

"Well, then text her and tell her you *do* want her to make breakfast."

Lucy picked up her phone from the nightstand and started a text. Then she locked the screen. "No, you're right. I need to practice tomorrow morning. I'm so far behind."

"Don't worry. You'll see Maggie at dinner. I'm cooking because she has a late class tomorrow." Liz continued her inspection of the ceiling, but she could feel Lucy's green eyes boring into the side of her face. Finally, she turned in her direction. "Yes?"

"I'll miss Maggie, but maybe we could cuddle tonight," Lucy suggested in her sweetest voice.

Liz regretted having her hands behind her head, because Lucy claimed her breast as a pillow. Left with no other choice, Liz put her arms around her.

"That's nice," Lucy murmured, snuggling into Liz's shoulder.

Moments later, her breathing changed, and Liz knew she was sound asleep.

Liz wondered what she'd been thinking to bring Maggie into the relationship. Having a wife like Lucy was more than enough to handle. When Liz had decided to do a second residency in oncology immediately after completing a grueling surgical residency, Erika had said she was a glutton for punishment. Maybe she was right.

Of course, I was right! And you haven't changed a bit, said a voice in Liz's head.

Oh, shut up, Erika!

As clearly as if she were in the same room, Liz could hear her old friend chortling with *Schadenfreude*.

Chapter 14

Maggie watched Lucy take the tablet right out of Liz's hands, something she would never dare to think of, never mind do. When Liz was busy, she was intolerant of affection, but with her radiant smile, Lucy could get away with anything. Like a cat, she assumed she was always welcome and would plop into Liz's lap whenever she wanted. Her mere presence demanded kisses and stroking.

Liz had her own role as a pet. While she read or half-heartedly watched TV, she'd lay her head on Lucy's lap like an affectionate puppy. Lucy would absently wind her gray hair in her fingers. She even scratched behind her ears. The petting seemed to calm Liz, mesmerizing her until she lay spellbound.

Maggie tried to figure out how she fit into this little menagerie. Their re-entry into "normal" life had been delayed. Except for Maggie, who'd had to teach her usual Monday classes, their weekend had been extended. Lucy had signed up for online training, and it was Liz's usual day off. Tomorrow, they'd all go back to their routine. To the outside world, appearances would remain the same, but everything had changed.

"Maggie, you're very quiet tonight," Lucy observed, climbing off Liz's lap. She sat down next to Maggie and gave her a penetrating look. "What's going on?"

"Nothing. Just enjoying our time together before you go back to work tomorrow. It's like we've been in a little bubble of happiness. We've changed, but the rest of the world hasn't. What do we tell people?"

"Nothing," Liz said, not looking up from her tablet. "It's no one's business what we do in bed."

Maggie leaned forward to see Liz's face. "But this is as bad as it was in college. We couldn't tell our friends or families. If anyone found out we were sleeping together, we would have been thrown out of school!"

"That was then," Liz said, her eyes still on her tablet. "Now, no one gives a shit what we do."

"Not us, maybe, but Lucy could lose her job if people find out."

Liz sat up and finally closed her tablet. "Yes, I guess she could."

Maggie glanced at Lucy and saw that all the color had left her face. "Could they really fire you?"

"Possibly. What could make it even worse is you work for the church, too."

"Not really. I don't take a salary for leading the choir."

"You return what we pay you as a donation to the church, but technically, you're a church employee. There are rules against a rector being sexually involved with an employee or a congregant. Not like I haven't pushed the boundaries before. Erika and I were openly living as a couple before we married. Liz and I barely made it through the one year waiting period, but the bishop kept asking if I was involved in your breakup."

"What did you say?" Maggie asked, curious.

"Nothing. I was lying by omission, of course."

"I could resign as music director," Maggie offered. "I don't need the job. After all, I was the one who seduced the rector."

Liz laughed. "You say it so proudly. Like it's an accomplishment."

"Well, it is. Look how long it took you to get Lucy into bed."

"She was showing respect for Erika's memory and healing from grief," Liz countered.

"You mean you're not as resistible as you think you are?" Meanwhile, Lucy's pallor made her freckles more prominent. Her mind clearly wasn't on their banter. "Sorry, Lucy. You're the one with the most risk here. We shouldn't be joking about it."

Lucy came back to the conversation. "No, Maggie, you shouldn't resign. That's not going to help anything, and it's the least of our problems."

"She's right," Liz said. "Your resignation would be meaningless. No one really cares about the music director's sexual preferences. The rector is judged by a higher standard. She's supposed to set an example for the congregation. In every other way, Lucy leads a model life."

"Can we stop talking about this?" Lucy begged, getting up. "I don't want to be awake all night worrying."

Maggie reached for her hand. "I'm sorry I brought it up."

"You only asked a question. I just don't have any answers right now." Lucy picked up her phone and left. Maggie got up to head after her.

"Let her go," said Liz.

"But I upset her."

Liz shook her head. "You pointed out the reality she needs to face. No one really cares what you and I do. As women of a certain age, we're invisible. But Lucy is in a position of moral authority. Fortunately, her church is liberal. Her bishop might give her some grief, but the little prick loves her as long as she rakes in money singing in the cathedral. Even so, we need to be very careful. I don't think Lucy's ready to give up being a priest."

"Liz, go to her. She's frightened."

Liz firmly held her gaze. "I can't fix this, Maggie. Neither can you. The only thing we can do to help is to be discreet and proceed with caution."

Maggie knew Liz was right, but her tough stance surprised her. A moment ago, she was indulging Lucy's kittenish ways, and now she refused to comfort her. "I'm sorry, Liz, but if you won't go to Lucy, I will."

Liz huffed in frustration, but she got up. "All right, we'll *both* go."

✻✻✻

At breakfast, Maggie gave Lucy a pep talk about embracing her power. "You can get away with a lot by looking supremely self-assured." Lucy could hear echoes of her mother's advice on how to achieve stage presence, so she didn't argue when Maggie suggested she leave on her deep red nail polish. It looked as fresh as when she'd put it on, and there wasn't a single chip anywhere. She put on the tapestry jacket Maggie had insisted she buy in the thrift store. The colors went perfectly with the color of her polish and matching lipstick. She looked in the mirror and saw a lush, feminine, and confident woman.

Many younger female clergy would wear anything except a black suit. They assumed that the collar was enough to identify their status. They dressed up their clerical blouses by wearing colorful jackets, patterned over-blouses and cardigans. Reshma did this exceptionally well. Her choice of bright motifs was also a nod to her African heritage. Although Susan's collared blouses were always black, even she wore pretty sweaters and blazers. Both Reshma and Susan would be at the clergy meeting that morning. Lucy hoped her sister priests would give her honest feedback on her new look.

Lucy was the first one to arrive in the meeting room. She took her usual seat at the head of the table. Tom was now officially co-rector, but he demonstrated his respect for her authority by *never* sitting in her chair. After running a large, affluent church, he had nothing to prove, whereas Lucy, being female, had needed to assert herself from the moment she'd arrived at St. Margaret's.

Reshma did an exaggerated double take at the door. "N-i-i-ice!," she said, swaying her hips as she bogeyed her way into the room, "Mother Lucy, you have proven once again that you are a fashion icon!" She waved her hand like it had been burned. "You are so hot I can barely stand it!" Obviously, the most junior member of St. Margaret's clergy wholeheartedly approved of the change in Lucy's appearance. "Are those your real nails?" Lucy nodded and extended her fingers so Reshma could admire them. "Color is so much fun, isn't it?" Reshma said with a conspiratorial wink.

"And you use it better than anyone I know."

"No way! When you dress up for your concerts, you put every woman in the room to shame."

"Thanks, Reshma. You're kind."

"I always try to be kind, but I have eyes." Reshma hugged Lucy around her shoulder. "Maybe we can go to the shops sometime."

"I'd like that," said Lucy.

Tom came and grabbed his cheeks, aping extravagant appreciation. "Oh, Lucy, you are a diva! If this is what a long weekend does for you, you should go away more often."

Lucy could feel her face warm. "Tom, stop."

"I will not stop! Honey, you look absolutely *fabulous*!" He took out his phone. "I've got to take a picture and send it to Jeff. We should do a piece in *Vogue*. 'What the well-dressed rector is wearing this season.'" Before Lucy could protest, Tom had snapped the photo.

"Okay, everyone. Let's settle down," Lucy urged, beginning to wish she hadn't tried this experiment. She was used to being the center of attention when she sang, but not in the weekly clergy meeting. Plus, the fuss implied that she looked dowdy when she wore her usual outfit.

Susan finally arrived. "What's going on?" Lucy couldn't tell if her former lover found her appearance attractive or appalling. She couldn't take her eyes away from Lucy's dark nails.

"Susan!" Lucy said sharply to divert her attention from her hands. She added in a milder voice: "Susan, will you pray us into the meeting?"

"Of course, Lucy."

They moved through the agenda quickly and began planning the holiday liturgies. Tom shyly asked if he might get away with Jeff before Christmas. "We have our eye on a little cruise of the intercoastal. Something romantic. Since I came out of retirement, Jeff has been so supportive of my return to active service. I feel I owe him a little attention."

"I think we ladies can manage," said Lucy, looking at her female colleagues in turn. "Susan can take the midnight mass, and I'll do Christmas Day." Reshma barely hid her disappointment that the big events were going to the senior clergy. "Reshma, youth formation is your project. Will you do the afternoon Christmas Eve service with the children's pageant?"

Reshma instantly brightened. "I've been working with Simone Ballou and Cherie Harrison on refreshing the costumes. I don't sew very well, but those two are geniuses with a needle. It's not an easy thing because the kids come in all sizes. Traditionally, the roles have been assigned by how big or small the costume is."

"And so it has been since Christmas pageants began," said Tom. "But now we have girls playing shepherds, even the Magi!"

"And why not? In the past, the only role for girls was Mary," said Susan. "That certainly wasn't fair!"

"Either we show that God is genderless and color blind, or we reinforce that the Trinity is a white, male club!" Reshma said in a surprisingly strident tone. Lucy had never heard her curate espouse such feminist views. She'd been a charity student at an Episcopal boarding school, where she'd absorbed the dominant culture along with the white students. Tiffany, her progressive girlfriend, was apparently giving her an alternative education.

Lucy felt Tom's eyes on her. When she looked up, he said, "Lucy, can you spare a few minutes for me after the meeting?"

"Of course, Tom."

The meeting was essentially done, so Lucy asked Susan to say the concluding prayer. Before Reshma left, she whispered into Lucy's ear, "Whenever you want to go shopping, just let me know." Lucy had Maggie for that, but it would be a good bonding experience to shop with Reshma. It might also help her young charge see herself more as an equal and not merely Lucy's protegée.

"Thank you, Reshma, I will let you know."

Tom had patiently waited until the women left. When they

closed the door behind them, he smiled kindly. "I love your new look, Lucy."

"Maggie Fitzgerald needed a thrift shop fix, so she dragged me along. We were trying to forget the horror of the election."

"Did it help?"

"Buying new outfits always helps."

"Finally, the glamorous opera diva and the effective rector achieve integration." Lucy hadn't thought of it that way, but Tom was right. "Is that also why, after all these years, you finally decided to paint your nails a color people will notice?" It was certainly a pointed question, and one that Lucy could choose not to answer. Tom's canny smile meant he already suspected something. His calm eyes made her want to tell him, but still she hesitated. "Lucy, I sense you testing limits. I know you can be bold. No one gets to sing on the stage of the Metropolitan without supreme confidence."

"And training. My mother probably overtrained me to ensure I would never falter."

"I bet she did, and she mostly succeeded," Tom said, "but there's something else going on here that I just can't put my finger on. I offer myself as a sounding board because you've chosen me as your spiritual advisor."

"What are you sensing, Tom?" Lucy asked, using the old therapist's trick of answering a question with another question.

"You're testing a new role, not just a costume."

"I am auditioning a less conservative look. How can I say I advocate for women in the clergy and then dress in the female equivalent of what English vicars have worn for a hundred years."

"Lucy, I wholeheartedly applaud the sartorial adjustment. Yes, you should celebrate your femininity. You are much too classy to go overboard, so good, but this is certainly an abrupt change. Now, what's going on?"

How can he know? Lucy wondered. Tom's long years as priest had taught him to be remarkably perceptive. Unlike some gay men, who mocked femininity with drag, Tom seemed to understand the significance of women's clothing. After a long moment of consideration, Lucy decided to tell him the truth. She gazed directly into his blue eyes. "Maggie Fitzgerald has become more than my thrift shop buddy."

Tom gave no sign of surprise other than to draw a quick, short breath. "Interesting." He sat back slightly as if withdrawing from something too hot to handle.

"I'm sure you'll understand better than most, especially given your history with Erika and Liz." The veiled accusation had jumped out of Lucy's mouth without any consideration. Lucy was glad she'd put her shocking new knowledge on the table. It would also prevent Tom from thinking he had the upper hand.

His usually rosy cheeks flamed scarlet. "She told you? I'm surprised. Usually, Liz is so discreet."

"In fairness, I pried it out of her. She insisted it was irrelevant because it happened so long ago."

"That's true," said Tom, nodding. "Erika and I were still graduate students at Yale. Liz was a surgical resident." He studied her critically. "You don't seem overly bothered by it."

"Oh, I was at first. I was furious that people I trusted the most had been keeping something so important from me."

"What made you change your mind?"

"I believe Liz when she said she wasn't deliberately keeping it from me, although I'd asked her several times if she'd ever been involved in a threesome. She tried to convince me that it didn't matter because the ethos back then was different."

"It was. Everyone was experimenting. Then HIV started killing gay men and ushered in a new Puritanism. Liz figured out she was exclusively a lesbian. Erika followed soon afterwards, and I decided to go to seminary."

"Why didn't you tell me?"

Tom's rosy complexion darkened even more. He hadn't expected to be on the hot seat. "I considered it, but as time went on, it just seemed too complicated and irrelevant to our work together. Please forgive me, Lucy. I meant no harm."

"I know, Tom. And I don't hold it against you. I only wish Erika or Liz had told me."

"I'm sure they had their reasons. It's in the past, Lucy. Let it stay there. What's more important is what's going on now. I can see from the change in your appearance you seem invigorated, even liberated by this new development."

"I am, but there are so many unresolved issues. In my role as a priest, I preach marital fidelity. It's part of the marriage vows. How can I lecture my pre-marital couples on the virtue of monogamy when I myself don't practice it?"

"Many of us behave in ways that are at odds with church doctrine. Yes, but let's look at scripture. What conservatives call 'Biblical marriage' goes far beyond a union between one man and one woman. In the Old Testament, there are many examples of how people bond sexually. It was common for men to have multiple wives. Of course, there is also the relationship between Jonathan and David, who was also married to a woman."

"There are commandments prohibiting adultery or coveting another man's wife."

Tom looked slightly impatient. "As a trained theologian, you know as well as I do that those commandments refer to a man's property rights. Another man having sex with his wife *disenfranchises* him from his *property*. Patriarchal domination at its most blatant." Tom rolled his eyes. "Lucy, you are an expert on this subject. Do we really need to discuss this?"

"No, Tom, but it's one thing to discuss it in theory. Another to be living it."

"Understood. It's hard enough to be in a relationship with one person, never mind two! And there are all kinds of status questions.

Is the third party less than the married couple? Is Maggie, Liz's former wife, now 'the other woman'?"

"Exactly. Nothing is clear."

"Lucy, I have often heard you say to a troubled church member or therapy client, 'sometimes we just need to sit with the uncertainty.' Nothing could be truer at this moment. We just had a cataclysmic election. The leaders of the MAGA movement are nihilists and chaos agents. The old norms were smashed long ago. We used to hold our Constitution and the rule of law sacred, but no more."

"Which is why what I've done is so frightening. Shouldn't we cling harder to the certainties we had?"

"No, because they're just tools. Yes, we must have some agreement about which rules we should follow, or society will fall apart. But we've been through many cycles of progress and regression. Punitive rules dictating strict sexual behavior are a function of fear, not growth. The Church hasn't always agreed that same sex relationships are wrong, as John Boswell convincingly showed. Never mind the Jonathan-David conundrum."

Lucy smiled, realizing they'd fallen into the trap of debating like theologians. Too bad Liz and Erika weren't there to add their pointed opinions.

"Why are you smiling?" asked Tom, mirroring her expression.

"I was thinking how much Liz would enjoy this conversation... and Erika."

Tom gazed out the window to the churchyard where Erika was buried. "Yes, they would. That was the one thing we discovered when we were a threesome. Our mutual intellectual curiosity was the attraction. The physical came along for the ride. When we couldn't provide the emotional and erotic connection each of us craved, we moved on. That's not the case here. You had a deep, multi-layered bond with Erika, and now with Liz."

"I do, and I get something else from Maggie...something I haven't figured out yet."

"You will," said Tom confidently. He studied her face. "I hope you're not disappointed that I didn't condemn you and give you a stern order to reform."

"Kind of like calling the kettle black, isn't it?"

"No, because my 'mischief,' if you want to call it that, is in the long distant past. You are living it."

"Even calling it 'mischief' is a mild condemnation."

"Not really. Mischief has the element of fun, and it usually isn't harmful."

"That's my greatest fear...that someone will get hurt or won't get what she needs, including me."

"That's inevitable when human beings are involved." Tom sighed deeply. "It won't be easy, Lucy. You'll have to make up your own rules because there are few norms to follow, and most are negative. The harder part will be figuring out how to reconcile your new arrangement with your role in the community. Do you tell people or not? If you do, how do you decide whom to trust with the truth?"

"Our families and friends could be shocked, never mind the congregation."

"The burden of secrecy will be difficult, especially for Maggie because she was the wife. You must be careful. You each have a prominent role in Hobbs and in the larger world. You don't need a scandal on top of the internal dynamics."

"I'm already a target because of my book," said Lucy. "Another bullseye on my back won't help anyone."

"Certainly not," Tom agreed.

"Believe it or not, the worst moment was when I realized I could give absolution to Liz and Maggie, but not myself."

Tom shook his head. "You didn't need absolution, Lucy. Love is never wrong when it is given freely and without the intent to use or abuse others. Knowing all of you, I can't believe any of you would deliberately harm the others." He reached across the table with his palms open wide. "Dear Lucy, thank you for the gift of your honesty."

Lucy put her much smaller hands in his. "Thank you, Tom, for listening and for being here for me."

"I am always here for you as a priest and your friend."

Lucy finally let go of his hands to wipe a tear from her eye.

Chapter 15

Maggie heard a large vehicle pull into the driveway and craned her neck to see out the window. Liz came out of the house to take the box from the driver. Something she said made him laugh loud enough for Maggie to hear. Liz remained to chat with him. It still puzzled Maggie that an introvert like Liz talked to strangers but could be nearly mute with those she loved.

The oven timer sounded. Maggie left the window to check the pumpkin-raisin breads she was baking. She made them for Liz. With cream cheese, it was one of her favorite breakfasts. Maggie set the loaves on a wire rack to cool and went back to the papers she was grading. This year's modern drama class was full of lazy kids, who'd signed up for the course thinking it would be an easy A. She hated to break it to them, but she gave out few As and certainly didn't grade on a curve. She found her students' casual attitude to their education increasingly frustrating. Maybe taking a semester off would ease her cynicism.

A loud sound made her jump. Someone was at the door. She knew which door to answer because when Sam had renovated the house and designed the garage apartment, she'd installed different ringers. The bell at the door to the connector was a pleasant two-note chime. The doorbell at the top of the garage stairs was an annoying old-fashioned buzzer that could wake the dead. Given Sam's perverse humor that had probably been the intention.

When Maggie opened the door, she found Liz on the landing with the box. "This just arrived for you. Mind if I come in?"

"You can, but don't mind the mess."

"I won't look," Liz promised, but her eyes swept the room, taking in the stacks of books and papers. She held out the box. "A present."

"But, Liz, you don't usually give presents."

"I don't give presents for special occasions. I give them when people need them. When you open it, you'll understand why I didn't ask for gift wrap."

Maggie moved some piles of books so Liz could set down the box. "I can't wait to see what you think I need," she said without skimping on the sarcasm.

Liz took a razor knife out of her pocket. She neatly slit the paper tape and took out a smaller box. The illustration on the front showed a series of graduated, gently pointed, color-coded rods, each with a round base. Their shape and texture suggested they were soft and pliable. "Dilators," Liz explained when she realized Maggie didn't know what to call them. "To stretch the vaginal opening and walls."

"It says they're pelvic exercisers."

"Same difference," Liz said, taking more items out of the box. The bottles turned out to be lubricants and cleaners for the devices.

"Thanks, I guess," said Maggie skeptically. She lowered her glasses to read the description on the back of the box. She could tell that her tepid response to the gift was frustrating Liz.

"If you're not interested, I can return them."

"It depends. You think I need them. Are you recommending them as a doctor?"

"No, as your lover. You'll have a lot more fun if it doesn't hurt."

"Did you need to use these things?"

"Something like it. When Lucy first introduced me to her toys, I hadn't had a dick inside me for over forty years."

"Tom?"

"Yep. That blew Lucy's mind, didn't it?"

"Mine too, actually." Maggie replaced the dilators in the shipping box. "Sorry if I seemed ungrateful."

"Maybe I should have asked first," Liz admitted. Lucy really had reformed her. It took a lot for Liz to admit a mistake.

"That would have been nice, but I appreciate the thought."

Liz eyed her with an arched brow. "I was kind of surprised you liked the dildos. You always claimed to be a 'natural' woman."

Maggie shrugged. "People change."

"I'm glad. Making love one way all the time is like fucking in the missionary position."

Maggie wondered how Liz guessed that weekly sex with Barry had always been conventional intercourse. The thought of giving him a blow job made her gag. "It just seems weird practicing to have sex."

"Trans women have to do it every day or their neovaginas close up."

"Must be awful."

"If it's important enough to you, you do it. And we don't have it easy, either. Women's bodies change as we age. We don't need our vaginas to stretch for sex or childbirth, so they atrophy and become inelastic. Even our labia minora shrink. In some women they disappear."

"I don't believe it!"

"I'll show you with a mirror sometime."

"Do you examine me while we make love?"

Liz shrugged, but her little grin revealed the truth. "When you use the dilators, take it slow. Don't get too ambitious or try to force it. Use lots of lubricant."

Maggie gave Liz a kittenish smile. "Maybe you could help me." She suggestively stroked Liz's crotch, but she subtly moved away from Maggie's hand.

"You saw what the box says. It's exercise. Besides, we need to decide about pairing off. That's where we could get into big trouble, especially in the beginning. Lucy thinks we should have a family meeting to figure out things like that."

"Sounds like a good idea." Maggie replaced the items in the box and moved it off the table.

"Why don't you sit down? I just took some pumpkin-raisin breads out of the oven."

Liz smiled. "I could smell something good when I came in."

"They're probably cool enough to eat. I can make you a cup of tea." Liz looked at her watch. While she'd been grading papers, Maggie had lost track of time, but she guessed it was around four. "I have some cream cheese. Let me take it out of the fridge." She turned around to find Liz standing behind her.

"I wish you'd told me when we were married that you were having problems."

"When it got bad, we were fighting all the time and weren't having sex. I figured, why bother?"

"I know you slept with that kid to get back at me, but it must have been so painful and humiliating when he couldn't get in." Liz's look of sympathy was so touching that Maggie leaned against Liz's body until she took her in her arms. Her flannel shirt smelled of wood smoke. She must have just started a fire in the main house. "Maggie, you could have come to me. I could have helped you." Liz said that now, but when the cancer had returned, Maggie had to lay siege to the waiting room at the practice and demand to be seen.

"It's okay, Liz," said Maggie, finally releasing her, "I'm just glad to be home."

"Me too. You could move into the house with us. We have plenty of room. I'm sure Lucy wouldn't mind."

Maggie wasn't as sure as Liz seemed to be. "Liz, it's sweet of you to ask, but I like having my own place. Here, I can leave my books and papers around without you giving me filthy looks. If I've had enough company or I'm tired, I can come here and close the door. Best of all, it's *mine*." Of course, that wasn't completely true. Liz owned the real estate. It was Lucy's name on the deed, not Maggie's. They could ask her to leave at any time. "But maybe we should have a lease."

Liz blinked several times. "Maggie, when I said the key to the apartment was yours to keep, I meant it. Don't you trust me?" she asked in an injured tone.

"One thing I know about you Liz is that you always keep your word." Maggie gently stroked Liz's shoulder to mollify her. "Honey, I trust you, but I've been burned before. What if something happened to you and Lucy decided she didn't want a tenant? My own daughter threw me out of the house that *I'd bought for her.* Sam told me I could live with her forever."

"Maggie, Sam said you could live in the house. She offered to sell it to you at a great price. You turned her down. You don't really think we would ask you to leave. Why are you feeling so insecure?"

"You and Lucy are married. I'm just the ex. I know it's irrational, but what if we have a fight?"

"If we have a fight, we work things out. Like the adults we are. We're the ones setting the rules."

Maggie nudged Liz away from the counter, so she could brew the tea and cut some slices of bread. "Go sit down. I know how you like your tea. I'll fix it for you."

Liz pulled out a chair. After Maggie set the tea and pumpkin bread slathered with cream cheese in front of Liz, she kissed the top of her head. "It's not easy to trust again after all that's happened, but I trust you, Elizabeth Anne Stolz."

"Since my mother died, no one calls me by my full name except you and Lucy, and then only when I've done something outrageous."

"You have done something outrageous, actually two things. You brought me into your marriage...and gave me pelvic exercisers so you can fuck me."

Liz grinned at the acknowledgement of her naughtiness and raised her glass. "Yes, I did, didn't I?"

❅❅❅

After cleaning up from dinner, Liz found Lucy and Maggie stretched out on the two sofas living room, watching the evening news.

"Uh, any chance one of you could make some room for me?" she asked. Instantly, they each sat up leaving Liz in the dicey position of choosing where to sit. Lucy's adult smile couldn't hide the child-like pleading in her green eyes. Liz imagined the Shrek character, Donkey, jumping up and down, insisting, "Pick me!" Maggie's sphinxlike smile was almost a dare, yet it, too, was full of vulnerable expectation. Liz suddenly perceived that their lives would now be fraught with hundreds of subtle and not-so-subtle choices. To avoid offending either one of them, Liz chose to sit alone in the club chair. The childlike expectation in Lucy's eyes dimmed somewhat, but she clearly approved of Liz's Solomon-like solution.

Maggie picked up the remote and turned off the TV. "I hope I left the kitchen in the order to which you are accustomed, Dr. Stolz."

"You are certainly a neater cook than Lucy, but you use a lot of pots."

Maggie grinned slyly. "Aren't you the one who always says, 'the right tool for the job'?"

"Touché."

"Why didn't I ever think of saying that?" said Lucy, smiling at Maggie.

They were in cahoots again, and Liz didn't like it. "Lucy, you're just a messy cook. When you use flour, the kitchen looks like a blizzard hit."

Maggie smiled in Lucy's direction. "It's all right, Lucy, I'm messy too. It's not easy living with a neat freak. That's why I'm keeping my own space."

Liz got up and switched the TV on. "Go back to your news show. I can't stand to watch anyway."

"Stop there," ordered Lucy, showing her palm. Liz instantly froze. "What's this about Maggie keeping her own space? What's the alternative?" Her narrowed eyes meant she had no tolerance for equivocation.

"I told Maggie she could move into the house, but she's not interested, so it's a moot point." The furrow between Lucy's brows grew deeper. "I guess I should have asked you first," Liz added.

"This shows why we need a family meeting," Lucy said, grabbing the remote to switch off the TV. "Liz, sit down. Let's figure out when to have it."

"How about now?" Maggie suggested.

"I think we need time to prepare our questions," said Lucy. "And we should meet on neutral territory, like my office."

Liz stared at Lucy in disbelief. "That's church property. It's like saying we should meet in the conference room at the practice. Neutral, my ass!"

"I'm sorry, Liz. It just seemed like a good space."

"We sound like warring countries arguing about the shape of the table at the peace conference," Maggie said. "Why not meet here? Liz created this space for all of us by hanging up the TV."

"Here is fine with me," Liz said, still glaring at Lucy.

Lucy huffed, but then she let out a sigh. "Fine with me too."

"May I make a suggestion?" Maggie asked in a meek tone guaranteed to get their attention. "When I'm directing a play and the actors are frustrated or upset with one another, I have the cast and crew do some exercises. Want to try it?"

"As long as we don't have to sing 'Kumbaya,'" Liz said in a grumpy tone.

Maggie laughed. "No, Liz, but we can sing it later if you like. Come on, everyone stand up."

Liz reluctantly got to her feet. She hated group exercises and usually felt like a fool for participating, but she didn't want the others to think she was being uncooperative. Maggie led them through stretching and relaxation exercises that loosened tense muscles. She guided them through some deep breathing. When she told them to open their eyes, even Liz had to admit she felt more relaxed.

"Thank you, Maggie," Lucy said, looking refreshed. "That was wonderful. I'll have to try that with my therapy groups." Maggie glowed under the compliment.

"Let me get my laptop to take notes," Liz said, getting up.

"That's a humble role for a surgeon," Maggie called to her.

Liz turned around. "Why? Doctors are always taking notes."

When Liz returned from her office, she found Maggie explaining to Lucy why she wanted to keep her own apartment instead of moving into the house.

"I wish I had a place to escape," Lucy said with a sigh.

Liz sat down and opened her laptop. "You do. The apartment at the beach house."

"The beach house reminds me too much of Erika. At least, when you're there, Liz, it's a distraction, and I don't feel as sad."

Liz typed some notes: *lease to the garage apartment, beach apartment, private space...*

"I understand, Lucy," said Maggie. "I'd find that difficult too, but everyone needs their own space."

"I took over the seashore room as an office. I sometimes sleep there when Liz is restless. I put the queen-sized bed that Liz built for Erika in it."

"Her furniture coming home," Maggie said, nodding in approval.

"We're getting too specific," said Liz. "Let's figure out the big picture items first."

"Liz, I thought I was leading this meeting," said Lucy, irritated.

"That's right, Liz," Maggie agreed. "You don't need to take over *everything*."

Liz compressed her lips to avoid saying what she was thinking, but they both looked at her seemingly expecting a reaction. "Go on, Lucy, lead! I'll shut up and play scribe."

Ignoring her, Lucy turned to Maggie. "Maggie, tell us your biggest concern."

"I'm living here on your goodwill. I don't even have a lease. If we have an argument, you could ask me to leave."

"You told me you're not worried about that," Liz protested. "You said you know I keep my word."

"And you do, but I have no legal status in this relationship. You two are married. I'm just the ex. I have no claim on anything here."

Liz wrote in her notes: *Maggie's relationship status, feeling insecure living here.* Maggie went on, recounting the many times she'd given up her home, going back to being forced to sell the Connecticut house after her divorce from Barry. Liz, who knew the details, was bored and secretly checked her text messages and emails. Lucy got her attention by asking, "Liz, what's your biggest concern?"

Surprised to be called on next, Liz had to think for a minute. "I worry about someone feeling left out. When we have sex, someone is left being a spectator. There are ways to be more inclusive when we're in bed, but what about pairing off? The day we came home from Moosehead, Maggie encouraged me to spend time alone with Lucy. But what if I wanted to sleep with Maggie? Or you two wanted to make love without me? In my mind, I say 'oh that's fine.' But I might feel jealous that you two were sharing something I couldn't be a part of."

Liz sensed that Lucy had been watching her intently as she spoke. 'Being fully present' they called it in clergy circles.

"Liz, thank you for your honesty," Lucy finally said. "I share those fears, but there will be times that I need to be alone with you. I need our intimacy, to touch you, not just physically, but emotionally and spiritually, and I don't mean in the religious sense. I'm still getting used to being Maggie's lover. I don't know what I need from her but I hope to find out. It's probably easier for you, Liz, because you've been married to each of us. You're what we have in common. I just don't want anyone to get hurt or lose either one of you." Her voice broke on the last sentence.

Liz opened her mouth to speak, but Maggie jumped in first. "Lucy, part of the reason our marriage broke up was I didn't give Liz enough sex. When I was married to a man, I saw sex as a duty. While I was going through the fertility treatments, it was a mechanical act to conceive a child. Liz is a considerate, skilled, and generous lover, but when she pressured me, I turned her away. The more she asked, the less interested I became. Maybe I'm just not as sexual as you two."

Liz grinned rakishly. "I don't know, Maggie. When we were up at the lake, you seemed very interested."

"I was. It had been months since I'd had sex."

"Maybe you enjoyed sex more because you allowed yourself to discard some of your inhibitions?" Lucy ventured.

"Yes, of course. Being with two lovers was a novelty. Your inventive toys were fun. My sex drive was never as high as Liz's, and the Tamoxifen depresses it even further. It would break my heart when she'd beg me for sex. Lucy, it's a relief that you can satisfy her needs. I don't have to be in bed with you every time you have sex or sleep with you every night. Honestly, I prefer sleeping alone."

"You do?" Liz said, surprised.

"Yes, and I sleep better. I know this might sound crazy, because not long ago I was so jealous of Lucy I could hardly see straight. But I wasn't jealous because Liz was having sex with you, Lucy. I was jealous because she loved you, not me. She was giving you attention, not me. Taking care of you, not me. Now, I see her paying attention to me and taking care of me too, and that was before we landed in bed together. I can see that she loves me."

Liz swallowed the lump in her throat. "I do love you, Maggie, and I always have."

Maggie's voice was shaky too. "Finally, I can believe you when you say it."

"But I'm the one coming out ahead here," Liz said. "I get to be with the two women I love. What do you and Lucy get out of it?"

"I get to have sex with my best friend," said Lucy.

Liz pouted. "I thought I was your best friend."

"You're my wife, my lover, and my soulmate, but Maggie is my best friend." In a lovefest worthy of the Barbie movie, Maggie and

Lucy beamed at one another. Liz rolled her eyes. Lucy, who missed nothing, caught her. "See, Liz? You don't get this part. This is where I can't go with you."

Maggie nodded in agreement. "There are a lot of places Liz won't go...the nail salon, the spa to have a facial, the thrift shops. Any shopping for something she doesn't need this minute. I can't wait to play with Lucy's hair and do our nails together. You know, all the girly things you hate, Liz."

Lucy's eyes smiled but not her mouth. "We can tie Liz down and give her a pedicure later." Maggie giggled, and Liz glared at her. Lucy went back into therapy mode. "What I'm hearing you say, Maggie, is your biggest concern is security. You feel vulnerable because you don't have a lease for the apartment or legal status in the relationship."

"I've had to give up my home so many times. I just can't be homeless again."

Liz bolded the note about the garage apartment she'd written earlier. "I'm sure we can work something out," she said. "For the sake of Lucy's reputation, it's probably better that you don't move in here. No one needs to know what we do in bed."

Lucy looked sheepish. "Someone already knows."

"Who?" Liz and Maggie asked in unison.

"I told Tom today."

Liz slammed her laptop shut. "Fuck! You told Tom? Oh, Lucy! Why did you do that?"

"Mostly because he guessed. And after all, he is my spiritual advisor. We don't have to make a public announcement, but we can't hide the facts from our closest friends and family. That would be living a lie."

"She's right, Liz. It would be going back into the closet, like when we were in college." Maggie turned to Lucy. "But can you trust Tom?"

Lucy shrugged. "Do I have a choice?"

Liz finally calmed down and opened her computer. "I trust Tom. Look how long he kept our secret. But there are some people we can't tell because they won't understand. Brenda is a lesbian, but she's so traditional. Cherie, too. Except for the fact that Brenda is female, they would be your typical cop family. Maggie, I think your kids would freak out if they knew."

"Oh, you should have heard them when I tried to reconcile with Barry."

"You tried to reconcile with that *asshole*?" Liz asked incredulously. "When did that happen?"

"I'll tell you later."

Liz shook her head. "Never mind. It doesn't matter. You're here now, with me."

"With *us*," Lucy corrected "Let's skip the possessiveness, please. We're in this *together*." She looked at each of them to reinforce the point. "I'm sorry I told Tom without consulting you first. Let's hold off on telling other people until we agree on who to tell and when so we can all be prepared for the fallout."

They all agreed that was a good idea. Reviewing the brief list of items on her laptop screen, Liz realized that some people had to know. "If Maggie wants a lease, I need to talk to Harriet."

"Of course, you need to talk to your lawyer," said Maggie, "but that doesn't mean you need to tell her we're all sleeping together."

Liz struggled to look patient. "Of course not, it's about real estate, not the sex, just like marriage."

"Isn't she romantic?" Maggie asked, looking to Lucy for sympathy.

"Romance is for opera," Liz flatly said. "According to Project 2025, our right to marry may be in danger. I need to make sure we are all protected."

Lucy stared at Liz. "And who appointed you the person to do the protecting? Now you sound like *him*. Lucy lowered her voice and mimicked a Queens accent. 'I'm going to protect the women whether they want it or not.'"

"Lucy, that's not how I meant it," Liz protested. "As I said, making sure everyone is treated fairly and protected is my highest priority."

"Let her go there, Lucy," Maggie advised calmly. "She's good at it, and she lives to be the competent, strong one who takes care of helpless ladies like us."

"I'm not helpless!" Lucy protested.

"We know, Lucy." Maggie let out a big sigh. "I'm sorry, kids, but I'm exhausted, and tomorrow is my long day with three classes. Can we continue this another night?"

"I think we made a good start," Lucy said. "Why don't we talk again on Thursday night? I don't have any meetings."

"That's fine," Maggie said. "All my classes are in the morning. I could make dinner for five, so we could start the meeting earlier."

Liz grudgingly agreed to the meeting and added some final notes to the list.

Chapter 16

Lucy rushed downstairs to grab some breakfast while Liz was in the shower. She found Maggie sitting in the breakfast nook with sections of *The New York Times* spread open on the table. Liz had accused Maggie of being a tree killer and called Lucy a Luddite when she admitted that she too enjoyed browsing the physical paper, but she'd resubscribed to the print edition, which she'd paused after the divorce. Despite the little digs, she seemed to enjoy indulging her "wives."

Maggie raised her face for a kiss. "Good morning, Lucy dear. You look like you're in a hurry today." She collected the newspaper into a neat stack.

"I have an early meeting. I gave up trying to put my hair in a French braid, because I'm all thumbs this morning."

"Sit down. I'll do it." Lucy loaded the toaster and sat down on the bench next to Maggie. "Turn around." Maggie took out the elastic and skillfully wound Lucy's hair into plaits. Her gentle hands created a warm tingling pleasure that spread over Lucy's body. She never wanted it to stop. "There," said Maggie, winding off the braid. She moved it aside and planted a warm kiss on the back of Lucy's neck. "I never realized you had so many freckles."

"Yup. They're everywhere. Thank heavens for concealing foundation." Lucy got up to rescue her raisin bread from the toaster. Although Maggie made sure their kitchen was supplied with fresh baked goods, sometimes Lucy had a craving for her old breakfast standby.

"How was your practice this morning?" Maggie asked.

"Okay. Liz says I'm singing sharp to compensate for my voice darkening. The curse of living with someone who has perfect pitch."

"Don't take her seriously. She likes to think she's an authority on everything."

Lucy bristled at hearing Liz criticized. She was glad that, instead of joining morning singing practice, Maggie had chosen an extra hour of sleep. On dark winter mornings, Lucy was often envious of Maggie, asleep upstairs, but her morning vocal routine went back to childhood. Her mother would wake her to sing scales and arpeggios before school. Now, her daily practice was so engrained that she often woke before the alarm sounded. Liz would follow her down to the media room and sit in the last row of home theater seats, listening even to the boring parts before Lucy rehearsed the works she was preparing to perform. That special time with Liz was sacred and private, not to be shared anyone, not even Maggie.

"I pay attention to what Liz says because she knows what she's talking about," Lucy said, cutting her toast into triangles. "She can read a score like a conductor and knows how each aria is supposed to sound."

"Good morning, ladies," said Liz, coming into the kitchen. She was dressed for work in a pristine button-down shirt and perfectly pressed chinos. She hung her blazer on the back of a chair.

"There's pumpkin bread over there," Maggie said. "I put out the cream cheese, so it's not ice cold."

"Thank you," said Liz, bending to kiss her. Lucy leaned back to get a kiss too. Liz smiled and gave her a prolonged, sensual kiss.

"What have you two been up to this morning?" Maggie said lightly when they finally parted.

Liz took a carton of half and half out of the refrigerator. "Don't worry, we weren't getting it on during practice. I'm trying to make up for yelling at her in practice this morning."

Maggie turned to Lucy and theatrically mocked surprise. "She yells at you, and you still kiss her like that?"

"The Boston production of *Die tote Stadt* is only a few months away," Liz said. "She needs to know she's singing sharp so she can do something about it. Better me than listen to the critics' complaints."

Maggie shook her head. "You two have the strangest relationship."

"Actually, we don't," Liz said, stirring her coffee. "It's simple. Lucy gives the orders, and I obey."

Maggie glanced at Lucy for confirmation. "She's kidding. That's just a little game we play."

"I'm not sure about that, Lucy," Maggie said, narrowing her eyes. "In bed, you call the shots."

"Not always. There's a reason they call it 'sweet surrender'. Feeling powerful and strong excites Liz. And I like to be taken. Works for us."

"Evidently," Maggie said dryly. "Your orgasms are a thing to behold."

Liz cut herself a piece of pumpkin bread and sat down. "Sex wasn't meant to be a spectator sport. We should try some more inclusive positions." As usual, Liz had reduced a complicated emotional situation to how to solve a technical problem.

Lucy tried to bring the conversation to a higher level. "Otherwise, we're committed to transparency. We tell each other everything, with kindness, of course. Liz knows when I manipulate her, so it's harmless."

Liz made a deep courtly bow. "She is my lady, and I am her knight."

"She adores you. Lucy, what did you do to her?"

Lucy thought for a moment. "I sang to her. Music is the way Liz sublimates her emotions. Listening to it allows her to process her feelings safely."

Maggie, who'd been listening intently, nodded. "That's Aristotle's definition of tragedy. It's more, of course. But she's open to you in a way she never was to me."

Lucy understood what Maggie was trying to say. "Because I let her be herself. I might point out a behavior that's not working for her, but it's her job to change it, not mine." Lucy stopped rubbing

Liz's thigh because she sensed it was arousing her. There was no time to do something about it. Liz was due at the office soon, and Lucy still needed to put on her makeup.

Liz looked disappointed when Lucy's hand moved away. "It's not even fun to be bad anymore, because she just ignores me."

"So that's your secret, Lucy? You ignore her?"

"Yes, when she's being naughty and doing something to get my attention, like speeding on the highway. She knows it's wrong, even dangerous. If I ignore her, like a kid acting out, she stops."

While Lucy had been talking, Liz had inhaled the slice of pumpkin bread. She got up to refill her coffee. "Maggie, tell me. How would you feel if your wife tried to modify your behavior?"

"Well, you did. You tried to get me to think and act more like you. And you know Lucy's not doing it to hurt you. She's trying to save you from yourself."

"But I have an image to uphold. Liz Stolz, chick magnet and heartbreaker." Liz was kidding, of course, but Maggie burst out laughing.

Liz looked stunned. After a moment, she dumped the coffee from her mug into her travel mug. "I have early appointments. See you later." Liz grabbed her jacket from the chairback and hurried out.

After she left, Maggie said, "That went well."

Lucy sighed. "I know you try to assert yourself to protect your boundaries, but you don't always need to confront people, especially when they're sensitive about something."

Maggie waved dismissively. "Oh, Liz doesn't even notice."

"You know that's not true. Liz has internalized all that male behavior. The thing men hate most is being laughed at by women. You might not see it, but Liz's ego is fragile like a man's." Lucy sighed in frustration. "I don't know why I'm telling you this. You know her better than I do!"

"Not sure about that, Lucy. You get her."

"You mean, I see her. And you do too, but you two are so entrenched in your old behaviors, you can't get past them. And you're still angry...both of you. She hasn't forgiven you for leaving her in college. You haven't forgiven her for falling in love with me. One of the things I worry about is this sex thing getting in the way of your healing. It's easier to have an orgasm than confront resentment."

Maggie had been listening thoughtfully. "I guess it's good to have a resident therapist."

Lucy vigorously shook her head. "I don't like being in the middle or pushed into doing therapy with my partners. That's my job, not what I want to do in my home, with the people I love."

"Of course not."

"Maggie, you are extremely perceptive about human behavior and emotions. That's what makes you such a great actress and director. Try looking at the dynamic between you and Liz from that point of view. It will open your eyes to a lot of things you never saw about her...and yourself."

That statement seemed to make a big impact. Maggie's hazel eyes steadily held Lucy's gaze. For the first time, Lucy saw the unvarnished Maggie, the frightened girl jockeying with her siblings for attention, who desperately wanted everyone's approval. Everything she'd done in her life had been to serve that goal, and yet she'd only managed to defeat herself and push people away. Although Lucy could see this clearly, it was something Maggie must figure out for herself.

"We can talk about this later. I need to get ready for the day," Lucy said, getting up.

"Lucy, I'm sorry."

"Don't be sorry, Maggie. Fix it!" Lucy could feel Maggie's eyes on her back as she left the room. She'd spoken more sharply than she'd intended, but a harsh tone was sometimes necessary for people to hear the message. She'd kiss Maggie before she left for work to make amends.

❊❊❊

Maggie, answer your goddamn phone! Liz had memorized Maggie's school schedule, so she knew she wasn't in class. They'd agreed to hold their "family meeting" that night because Maggie only had morning classes and would be home early.

"Liz, is everything okay?" Maggie asked anxiously when she finally answered.

"Yes, but you were so fucking annoying this morning I forgot to ask you and Lucy something important. Hang on while I get her on the line." Before Maggie could respond, Liz put her on hold.

"Liz, what a nice surprise," Lucy said. "I was just about to take a break. How are you?"

"I have Maggie on the other line. Hold on. There's something I need to talk to you about. Do you have time now?"

"Yes, I have twenty minutes before my next meeting."

"Okay. Good. Hold on." Liz connected the calls. "Sorry for the interruption in your day. Since we agreed to consult the others before telling anyone I needed to talk to you. I made a date with Olivia to have drinks this afternoon. Maggie, you still okay to make dinner?"

"Yes, that was my plan."

"Make it for seven. I should be home by then."

"Liz, you're not thinking of telling Olivia?" asked Lucy anxiously. "She's on the vestry. If she tells anyone, I'm out of a job."

"You told Tom," Liz reminded her.

"I'd trust Tom before I'd trust Olivia," Maggie said. She'd never been an Olivia fan, so her negative reaction was unsurprising.

Expecting pushback, Liz had already formulated what she considered a compelling argument. "Olivia manages our investments. We trust her with our life savings, which are significant. Why can't we trust her with our little secret?"

"Olivia does a great job of handling our money. I just don't like her," Maggie admitted. "I'll go with your judgment, Liz, but why is this such an emergency that you had to call us?"

"Ordinarily, I'd just go ahead and apologize later, but I'm trying to play by the rules. Shocking, I know."

"It's not really your style," Maggie agreed. "Is it really necessary that you tell Olivia?"

"This threesome has financial implications. First, we need to get Maggie a lease, but we should also talk about how we share expenses, deal with property, and inheritance. I want to run some ideas by Olivia. I'm sure she'll have suggestions. Where money is concerned, Olivia can be very creative."

There was a long silence before Maggie spoke. "Liz, aren't you getting a little ahead of yourself?"

"Eventually, we'll have to tell her. This way, we can begin making some plans."

"I don't know, Liz...." said Lucy, who clearly had the most to lose if Olivia told anyone in the congregation.

"Lucy, I'm asking you to trust me on this."

"I do trust you, Liz, but you have no control over what Olivia might do, and I'm not ready to give up being a priest."

"I promise you won't have to, at least not because of Olivia."

Liz could feel Lucy struggling on the other end of the line.

"Maggie's already given her consent," Lucy finally said. "I need a few minutes to think about it. What time are you going to Olivia's?"

"I told her I'd be at her house around four o'clock." Liz glanced at her watch. It was only two-thirty. There was plenty of time for Lucy to digest the idea or come up with more objections.

"Ladies, I have to go," said Maggie. "You two figure it out. I'll talk to you later. I love you both." The phone clicked as she left the call.

Lucy was so quiet that for a moment, Liz thought she wasn't there. "Luce...?"

"Liz, be honest. Do you really need to bring Olivia into it?"

"Well, I could pretend I'm asking for a friend." She grinned and she could bet Lucy could hear it through the phone.

"Oh!" said a frustrated Lucy in mock disgust. "Liz, this is *serious*."

"I won't say that we're sleeping together, only that I want to provide Maggie with some assurances."

"Olivia is extremely perceptive," said Lucy. "She'll guess what's going on."

"Of course, she will. Though she's not as intuitive as you are. She just observes people carefully and figures out what makes them tick. That's how she turned the Enright Fund into a goldmine. But in this situation, she has responsibility as a fiduciary and needs to hold certain things confidential."

"Liz, you're in a different situation. You've had multiple partners since you bought Hobbs Family practice. If people find out about us, they might gossip a little, but it won't end your career as a doctor. Same with Maggie. She's an actress. Theater people are supposed to have scandalous affairs. But if Olivia tells anyone, it will be the end of my ministry at St. Margaret's."

"Lucy, no one really cares what we do. In their minds, old women don't matter. They probably can't even imagine we have sex."

"Liz, everything you say may be true, but it's my job on the line."

Liz knew Lucy was right. If Olivia told anyone, Lucy could lose her job. Of course, their financial planner would likely tell her lover, which meant Liz's partner, Amy, would also know. The more people who knew about it, the more likely the secret would get out and everyone would know.

"Liz? Are you still there?"

"Yes, Lucy. I'm thinking."

"Let me see your face," Lucy ordered. Liz impatiently opened a video chat. When Lucy appeared on the screen, her green eyes were clouded with worry. "Liz, I love you with all my heart, and I trust you absolutely, but we are playing with fire. It can get out of control very quickly. You say you want to protect us. Don't put us into danger without being sure you know what you're doing. That's all I'm going to say. *You* decide."

Liz felt the weight of the burden Lucy had placed on her. "Lucy, I know it's risky. Everyone assumes the worst of Olivia, but you know her. She's not a bad person."

"No, she's not, but she meddles where she shouldn't. Remember when she went around me to the bishop?"

Until the reminder, Liz had forgotten about that episode, but Lucy never would. "She didn't do it to hurt you, Lucy. Her intentions were good. She was concerned you were overworked. She didn't understand the organization of your church. In her mind, going to your boss and asking him to lighten your load was helping you."

"It was not her business to go directly to the bishop, even as a member of the vestry."

"No, it wasn't, and you're right, as always."

"Liz, it's not about being right. It's about making a good decision. You may think you can trust Olivia. She's fiercely loyal to you because you accepted her when no one else would. She respects you and sees you as an equal. If anyone can convince her she needs to keep her mouth shut, it's you, but can she do it?"

"There's risk involved, but in this case, the benefits are worth it."

Lucy still didn't look convinced. She searched Liz's eyes. Finally, she said, "All right, sweetie. You figure it out. I trust you but pay attention and trust your gut. Olivia is clever and extremely perceptive. If you have even the smallest doubt, don't do it." Lucy air kissed the screen. "I love you."

"I love you too."

Liz was distracted after the conversation. Lucy's concerns had punched through her ironclad resolve. She occupied herself with paperwork for the hour before she presented herself at Olivia's obscenely large Pseudo-Victorian on Gull Island.

Olivia had lured Liz to her lair with the promise of martinis. She always used outrageously expensive gin, which made them particularly good. The first-rate alcohol was usually accompanied with equally impressive savory snacks. Liz regretted that she needed to forego the garlic-stuffed olives, her favorite. Lucy might not mind, but Maggie turned up her sensitive nose at second-hand garlic.

"Hello, my dear," said Olivia, opening the door. Usually, she used the door camera and remote lock to admit visitors, but she always came to the door for Liz. Olivia kissed her on both cheeks. "It's so good to see you! Everyone's been in hiding since that horrible election!"

"A reasonable response to a disaster, don't you think?"

"Can we just leave the country until he's gone?" Olivia asked in a completely serious tone.

"Some people are threatening, but honestly, there's no place to hide. The stuff he's promised to do will affect the entire world. The only thing we can do now is rest up for the fight. We went up to Moosehead for the weekend."

Olivia closed the door behind them. "Amy told me you'd gone up there to see the Aurora, but you didn't need to travel that far. We saw the lightshow right from the deck." Liz followed her hostess to the enclosed porch, where an electric fireplace that looked incredibly realistic pumped out comforting warmth. "I know you're punctual when you haven't been way laid by a patient, so I took the chance of mixing the martinis." Olivia gestured to an artistically designed carafe chilling in an ice bath. "I'm sorry to say this, Liz, but you look like you *really* need one."

Liz took her usual place on the wicker settee. She knew that Olivia liked assigned seating from being in C-suites, where someone's position at a conference table signaled their power. Dominating every situation was important to Olivia, so Liz went along with this harmless preference.

Liz gratefully accepted a martini in a perfectly chilled glass. "I think the entire country could use a good stiff drink. In my opinion, his supporters will get what they voted for and end up being sorry."

"Unfortunately, we'll all suffer along with them."

"Yes, we will." Liz took a sip of the martini, barely restraining herself from reacting to the overbearing piney taste. "New gin?"

"Yes, handcrafted right here in Maine. It was highly rated. What do you think?" asked Olivia, hovering. Liz felt privileged that Olivia would ask her opinion and allow her insecurities to show. She considered Liz part of an elite sorority of self-made women, which automatically entitled her to a modicum of respect. With others she presented monolithic confidence in her carefully acquired sophistication. Olivia handed Liz the bottle of gin so she could read the label. "I'm trying to find substitutes for my favorite imports. When he slaps on those tariffs he promised, we may find many things hard to get. I want to be prepared for the worst."

"I know what you mean. Ellie told me our dryer is on its last leg, so I ordered a new laundry set. Even if things are assembled here, they're full of parts from Mexico or Asia. I don't want to spend double for something after he gets into office and starts wrecking the economy."

Olivia gazed into her martini and sighed deeply. "Republicans used to be for fiscal responsibility and lower taxes, but all they do is give unnecessary tax cuts and run up the deficit. Then the Democrats come in to fix it, which they always do." Liz nodded, but she wondered why Olivia, who understood finance inside and out, had only recently come to this conclusion. Proof that people's beliefs weren't always tied to facts.

Olivia tasted her martini and pronounced it, "decent." To Liz's taste, the juniper flavor was much too forward. She guessed from Olivia's face that she thought the same, but she was waiting for confirmation. With a faux smile, Liz set the terrible martini aside.

Olivia did the same. "I don't know what we'll do if we can't get certain things, but for now I'm going to enjoy the peace while we have it and enjoy the holidays."

"Is your family coming for Thanksgiving?"

"Yes, my ex-daughter-in-law and her girls. Amy's parents and brother are coming to us too."

Lucy had facilitated Olivia's reconciliation with her family. It came as a relief that it still held. The relationship with Amy, however, remained a puzzle. Inviting Amy's family indicated not only stability, but a deepening of their partnership. *None of my business,* Liz told herself firmly when she found herself speculating further.

"We're also having a big crowd. Lucy invited Tiffany's parents, now that she's decided Brad Taylor isn't so bad after all. And Maggie's daughter, Sophia will be moving up here for her new job. After Thanksgiving, I'm going to help her move."

"That's what I admire about you, Liz. You are so loyal, even to someone who made your life hell." Of course, Olivia had sided with Liz over Maggie during the divorce, and her bad opinion of her had persisted.

"Olivia, we both acted badly."

"I'm sorry, but cheating on you with her boy toy wasn't equal to ogling Lucy's anatomy. Everyone stares at Lucy because she's beautiful."

Liz appreciated Olivia's loyalty, but now it could be a liability. "Yes, but I wasn't exactly discreet. Maggie had a right to be annoyed. We're trying to get past it."

The set of Olivia's mouth meant she wasn't buying this explanation. "I admire your ability to forgive. I couldn't do it." Liz could bet that Olivia never let go of a grudge. At a benefit event for the Gun Victims Fund, one of Olivia's Wall Street friends had confided that he still dreaded retribution for his disloyalty during her downfall.

Liz decided to turn the conversation away from the past. "I'm sure you didn't invite me today just to taste your craft gin."

"Which isn't very good, is it?"

Liz shook her head.

"Liz, I'm glad I can always count on you to tell me the truth." Olivia snatched Liz's glass out of her hand. "Give me that awful stuff, and I'll mix up another batch." She fished the vacuum bottle out of the ice. "I'll be right back."

While Olivia was in the kitchen, Liz thought about the conversation with her wives. Lucy was right. Liz held her future in the church in her hands. If she made the wrong decision, and the information about them leaked out, it would be a disaster.

Olivia returned with clean glasses and a new batch of martinis. "Liz, I have an idea I want to run by you," she said, pouring the drinks. "Everyone is so angry and divided. I thought a town event during the holidays might help bring people together."

"Great idea, Olivia. What did you have in mind?" Liz sipped the fresh martini, relieved to taste Olivia's usual excellent gin.

"Whatever we do needs to fit in with people's other holiday plans. I was thinking of a reception, with food provided by local eateries. The Christmas parade ends at the safety building. We could move out the fire trucks and ambulances and hold it in the garage."

"But does the town have that kind of money?" Liz asked, knowing that, Olivia, the town manager, would have the numbers right at hand.

"It does, but I wouldn't burden residents with the expense. I'd put up most of the money myself but ask for donations for the rest." Olivia gave Liz a significant look.

"Of course, I'll be glad to contribute."

"Thank you, Liz. I knew I could count on you. Fortunately, everyone's investments have done well this year. We might as well spend the money before that man wrecks the economy, and our portfolios shrink to nothing." Liz's ears perked up. If anyone would know what would happen in the financial markets, Olivia would. "Of course, I'll make adjustments to your portfolio as situations arise, but if the world markets crash like in 2008, we may all be in trouble."

"You think it's a realistic possibility?"

Olivia shrugged. "At this point, your guess is as good as mine. Part of me says he won't do half of the crazy things he's threatened. The wiser part says, of course, he will, *every...single...thing*, the crueler and more destructive the better. He ran on punishing his enemies, and he will, along with the rest of us. I think we should prepare for the worst."

Liz took a large gulp of martini. "I was afraid you'd say that."

"Right now, there's little we can do except plan ahead."

When they finished the first round of improved martinis, Olivia got up to mix more. Liz took a few minutes to check the phone messages before following Olivia into the kitchen. Olivia looked up from measuring off the gin. "You know, Liz, you're one of the few people I allow to wander around my house."

"I'm aware that it's a privilege."

Olivia smiled warmly. "I trust you, Liz. You are honest and loyal. What you say you'll do, gets done, no ifs, ands, or buts. I value our friendship immensely. Maybe I don't say it often enough."

"Thank you, Olivia. I feel the same, which is why I'm going to share something private."

Olivia's eyes glittered with anticipation. As much as she liked juicy gossip, she loved confidences even more. "I'm honored, Liz. You know your secrets are safe with me."

Liz took a moment to compose her thoughts but finally decided on the direct approach. "Lucy and I have brought Maggie into our relationship."

Olivia blinked, which meant she was surprised, a rare event. Having made a career of anticipating what would happen in the financial markets, she took pride in always being in the know. The fact that this detail had escaped her notice clearly intrigued her. "You mean you're a threesome now? Oh, Liz, you are such a stud having two wives!"

"It's not a harem, Olivia. We're equals in this partnership, which is why I'm talking to you."

Olivia's blue eyes twinkled. "You want my advice," she concluded with obvious satisfaction. "Tell me more."

"For obvious reasons, Maggie feels insecure. She lives in that garage apartment on my goodwill. Not that I can rent it to someone else. It's not a legal apartment, but Maggie's been made homeless too many times by people she's loved."

"That's because she trusts other people to provide her security. I would never leave my fate in the hands of others the way she has."

"I was one of those others," Liz reminded her.

"Yes, but you are a straight arrow. No matter how angry you are, you always try to do the right thing." Olivia peered at Liz. "But don't get any ideas about divorcing Lucy. No matter what, you *must* remain married to her for the sake of her position in the church." The brisk tone of her advice made it sound like an order.

"We already figured that out. Maggie seems to have no problem with it. We're equals, but we have different needs. When Sam left, Maggie realized that finding status through a relationship can be a mixed bag."

"Well, it's about time she figured that out," Olivia said in her typical judgmental tone. "Some women never do. No one is coming to save Maggie Fitzgerald, not even the heroic Dr. Stolz, although she certainly tries."

"I do not!" Liz protested indignantly, which made Olivia laugh out loud. "But it's a good thing Maggie understands and doesn't expect me to marry her. Obviously, I can't."

Olivia added more ice to the cooler. "No, you can't, but you could form a corporation." The idea was not only brilliant, but so obvious that Liz wondered why she hadn't thought of it. "You could create a holding company and merge your assets. I'm sure Melissa can advise you on trusts for your heirs. It doesn't have to be complicated."

"Olivia, I could kiss you!"

Olivia turned and gave Liz a sultry smile. "Then what are you waiting for?"

Startled, Liz gave her a quick kiss.

Olivia giggled almost coquettishly. "Next time, you'll have to do better, but it seems you already have enough women to manage, *Dr. Stud.*"

***

At dinner, Liz described Olivia's scheme to create a corporation. Maggie had every confidence in Liz's ability to take care of their money. Liz had learned management and finance from growing up in the family business, and she was good at it. That's why Maggie had trusted Liz to invest the proceeds from the sale of her Greenwich Village coop. Under Liz's watch, the small nest egg had grown into a sum Maggie had never dreamed of, enough to buy a house for cash in a nice suburb of Portland and still have plenty to live comfortably.

Once Maggie got the gist of Olivia's plan, she lost interest in the details. Liz's body language and Lucy's responses were far more compelling. Money wasn't Lucy's forte, either, but she'd needed to learn the rudiments of finance after being defrauded by her agent. Her blank expression meant she didn't understand what Liz was saying any more than Maggie did. Plus, the poor woman looked exhausted.

"Tired, Lucy?" Maggie asked when Liz finally took a breath.

"I am. I had some heavy-duty meetings today."

"Liz, can't we save the rest of this discussion for another time?" Maggie made big eyes to emphasize the point, but Liz was on a roll. Maggie repeatedly glanced in Lucy's direction so Liz would get the message.

"Okay," Liz finally said, realizing she was wasting her breath. "Let me clean up the kitchen." She started to get up, but Maggie stopped her with a restraining hand.

"No, you won't. Sounds like you've done enough work today for three people." Maggie smiled, amused by her own cleverness.

"Yeah, I guess I did." Liz sat down again. "Hope you both think I'm doing a good job." Maggie caught a glimpse of a younger Liz, who needed reassurance. Her indomitable surgeon's confidence hadn't completely defeated the self-doubt that most women felt.

Maggie began clearing the table. "Liz, I'm sure you've got it covered. Right, Lucy?"

Realizing she'd been addressed, Lucy woke from wherever her mind had gone and nodded.

"Oh, Lucy, you look exhausted," said Maggie with a sympathetic frown. "Why don't we postpone tonight's meeting? It's kind of late to start."

Lucy attempted a smile. "We've already covered a lot of ground. That counts as a meeting, don't you agree?"

Liz shrugged. "Works for me."

Maggie collected the plate. "Lucy, why don't you turn in early? You too, Liz. I'll take care of the kitchen."

Before they left, they helped her clear the table and put away the leftover food. Loading the dishwasher, Maggie realized how completely their lives had changed. Part of her had assumed that when they got home, everything would go back to the way it had been, but the threesome idea had taken on a life of its own. It was beginning to feel *normal*.

The only uncomfortable part was watching her partners' unguarded interactions. Their almost wordless communication was puzzling. Occasionally, Maggie felt left out because she had no idea what they were saying to one another. She was surprised by Lucy's sudden fits of pique but intrigued by the little coquettish giggle she reserved for Liz. Seeing someone in the throes of orgasm always provided a different perspective, but Lucy's climaxes were totally unself-conscious. She came like she listened, with her entire body.

Thinking about Lucy's deep, expansive orgasms made Maggie tingle. While she was wondering if her "wives" were too tired for sex tonight, long arms encircled her waist. She instantly knew they belonged to Liz. Like radar, Maggie could always sense her presence. Lucy's footfalls were lighter and ethereal. Liz's larger body mass was more intrusive. Even the feel of the air when she moved was distinctive.

"Hi there," Liz whispered from behind. She lightly massaged Maggie's crotch through her jeans.

Maggie leaned back, confident her weight would be supported. "I was just thinking about you."

"You were?" asked Liz, stealthily unzipping Maggie's jeans. Her hand slid into her panties. Her fingertips touched so gently, like the brush of fairy wings. Meanwhile, her tongue lazily explored the folds of Maggie's ear. She knew how much Maggie liked to have her ears kissed. "I was sent to tell you that it's time for bed," Liz whispered on a warm breath. "I have some of that nice lubricant you like, but from the feel of things down here, you won't need it."

Maggie could both feel and hear the slickness between her legs. Between frequent sex and making herself come, her natural moisture was returning. Liz steadily increased the pressure of her touch until it was obvious an orgasm was near. "Do you want to come?" she whispered into her ear.

"No, let's go upstairs."

Liz carefully zipped up Maggie's jeans. "Lucy's waiting for us."

They took the elevator to the third floor. Liz took advantage of the slow ascent to tongue kiss Maggie like they were back in their college dorm. Liz had never really been kissed before Maggie taught her how. The enthusiasm was the same, but Liz's adult kisses were decidedly more refined.

Liz opened the door to the bedroom, which was dark except for some strategically placed candles. The incense was a spicy-sweet, exotic scent that did not come from a church. While Maggie had been doing the dishes, they'd been setting the scene. Lucy lay on the stack of pillows in a diaphanous nightgown that revealed every perfect curve of her body. It was so sexy that Maggie couldn't wait to get it off her. When Lucy opened her arms, Maggie wanted to fall into them, but Liz grabbed her by a belt loop and pulled her back. "These need to go," she ordered, unzipping the jeans and pulling them down. She yanked off Maggie's wooly socks and tossed them over her shoulder. After she freed Maggie of her panties, she teased her with her tongue. At the very moment Maggie was about to come, the motion suddenly stopped.

"Lucy, you can have her now."

"You devil!" Feeling cheated, Maggie gently punched Liz's shoulder.

"Yes, she can be a devil." Lucy beckoned with her eyes. "Come here, Maggie. Let me take care of you." A pull of the strings of her bodice invited Maggie to enjoy her breasts. While Maggie sucked first one pert nipple, then the other, she was startled to be entered from behind.

"Hmm. You've been exercising," Liz said, probing deeply. "I didn't think you could take this much." Her fingers simultaneously teased Maggie on the outside.

When the orgasm erupted, Maggie saw vibrating colors and stars, until Liz finally stilled the motion and gently withdrew.

"Well, that was a good start. Let's see what else you have for us."

"Liz, take your clothes off and join us," Lucy ordered.

Liz made a low, courtly bow. "As you wish, my lady." She stripped quickly, tossing her clothes on the nearby chair.

Liz's mission became clear. She meant to prove there were ways to make love and not leave one partner a spectator. That night, Maggie was introduced to positions she'd only read about in books. They joined in so many ways, some unexpected, others completely obvious. With her martial arts skills, Lucy moved them around like playing pieces on a board. The dance reminded Maggie of a statue of the three graces she'd seen in Milan, whose intent was certainly no innocent frolic. In the sculpture, one woman caressed the breast of another, while two of them touched their ecstatic faces together.

Tonight, they were the living embodiment of that perfect erotic moment.

Chapter 17

The expiration date on Sophia's visit had come and gone. Maggie's elder daughter had arrived the week before Thanksgiving, and this time, she'd accepted Liz's invitation to stay in the main house. For eight difficult days, they'd all managed to pretend that Maggie was merely the ex-wife, living in the garage apartment because housing was scarce.

Maintaining this fiction was exhausting. Maggie had to restrain herself from blowing a kiss to Liz or giving Lucy's heart-shaped buttocks a quick caress when she passed. It was torture because Maggie hadn't felt so horny since she was a teenager. She wanted to touch Liz and Lucy at every opportunity. With Sophia there, her partners were painfully off limits. Tonight, things could finally go back to normal.

Handing up the plates while Sophia stacked them in the cabinet, Maggie heard Liz coming up the stairs. She'd generously agreed to move the boxes that Sophia had shipped up to Maine. She set the last carton on a kitchen chair. "Well, that's it. Thank God, because my knee is about to give out. Must have some 'weathah' comin' in." She sounded exactly like an old Mainer.

Sophia looked down at her from the step ladder. "Science has never been able to find a connection between aches and pains and a storm approaching."

"I know, but generations of old people can't be wrong." Liz folded her arms on her chest while she surveyed their progress. "Looks like you two have the situation under control. I'm going home to get dinner started. You okay here, Maggie?"

"Yes, thank you, Liz." Maggie wanted to kiss her, even if only on the cheek, to show her appreciation for all her hard work. The little twinkle in Liz's eye indicated she'd gotten the message. As soon as Sophia's back was turned, Liz puckered up and winked.

"Are you coming for dinner, Phi?" she asked. Maggie widened her eyes to let Liz know the invitation was not appreciated.

"Thanks, but no thanks, Liz. I need the time to get settled in. I only have the weekend before my first day at work."

"Okay," said Liz, holding Maggie's gaze with a wry grin. "If you change your mind, you're welcome. We have plenty."

Maggie grimaced to communicate that Liz should stop encouraging her. Ignoring the body language and Maggie's worries about Sophia finding out, Liz kissed her cheek. "Later."

After Liz left, Maggie became aware that Sophia was studying her. "It's nice to see you getting along. For a while there, I thought you'd never forgive her."

"Neither did I," Maggie admitted, "but things change."

Sophia clambered down from the ladder. "You know, I'd like to take a break. My legs ache."

"Good idea. I'll make some tea." The electric tea pot was one of the first things Maggie had unpacked, so she knew exactly where to find it. She'd also stopped by the supermarket to pick up some kitchen necessities. Thanks to her mother, Sophia now had milk in the fridge, sugar, tea and coffee, and a collection of fresh herbs and spices, not that she had time to cook.

Maggie had tried to teach both of her adopted daughters how run a household, but Sophia made a better oncologist than housekeeper. Her daughter's professional achievements filled Maggie with pride, but like most feminist women of her generation, she'd grown up thinking she could have it all. It was nothing but propaganda. When the adoption agency called to say that two girls from Romania were available, Maggie had given up her Broadway dreams to raise her daughters. That's why she cut off anyone who criticized Lucy for giving up her infant daughter to save her singing career. Maggie understood her sacrifice.

When the electric teapot clicked, indicating it had come to

temperature, Maggie poured the hot water into two battered Baylor University Medical Center mugs.

"If you'd like something to eat," Maggie said, filling the lab beaker that Sophia used as a creamer with milk for their tea, "I brought a banana bread."

"Thanks, I'll save it for breakfast. I'll skip the extra calories."

Sophia had an attractive figure, but she was right about the extra calories. Alina's PTSD and chronic anxiety left her too thin, but Sophia had the opposite problem. As the elder, she'd needed to look after both herself and her younger sister while they were trapped in the overcrowded Romanian orphanage. Instinct forced her to take care of herself first. She had natural good looks—well-proportioned features, smooth raven hair, and a clear, olive complexion. Maggie had tried to pass along her beauty secrets to both daughters. Alina was a willing student, but whenever Maggie had suggested that Sophia put on some makeup, she'd snarled and said that she was too busy saving lives to worry about looking pretty.

"I hope this new job isn't a mistake," Sophia said, carefully straining the liquid out of her teabag with her spoon. "I know I'm a good oncologist, but managing an entire department is a big deal."

"Liz thinks you're ready."

"She says she was scared shitless when she became the youngest chief of surgery at Yale. She pretended she owned the role until she did."

Maggie translated the idea into the popular formula. "Fake it until you make it."

"Yup." Sophia looked thoughtful. "Mom, I'm glad you're living over there. I admit I was worried when you first moved in."

"Why?"

"Well, you've been a vagabond since your divorce. First, you buy a house with Alina, then you move in with Sam, move back in with Alina, who throws you out in a fit..."

"To be fair, Sophia, I'd sold the house to Alina and Steve when I thought I'd found my forever home with Sam."

"That's my main worry. Lesbian relations are so volatile. They don't last."

Maggie bristled at hearing the old myth come out of her daughter's mouth. She tried to speak calmly. "Well, let's look at the facts. I was married to Liz almost as long as I was married to your father. We've known each other for over fifty years and still care deeply. I'd call that a durable relationship. Wouldn't you?"

"At first, I thought you'd moved in with Liz because you were desperate. I assumed when you'd find something better, you'd move on."

"But as you saw, the apartment is spacious. The setting is beautiful. Why would I leave?"

"You could do better. You certainly have the money to live by the ocean."

"In fact, Lucy offered me the apartment next to her beach house, but I turned it down." Maggie wondered why Sophia was suddenly so worried about where she lived. It wasn't as if she were a bag lady in a homeless encampment. "Sophia, what's your concern?"

Sophia trained her dark eyes on her. "I just hope you're not waiting for Liz to take you back, like you waited for Dad. I still can't believe you humiliated yourself like that." This was one of those times when Maggie regretted teaching her daughters to speak their minds. Before barking out a response, she took a deep breath. Sophia was tougher than Alina, but not always. Sometimes, she still saw the vulnerable little girl clutching her little sister's hand.

"I'm not waiting around for Liz," said Maggie, staring into her teacup.

"Good, because she's married to Lucy now, and they seem really happy." When Maggie looked up, Sophia was peering deeply into her eyes. "So, Mom, are you seeing anyone?"

Maggie had to resort to her acting skills so that Sophia wouldn't read everything she was thinking. This interrogation was getting much too close for comfort.

"Not at the moment," Maggie replied casually. "I'm too busy with school and acting, and you know how it is. The harder you look, the less likely it is you'll find anyone." Maggie was commiserating with someone who never had time for a relationship. To her knowledge, Sophia had never had a steady partner.

"You're a young seventy-one, Mom, and still beautiful. You're a good catch for anyone, male or female." In reply, Maggie simply stared at her daughter. "I know what you're thinking, Mom. Who am I to tell you what to do, but I worry about you."

"As far as I know, Phi, I am still *compos mentis* and can decide how to lead my life. If I need advice, I'll let you know." Maggie's tone was colder than she'd intended, but instead of taking the hint, Sophia continued. Like Liz, she never knew when to let go of an argument.

"Mom, you're not going to meet anyone holed up in the woods with a married couple."

"Sophia, that's enough! I don't tell you how to run your life. I'll thank you not to tell me how to run mine. Allow me to take responsibility for myself. That's how to show respect, especially for your mother."

"Fine, Mom. But that doesn't mean I don't have an opinion. I think it's weird that you're living with your ex-wife. I'm sure people talk."

"Do you think I care?" asked Maggie, exasperated that she couldn't get Sophia to back off. At this point, she just wanted to blurt out the truth. She only hesitated because she'd promised to discuss it with the others first.

"I'm sure Lucy cares. She has her church to worry about."

"Sophia, it's none of your business, *do you understand*?" Maggie enunciated the words with precision, hoping the message would be clearer.

"Yes, Mom, I understand, but I worry about you. Now that Dad's dying, you and Alina are all I have!"

"Your father is *dying*?" Maggie repeated, knocked back by the shock. "I thought he was cancer free."

Sophia assumed her doctor's voice. "Not quite. He was in remission, but the cancer was stage four when they found it. They'd been giving him anti-androgen drugs to keep the cancer in check, but eventually it figures out how to get around them. His PSA suddenly shot way up, so they did a scan and found the cancer had metastasized to two ribs and the spine."

Maggie was afraid to ask the dreaded question, but she did. "How long does he have?"

"It's still what we call 'low volume,' so it's hard to tell, but maybe a year. Two, if he's really lucky."

"I'm sorry, Sophia," said Maggie and meant it sincerely. Barry might be a clumsy fool, but he'd stood by her during all those awful fertility treatments. He'd agreed to adopt two at-risk orphans, so Maggie could realize her dream of motherhood. It wasn't his fault she hadn't loved him. "Have you told Alina?" Maggie asked cautiously.

"Not yet. You know how she freaks out when something's wrong with any of us."

"We should probably tell her together."

"As you might imagine, I've gotten pretty good at breaking bad news. In my line of work, it's a job requirement." Sophia's tone was brave, but she looked grim. "I'm going up to Alina's this weekend. Maybe you can come with me."

Maggie nodded. She'd lost her taste for arguing about living with Liz and Lucy, or for explaining the situation to Sophia. This wasn't the time.

❋❋❋

Lucy had spent the entire day moderating church disputes and listening to people in emotional and spiritual distress. The last thing she wanted to do was more counseling, but Maggie was so distraught. "I just wanted to say, no, I'm not waiting for Liz to take me back because she already has!"

"Be glad you didn't say it, Maggie. Besides being provocative, a statement like that would have shut down any meaningful conversation. And yes, the agreement to consult all of us before telling people applies to everyone, even family."

Beside her, Liz loudly cleared her throat. "Maggie, I'm sorry to hear about Barry. Most prostate cancers are slow growing. The longer they keep it low volume, the better the chance that he'll die of something else first."

Maggie gave Liz a filthy look. "You never liked him."

"It's nothing personal. I lost out to him because he had a dick, but in the end, I ended up with his wife and his kids. *Schadenfreude* is my guilty pleasure." Liz raised her whiskey glass.

"Liz..." Lucy warned gently. "No one deserves cancer."

"Of course not. Maggie, I don't know the details, but if Barry has no other comorbidities, Sophia's prognosis may be overly pessimistic."

"Let's hope you're right. I have my own issues with Barry, but I don't wish him any harm." Maggie poured herself and Lucy another glass of wine. "I've decided to go with Sophia on Saturday when she tells her sister. Alina will freak out, but we *must* tell her. Remember when she found out about my cancer recurrence after the fact? She wouldn't speak to you or Sophia for months afterwards."

Lucy wondered which was worse, shocking people or withholding the facts and risking their fury when they finally learned the truth.

"Lucy, I'd like you to come."

"Me?" Lucy cuddled back under Liz's protective arm. This was their first night together since Sophia had left. Lucy had been looking forward to a quiet night with her partners. Now, the evening had become about Maggie's crisis.

"Alina looks up to you, Lucy," Maggie explained. "You helped her pull her out of the wreckage she made of her marriage. I could really use your help."

Of course, Lucy wanted to help, but she knew involving herself professionally was inappropriate. "I'll come as Alina's friend, but not as a counselor or a priest."

"I'm not expecting you to wear your collar."

"Good because I won't," replied Lucy with a firm look.

"I'll come too," Liz volunteered.

"Liz, I love you dearly, but..." Maggie began, which meant that something unflattering was coming, "...you can be so tactless sometimes."

"But not in medical situations," Liz replied evenly. "After all these years, I've gotten pretty good at delivering bad news."

"You're a great doctor, Liz, but where Barry is concerned, your hatred of him always comes through."

Lucy reached out and took Maggie's hand. "Maggie, Liz is kindly offering her help. Give her the benefit of the doubt. She's bailed you out before when Alina had problems. It might be good to have her there."

"That's true. Liz even drove to Logan in a blizzard to pick her up."

"That was quite a night," said Liz, remembering. "But Sophia was going up alone to see her sister. She invited you, and now there are four of us. How do we invite ourselves without being obvious?" Liz thought for a moment before her face lit up. "When in doubt, bring food! We could bring some frozen dishes and say we're coming to restock their freezer."

Maggie instantly warmed to the idea. "I'll offer to make dinner for all of us. Steve will like that. Alina doesn't cook much since she's been on this new assignment. During the week, the family lives on our harvest dinners."

"At least, the kids are getting healthy food," said Liz. "But are we going to tell them about us?"

They both looked at Lucy.

"Maggie, I'm so proud of you that you didn't tell Sophia for the wrong reasons, especially because of Barry's illness. I don't think Alina needs to hear about our living arrangements on top of the bad news about her father."

Liz scowled. "And why do we have to confess what we do in bed or explain our relationship to anyone? We're all adults. We're not breaking any laws or hurting anyone. We don't tell people about Lucy's toy collection. Why do they need to know we sleep together?"

"You told Olivia," Maggie reminded her.

"It was a need-to-know situation. She needed the context to give us advice. But honestly, I dread facing our lawyers. Of course, Harriet already thinks I'm crazy. This will be the third marital agreement she's drawn up for me."

Maggie looked unsympathetic. "Maybe you should stop getting married."

Lucy just wanted this conversation concluded so they could go to bed. "Maggie, why don't you propose your plan to Alina and let us know?"

"I'll tell her to expect the three of us, and we'll make dinner for them. Katrina and Nicki will be glad to see us. Between the election and figuring out our situation, I've barely seen them."

"We have a plan," Lucy said, getting up. "And now I'm going to bed. Five AM comes early."

Liz got up too and turned to Maggie. "Well? Are you coming?"

"Thank you, yes. I need a cuddle tonight."

"Me too," said Lucy.

Liz just rolled her eyes.

❋❋❋

Liz watched Lucy look around Alina's kitchen with barely disguised disgust. Only Maggie had been there recently, so the state of the house came as a shock. Sophia, who'd arrived earlier, was scrambling to help her sister put things in order.

"I'll just put these trays downstairs in your freezer," Liz said, trying to ease herself out of the frenzied activity. She got halfway down the stairs before the girls began following her.

"Thank you for bringing us dinners, Grandma Liz," Katrina said formally.

"You're welcome, Trina. I heard you like them."

"We love them! It's the only time Mommy cooks." The girl's honest remark made Liz worry about their nutrition. She hoped Alina didn't bridge the gaps with fast food.

"Does your mom make salad for you and veggies?"

"Sometimes. I learned how to make salad too," Katrina said proudly.

"It's fun, isn't it?" The seal around the freezer had formed a vacuum. Liz set the trays on top to use two hands. "You can put all kinds of different vegetables in a salad, not just tomatoes."

"Mommy says she's going to ask you how to grow tomatoes this summer," Nicky said.

"She's afraid there won't be enough food to buy, like in the pandemic," Katarina explained.

Liz knew the girls were smart and paid attention to everything. It saddened her that worry about the political situation had infected even the youngest generation. "I can teach you how to grow lots of veggies in containers. Or I can bring up my rototiller and clear a patch for a real garden if your mommy doesn't mind me digging up the lawn. Which would you like?"

"Both!" said Nicky happily. Of course, she did. That kid had an enthusiasm for life that nothing could dampen.

Liz enrolled the kids in helping her bring more trays of food into the basement. When they returned to the kitchen, the adults were speaking in hushed tones. From their somber expressions, Liz guessed Sophia had already shared the sad news about Barry's failing health and bent down to whisper into Katrina's ear, "Why don't you go watch TV with your sister and let the grownups talk?"

Katrina eyed her cautiously. The curious kid would have preferred to stay and listen. Liz leaned on her knees and peered into her eyes to reinforce that it was more than a suggestion. Finally, the girl took her sister's hand and headed down the hall. After they left, Liz leaned in the doorway and listened. Maggie and Sophia should take the lead in this conversation, but when Alina asked how long her father had to live, Liz decided to insinuate herself.

"I've known patients with prostate cancer to live well past their stated expiration date." She gave Sophia a conciliatory look with the hope of averting an argument. "Different people have different outcomes. No doctor can predict with certainty how long someone will live. It's just a guess."

"More than a guess," insisted Sophia, clearly annoyed to have her answer pre-empted. "A prognosis is informed by data."

Liz smiled to smooth her feathers. "I don't know all the details like you do, Phi."

Sophia took a deep breath and looked directly into her sister's eyes. "Liz is right. We don't know the exact time Daddy has left, but we do know that it's not long, so we should be prepared." Fortunately, she didn't add, for the worst.

Alina twisted away from her sister and sought refuge in Maggie's arms. Lucy soothingly made circles and figure eights on the young woman's back, while she cried. Finally, Alina brushed away her tears with her fists. "We should go see Daddy before Christmas."

Across the room, Steve's eyes grew wide. Alina heading to the west coast would leave him with the responsibility for looking after the girls.

"Don't worry about the kids," Liz said without stopping to think. "We'll look after them, right Lucy?"

Lucy nodded and smiled graciously. "Of course."

"But they'll miss school," Alina said, perceiving the flaws in the plan.

"No they won't," Liz said. "I can drive them to their sitter and pick them up. That's one benefit of being semi-retired. My schedule is flexible."

"You're busy, Liz," Alina said. "That's too much for you."

Liz shook her head. "Never too busy to help family."

Alina left the security of Maggie's arms and went to Liz. "I worried when you and Mom divorced that we'd lose you, but you've always been there for us. Thank you."

Liz enfolded her in a sturdy embrace. "You're welcome. I'm always here for you," she whispered into the young woman's ear. "I wish the news were better."

"What did you mean when you said you can't say how long he has?" she asked, looking directly into Liz's eyes.

"Your sister probably knows more about the situation than I do, but men can live a long time with prostate cancer. In most cases, the older you are, the slower it grows. Some men can even outlive it and die of something else." Sophia's pursed lips indicated she didn't approve of Liz's version of the prognosis, but like all medical personnel, she'd been taught never to argue with a senior doctor. Instead, she looked at the clock. "Mom, if you're going to make dinner, you should get started. I need to get home at a reasonable hour. Tomorrow is my first day at the new job."

The others drifted into the living room. Sophia and Liz stayed behind to help Maggie. She handed Liz some onions to chop. Every knife Liz tried was dull. She found a porcelain cup without glaze on the bottom and ran the edge of the chef's knife along it.

Sophia watched. "I never knew you could do that," she said admiringly.

"If you know where to look, there's always a solution," Liz said, demonstrating the angle at which to hold the knife.

"I can see why Mom keeps you around."

"Yes, she can be useful."

Sophia couldn't help but notice the loving look Maggie beamed in Liz's direction. "Mom, I finally figured out you're in some weird ménage with Liz and Lucy. I don't want to know what you do in private, but you seem happier than I've seen you in a long time."

"Because I am."

Sophia turned to Liz. "For God's sake, just don't hurt her. She's already been through enough."

"I swear to you, Sophia, I would never deliberately hurt your mother. She's literally my oldest friend, and I love her. Lucy is the soul of kindness, and she loves your mother too. You have nothing to fear from us."

Sophia didn't look convinced, but her brow smoothed, and she nodded to acknowledge she'd heard. "Just don't tell, Alina. She won't understand."

"Eventually, we'll tell her," Maggie said, "but not today. The news about your father is hard enough."

Sophia drew a long breath. "Mom, what can I do to help?

Maggie handed her the bag of potatoes. "Peel these."

"Hold on," said Liz. "I'll sharpen a paring knife."

Maggie smiled at her daughter. "See? She is useful."

Chapter 18

"Thank you for coming," said Lucy, reaching up to embrace the tall redhead. Their resemblance was uncanny. Except for her blue eyes and height, Emily Bartlett could be her mother's much younger self.

"You don't have to thank me, Mom. Now is a good time to come home. Classes are over until the new year. When Katrina called me, it was like a command performance. How could I refuse?"

"Katrina and Nicky are your biggest fans." Lucy hooked her arm in Emily's and led her into the kitchen. "They'll be so excited to see you."

"Where are they?"

"They'll be here soon. Liz drove to Scarborough to pick them up." Lucy gestured to a plate on the island. "Liz made those blueberry muffins for you. Help yourself while I make us some coffee."

"You don't have to wait on me, Mom. I have my own place now. I even know how to cook, thanks to Denise. Since *Opa* told me about Ferraro's, I cheat sometimes. Not regularly. I can't afford fancy takeout on a junior professor's salary. Of course, all those Italian specialties will be even more expensive if he puts on those tariffs."

Lucy was impressed that her neurodiverse daughter was so aware of the political situation. She credited Denise, Emily's ex-girlfriend, who'd encouraged her to read the New York Times every day and discuss the news as a way of improving her social skills.

Although Denise had been good for Emily, Lucy was glad that she'd moved on both for Emily's sake and the future of her career. Hobbs had been a good place for Denise while the pandemic shut down music and theater, but Denise couldn't build her singing career hibernating in a small town in Maine. Lucy had too much invested in helping Denise learn how to sound like a natural alto instead of the countertenor she was before she'd transitioned.

Fortunately, Denise's baritone boyfriend had helped her get a contract job at Milan's LaScala opera house, which meant she could stay in Italy for a while. With all the backlash against trans that the incoming administration had encouraged, staying away from the US made sense.

"Have you heard from Denise?" Lucy asked casually.

With her mouth full of muffin, Emily could only nod. Lucy was glad but not surprised to hear that Emily and Denise were speaking again. Their on-again, off-again romance had always been less important than their bond over being so different and their shared love of music. "Denise is coming to Boston to get the rest of her clothes," Emily explained after swallowing what she'd been chewing. "She's afraid to travel in and out of the country once he gets into office."

"Unfortunately, she's right to be worried." Lucy brought their coffee cups to the table. She watched Emily add what she would consider too much sugar, but she didn't say anything. Even mild criticism could make Emily withdraw and become sullen.

"Things won't get that bad, will they, Mom?" Emily's eyes anxiously searched Lucy's face.

Lucy usually moderated what she said to Emily because of her high-end autism. But Emily was no longer the frightened teenager Lucy had rescued from a homeless shelter. She'd grown into a savvy, politically aware young woman. Maybe it was time to speak to her like one.

"Yes, honey, I am afraid. I'm afraid for everyone who isn't an able male, white, heterosexual, and Christian."

"That includes us. But what can we do?"

"Right now, not much. We can support one another and be as kind as we can."

Emily tapped up the muffin crumbs with her fingertips. "Are you worried, Mom? *Project 2025* calls for abolishing same-sex marriage. You don't think that will change how Liz feels about you. She'll still love you."

The statement chafed uncomfortably close to the truth. Before Maggie had left for California, they'd agreed to tell their children about the change. Maggie didn't want the unsettling news to disrupt Alina's visit with her dying father. She'd decided to wait to wait until their return and tell Alina with the support of her partners. Lucy wished for Liz's solid presence while she broke the news to Emily, but once the kids arrived, meaningful conversation would be difficult. Lucy decided to seize the moment. "Emily, there's something I need to tell you..." Lucy began. The preamble sounded ominous, so she hurried to add, "...nothing bad."

Emily looked up from preparing her coffee to show she was listening. Unlike some of the responses she'd learned to blend in socially, this one seemed natural. "What's up, Mom?"

"We really like having Aunt Maggie here. She looks after the house when I'm traveling. She cooks for us. So she became more and more a part of our lives until we..." Lucy just couldn't say it.

"...became a throuple," Emily said, grinning. "Denise and I took bets on how long it would take."

Lucy had to remind herself to close her mouth. "What?"

"Denise won. She doesn't miss a thing," said Emily, reaching for another muffin. "I owe her twenty dollars."

"You made a bet?" asked Lucy, although she'd heard perfectly.

Emily's blue eyes grew large. "Did we do something wrong?" she asked gravely. "I'm sorry."

"No, sweetie, not at all. I'm just surprised you would even think about such a thing."

"Why, Mom? I'm smart, you know." Lucy nearly burst out laughing at the understatement. Emily's high IQ was in the genius range. "Denise was the first to guess it would happen, but when I paid attention, I saw it too. Aunt Liz loves you so much, but I could tell she never stopped loving Aunt Maggie."

Lucy managed to compose herself. "And what do you think about it?"

"I think it's cool that you all love each other." Lucy hadn't known what to expect when she told Emily. Changes sometimes upset her, but she could also be coldly objective. Of course someone as different as Emily wouldn't see anything wrong with the unusual arrangement. Why did other people find it so shocking?

"Thanks for being so understanding...and accepting," Lucy said, gingerly reaching out for Emily's hand. Physical contact, even from her mother, wasn't always welcome.

"I love you, Mom, and I love Aunt Liz and Aunt Maggie. It's all good."

The sound of voices from the hall meant Liz had returned with the children. Nicky tackled Emily and hung on like a terrier. Katrina waited until Nicki moved away before wrapping Emily in a suffocating hug. "Grandma Liz is going to take us to the Christmas Prelude in Kennebunk. Are you coming?" the girl asked solemnly.

Emily bent down to be at eye-level with Nicky. "Of course, I am! I love the Christmas Prelude."

"Grandma said we can see Santa Claus," Nicky said in an excited voice, "and tell him what we want for Christmas!"

"That sounds like fun," Lucy said. "Can I come too?"

"Grownups don't need to talk to Santa," Katrina informed Lucy in a matter-of-fact tone.

"Why not? Otherwise, how will he know what I want for Christmas?" Lucy countered, playing along.

"Aunt Lucy just wants to do Christmas shopping," said Liz with an eyeroll. "But we'll need to dress warmly. Getting cold out there." She bent to kiss Lucy. "You sure you're okay with this idea?"

Lucy pulled her closer so she could whisper into her ear. "Emily knows."

Liz's brows went up. "She does?" she whispered back. "Did you tell her?"

"No, she figured it out. She and Denise had a bet on how long it would take."

Liz chuckled. "Well, good. Saves us the trouble of making an announcement." She gave Emily a warm pat on the shoulder. "Welcome home, kid. Can you stay a while?"

"I'd like to stay until after Christmas if that's okay." Lucy's heart took a leap of joy at the idea that her daughter was home again.

"Of course, it's okay," Liz assured her. "Now, who's ready for blueberry pancakes?"

Three young hands shot up.

***

While Maggie and her daughters sat with Barry in the solarium of his Santa Cruz home, his second wife hovered outside the door. Like his other love interests since the divorce, Heather was young enough to be his daughter. Her bleach blond hair, plumped lips, and blue eyes made her the personification of the right wing ideal of female beauty. Maggie hoped that Barry hadn't gone over to the dark side, but given his sorry state, he would never live to vote in another major election.

Maggie tried not to stare at the man she'd once called her husband. She hadn't seen him in a dozen years, not since Sophia's graduation from medical school. Recent pictures had shown him with a full head of hair. That was before the chemo and anti-androgen drugs. The high school quarterback's muscular limbs were now sticks, but his belly and face were bloated. These obvious signs of decline suggested the end was near. Against all hope, Maggie had known that Liz was trying to be kind when she'd said a prognosis is just a guess. Sophia's estimate of Barry's life span was probably more accurate.

Alina couldn't take her eyes off her father. When Barry's new wife went into the kitchen to prepare lunch for her guests, Alina jumped up to help as if she couldn't wait to get out of the room.

"She's taking it hard," Barry said with a sigh, watching his adoptive daughter retreat.

"It's not easy to watch your parent suffer from cancer," Sophia said in a surprisingly unsympathetic tone. "I tried to prepare her, Dad. I really did."

Barry narrowed his eyes as he turned to his elder daughter. "I'm sure you did, Phi. You're a good doctor."

She glanced away rather than meet his gaze. "Except we might not be here if you'd listened to me and had your prostate removed."

He sighed deeply. "I wish I had done a lot of things. Too late now." Barry focused his eyes on Maggie. They looked strikingly blue against his jaundiced complexion. On the ride from the airport, Sophia had tried to prepare them for Barry's condition, explaining that stress on his liver had turned his skin yellow. "Phi, would you mind giving your mom and me a few minutes alone?"

Indignant at being dismissed, Sophia gave Maggie a sharp look, but her tone was mild. "Sure, Dad. I'll go see if Heather needs any help."

After Sophia left, Barry took a moment to gather his thoughts. "I want to thank you for coming all this way to see me. I thought I might never see you again before..." His voice broke. The deep sadness in his eyes made Maggie's eyes sting. She had to draw on her acting skills to hold back the tears.

"It's not over yet," she said, trying to sound encouraging.

"Not yet, but it will be soon." He heaved out a big sigh. "The chemo is awful, and it's not working anyway. I don't know how Phi can live with herself filling people with that shit. It's all heavy metals. Pure poison." As a chemical engineer, he would know. "It's not so bad going in, but when it starts working a few days later, you can barely get out of bed. You lie there, waiting for it to end and wonder if the gain is worth the pain."

"Oh, Barry, I'm so sorry!"

"I'm sorry too...about a lot of things." He swallowed loud

enough for Maggie to hear. He was holding back tears too. "Mostly, I'm sorry I couldn't be what you needed."

"It wasn't your fault. I couldn't be what you needed. You thought by marrying the popular girl, you were getting the perfect wife. I thought by marrying the football hero with a bright future, I was getting the perfect husband. We fell in love with what our parents wanted for us, not with each other."

"God knows, I tried," Barry said, reaching for her hand. His felt cold.

"I know you did. You were so generous and brave to take on the girls. We both knew they would have so many problems"

With a smile, he glanced toward the dining room, where their daughters were setting the table. "But they both turned out all right."

"Yes, they did. I'm so proud of them."

"Me too. I love them to pieces." He focused his eyes on Maggie's face. "I want you to know that I really wanted it to work. I loved you."

This time, Maggie couldn't stop the tear before it made a wet trail down her cheek. She impatiently brushed it away with her fingertips. "You have nothing to be sorry for. You were a good husband. You stuck by me through all those awful fertility treatments. You went along with adopting the girls. You always took care of us."

"That's not true. I got so tired of trying. When I realized nothing could ever be enough, I had to escape. I just wish I had been honest with you instead of cheating."

"Please stop blaming yourself. I cheated on you too."

He looked surprised and curious. Fortunately, he didn't ask for the details, not that they mattered. It had happened so long ago. "We were both trying to get what we needed but couldn't get from each other," said Maggie.

Barry let go of her hand and sat back. He closed his eyes for a moment as if trying to rest so he could go on. Finally, he opened them again. "Sophia tells me you've gone back to Liz."

Maggie panicked and gave him the usual excuses for living in her ex's garage. "Rentals are hard to find and so expensive." His blue eyes nailed her for the dishonesty, but she babbled on. "It's a nice place. She built it for her mother, but she never stayed there. Not even once."

"Happens," Barry said, releasing her from his gaze. "I fixed up a space here for my mother. She died before the work was finished. Heather can get good rental income if she wants to rent it. The taxes here are unbelievable." He stopped to take a breath. "I'm sorry I forced you to sell the Connecticut house. It was expensive to live out here, and I needed the money."

"Barry, we don't need to confess all our sins," Maggie said, patting his arm. "Let's just enjoy our time together."

"Good idea," he said with a nod. "But I'm glad you're back with Liz. She got Phi that good job in Boston. Phi told me she got Alina's meds sorted out. She takes good care of you and the girls. And she's what you always wanted."

Maggie studied Barry, wondering what he knew. "You know that Liz is married to another woman?"

"To a minister, right? Hopefully, that keeps her out of mischief." He grinned. Maggie couldn't believe she was having this bizarre conversation with her ex-husband. Fortunately, Heather came to the door to call them to lunch. After she left, Barry struggled to his feet with Maggie's help. He leaned heavily on her arm to reach his walker. Before they entered the dining room, he suddenly grabbed Maggie's hand and pressed it to his lips. "Maggie, I'm glad you came. Thank you. Thank you so much. Please take good care of yourself and our girls."

Maggie swallowed a lump in her throat. "I will," she promised.

❖❖❖

Liz wished the lighting were better. Not only was it hard to see what they were doing, but this deserted area outside of Logan airport was notorious for drug and gang violence. Liz kept her pistol close while she helped Denise unload her storage locker. Given the shady reputation of the place, she was glad she could legally carry a gun. Since she'd been hauled off to jail during a raid on the strip club where she'd taken Erika for her bachelorette party, she made sure to keep her Massachusetts permit current.

Lucy glared through the window whenever Liz went by the passenger side. She was still fuming after being ordered to stay inside the truck with the doors locked. Not only was the place dangerous, but the December night was shockingly cold. It was early for such low temperatures. Denise almost never wore pants because she wanted to show off her slender, shapely legs. Tonight, she'd made a concession to the weather and was wearing jeans.

Liz maneuvered the last box into the back of the truck. "I don't want to make another trip, so I'm glad it all fits." After a quick check for clearance, she closed the tailgate. "How much will it cost you to ship all this stuff?"

"Too much," Denise admitted, "but I'm not taking any chances. I don't know when I'll be able to come back."

"I hope for everyone's sake, it's soon. You don't want to be cut off from performing in the US. That will hamper your career." She cautiously looked around. "Let's get out of here. I don't like this place."

"That's why it was cheap," Denise explained, getting in behind Lucy.

Liz hauled herself into the driver's seat. Denise leaned through the gap between the front seats. "Thank you, Liz. And you too, Lucy."

"I didn't do anything, but you're welcome," said Lucy briskly. Obviously, she was still resentful for being told she couldn't help.

They drove to the kiosk to drop off the keys. After the sleepy attendant passed them a clipboard for Denise to sign, Liz looked for the exit. "Denise, can you set your GPS for the shipping terminal? I was there with Sam last year, but we came from a different direction."

"I can do it," Lucy volunteered, determined to be helpful.

They finally found the terminal. While Denise made the arrangements, Liz and Lucy sat in the truck. "Denise's flight isn't until nine-thirty," said Liz. "Are you okay with taking her out to dinner?"

"As long as we don't stay out too late. Reshma asked me to take morning prayer tomorrow."

"Anything but airport food," Denise said when she learned of the plan. "Now that La Scala hired me for the season, I miss the traveling, but I *don't* miss airports."

"But you're still doing the summer festivals?" asked Lucy.

"Yes, but as long as he's in office, I'm not coming home. Like it's up to me! My passport shows my chosen gender. They might not even let me in!" Denise sighed. "You two should come visit me before travel becomes complicated. Rinaldo's condo is too small for guests, but I know some wonderful small hotels nearby."

Liz could feel Lucy staring at the side of her face and knew she was waiting for her to say something. "Would you mind if we brought someone else along?" Liz finally asked.

"Emily? She's talked about coming to visit."

Liz engaged Denise's eyes in the mirror. "Actually, I was thinking of Maggie Fitzgerald."

"Hah! I knew it! That means Emily owes me twenty bucks. No, I don't mind. In fact, I'd love it. Did you know that Maggie emails me regularly?"

"No," said Lucy, surprised. "I didn't know you'd become such good friends." When Maggie had returned to her role of music director of St. Margaret's after Denise left to pursue her singing career, they'd locked horns over unacknowledged competition and differences in musical style.

"Glad to hear it," Lucy said.

"She asks my advice on music, but most of her emails are gossip about what's going on in Hobbs. I'm surprised she didn't tell me about your new *arrangement.*"

"We made a pact to agree before we tell anyone," Lucy explained. "For obvious reasons, the information is sensitive."

"I understand, and no one will ever hear it from me. Don't worry, Lucy. I have your back just like you had mine."

Lucy turned to Liz. "Liz, what do you think about a trip to Milan after Christmas? I'll be burnt out from all the services. Tom will be in Florida, but I'm sure Susan and Reshma can manage."

Liz shrugged. "I said I'd travel with you wherever you go. We can ask Maggie when we get home."

"Lucy, I know you've sung at La Scala many times, but I'd love to show Liz and Maggie backstage."

"You know how it is, Denise. When you're there for a performance, you're in and out, and one dressing room becomes like another. I wouldn't mind a backstage tour, either."

"Perfect. I'll look for accommodations as soon as I get home."

"Lucy, any luck finding a place to eat?" Liz asked, "otherwise I'm just driving around in circles."

"There's a tavern nearby with a four-and-a-half-star rating, serving American food. The prices seem reasonable."

"At this point, I don't care what I eat," Liz growled. "I'm starving."

"Don't believe a word she says," Lucy confided to Denise. "She's always starving, and she cares very much about what she eats."

A low chuckle emerged from the backseat.

Chapter 19

Maggie stared at the pile of papers in front of her. They were only at the beginning of their document review. Liz had insisted everyone read the advance directives first to make sure the end-of-life instructions were correct. Next was the power of attorney. Liz explained that it gave each of them the right to act on behalf of the others. So far, Maggie had been keeping up, but when Liz got to the document forming their corporation, her mind began to wander.

She thought of the visit to California to see Barry. After their private talk, his eyes kept seeking hers. He looked sad and contrite, as if begging forgiveness. Yet it was she who should be asking forgiveness for using him to pretend she was someone she wasn't. Before they'd left, Maggie had hugged his skeletal frame and kissed his cheek, probably for the last time. She was glad that she'd come in person to say goodbye, but it was a sobering reminder that time was not promised.

"How are you doing there, Maggie?" Liz asked, sensing her distraction. Maggie wondered how Liz could tell she wasn't keeping up, then realized she hadn't been turning the pages fast enough. For someone who could be oblivious to her surroundings, Liz was remarkably observant.

Maggie was becoming impatient. "Liz, you've read every word of these documents. Why can't you just explain them to us?" Lucy looked up and smiled conspiratorially.

"You need to know what you're signing tomorrow," Liz insisted. "These documents merge our wealth: this house, Lucy's beach house, all our investments. Everything we own will be held by this corporation. This is huge!"

"I know it is, but you understand it, and I don't." Liz glanced at Lucy looking for sympathy.

"I'm sorry, Liz, but I don't understand either," Lucy admitted. "I'm just reading words on the page to make you happy."

Liz separately tapped each finger of her right hand on the table-top. Maggie could bet she'd learned that calming trick from Lucy. Finally, Liz said, "I don't want to hear either of you say later that you didn't fully understand what you were signing."

Lucy directly held her gaze. "Liz, we already agreed that we want to do this. You always say if there's no good will, a contract is not worth the paper it's printed on." A nostalgic smile came to Liz's lips, and Maggie recognized one of her mother's business maxims.

"That's true, but it's important for us all to be on the same page. All right, I'll do my best to summarize the key points."

Maggie took off her glasses and sat back to watch Liz do what she did so well—explain complicated things in a way anyone could understand. Maggie often wondered if she'd missed her calling and should have been a teacher instead. Of course, as chief of surgery in a large teaching hospital, she'd had plenty of opportunities.

"We're keeping the existing bank and investment accounts both for tax reasons and to maintain their identity should anyone want out of this arrangement."

"Like the prenup," said Maggie, trying to show she was paying attention.

"That still pisses you off, doesn't it?" snarled Liz.

"You didn't ask Lucy to sign one."

Lucy reached for Maggie's hand. "It's in the past, Maggie. Let it go."

Liz didn't look willing to let it go, either. "Maggie, I didn't know better when I married you. Harriet advised it, and I followed my lawyer's advice. It protected you too because you kept your own wealth."

"So why should we do this if that arrangement was so great?" Maggie asked.

"Because it shows that we trust one another," Lucy explained.

"It means we've decided to be a family and pool our resources. Every month, we'll pay a fixed amount into a separate account to cover our common expenses like food. No more paying out of your pocket for groceries."

"I feel like I'm watching a corporate merger or something equally unromantic," Maggie said, crossing her arms on her chest. The closed gesture was deliberate.

"Well, that's what we're doing," Liz conceded, "but it's the closest we can get to being married."

"I was expecting some kind of ceremony, where we pledge ourselves to one another." She glanced at Lucy. "That's your department, isn't it?"

Lucy looked sad. "There are no services for joining three people. Maybe afterward, we can pray together."

Maggie looked at each of them in turn. "For the first time, I'm nervous. This is real. We're a throuple."

"Getting cold feet?" Liz asked, peering directly into Maggie's eyes. "We don't have to do this."

For the first time, Maggie realized why Liz had gone to the trouble of involving her lawyer and financial advisor. "I asked for a lease, and you're going through all this for me?" Unexpectedly, tears came to her eyes. She dabbed them with a napkin left over from dinner. When she looked up, Liz was watching her with a little pucker between her brows. "No, Liz, these aren't stage tears. They're real."

"I wasn't doubting you, Mag. I'm just glad you finally got it. Because the lawyer's costs for this are going to be astronomical."

"Liz!" Lucy hissed and put her arm around Maggie. "She's showing her appreciation for your efforts to make her feel wanted and safe."

Liz came around the table to where Maggie sat and leaned on her knees, so she could see Maggie's face. "I'm sorry, Maggie. Like you always say, I'm stupid when it comes to women."

Maggie murmured, "Yes, you are, but I love you anyway."

"That's two of us," Lucy said, "but, Liz, try to be a little more sensitive."

***

While they were waiting for Maggie to return from the ladies' room, Liz studied the women sitting across the table. In the center was Harriet Keene, Liz's lawyer since she'd first bought the practice in Hobbs. Like so many women in town, she used to be a highflyer, negotiating multi-million-dollar real estate deals in Boston. She'd come to Portland during the building boom thirty years ago. Now, she pretended to be a small-town lawyer doing property transfers and wills, not unlike the way Liz pretended to be a country doctor. Beside Harriet sat Olivia Enright, once known as the "Female Wolf of Wall Street." On Harriet's other side was Melissa Morgenstern, one of the country's foremost trust attorneys. This morning, she was demonstrating that she'd adjusted to life in Hobbs by leaving her power suit at home and wearing business casual.

These women had come together, without question, to help Liz and her two partners do something unheard of, or at least very un-traditional. None of them had yet called her crazy, except Harriet, but she'd said it with a big smile and a hug of congratulations. While they waited, they talked about plans for Christmas, now less than a week away. The select board had approved Olivia's scheme to hold a party at the safety building after the Christmas parade. It would be catered by the town's restaurants, but paid for by private donations, just as Olivia had envisioned. Everyone at the table had contributed generously.

Sitting beside Liz, Lucy answered text messages. With all the special liturgies, the holidays were a busy time of year for St. Margaret's clergy. The staff was busy with pastoral visits and coun-seling because the holidays dredged up pain for people who'd lost loved ones or were alone. They worked with the town departments to create a sense of community. On Christmas day, the priests would be at the firehouse, serving the meal the firemen cooked. Seats at the table were offered free to anyone who reserved a place. Liz and staff from the practice would be there too. Maggie and Tony would provide the entertainment.

Maggie returned to the table. "Sorry to keep you all waiting."

"With this bunch, you can always count on us using the time profitably," Harriet said affably. "We've got the holidays all planned."

"Glad to hear it. I've still got my Christmas cookies to bake."

"Somehow it all gets done," said Olivia. "Like they say, 'need something done? Ask a busy person.'"

Harriet tapped her papers into a neat stack. "Okay, let's get started." She looked directly at Liz. "I have to say, Liz, I've seen you do some unusual things, but this one's a doozy. Are you all sure you want to do this?"

Three heads nodded.

"Before you sign anything, I want you to double check that I got your names right." She read them off, "Elizabeth Anne Stolz, Margaret Mary Fitzgerald, and Lucille Margaret Bartlett. Hmm, I hadn't realized you two shared a name. More than that apparently." She peered at Liz.

"The names are correct," Liz said impatiently. She was anxious and wanted to get this done.

"Well, we all know who's who," Harriet said with a reassuring smile, "but we want to make sure, for the sake of the filing, that the documents are accurate. We don't want someone trying to exploit a minor error to break the agreement. As we discussed, Liz and Lucy will remain legally married, but their marital assets, including their houses, will be held jointly by the three of you." She handed out Harriet and Morgenstern pens to everyone. "The documents include the revisions to your wills to name the remaining partners your heirs. Your natural heirs, children, grandchildren, nieces and nephews, are now covered by the trusts you funded from your assets. Before you sign, does anyone have any questions?"

"No," said Maggie, staring at the too fat ball-point pen that didn't feel right in her fingers. "Liz forced us to read all the documents last night."

"I know," said Melissa sympathetically, "it can be torture, even when you do it for a living."

The room was completely silent as Liz, Maggie, and Lucy signed the papers and passed them around the table for the others to witness. Because Olivia and the attorneys were named as trustees, Harriet called in two of her paralegals as witnesses. The only sound in the room was the light scratching of pens on paper. Liz realized she'd been holding her breath watching Maggie and Lucy sign. An admin efficiently collected the documents into folders for each of them. Along with the many agreements Liz had signed over the years, the originals would remain in Harriet's safe.

"The LLM Corporation is now fully executed and will be filed with the state of Maine this afternoon," Harriet said. "You are now the closest thing to being married that we three could manage. Congratulations, ladies."

"Hear, hear," said Olivia and started to clap. "And just to embarrass Liz, I've brought some champagne." She left to get the bottle. "Look at these nice plastic glasses I found. You can hardly tell them from the real thing. Feel the weight of them." As usual, she handed the bottle to Liz to open. "Here you go, Dr. Stud."

Liz gave her a filthy look. She'd futilely hoped she'd forgotten the new nickname. But Olivia never forgot a thing. The cork released with a satisfying pop. Liz returned the bottle to Olivia to serve. Of course, it was expensive champagne, not something off the shelf in the supermarket. It was so dry that Liz's mouth puckered.

"Liz, this was one of my most interesting projects," Melissa said, cornering her. "But what will you tell people?"

"Nothing," Liz replied instantly. "It's none of their business. As far as they're concerned, I'm married to Lucy, and Maggie is my tenant, just like before. For the sake of Lucy's job, that's all we can say. Eventually, we may tell close friends, but for now, mum's the word."

"That's got to be hard for you, Maggie," Olivia said in a surprisingly sympathetic tone.

"It is. Being married to either of these two amazing women would impress people. Lucy's job is more important than me shouting from the rooftops that I'm an equal partner. At this point in my life, who cares? I'd rather be known for my teaching and acting than who my spouse is."

"Congratulations, Maggie. I married Michael Enright for his WASP name and connections. Now, no one even remembers him."

"But they sure remember you," said Harriet, grinning. "Here's to the LLM corporation and its partners. May they live long and prosper."

Liz, who never turned down a *Star-Trek*-inspired toast, raised her glass.

❋❋❋

Lucy waited until they were alone in the foyer to the parking lot entrance to kiss her partners. She'd needed privacy to fully express the depth of her feelings. She made sure to hug Maggie especially tight because she needed applause and public acclaim like air to breathe. Foregoing the status of an official wife was an incalculable sacrifice. Some might say it was an act of desperation, but Lucy knew it was a profound gift of love.

The practical matters Liz had insisted needed to be addressed were behind them now, but they were still finding their way. *Learn to sit with the uncertainty*, Lucy reminded herself as they headed out to the parking lot.

"Let's have a nice lunch to celebrate," Liz suggested. "LaScala is open for lunch during the holidays."

Maggie stopped them with a hand on their arms. "I want to go to church first and pray."

Lucy knew she couldn't bring them to St. Margaret's. At that hour, the altar guild would be preparing the sanctuary for Sunday services. "We can't go to St. Margaret's, but I can let us into the summer chapel."

"I'd rather just go to the ocean and commune with nature," said Liz.

"At the summer chapel, we can have both," Maggie said. "We can pray and then go to the ocean."

Lucy noted as they approached the entrance to the chapel grounds that the red, white, and pale blue Episcopal flag was sun bleached and tattered. Once it made her heart sing to see the flag flying outside her church, but now she wondered what the future would bring. Churches all over the state were closing, their buildings being repurposed as community and arts centers, even homeless shelters. While most congregations were declining, hers had grown. She was still an ordained priest, but she no longer believed in everything the Church preached.

After Liz drove through the iron gate, Lucy closed it again so passing tourists wouldn't think the church was open to visitors. Locking the gate behind them suddenly became a metaphor for how her church role had trapped them in secrecy. With a heavy heart, she unlocked the heavy door of the stone chapel and put on the lights. The interior was as cold and damp as would be expected for a late December afternoon. Lucy and the maintenance workers were the only people who'd been in the building since services had ended in September.

Maggie knelt at the communion rail, but Liz protested that her bad knee wouldn't tolerate that position. Lucy knew there was more to it.

"It's okay. God doesn't require groveling. We can stand together." She reached out and took their hands in hers. "I didn't compose any prayers, so bear with me while I figure out what to say."

"I'm sure you'll do fine," Maggie said confidently.

Lucy's heart was so full that her eyes stung. She swallowed hard to keep back the tears. For a long moment, she wondered whether she could do this. She closed her eyes and silently prayed for inspiration. She spoke aloud the words that began to form in her mind.

"Divine One, I stand here, not as your priest, but as your daughter, Lucy. I stand here with my sisters, Liz and Maggie, to ask your blessings on our new family. You have shown us in scripture that there are many ways to love and be committed. David loved Jonathan. Ruth pledged herself as kin to her mother-in-law, Naomi, saying 'Where you go I will go, and where you stay I will stay. Your people will be my people and your God my God.' I give this same pledge to these women. As Abraham and Jacob took several women to be their wives, so do we. We know it is not the teaching of the Church, which barely acknowledges the marriage of two women, but you have brought us together to love and care for one another. Therefore, I, Lucy, give my body and all my worldly goods to Liz and Maggie to be shared equally and with love."

Maggie picked up on the cue. "I, Maggie, give my body and all my worldly goods to Liz and Lucy to be shared equally and with love."

Liz made a little face, but she repeated the words.

"Now, let's all pray silently to God to give us the grace to make this work," Lucy said and closed her eyes. She could feel Liz beside her, shifting from one foot to the other. Either she was being as impatient as always with religious rituals, or her knee was really bothering her. Lucy squeezed her hand. She was pleased when Liz squeezed back. Lucy squeezed Maggie's hand too and got the same response. They prayed until Liz became obviously twitchy. Lucy decided it was time to end the impromptu service. "We thank you, Divine One, who loves us more than we can ever imagine, for your many blessings, especially for the gift of these companions, and the grace to go forward in love, respect, and peace. Amen."

Maggie and Liz solemnly repeated, "Amen." They all kissed one another.

"Nice service, Lucy," said Maggie, embracing her. "Did you really just make it up?"

"Completely spontaneous, if you can believe it."

Maggie gave her another hug. "You should ad lib more often. That prayer was right on point and truly inspiring."

"I think it's colder in here than it is outside," Liz said on a cloud of vapor. "Let's go down to the oceanside chapel."

As Lucy locked the doors, she realized that Liz was right. It was warmer outside because the winter sun was shining brightly. They walked down the stone path to the stone altar by the sea wall, where they stood watching the ships go in and out of the harbor. The red-sailed tour boat that would operate until Christmas came out of the harbor. You could set a watch by its transits.

"This is my church," Liz said gesturing to the water below, "the ocean, the pines, the rocks, the big sky overhead..."

"I didn't know you were a pantheist," Maggie said.

"Oh, she's not," Lucy said, burrowing deeper into her scarf. "She just finds churches too confining. They're not big enough for her idea of God, and she's right. The Church isn't big enough for what we've done today."

Maggie nodded thoughtfully but said nothing. They kept the silence until Lucy began to visibly shiver, and Liz put her arm around her. The bright sun was deceiving because it had done little to raise the air temperature. The brisk wind off the ocean wasn't helping.

"I'm too cold to stand out here any longer," Lucy finally admitted.

Liz took her hand and stuck it into her pocket. "Let's head for LaScala. I'm hungry."

Maggie cocked a brow. "You're always hungry."

"Not always. After sex, I'm ravenous with you two burning up all my energy. But I wouldn't trade you for anything."

Before they headed to the car, Liz reached out for Maggie's hand and put it into her other pocket.

Epilogue

Maggie had insisted that they couldn't leave Milan without visiting the Gallerie d'Italia to see *Le Tre Grazie*, Conova's eighteenth-century marble rendering of the three graces. Although three beautiful women dancing was a common theme in neo-classical sculpture, the erotic intention of this statue was too obvious to ignore. The intertwined female figures, one tenderly supporting the breast of her companion, were clearly in love.

Now, Denise was taking them to see backstage at the famous opera house across the plaza. Following Lucy and Maggie down the stairs, Liz zipped up her down coat. "I'm glad you warned us about the weather. It is almost as cold in Milan as it is in Maine."

"I was surprised myself," said Denise. "Thanks for helping me get my winter clothes out of the storage locker in time."

"No problem. Glad to help." Liz smiled warmly. "Can't have you shivering over here."

"Winter is a good time to visit Milan. There aren't many tourists."

"Once he gets into the office, the tourist traffic will probably plummet. I won't be surprised to see new travel bans. People who've overstayed their visas will be afraid to leave the country."

"Rinaldo and I are glad you could visit before the inauguration."

"It's only a short trip, a little honeymoon with my best girls."

Denise turned to watch Maggie and Lucy walking through the Piazza della Scala. "They look like they're enjoying themselves. Here, no one thinks twice about them walking arm in arm. It's so much more civilized. You should consider moving to Europe. Lucy would be right at home. She's lived here before."

"I'm not ready to move," Liz said. "Someone needs to stay and fight."

Denise searched Liz's eyes. "Liz, I admire your bravery, but as a trans woman, that's not something I can afford."

"I know. Now that I'm living a life no one understands, I finally understand."

"Quite an experience, isn't it? But you seem happier."

"I finally have everything I've ever wanted."

Liz offered her arm to Denise, who blushed a little and glanced around. "Are you sure?" she asked anxiously.

"Absolutely," Liz assured her. "I'm always proud to be seen with a beautiful woman."

Blushing a little, Denise threaded her arm through Liz's. "You're so gallant. Do your partners appreciate how attentive you are?"

"Oh, I think so."

Denise pulled Liz closer. In turn, Liz affectionately pressed Denise's arm to her body. They'd been walking more slowly than the others, and they'd gotten far ahead of them. They'd paused to take in the monument to Leonardo da Vinci. Lucy turned around and waved vigorously.

"I think they want us to pick up the pace," Denise observed.

"Don't worry. They'll wait for us."

"You seem so sure."

"I am."

Maggie turned around and put her hands on her hips to show her impatience. She said something that reduced Lucy to laughter. Obviously, they were still whispering to each other. Liz smiled indulgently, knowing their little confidences were harmless.

"They really want you to go with them," said Denise, releasing Liz's arm. "I'll meet you at the stage entrance. Lucy knows where it is."

Liz hurried down the stairs to catch up with her wives. Each offered an arm. Flanked by the people she loved most, she allowed them to lead her forward.

Also by Elena Graf

HOBBS SERIES

HIGH OCTOBER

Liz Stolz and Maggie Fitzgerald were college roommates until Maggie confessed their affair to her parents. When Maggie breaks her leg in a summer stock stage accident, she lands in Dr. Stolz's office. Is forty years too long to wait for the one you love?

THE MORE THE MERRIER

Maggie and Liz's plans of sitting by the fire, drinking mulled wine, and watching old Christmas movies get scuttled by surprise visits from friends and family.

THIS IS MY BODY

Professor Erika Bultmann, a confirmed agnostic, is fascinated by Mother Lucy, the new rector of the Episcopal Church, especially when she discovers Lucille Bartlett was a rising opera star before mysteriously disappearing from the stage.

LOVE IN THE TIME OF CORONA

Police Chief Brenda Harrison shows an interest in Liz's biracial PA, but first Cherie needs to get past her loathing for all law enforcement since a state trooper shot and killed her sister.

THIRSTY THURSDAYS

Liz Stolz initiates Thirsty Thursdays, a weekly cocktail party on her deck, so her friends can socialize safely during the pandemic. Pretentious, overbearing Olivia Enright pursues Liz's friend, architect Sam McKinnon, and tries to push her way into the tight-knit group.

THE DARK WINTER

Erika hires Sam to build a soundproof practice room for Lucy. Fortunately, the early Christmas gift is ready before tragedy strikes. As the women of Hobbs pull together to help a beloved friend deal with her loss, the dark winter brings tension and realignment in their small community.

SUMMER PEOPLE

Melissa Morgenstern, a high-profile lawyer from Boston, is spending the summer with her widowed mother. She's doing some trust work for Liz who introduces her to the attractive Courtney Barnes, Hobbs Elementary's new assistant principal. The arrival of Susan, Lucy's ex, complicates her deepening relationship with Liz.

STRANDS

Cherie hears her biological clock ticking and would like to start a family. When a shocking tragedy creates an opportunity for her and Brenda to become parents, their friends need to step up to make it happen.

THE RECTOR'S WEDDING

The sudden opportunity for Lucy to return to her singing career throws everything in her life into doubt—her vocation as a priest, her settled life in Hobbs, even her upcoming marriage to the woman she loves.

THE VANISHING BRIDGE

Rev. Susan Gedney tries to rebuild trust after her humiliating exit from Hobbs. Bobbie Lantry always needs to rush away to take care of a mysterious elderly woman. They need to share their secrets, but do they dare?

EXTENDED CAPACITY

A school shooting was a nightmare that only happened in other towns until it came to Hobbs. Liz finds herself in the middle when the shooter's identity is revealed. The town is shocked to learn how the shooter got into the school.

RIP TIDE

A small town in Maine has begun to recover from a school shooting when another mass shooting and divisive politics threaten to divide friends and end relationships. Town doctor Liz Stolz and Episcopal rector Lucy Bartlett, used to bringing people together, find their own alliances threatened.?

About the Author

In addition to the Hobbs series of contemporary novels set in a small town in Maine, Elena Graf has published four historical novels set in twentieth-century Europe. Two of the titles in the Passing Rites series have won Golden Crown Literary Society and Rainbow awards for best historical fiction. She pursued a Ph.D. in philosophy but ended up in the "accidental profession" of publishing, where she worked for almost four decades. She lives in coastal Maine.

Find out about events and new books at her website, elenagraf.com. You can write to Elena at elena.m.graf@gmail.com. Or find her on Facebook.

www.ingramcontent.com/pod-product-compliance
Lightning Source LLC
Chambersburg PA
CBHW052028220726
48293CB00015B/438